THE HOLLOW MAN

BOOKS BY DAN SIMMONS

Carrion Comfort
Children of the Night
The Fall of Hyperion
Hyperion
Phases of Gravity
Prayers to Broken Stones
Song of Kali
Summer of Night

THE HOLLOW MAN

Dan Simmons

BANTAM BOOKS

New York ○ *Toronto*
London ○ *Sydney*
Auckland

THE HOLLOW MAN
A Bantam Book / October 1992

Grateful acknowledgment is made for permission to reprint the
following:

"Elegy for Jane," copyright © 1950 by Theodore Roethke. Reprinted
by permission of Doubleday, a division of Bantam Doubleday Dell
Publishing Group, Inc.

Illustration from Foundations of Mechanics by R. Abraham and
J. Marsden. Copyright © 1978 by Addison-Wesley Publishing
Company, Inc. Reprinted by permission of the publisher.

"The Hollow Men," from Collected Poems, 1909–1962 by T. S.
Eliot. Copyright © 1936 by Harcourt Brace Jovanovich, Inc.
Copyright © 1964, 1963 by T. S. Eliot. Reprinted by permission of
the publisher.

Book design by Beth Tondreau Design

No part of this book may be reproduced or transmitted in any form
or by any means, electronic or mechanical, including photocopying,
recording, or by any information storage and retrieval system, without
permission in writing from the publisher.
For information address: Bantam Books.

Library of Congress Cataloging-in-Publication Data
Simmons, Dan.
    The hollow man / Dan Simmons.
       p.   cm.
    ISBN 0-553-08252-3
    I. Title.
    PS3569.I47292H64   1992
    813'.54—dc20   92-8086
                                                       CIP

Published simultaneously in the United States and Canada

Bantam Books are published by Bantam Books, a division of Bantam
Doubleday Dell Publishing Group, Inc. Its trademark, consisting of the
words "Bantam Books" and the portrayal of a rooster, is Registered in
U.S. Patent and Trademark Office and in other countries. Marca
Registrada. Bantam Books, 666 Fifth Avenue, New York, New York
10103.

PRINTED IN THE UNITED STATES OF AMERICA

BVG   0 9 8 7 6 5 4 3 2 1

ACKNOWLEDGMENTS

The author would like to thank the following people for turning an impossible task into a merely difficult one:

Sue Bolton and Edward Bryant for reading the book that was written rather than the one that was expected by others. Tabitha and Steve King for the long, cross-country reading marathon . . . and for the helpful words that followed. Niki Gernold for demonstrating the mechanics of telepathy. Betsy Mitchell for showing the courage of our shared convictions. Ellen Datlow for liking (and buying) the story that began it all, lo these ten long years ago. Richard Curtis for eschewing obfuscation via quintessential professionalism. Mathematician Ian Stewart for provoking a passionate response from a mathematical illiterate. Karen and Jane Simmons for their love, support, and tolerance as I perversely kept trying to turn a merely difficult task back into an impossible one.

In addition to these wonderfully alive people, I must thank several who are no longer with us:

Dante Alighieri, John Ciardi, T. S. Eliot, Joseph Conrad, and Thomas Aquinas

All of whom have explored, far more eloquently than my powers would ever allow, the obsessive theme of—

> Wandering between two worlds, one dead
> The other powerless to be born

Thou shalt prove how salty tastes another's
bread, and how hard a path it is to go up and down
another's stairs.

—Dante, *Paradiso XVII*

Eyes I dare not meet in dreams
In death's dream kingdom
These do not appear.

—T. S. Eliot, *The Hollow Men*

THE HOLLOW MAN

Shadow at Evening

Bremen left the hospital and his dying wife and drove east to the sea. The roads were thick with Philadelphians fleeing the city for the unusually warm Easter weekend, so Bremen had to concentrate on traffic, leaving only the most tenuous of touches in his wife's mind.

Gail was sleeping. Her dreams were fitful and drug-induced. She was seeking her mother through endlessly interlinked rooms filled with Victorian furniture. Images from these dreams slid between the evening shadows of reality as Bremen crossed the Pine Barrens. She awoke just as Bremen was leaving the parkway, and for the few seconds that the pain was not with her, Bremen was able to share the clarity of sunlight falling across the blue blanket at the foot of her bed; then he shared the quick vertigo of confusion as she thought—only for a second—that it was morning on the farm.

Her thoughts reached for him just as the pain returned, stabbing behind her left eye like a thin but infinitely sharp needle. Bremen grimaced and dropped the coin he was handing the tollbooth attendant.

"Something wrong, pal?" Bremen shook his head, fumbled out a dollar, and thrust it blindly at the man. Tossing his change into the Triumph's cluttered console, he concentrated on pushing the little car up through its gears while shielding himself from the worst of Gail's pain. Slowly the agony faded, but her confusion washed over him like a wave of nausea.

She quickly gained control despite the shifting curtains of fear that fluttered at the edges of her consciousness. She subvocalized, concentrating on narrowing the spectrum of what she shared to a simulacrum of her voice.

Hi, Jerry.

Hi, yourself, kiddo. He sent the thought as he turned onto the exit of Long Beach Island. Bremen shared the visual—the startling green of grass and pine trees overlaid with the gold of April light, the sports car's shadow leaping along the curve of the embankment as he followed the cloverleaf down to the road. Suddenly there came the unmistakable salt-and-rotting-vegetation scent of the Atlantic, and he shared that with her as well.

Nice. Gail's thoughts were slurred with the static of too much pain and medication. She clung to the images he sent with an almost feverish concentration of will.

The entrance to the seaside community was disappointing: dilapidated seafood restaurants, overpriced cinder-block motels, endless marinas. But it was reassuring in its familiarity to both of them, and Bremen concentrated on seeing all of it. Gail began to relax a bit as the terrible swells of pain abated, and for a second her presence was so real that Bremen caught himself half turning to speak to her in the passenger's seat. The pang of regret and embarrassment was sent before he could stifle it.

The driveways of beach homes were filled with families unpacking station wagons and carrying late dinners to the beach. The evening shadows carried the nip of early spring, but Bremen concentrated on the fresh air and the warmth of the low strips of sunlight as he drove north to Barnegat Light. He glanced right and caught a glimpse of half a dozen fishermen standing in the surf, their shadows intersecting the white lines of breakers.

Monet, thought Gail, and Bremen nodded, although he had actually been thinking about Euclid.

Always the mathematician. Gail's voice faded as the pain returned. Half-formed sentences scattered like the spray rising from the white breakers.

Bremen left the Triumph parked near the lighthouse and walked through low dunes to the beach. He threw down the tattered blanket that they had carried so many times to just this spot. A group of children ran past, squealing as they came close to the surf. Despite the cold water and rapidly chilling air, they were dressed in swimsuits. One girl of about nine, all long white legs in a suit a year too small, pranced on the wet sand in an intricate and unconscious choreography with the sea.

The light was fading between the venetian blinds. A nurse smelling of cigarettes and stale talcum powder came in to change the IV drip and to take a pulse. The intercom in the hall continued to make loud, imperative announcements, but it was difficult to understand them through the growing haze of pain. Dr. Singh arrived about six P.M. and spoke to her softly, but Gail's attention was riveted on the doorway where the nurse with the blessed needle would arrive. The cotton swab on her arm was a delightful preliminary to the promised surcease of pain. Gail knew to the second how many minutes before the morphine would begin to work in earnest. The doctor was saying something.

". . . your husband? I thought he would be staying the night."

"Right here, doctor," said Gail. She patted the blanket and the sand.

Bremen pulled on his nylon windbreaker against the chill of coming night. The stars were occluded by a high cloud layer that allowed only a bit of sky to show through. Far out to sea, an improbably long oil tanker moved along the horizon. Windows of the beach homes behind Bremen cast yellow rectangles on the dunes.

The smell of steak being grilled came to him on the breeze. Bremen tried to remember whether he had eaten that day or not. His stomach twisted in a mild shadow of the pain that still filled Gail even now that the medication was working. Bremen considered going back to the convenience store near the lighthouse to get a sandwich, but remembered an old Payday candy bar he had purchased from the vending machine in the hospital corridor during the previous week's vigil. It was still in his jacket pocket. Bremen contented himself with chewing on the rock-hard wedge of peanuts while he watched the evening settle in.

Footsteps continued to echo in the hall. It sounded as if entire armies were on the march. The rush of footsteps, clatter of trays, and vague chatter of aides bringing dinner to the other patients reminded Gail of lying in bed as a child and listening to one of her parents' parties downstairs.

Remember the party where we met? sent Bremen.

Mmmm. Gail's attention was thin. Already the black fingers of panic were creeping around the edge of her awareness as the pain began to overwhelm the painkiller. The thin needle behind her eye seemed to grow hotter.

Bremen tried to send memory images of Chuck Gilpen's party a decade earlier, of their first meeting, of that first second when their minds had opened to one another and they had realized *I am not alone.* And then the corollary realization, *I am not a freak.* There, in Chuck Gilpen's crowded town house, amid the tense babble and even tenser neurobabble of mingling teachers and graduate students, their lives had been changed forever.

Bremen was just inside the door—someone had pressed a drink in his hand—when suddenly he had sensed another mindshield quite near him. He had put out a gentle probe, and immediately Gail's thoughts had swept across him like a searchlight in a dark room.

Both were stunned. Their first reaction had been to increase the strength of their mindshields, to roll up like frightened armadillos. Each soon found that useless against the unconscious and almost involuntary probes of the other. Neither had ever encountered another telepath of more than primitive, untapped ability. Each had assumed that he or she was a freak—unique and unassailable. Now they stood naked before each other in an empty place. A second later, almost without volition, they flooded each other's mind with a torrent of images, self-images, half memories, secrets, sensations, preferences, perceptions, hidden shames, half-formed longings, and fully formed fears. Nothing was held back. Every petty cruelty committed, sexual experiment experienced, and prejudice harbored poured out along with thoughts of past birthday parties, former lovers, parents, and an endless stream of trivia. Rarely had two people known each other as well after fifty years of marriage.

A minute later they met for the first time.

The beacon from Barnegat Light passed over Bremen's head every twenty-four seconds. There were more lights burning out at sea now than along the dark line of beach. The wind had come up after midnight, and Bremen clutched the blanket around himself tightly. Gail had refused the needle when the nurse had last made her rounds, but her mindtouch was still clouded. Bremen forced the contact through sheer strength of will.

Gail had always been afraid of the dark. Many were the times during their nine years of marriage that he had reached out in the night with his mind or arm to reassure her. Now she was the frightened little girl again, left alone upstairs in the big old house on Burlingame Avenue. There were things in the darkness beneath her bed.

Bremen reached through her pain and confusion to share the sound of the sea with her. He told her stories about that day's antics of Gernisavien, their calico cat. He lay in the hollow of the sand to match his body with hers on the hospital bed. Slowly she began to relax, to surrender her thoughts to his. She even managed to doze a few times without the morphine, and her dreams were the movement of stars between clouds and the sharp smell of the Atlantic.

Bremen described the week's work at the farm—what little work he had done between hospital vigils—and shared the subtle beauty of the Fourier equations across the chalkboard in his study and the sunlit satisfaction of planting a peach tree by the front drive. He shared memories of their ski trip to Aspen the year before and the sudden shock of a searchlight reaching in to the beach from an unseen ship out at sea. He shared what little poetry he had memorized, but the words kept sliding into pure images and purer feelings.

The night drew on, and Bremen shared the cold clarity of it with his wife, adding to each image the warm overlay of his love. He shared trivia and hopes for the future. From seventy-five miles away he reached out and touched her hand with his. When he drifted off to sleep for only a few minutes, he sent her his dreams.

Gail died just before the first false light of dawn touched the sky.

A Banner There Upon the Mist

Two days after the funeral, Frank Lowell, the head of the mathematics department at Haverford, came to the house to assure Bremen that his job would be kept safe no matter what he decided to do in the coming months.

"Seriously, Jerry," Frank was saying, "there's nothing to worry about in that area. Do what you have to do to put things back together. Whenever you want it back, it's yours." Frank smiled his best little-boy smile and adjusted his rimless glasses. He seemed to have a chubby thirteen-year-old's cheeks and chin behind the mat of beard. His blue eyes were open and guileless.

Satisfaction. A rival removed. Never really liked Bremen . . . too smart. The Goldmann research made him too much of a threat.

Images of the young blonde from MIT whom Frank had interviewed the summer before and slept with through the long winter.

Perfect. No more need for lying to Nell or inventing conferences to fly to over long weekends. Sheri can stay in town, near campus, and she'll have the chair by next Christmas if Bremen stays away too long. Perfect.

"Seriously, Jer," said Frank, and leaned forward to pat Bremen's knee, "just take whatever time you need. We'll consider it a sabbatical and keep the position open for you."

Bremen looked up and nodded. Three days later he mailed in his letter of resignation to the college.

Dorothy Parks from the psychology department came on the third day after the funeral, insisted on making dinner for Bremen, and stayed until after dark, explaining the mechanisms of grief to him. They sat on the porch until darkness and chill drove them inside. It was beginning to feel like winter again.

"You have to understand, Jeremy, that stepping out of one's usual environment is a common mistake made by people who've just suffered a serious loss. Taking too much time off from work, changing homes too quickly . . . it all seems like it might help, but it's just another way to postpone the inevitable confrontation with grief."

Bremen nodded and listened attentively.

"Denial is the stage you're in now," said Dorothy. "Just as Gail had to go through that stage with her cancer, now you have to go through it in your grief . . . go through it and get past it. Do you understand what I'm saying, Jeremy?"

Bremen lifted a knuckle to his lower lip and nodded slowly. Dorothy Parks was in her mid-forties but dressed like a much younger woman. This night she wore a man's shirt, unbuttoned quite low, tucked into a long gaucho skirt. Her boots were at least twenty inches tall. The bracelets on her wrist jingled as she gestured. Her hair was cut short, dyed a red impinging on purple, and moussed into a cockscomb.

"Gail would have wanted you to deal with this denial as quickly as possible and get on with your life, Jeremy. You know that, don't you?"

He's listening. Looking at me. Perhaps I should have left that fourth button closed . . . just be the therapist tonight . . . worn the gray sweater. Well, shit with that. I've seen him looking at me in the lounge. He's smaller than Darren was . . . not as strong looking . . . but that's not so important. Wonder what he's like in bed?

Images of a sandy-haired man . . . Darren . . . sliding his cheek lower on her belly.

It's okay, he can learn what I like. Wonder where the bedroom is here? Second floor somewhere. No, my place . . . no, better a neutral place the first time. Clock ticking. Biological clock. Shit, whatever man came up with that phrase ought to have his balls cut off.

". . . important that you share feelings with your friends, with someone close," she was saying. "Denial can only go on for so long before it turns the pain inward. You'll promise you'll call? Talk?"

Bremen lifted his head and nodded. At that second he decided beyond any doubt that the farm could not be sold.

On the fourth day after Gail's funeral, Bob and Barbara Sutton, neighbors and friends, called again to express their sympathies in private. Barbara wept easily. Bob shifted uneasily in his chair. He was a big man with a blond crew cut, a permanent flush to his round face, and fingers that looked as short and soft as a child's. He was thinking about getting home in time to watch the Celtics game.

"You know that God doesn't give us anything we can't bear, Jerry," Barbara said between bouts of weeping.

Bremen considered that. Barbara had a premature streak of gray in her dark hair and Bremen followed the sinuous line of it back from her forehead, under her barrette, and out of sight around the curve of her skull. The neurobabble from her was like a surge of superheated air from an open hearth.

Witnessing. Wouldn't Pastor Miller think it wonderful if I brought this college professor to the Lord. If I quote Scripture, I'm liable to lose him . . . oh, wouldn't Darlene have a fit if I came to Wednesday-night services with this agnostic . . . atheist . . . whatever he is, ready to come to Christ!

". . . He gives us the strength we need when we need it," Barbara was saying. "Even when we can't understand these things, there's a reason. A reason for everything. Gail was called home for some reason the Good Lord will reveal when our time comes."

Bremen nodded, distracted, and stood. Somewhat startled, Bob and Barbara stood also. He moved them toward the door.

"If there's anything we can . . ." began Bob.

"Actually, there is," said Bremen. "I wonder if you might take care of Gernisavien while I go away for a while."

Barbara smiled and frowned at the same time. "The kitty? I mean, of course . . . Gerny gets along with my two Siamese . . . we'd be happy to . . . but how long do you think . . ."

Bremen attempted a smile. "Just a while to sort things out. I'd feel better if Gernisavien were with you rather than at the vet's or that cat boarding place on Conestoga Road. I could drop her off in the morning, if that'd be okay."

"Yeah," said Bob, shaking Bremen's hand again. *Five minutes until the pregame show.*

Bremen waved as they turned their Honda around and disappeared down the gravel drive. Then he went into the house and walked slowly from room to room.

Gernisavien was sleeping on the blue blanket at the foot of their bed. The calico's head twitched as Bremen entered the room and her yellow eyes squinted accusingly at him for awakening her. Bremen touched her neck and went to the closet. He lifted one of Gail's blouses and held it to his cheek a second, then covered his face with it, breathing deeply. He went out of the room and down the hall to his study. Student test booklets remained stacked where he had left them a month earlier. His Fourier equations lay scrawled where he had chalked them in a burst of two A.M. inspiration the week before Gail had been diagnosed. Heaps of manuscripts and unread journals covered every surface.

Bremen stood for a minute in the center of the room, rubbing his temples. Even here, a half mile from the nearest neighbor and nine miles from town or the expressway, his head buzzed and crackled with neurobabble. It was as if all of his life he had heard a radio tuned softly in another room and now someone had buried a boom box in his skull and turned the volume to full. Ever since the morning Gail had died.

And the babble was not only louder, it was *darker*. Bremen knew that it now came from a deeper and more malevolent source than the random skimming of thoughts and emotions he had held access to since he was thirteen. It was as if his almost symbiotic relationship with Gail had been a shield, a buffer between his mind and the razor-edged slashings of a million unstructured thoughts. Before last Friday, he would have had to concentrate to pick up the mélange of images, feelings, and half-formed language phrases that constituted Frank's thoughts, or Dorothy's, or Bob and Barbara's. But now there was no shielding himself from the onslaught. What he and Gail had thought of as their *mindshields*—simple barriers to mute the background hiss and crackle of neurobabble—were simply no longer there.

Bremen touched the chalkboard as if he were going to erase the equation there, then set down the eraser and went downstairs. After a while Gernisavien joined him in the kitchen and brushed up against his legs. Bremen realized that it had grown dark while he was sitting at the table, but he did not turn on the light as he opened a fresh can of cat food and fed the calico. Gernisavien looked up at him as if in disapproval of his not eating or turning on a light.

Later, when he went in to lie on the couch in the living room to wait for morning, the calico lay on his chest and purred.

Bremen found that closing his eyes brought on the dizziness and impending sense of terror . . . the sure knowledge that Gail was here somewhere, in the next room, outside on the lawn, and that she was calling for him. Her voice was almost audible. Bremen knew that if he slept, he would miss the instant when her voice reached the threshold of his hearing. So he lay awake and waited as the night passed and the house creaked and moaned in its own restlessness, and his sixth night without sleep passed into the gray chill of his seventh morning without her.

At seven A.M. Bremen rose, fed the cat again, turned the kitchen radio on full, shaved, showered, and had three cups of coffee. He called a cab company and told them to have a taxi meet him at the Import Repair garage on Conestoga Road in forty-five minutes. Then he set Gernisavien in her travel cage—her tail thrashed since the cage had been used only for trips to the vet in the two years since her disastrous flight out to California on the visit to Gail's sister there—and then he carried the cage out to the passenger seat of the Triumph.

He had bought the eight jerricans of kerosene on Monday, before dressing for the funeral. Now he lugged four of them to the back porch and twisted off their lids. The sharp fumes sliced through the cold morning air. The sky suggested rain before nightfall.

Bremen began with the second floor, dousing the bed, the quilt, the closets and their contents, the cedar chest, and then the bed again. He watched the white paper wrinkle and darken in the study as he slopped liquid from the second jerrican, and then he left a trail down the stairs, soaking the dark banisters that he and Gail had so painstakingly stripped and refinished five years before.

He used another two cans on the downstairs, sparing nothing— not even Gail's barn coat still hanging on the hook by the door— and then he went around the outside of the house with the fifth can, soaking front and back porches, the Adirondack chairs out back, and the doorway lintels and screens. The final three cans were used on the outbuildings. Gail's Volvo was still in the barn they used as a garage.

He parked the Triumph fifty yards down the drive toward the road and walked back to the house. He'd forgotten matches, so he had to go back into the kitchen and rummage in the junk drawer for them. The kerosene fumes made tears stream down his cheeks and seemed to cause the very air to ripple, as if the butcher-block table and Formica counter and tall, old refrigerator were as insubstantial as a heat mirage.

Then, as he retrieved the two books of matches from the tumble of stuff in the drawer, Bremen was suddenly and blissfully certain of what he should do.

Stand here. Light them. Go lie down on the couch.

He had actually removed two matches and was on the verge of striking them when the vertigo struck. It was not Gail's voice denying him the act, but it was *Gail.* Like fingers scratching wildly on a pane of Plexiglas that separated them. Like fingers on the mahogany lid of a coffin.

You aren't in a coffin, kiddo. You were cremated . . . as per your request when we drank too much three New Year's Eves ago and got all weepy about mortality.

Bremen staggered to the table and closed the cover of the matchbook over the two matches, ready to strike them. The vertigo grew worse.

Cremated. Pleasant thought. Ashes for both of us. I spread yours in the orchard out beyond the barn . . . perhaps the wind will carry some of mine there.

Bremen started to strike the matches, but the scratching intensified, grew magnified, until it roared in his skull like a runaway migraine, shattering his vision into a thousand dots of light and darkness, filling his hearing with the scrabbling of rats' feet on linoleum.

When Bremen opened his eyes, he was outside and the flames were already working on the kitchen and a second glow was visible in the front windows. For a moment he stood there, his headache throbbing with each pounding of his pulse, considering going back into the house, but when the flames became visible at the second-story windows and the smoke was billowing out through the screens of the back porch, he turned and walked quickly to the outbuildings instead. The garage went up with a muffled explosion that singed Bremen's eyebrows and drove him back past the pyre of the farmhouse.

A line of crows from the orchard rose skyward, scolding and

screeching at him. Bremen hopped in the idling Triumph, touched the cage as if to calm the agitated cat, and drove quickly away.

Barbara Sutton was red-eyed as he dropped the cat off. A line of trees blocked the sight of smoke rising from the valley he had left behind. Gernisavien crouched in her carry cage, slat-eyed and suspicious, trembling and glaring at Bremen. He cut through Barbara's attempt at small talk, said that he had an appointment, drove quickly to the Import Repair shop on Conestoga Road, sold the Triumph to his former mechanic there at the price they had discussed, and then took a cab to the airport. Fire engines passed them as they drove toward the expressway to Philadelphia. He was only five minutes behind schedule.

Once at the airport, Bremen went to the United counter and bought a one-way ticket on the next flight out. The Boeing stretch 727 was airborne and Bremen was beginning to relax, seat reclined, beginning to feel that sleep might be permissible now, when the full force of everything struck him.

And then the nightmare began in earnest.

EYES

In the beginning was not the Word.

Not for me, at least.

As hard as it is to believe, and harder yet to understand, there are universes of experience that do not depend upon the Word. Such was mine. The fact that I was God there . . . or at least a god . . . is not yet relevant.

I am not Jeremy, or Gail, although someday I would share all that they had known and been and wished to become. But that does not make me *them* any more than watching a television show makes you that stream of electromagnetic pulses that is the show. Neither am I God, nor god, although I was both until that unanticipated intersection of events and personalities, that meeting of parallel lines that cannot meet.

I am beginning to think in mathematics, like Jeremy. Actually, in the beginning there was not the Number, either. Not for me. No such concept existed . . . neither counting nor adding nor subtracting, nor any of the supernatural divinations that constitute mathematics . . . for what is a number other than a ghost of the mind?

I'll cease the coyness before I begin to sound like some disembodied, alien intelligence from outer space. (Actually, that would not be too far from the mark, even though the concept of outer space did not exist for me then . . . and even now seems an absurd thought. And as far as *alien* intelligences go, we do not have to seek for them in outer space, as I can attest and Jeremy Bremen is soon to learn. There are alien intelligences enough among you on this earth, ignored or misunderstood.)

But on this morning in April when Gail dies, none of this means anything to me. The concept of death itself means nothing to me, much less its multifoliate subtleties and variations.

But I know this now—that however innocent and transparent Jeremy's soul and emotions seem on this April morning, there is a darkness already abiding there. A darkness born of deception and deep (if unintentional) cruelty. Jeremy is not a cruel man—cruelty is as alien to his nature as it is to mine—but the fact that he has kept a secret from Gail for years when neither thought that he or she could keep a secret from the other, and the fact that this secret is essential to the denial of their shared wishes and desires for so many years—this secret in and of itself constitutes a cruelty. One that has hurt Gail even when she does not know it is hurting her.

The mindshield that Jeremy thinks he has lost as he boards his airplane to a random destination is not exactly lost—he still has the same ability as ever to shield his mind from the random telepathic surges of others—but that mindshield is no longer capable of protecting him from those "dark wavelengths" he must now endure. It had not been the "shared mindshield," merely the shared life with Gail that had protected him from this cruel underside of things.

And as Jeremy begins his descent into hell he carries another secret—this one hidden even from himself. And it is this second secret, a hidden pregnancy in him as opposed to an earlier hidden sterility there, that will mean so much to me later.

So much to all three of us.

But first let me tell you of someone else. On the morning that Jeremy boards his aircraft to nowhere, Robby Bustamante is being picked up at the usual time by the van from the East St. Louis Day School for the Blind. Robby is more than blind—he has been blind, deaf, and retarded since birth. If he had been a more normal child physically, the diagnosis would have included the term "autistic," but with the terminally blind, deaf, and retarded, the word "autism" is a redundancy.

Robby is thirteen years old, but already weighs one hundred and seventy-five pounds. His eyes, if one can call them that, are the sunken, darkened caverns of the irrevocably blind. The pupils, barely visible under drooping, mismatched lids, track separately in random movements. The boy's lips are loose and blubbery, his teeth gapped and carious. At thirteen, he already has the dark down of a mustache on his upper lip. His black hair stands out in violent tufts; his eyebrows meet above the bridge of his broad nose.

Robby's obese body balances precariously on grub-white, emaciated legs. He learned to walk at age eleven, but still will stagger only a few paces before toppling over. When he does move, it is in a series of pigeon-toed lurches, his pudgy arms pulled in as tight as two broken wings, wrists cocked at an improbable angle, fingers separate and extended. As with so many of the retarded blind, his favorite motion is a perpetual rocking with his hand fanning above his sunken eyes as if to cast shadows into the pits of darkness there.

He does not speak. Robby's only sounds are animallike grunts, occasional, meaningless giggles, and a rare squeal of protest that sounds like nothing so much as an operatic falsetto.

As I mentioned earlier, Robby has been blind, deaf, and retarded since birth. His mother's drug addiction during pregnancy and an additional placental malfunction had shut off Robby's senses as surely as a sinking ship condemns compartment after compartment to the sea by the automatic shutting of watertight doors.

The boy has been coming to the East St. Louis Day School for the Blind for six years. His life before that is largely unknown. The authorities had taken notice of Robby's mother's addiction in the hospital and had ordered social-worker follow-ups in the home, but through some bureaucratic oversight, none of these had occurred for seven years after the boy's birth. As it turned out, the social worker who did finally make a home visit was doing so in relation to a court-ordered methadone-treatment program for the mother rather than out of any solicitude for the child. In truth, the courts, the authorities, the hospital . . . everyone . . . had forgotten that the child existed.

The door to the apartment had been left open, and the social worker heard noises. The social worker said later that she would not have entered, except that it sounded like some small animal was in distress. In a very real sense, that was the fact of it.

Robby had been sealed into the bathroom by the nailing of a piece of plywood over the bottom half of the door. His small arms and legs were so atrophied that he could not walk and could barely crawl. He was seven years old. There were wet papers on the tile floor, but Robby was naked and smeared with his own excrement. It was obvious that the boy had been sealed in there for several days, perhaps longer. A tap had been left on, and water filled the room to the depth of three inches. Robby was rolling fitfully in the mess, making mewling noises and trying to keep his face above water.

Robby was hospitalized for four months, spent five weeks in a county home, and was then returned to the custody of his mother. In accordance with further court orders, he was dutifully bused to the Day School for the Blind for five hours of treatment a day, six days a week.

When Jeremy boards the airplane on this April morning, he is thirty-five years old and his future is as predictable as the elegant and ellipsoid mathematics of a yo-yo's path. On this same morning, eight hundred–some miles away, as thirteen-year-old Robby Bustamante is lifted aboard his van for the short voyage to the Day School for the Blind, his future is as flat and featureless as a line extending nowhere, holding no hope of intersection with anyone or anything.

Out of the Dead Land

The captain had dimmed the seat-belt sign and announced that it was safe to move about in the cabin—urging everyone to keep their belts on while seated anyway, just as a precaution—when the true nightmare began for Bremen.

For an instant he was sure that the plane had exploded, that some terrorist bomb had been triggered, so brilliant was the flash of white light, so loud was the sudden screaming of a hundred and eighty-seven voices in his mind. His sudden sense of falling added to the conviction that the plane had shattered into ten thousand pieces and that he was one of them, tumbling out into the stratosphere with the rest of the screaming passengers. Bremen closed his eyes and prepared to die.

He was not falling. Part of his consciousness was aware of the seat under him, of the floor under his feet, of the sunlight coming through the window to his left. But the screaming continued. And grew louder. Bremen realized that he was on the verge of joining that chorus of screams, so he stuffed his knuckles in his mouth and bit down hard.

A hundred and eighty-seven minds suddenly reminded of their own mortality by the simple routine of an aircraft taking off. Some in terror recognized, some in full denial behind their newspapers and drinks, some buoyed by the routine of it all even as a deeper center of their brains drowned in the fear of being locked in this long, pressurized coffin and suspended miles above the ground.

Bremen writhed and twitched in the isolation of his empty row while a hundred and eighty-seven careening minds trampled him with iron-shod hooves.

Jesus, I should've called Sarah before the flight left. . . .

Son of a bitch knew what the contract said. Or should have. It isn't my fault if . . .

Daddy . . . Daddy . . . I'm sorry . . . Daddy . . .

If Barry didn't want me to sleep with him, Barry should've called . . .

She was in the tub. The water was red. Her wrists were as white and open as a sliced tuber. . . .

Fuck Frederickson! Fuck Frederickson! Fuck Frederickson and Myers and Honeywell, too! Fuck Frederickson! . . .

What if the plane goes down, oh shit and Jesus and goddamn, what if it goes down and they find the stuff in the briefcase, oh shit and Jesus, ashes and burned steel and bits of me and what if they find the money and the Uzi and the teeth in the velvet bag and the bags like so many sausages up my ass and down my gut, oh please, Jesus . . . what if the plane goes down and . . . And these were the easy ones, the fragments of language that cut Bremen like so many shards of dull steel. It was the images that lacerated and sliced. The images were the scalpels. Bremen opened his eyes and saw the cabin as normal as it could be, sunlight streaming through the window to his left, two middle-aged flight attendants beginning to hand out breakfasts twelve rows ahead, people lounging and reading and dozing . . . but the panicked images kept coming, the vertigo of it all was too great, so Bremen undid his seat belt, folded back the armrest, and curled up on the empty seat to his left, still being pummeled by the sounds and textures and discordant colors of a thousand uninvited thoughts.

Teeth dragging on slate. The burned ozone and enamel smell of a dentist's drill left too long on a rotten tooth. Sheila! Christ, Sheila . . . I didn't mean to . . . Teeth dragging slowly across slate.

A fist crushing a tomato, pulp oozing between spattered fingers. Only it is not a tomato but a heart.

Friction and lubricity, the slow, rhythmical thrust and pull of sex in the dark. Derek . . . Derek, I warned you. . . . Lavatory graffiti images of penis and vulva, Technicolor hues, moist and three-dimensional. Slow close-up of a vagina opening ahead like a cavern between moist portals. Derek . . . I warned you that she would consume you!

Screams of violence. The violence of horses. Violence without boundaries or pause. A face being struck, like a clay figure being pounded flat again, only the face is not clay . . . the bone and cartilage crack and broaden, the flesh pulps and ruptures . . . the fist does not relent.

"Are you all right, sir?"

Bremen managed to sit up, to clench his right hand on the armrest, and to smile at the flight attendant. "Yes, fine," he said.

The middle-aged woman seemed all wrinkles and tired flesh behind the tan and makeup. She held a breakfast tray. "I can check to see if there is a doctor aboard if you're not feeling well, sir."

Damn. Just what we need this morning . . . some feeb with epilepsy or worse. We'll never get the geese fed if I have to hold this guy's hand while he twitches and sweats all the way to Miami. "I'd be happy to have the captain check for a doctor if you're ill, sir."

"No, no." Bremen smiled and took the offered breakfast, pulled down the tray from the seat ahead. "I'm fine, honestly."

Goddamn, son of a bitch, fucking plane goes down, they find the sausages up my ass, motherfucker Gallego gonna cut Doris's tits off an' feed 'em to Sanctus for fucking breakfast.

Bremen sliced a bit of omelet, raised the fork, swallowed. The flight attendant nodded and moved on.

Bremen made sure that no one was watching, then spat the soft mass of omelet into a paper napkin and set it next to the tray of food. His hands shook as he set his head back against the seat and closed his eyes.

Daddy . . . oh, Daddy . . . I'm so sorry, Daddy. . . .

Pounding the face into a flattened mass, pounding the mass until the marks of knuckles in ridged flesh were the only features, pounding the flattened mass back into the crude shape of a face to pound it again. . . .

Twenty-eight thousand from Pierce, seventeen thousand from Lords, forty-two thousand from Unimart-Selex . . . the white wrist like a sliced tuber in the bathtub . . . fifteen thousand seven hundred from Marx, nine thousand from Pierce's backer . . .

Bremen lowered the left armrest and gripped it tightly, both arms straining with the effort. It was like hanging from a vertical wall . . . as if his row of seats were bolted onto the face of a cliff and only the strength of his forearms was holding him in place. He could hang on for a minute more . . . perhaps two minutes more . . . hold on for three minutes more before the tidal wave of images and obscenities and the tsunami of hates and fears washed him off. Perhaps five minutes. Sealed here in this long tube, miles above nothing, with no way to escape, nowhere to go.

"This is your captain speaking. Just wanted to let you know that we've reached our cruising altitude of thirty-five thousand feet, that it looks like clear weather all the way down the coast today, and that our flying time to Miami will be . . . ah . . . three hours and fifteen minutes. Please let us know if we can do anything to make your trip more comfortable today . . . and thanks for flying the friendly skies of United."

On the Joyless Beach

Bremen had no memory of the rest of the flight, no memory of the Miami airport, no memory of renting the car or driving out away from the city into the Everglades.

But he must have. He was here . . . wherever here was.

The rental Beretta was parked under low trees by the side of a gravel road. Tall palm trees and a riot of tropical foliage formed a green wall in front and on two sides of the car. The road behind him was empty of traffic. Bremen was sitting with his forehead against the steering wheel, hands on the wheel on either side of his head. Sweat dripped onto his knees and the plastic of the wheel. He was shaking.

Bremen pulled the keys, thrust open the door, and staggered away from the car. He stumbled into the foliage and fell to his knees a brief second before the cramps and nausea rolled over him. Bremen vomited into the undergrowth, crawled backward, was assailed by more waves of illness, dropped to his elbows, and continued to vomit until only noise came up. After a moment he dropped to his side, rolled away from the mess, wiped his chin with a shaking hand, and lay staring up through palm fronds at the sky.

The sky was a gunmetal gray. Bremen could hear the rasp of distant thoughts and images still echoing through his skull. He remembered a quote that Gail had shown him—something she had dredged up from the sportswriter Jimmy Cannon after she and Bremen had argued about whether prizefighting was a sport or not. "Boxing is a filthy enterprise," Cannon had written, "and if you stay in it long enough, your mind will become a concert hall where Chinese music never stops playing."

Well, Bremen reflected grimly, barely able to sort out his own thoughts from the distant neurobabble, *my mind's sure as hell a concert hall. I just wish it was only Chinese music playing.*

He got to his knees, saw a glint of green water down the slope through the shrubs, rose, and staggered that way. A river or swamp stretched away through dim light. Spanish moss hung from live oak and cypress trees along the shore and more cypress rose from the brackish water. Bremen knelt, skimmed away the crust of green scum from the water, and washed his cheeks and chin. He rinsed his mouth and spat into the algae-choked water.

There was a house—little more than a shack, actually—under tall trees fifty yards to Bremen's right. His rented Beretta was parked near the beginnings of a trail that wound through foliage to the sagging structure. The faded pine boards of the shack blended with the shadows there, but Bremen was able to make out signs on the wall facing the road: LIVE BAIT and GUIDE SERVICE and CABIN RENTALS and VISIT OUR SNAKE EMPORIUM. Bremen moved that way, shuffling along the edge of the river, stream, swamp . . . whatever that green-and-brown expanse of water was.

The shack was set up on cement blocks; from beneath it came a loam-rich scent of wet earth. An old Chevy was parked on the far side of the low building, and now Bremen could see a wider lane that ran down from the road. He paused at the screen door. It was dark inside, and despite the signs the place seemed more some

hillbilly's shack than a store. Bremen shrugged and opened the
door with a screech.

"Howdy," said one of the two men watching from the darkness.
The one who spoke had been standing behind a counter; the other
sat back amid shadows in the doorway to another room.

"Hello." Bremen paused, felt the rush of neurobabble from the
two men like the hot breath of some giant creature, and almost
staggered outside again before noticing the big, electric cooler. He
felt as if he had not drunk anything for days. It was the old kind
of cooler with a sliding top, bottles of cold pop resting in half-
melted ice. Bremen fished out the first bottle he uncovered, an RC
Cola, and went to the counter to pay for it.

"Fifty cents," said the standing man. Bremen could see him
better now: wrinkled tan slacks, a T-shirt that once had been blue
but had been washed to a near gray, rough, reddened face, and
blue eyes that *hadn't* faded looking out from under a nylon cap
with a mesh back.

Bremen fumbled in his pocket and found no change. His wallet
was empty. For a second he was sure that he had no money, but
then he fished in his gray suitcoat pocket and came out with a roll
of bills, all twenties and fifties from the looks of it. Now he remembered going to the bank the day before and removing the
$3,865.71 that had been left in their joint account after mortgage
and hospital payments.

Shit. Another goddamn drug dealer. Prob'ly from Miami.

Bremen could hear the standing man's thoughts as clearly as if
they had been spoken, so he replied in words even as he peeled off
a twenty-dollar bill and set it on the counter. "Uh-uh," he rasped,
"I'm not a drug dealer."

The standing man blinked, set a red hand on the twenty-dollar
bill, and blinked again. He cleared his throat. "I didn't say you
was, mister."

It was Bremen's turn to blink. The man's anger pulsed at him
like a hot, red light. Through the static of neurobabble, he could
sort out a few images.

Fucking druggies killed Norm Jr. as sure as if they'd put a gun to his head. Boy never had no discipline, no common sense. If his mommy'd lived, mighta been different. . . . Images of a child on a tire swing, the seven-year-old boy laughing, front tooth missing. Images of the boy as a man in his late twenties, eyes darkened, pale skin slick with sweat. *Please, Dad . . . I swear I'll pay you back. Just a loan so I can get on my feet again.*

You mean get on your feet until you can score another hit of coke, or crack, or whatever you call it now. Norm Sr.'s voice. When Norm Sr. had gone into Dade County to see the boy. Norm Jr. shaking, sick, deep in debt, ready to go infinitely deeper in debt to keep up his habit. *Over my dead body you'll get more money for this shit. You wanna come home, work at the store . . . that's all right. We'll get you into the county clinic. . . .* Images of the boy, the man now, sweeping dishes and coffee cups from the tabletop and stalking from the café. Memory of Norm Sr. weeping for the first time in almost fifty years.

Bremen blinked as Norm Sr. handed him his change. "I . . ." began Bremen, then realized that he could not say that he was sorry. "I'm not a drug dealer," he said again. "I know how it must look. The teller gave me the balance in fifties and twenties . . . our savings." Bremen popped the top off the RC Cola and took a long drink. "I just flew down from Philadelphia," he said, wiping his chin with the back of his hand. "My . . . my wife died last Saturday."

It was the first time Bremen had said those words and they sounded flat and patently false to him. He took another sip and looked down, confused.

Norm's thoughts were churned, but the red heat was gone. *Maybe. What the hell . . . fella can be strung out from his missus dyin' as much as from drugs. Suspicious of everybody these days. He looks like I did when Alma Jean passed on . . . he looks like hell.*

"You thinking of doin' some fishin'?" said Norm Sr.

"Fishing . . ." Bremen finished the drink and looked up at the shelves stocked with lures, small cardboard boxes of bobbers, and reels. He saw cane and fiberglass rods stacked against the far wall. "Yesss," he said slowly, surprising himself with his answer, "I'd like to do some fishing."

Norm Sr. nodded. "You need any tackle? Bait? A license? Or you got that already?"

Bremen licked his lips, feeling something returning to the insides of his skull. His scoured, bruised skull. "I need everything," he said, almost in a whisper.

Norm Sr. grinned. "Well, mister, you got the money for it." He began moving around, offering Bremen choices on tackle, bait, and rental rods. Bremen wanted no choices; he took the first of everything that Norm Sr. offered. The stack on the countertop grew.

Bremen went back to the cooler and fished around for a second bottle, feeling somehow liberated at the thought of that also going on his growing tab.

"You need a place to stay? It's easier if you stay out on one of the islands if you're gonna fish the lake."

Was that swamp he'd mistaken for the Everglades a lake? "A place to stay?" Bremen repeated, seeing in the reflecting glass of Norm Sr.'s slow thoughts that the man was sure that he was retarded in his grief. "Yes. I'd like to stay here a few days."

Norm Sr. turned back to the silent, seated man. Bremen opened his thoughts to the dark figure there, but almost no language came through. The man's thoughts churned like an infinitely slow washing machine turning a few rags and bundles of images, but almost no words at all. Bremen almost gasped at the newness of this.

"Verge, didn't that Chicago fella check out of Copely Isle Two?"

Verge nodded, and in a sudden shift of light from the only window, Bremen could see now that he was an old man, toothless, liver spots almost glowing in the errant touch of daylight.

Norm Sr. turned back. "Verge don't talk so good after his last stroke . . . aphasia is what Doc Myers calls it . . . but his mind's all right. We got an opening on one of the island cabins. Forty-two dollars a day, plus rental of one of the boats an' outboards. Or Verge could take you out . . . no charge for that. Good spots right from the island."

Bremen nodded. Yes. Yes to everything.

Norm Sr. returned the nod. "Okay, minimum three nights' stay, so there's a hundred-and-ten-dollar deposit. You gonna stay three nights?"

Bremen nodded. Yes.

Norm Sr. turned to a surprisingly modern electronic cash register and began totaling the bill. Bremen pulled several fifties from his wad of bills, shoved the rest into his pocket.

"Oh . . ." said Norm Sr., rubbing his cheek. Bremen could sense the reluctance to ask a personal question. "I imagine you got clothes for fishin', but if . . . ah . . . if you need somethin' else to wear. Or groceries . . ."

"Just a minute," said Bremen, and left the store. He walked up the narrow trail, past where he had vomited, back to the rental Beretta. There was a single piece of luggage on the passenger seat: his old gym bag. Bremen had no recollection of checking it through, but there was a claim check on it. He lifted it, felt the uneasy emptiness except for a single lump of weight, and unzipped it.

Inside, wrapped in a red bandanna that Gail had given him the previous summer, was a Smith & Wesson .38-caliber revolver. It had been a gift from Gail's policeman brother the year they had lived in Germantown and there had been break-ins up and down their block. Neither Bremen nor Gail had ever fired it. He had always meant to throw it away—it and the box of shells Carl had given them with the pistol—but instead had left it locked in the lower right-hand drawer of his desk.

Bremen had no memory of packing the thing. He lifted the pistol, unwrapped the bandanna, knowing that at least he would not have loaded it.

It was loaded. The tips of five slugs were partially visible in the round cradles of their chambers, gray-curved and pregnant with death. Bremen wrapped the pistol, set it in the bag, and zipped the bag shut. He carried it back to the store.

Norm Sr. raised his eyebrows.

"I guess I brought the wrong clothes for fishing," said Bremen, trying a grin. "I'll look on the racks over there."

The man behind the counter nodded.

"And some groceries," said Bremen. "I'll need three days' worth, I guess."

Norm Sr. walked over to shelves near the front of the store and began removing cans. "The cabin's got an old stove," he said. "But most guys just use the hot plate. Soup an' beans an' stuff okay?" He seemed to sense that Bremen was not up to making decisions himself.

"Yeah," said Bremen, finding a pair of work pants and a khaki shirt only one size away from his own. He carried them over to the counter and looked at his feet, frowning at his polished penny loafers. One glance around told him that this miraculous store did not stock boots or sneakers.

Norm Sr. retotaled the bill and Bremen peeled off twenties, thinking that it had been many years since he had been so pleased to make a purchase. Norm Sr. dumped the goods in a cardboard box, cartons of live bait going in next to bread and white-paper-wrapped packages of cold cuts, and handed Bremen the fiberglass rod he'd chosen for him.

"Verge's got the outboard warmed up. That is, if you're ready to go on out . . ."

"I'm ready," said Bremen.

"You might wanna move your car down from the road. Park it out behind the store."

Bremen did something that surprised even himself. He handed Norm Sr. the keys, knowing beyond certainty that the car would be safe with the man. "Would you mind . . . ?" Bremen could not conceal his eagerness to get going.

Norm Sr. raised his eyebrows a second, then smiled. "No problem. I'll do it right away. Keys'll be here when you're ready to leave."

Bremen followed him out the back door, onto a short dock that had been invisible from the front of the store. The old man sat at the rear of a small boat, grinning up toothlessly.

Bremen felt a sort of unhappiness unfold in his chest, rather like a tropical bird stretching its wings after sleep, revealing bright plumage. For a terrible second Bremen was afraid that he might cry.

Norm Sr. handed the carton of goods down to Verge and waited while Bremen clumsily stepped into the center of the boat, laying his fiberglass rod carefully along the thwarts.

Norm Sr. tugged at his nylon cap. "You all have a good time out there, hear?"

"Yes," whispered Bremen, sitting back on the rough seat and smelling the lake and the bite of motor oil and even the hint of kerosene on his clothes. "Yes. Yes."

EYES

Probably no one alive understands how the mind actually works as well as Jeremy. Besides having access to other minds since he was thirteen years old, Jeremy has blundered onto research that shows the actual mechanism of thought. Or at least a very good metaphor for it.

It is five years before Gail's death, Jeremy has finally finished his thesis on wavefront analysis, when a paper by Jacob Goldmann arrives on his Haverford desk. A note from his old roommate Chuck Gilpen is appended: *Thought you might like to see someone else's approach to this stuff.*

Jeremy comes home so excited that he can hardly talk. Gernisavien glares at him and runs from the room. Gail pours him a cold drink and sits him down at the kitchen table. "Slower," she says. "Talk more slowly."

"Okay," gasps Jeremy, almost choking on the iced tea. "You know my thesis? The wavefront stuff?"

Gail rolls her eyes. How can she not know his thesis? It has filled their lives and stolen their spare time for four years now. "Yes," she says patiently.

"Well, it's all obsolete," says Jeremy with an incongruous smile. "Chuck Gilpen sent me some stuff today by a guy named Gold-mann up in Cambridge. All my Fourier analysis is obsolete."

"Oh, Jerry . . ." begins Gail, real sorrow in her voice.

"No, no . . . it's *great!*" Jeremy is almost shouting. "It's wonderful, Gail. Goldmann's research fills in all the missing parts. I was doing all the right work, but on the wrong problem."

Gail shakes her head. She does not understand.

He leans forward, his face glowing. Iced tea spills onto the butcher-block table. He thrusts a stack of papers toward her. "No, *look,* kiddo, it's all right here. Remember what my work is about?"

"Wavefront analysis of memory function," says Gail automatically.

"*Yes.* Only I was stupid to restrict it to memory. Goldmann and his team have been doing basic research on holistic wavefront parameters for general human consciousness analogs. It started with a line of analysis developed in the thirties by a Russian mathematician, tied into some stuff done on rehabilitation anomalies following stroke effects, and led right up to my Fourier analysis of memory function. . . ." Despite himself Jeremy abandons language and tries to communicate directly with Gail. His mindtouch interferes with words, images cascading like printouts from an overworked terminal. Endless Schrödinger curves, their plots speaking in language infinitely purer than speech. The collapse of probability curves in binomial progression.

"No, no," gasps Gail, shaking her head. "Talk. Tell me in words."

Jeremy tries, knowing all the while that the mathematics that are so much chalky static to her would tell the story more clearly. "Holograms," he says. "Goldmann's work is based on holographic research."

"Like your memory analysis," says Gail, frowning slightly as she always does when they discuss his work.

"Yeah . . . right . . . only Goldmann's work has taken it beyond a synaptic memory-function analysis, taken it all the way to an analog of human thought . . . hell, the entire range of human consciousness."

Gail takes in a breath and Jeremy can see the understanding begin to blossom in her mind. He would like to reach in and substitute pure math for the sullied language constructs she uses to bridge her way to understanding, but he resists the impulse and tries to find more words himself.

"Does this . . ." says Gail and pauses. "Does this work Goldmann's doing explain our . . . ability?"

"Telepathy?" Jeremy grins. "Yes, Gail . . . *yes*. Hell, it explains almost everything that I was groping around like a blind man." He takes a breath, gulps down the last of his iced tea, and continues. "Goldmann's team is doing all sorts of complicated EEG studies and scans. He's been getting a lot of raw data, but I took his stuff this morning and did a Fourier analysis of it, then plugged it into various modifications of Schrödinger's wave equation to see whether it worked as a standing wave."

"Jerry, I don't quite see . . ." says Gail. He can feel her questing thoughts trying to sort out the mathematical jumble of his own thoughts.

"Damn it, kiddo, it *did* work. Goldmann's MRI-type longitudinal study of human thought patterns *can* be described as a standing wavefront. Not just the memory function of it, like I was piddling around with it, but *all* of human consciousness. The part of us that's us can be expressed almost perfectly as a hologram . . . or, maybe more precisely, sort of a superhologram containing a few million smaller holograms."

Gail leans forward, her eyes beginning to shine. "I think I see . . . but where does that leave the mind, Jerry? The brain itself?"

Jeremy grins, tries to take another drink, but only ice cubes rattle against his lips. He sets the glass down with a bang. "I guess the best answer is that the Greeks and the religious nuts were right to separate the two. The brain could be viewed as a . . . well, a kind of electrochemical wavefront generator and interferometer all in one. But the mind . . . ah, the *mind* . . . that is something much more beautiful than that lump of gray matter we call a brain." Despite himself Jeremy is again thinking in terms of equations: sine waves dancing to Schrödinger's elegant tune. Eternal but mutable sine waves.

Gail frowns again. "So there *is* a soul . . . some part of us that can survive death?" Gail's parents, especially her mother, had been fundamentalists, and now her voice takes on that slightly querulous tone that always enters in when she discusses religious ideas. The idea of a smarmy little cherub of a soul winging its way toward eternal stasis in heaven is appalling to her.

It is Jeremy's turn to frown. "Survive death? Well, no . . . ." He is irritated at having to think in words once again. "If Goldmann's work and my analysis of it are right and the personality is a complex wavefront, sort of a series of low-energy holograms interpreting reality, then the personality certainly couldn't survive brain death. The template would be destroyed as well as the holographic generator. That intricate wavefront that's *us* . . . and by intricate, Gail, well, my analysis shows more wave-particle variations than there are atoms in the universe . . . that holographic wavefront needs energy to support it just like everything else does. With brain death, the wavefront would collapse like a hot-air balloon without the hot air. Collapse, fragment, shred, and disappear."

Gail smiles grimly. "Pleasant image," she says softly.

Jeremy is not listening. His eyes have taken that slightly stigmatic look he gets when a thought is working him over. "But it's not what happens to the wavefront when the brain dies that's important," he says in a tone that suggests his wife is one of his students. "It's how this breakthrough . . . and by God, it *is* a breakthrough . . . it's how this breakthrough applies to what you call our ability. To telepathy."

"And how does it apply, Jerry?" Gail's voice is soft.

"It's simple enough when you visualize human thought as a

series of standing wavefronts creating interference patterns that can be stored and propagated in holographic analogs."

"Uh-huh."

"No, it *is* simple. Remember when we shared impressions of the ability just after we met? We both decided that it would be impossible to explain mindtouch to anyone who hadn't experienced it. It would be like describing—"

"Like describing colors to a person blind since birth," says Gail.

"Okay. Yeah. *You* know that the reality of mindtouch isn't anything like how they portray it in those silly sci-fi stories you read."

Gail smiles. Reading science fiction is her secret vice, a vacation from the "serious reading" she usually does, but she enjoys the genre enough that she usually chastises Jeremy for calling it "sci-fi." "They usually say it's like picking up radio or TV broadcasts," she says. "Like the mind's a receiver or something."

Jeremy nods. "*We* know it's not like that. That it's more like . . ." Again, words fail him and he tries to share the mathematics with her: out-of-phase sine waves slowly converging as amplitudes shift across graphed probability space.

"Sort of like having déjà vu with someone else's memories," says Gail, refusing to leave the flimsy raft of language.

"Right," says Jeremy, but frowns, considering, and then says "right" again. "The question that no one ever thought to ask . . . at least until Goldmann and his team . . . is how does anyone read his or her own mind? Neurological researchers are always trying to track down the answer to that by looking at neurotransmitters or other chemicals, or thinking in terms of dendrites and synapses . . . sort of like someone trying to understand how a radio works by tearing apart individual chips or peering into a transistor, without ever putting the thing together."

Gail goes to the fridge, returns with a pitcher to refill his iced tea. "And you've put the radio together?"

"Goldmann has." Jeremy grins. "And I've turned it on for him."

"How do we read our own minds?" Gail asks softly.

Jeremy molds the air with his hands. His fingers flutter like the elusive wavefronts he describes. "The brain generates these superholograms that contain the full package . . . memory, personality, even wavefront processing packages so that we can interpret reality . . . and even while generating these wavefronts, the brain is also acting as interferometer, breaking down wavefronts into component pieces as we need them. 'Reading' our own minds."

Gail's hands are clenching and unclenching as she resists the impulse to bite her nails in excitement. "I think I see. . . ."

Jeremy grabs her hands. "You *do* see. This explains so much, Gail . . . why stroke victims can relearn using different parts of their minds, the terrible effects of Alzheimer's, even why babies need to dream so much and old people don't. You see, the personality wavefront in a baby has such a greater need to interpret reality in that holographic simulator. . . ."

Jeremy pauses. He has seen the flicker of pain that crossed Gail's face at the mention of a baby. He squeezes her hands.

"Anyway," he says, "you see how it explains the ability we have."

She looks up, meeting his gaze. "I think I do, Jerry. But . . ."

He drains the last of his iced tea. "Perhaps we're genetic mutations, kiddo, the way we've discussed in the past. But if so, we're mutants whose brains do just what everyone else's brains do . . . break down the superholograms to understandable patterns. *Only our brains can interpret other people's wavefront patterns as well as our own.*"

Gail is nodding quickly now, seeing it. "That's why we have this constant static of people's thoughts . . . what you call neurobabble . . . isn't it, Jerry? We're constantly breaking down other people's thought waves. What did you call the hologram thing that does that?"

"An interferometer."

Gail smiles again. "So we were born with faulty interferometers."

Jeremy lifts her hand and kisses her fingers. "Or overefficient ones."

Gail walks to the window and looks out toward the barn, trying to absorb these things. Jeremy leaves her thoughts to her, raising his mindshield enough not to intrude. After a moment he says, "There's one other thing, kiddo."

She turns away from the window, holding her arms.

"The reason Chuck Gilpen had that research in the first place," he says. "Do you remember that Chuck's working with the Fundamental Physics Group out at Lawrence Berkeley Labs?"

Gail nods. "So?"

"So for the past few years they've been hunting down all those smaller and smaller particles and studying the properties that rule them to get a hook on what's real. What's *really* real. And when they get past the gluons and quarks and charm and color, and do get a glimpse of reality on its most basic and persuasive level, you know what they get?"

Gail shakes her head and hugs herself more tightly, seeing his answer even before he verbalizes it.

"They get a series of probability equations that show standing wavefronts," he says softly, his own skin breaking out in goose bumps. "They get the same squiggles and jiggles that Goldmann gets when he looks beyond the brain and finds the mind."

Gail's voice is a whisper. "What does that *mean*, Jerry?"

Jeremy abandons his iced tea with its melting ice cubes and goes to the fridge to get a beer. He pops the top and drinks deeply, pausing to burp once. Beyond Gail, the late-afternoon light is painting the cherry trees beyond the barn in rich colors. *Out there*, he shares with Gail. *And in our minds. Different . . . and the same. The universe as a standing wavefront, as fragile and improbable as a baby's dreams.*

He burps again and says aloud, "Beats the hell out of me, kiddo."

Lasciate Ogne Speranza,
Voi Ch'intrate

On the third day, Bremen rose and went out into the light. There was a small dock behind the shack, little more than two boards on pilings really, and it was here that Bremen stood and blinked at the sunrise while birds made riotous sounds in the swamp behind him and fish rose to feed in the river in front of him.

On the first day he had been content to let Verge ferry him across the river and show him his fishing shack. The old man's thoughts were a welcome change to Bremen's exhausted mind: wordless thoughts, images without words, slow emotions without words, thoughts as rhythmic and soothing as the put-putting of the ancient outboard motor that propelled them across the slow-moving river.

The shack had been more than Bremen had expected for forty-two dollars a day; beyond the dock the little structure boasted a porch, a tiny living room with screened windows, one sprung couch, and a rocking chair, a small kitchen with a half-sized refrigerator—there was electricity!—the bulky oven and promised hot plate, and finally a narrow table with a faded oilcloth. There was also a bedroom not much larger than the built-in bed itself, its single window looking out on an honest-to-God outhouse. The shower and sink were makeshift things in an open alcove outside the back door. But the blankets and folded sheets were clean, the three electric lights in the shack worked, and Bremen collapsed onto the sprung couch with an emotion very close to elation at having found this place . . . if one can feel elation while feeling a sadness so profound that it bordered on vertigo.

Verge had come in and sat on the rocking chair. Remembering his manners, Bremen had gone through the grocery sacks, found the six-pack of beer that Norm Sr. had packed, and had offered one to Verge. The old man did not refuse, and Bremen basked in the warm glow of the old man's wordless thoughts as they sat in the warm twilight and sipped their equally warm beers.

Later, after his guide had left, Bremen sat on the dock and fished. Not worrying about choice of bait or strength of line or what kind of fish he was going after, he had dangled his legs off the rough planks, listened to the swamp and river come alive with bullfrogs in the fading light, and caught more fish than he had ever dreamed of. Bremen knew that some were catfish from their whiskers, that several were longer, thinner, and tougher fighters, and that one actually looked like a rainbow trout, although he considered that unlikely . . . but he threw them all back. He had enough for three nights' dinners and he needed no fish. It was the *process* of fishing that was therapeutic; it was *fishing* that lulled his mind into some vestige of peace after the madness of the preceding days and weeks.

Later on that first day's night, sometime after it grew dark (Bremen did not consult his watch), he had gone into the shack, prepared a bacon, lettuce, and tomato sandwich for dinner, washed it down with another beer, cleaned the dishes and then himself, and had gone to bed, to sleep for the first time in four days, and to sleep, without dreaming, for the first time in many weeks.

On the second day Bremen slept late and fished from the dock through the morning, caught nothing at all, and was as satisfied as he had been the night before. After an early lunch he had walked along the bank almost to a point where the river drained into the swamp, or vice versa . . . he could not tell, and fished for a few hours from a bank. Again, he threw back everything he caught, but he saw a snake swimming lazily between the half-submerged cypress and for the first time in his life was not afraid of the serpent.

On the evening of the second day Verge came put-putting upriver, coasted into the dock, and let Bremen know through simple signs that he was there to take him fishing back in the swamp. Bremen had hesitated a moment—he did not know if he was ready for the swamp—but then had lowered his rod and reel to the old man and jumped carefully into the front of the boat.

The swamp had been dark and overhung with Spanish moss, and Bremen had spent less time paying attention to his fishing than in watching the huge birds flapping lazily overhead to their nests, or listening to the evening calls of a thousand varieties of frogs, and even watching two alligators move lazily through the dusk-tinted water. Verge's thoughts were almost one with the rhythms of the boat and swamp, and Bremen found it infinitely soothing to surrender the turmoil of his own consciousness to the damaged clarity of his fishing partner's damaged mind. Through some strange way Bremen had fathomed that Verge, although poorly educated and far from being a learned man, had been a kind of poet in his earlier days. Now, since the stroke, that poetry showed itself as a gentle cadence of wordless memories and as a willingness to surrender memory itself to the more demanding cadence of *now*.

Neither of them had caught anything worth keeping, so they came out of the swamp into a lighter darkness—a full moon was rising above cypress to the east—and tied up to the little dock at Bremen's shack. A breeze kept the mosquitoes away as they sat in companionable silence on the porch and finished the last of Bremen's beers.

Now, on the third morning, Bremen rose and came out into the light, blinking at the sunrise and wanting to get a little fishing in before breakfast. Bremen jumped down from the dock and walked a hundred yards south along the bank to a grassy place he had found the previous afternoon. Mist rose from the river and the birds filled the air with urgent cries. Bremen walked carefully, one eye out for snakes or alligators in the weeds along the bank, feeling the air warm quickly as the sun rose free of the trees. There was something very close to happiness turning slowly in his chest.

The Big Two-Hearted River, came Gail's thought.

Bremen stopped and almost stumbled. He stood, panting slightly, closing his eyes to concentrate. It had been Gail but had *not* been Gail: a phantom echo, as chilling as if her actual voice had whispered to him. For a minute the dizziness grew worse, and Bremen had to sit down quickly on a hummock of grass. He lowered his head between his knees and tried to breathe slowly. After a while the humming in his ears lessened, the pounding in his chest moderated, and the wave of déjà vu bordering on nausea passed.

Bremen raised his face to the sun, tried to smile, and lifted his rod and reel.

He did not have his rod and reel. This morning he had carried out the .38-caliber pistol instead.

Bremen sat on the warming riverbank and considered the weapon. The blue steel looked almost black in the bright light. He found the lever that released the cylinder and looked at the six brass circles. He clicked the cylinder shut and lifted the weapon higher, raising it almost to his face. The hammer clicked back with surprising ease and locked into place. Bremen set the short barrel against his temple and closed his eyes, feeling the warm sunlight on his face and listening to the buzz of insects.

Bremen did not fantasize that the bullet entering his skull would free him . . . would send him to some other plane of existence. Neither he nor Gail had ever believed in any life but this one. But he did realize that the gun, that the single bullet, were instruments of release. His finger had found the trigger, and now Bremen knew with absolute certainty that the slightest additional pressure would bring an end to the bottomless chasm of sorrow that lay under even this brief flash of happiness. The slightest additional pressure would end forever the incessant encroachment of other people's thoughts that even now buzzed around the periphery of his consciousness like a million bluebottle flies around rotted meat.

Bremen began to apply that additional pressure, feeling the perfect arc of metal under his finger, and, despite himself, converted that tactile sense of arc as a mathematical construct. He visualized the latent kinetic energy lying in the gunpowder, the sudden translation of that energy into motion, and the ensuing collapse of a much more intricate structure as the complex dance of sine waves and standing wavefronts in his skull died with the dying of the brain that generated them.

It was the thought of destroying that beautiful mathematical construct, of smashing forever the wavefront equations that were so much more beautiful to Bremen than the flawed and injured human psyche they represented, that caused him to lower the pistol, lower the hammer of the pistol, and toss it away from him, over the high reeds, into the river.

Bremen stood and watched the ripples widen. He felt neither elation nor sadness, satisfaction nor relief. He felt nothing at all.

He sensed the man's thoughts only seconds before he turned and saw him.

The man was standing in an old skiff not twenty-five feet from Bremen, using an oar as a pole to move the flat-bottomed boat out of the shallows near where the river entered the swamp (or vice versa). The man was dressed even less appropriately for the river than Bremen had been three days before: he wore a white lounge suit with a black shirt, sharp collars slashing across the suit's broad lapels like raven wings; there were layers of gold necklaces descending from the man's thin throat to where black chest hair matched the black satin of his shirt; he wore expensive black pumps of a soft leather never designed for any surface more hostile than a plush carpet; a pink silk handkerchief rose from the pocket of his white lounge suit; his pants were held up by a white belt with a large gold buckle, and a gold Rolex gleamed on his left wrist.

Bremen had opened his mouth to say good morning when he saw everything at once.

His name is Vanni Fucci. He left Miami a little after three A.M. The dead man in the trunk had borne the unlikely name of Chico Tartugian. Vanni Fucci had dumped the body less than twenty feet from where the skiff now floated, just back among the cypresses where the swamp was black and relatively deep.

Bremen blinked and could see the ripples still emanating from the shadowy place where Chico Tartugian had been pushed overboard with fifty pounds of steel chain around him.

"Hey!" cried Vanni Fucci, and almost overturned the skiff as he took one hand off the oar to paw under his white jacket.

Bremen took a step backward and then froze. For an instant he thought that the .38-caliber revolver in Vanni Fucci's hand was *his* gun, the pistol Bremen's brother-in-law had given him, the pistol he had just tossed into the river. Ripples still widened from that site of discard, although they were dying now as they met the river current and the small waves from Vanni Fucci's bobbing skiff.

"Hey!" shouted Vanni Fucci a second time, and cocked the pistol. Audibly.

Bremen tried to raise his hands, but found that he had only brought them together in front of his chest in a motion suggesting neither supplication nor prayer so much as contemplation.

"What the fuck are you doing here?" screamed Vanni Fucci, the skiff wobbling so much now that the black muzzle opening of the pistol moved from being aimed at Bremen's face to a point near his feet.

Bremen knew that if he were going to run, now was the time to do it. He did not run.

"I said what the fuck are you doing here, you goddamn fuck!" screamed the man in the white suit and black shirt. His hair was as black and shiny as his shirt and rose in tight ringlets. His face was pale under a machine tan and his mouth was a cupid's fleshy pout, now contorted into something resembling a snarl. Bremen saw a diamond gleaming in Vanni Fucci's left earlobe.

Unable to speak for a moment, due more to a strange exhilaration than from any surge of fear, Bremen shook his head. His hands remained cupped, fingertips almost touching.

"C'mere, you fuck," shouted Vanni Fucci, trying to keep the pistol steady as he tucked the oar tighter under his right arm and poled toward the bank, using his left forearm to steady himself against the oar. The skiff rocked again, but coasted forward; the muzzle of the pistol grew in size.

Bremen blinked gnats away from his eyes and watched as the skiff floated up to the bank. The .38 was less than eight feet away now and much more steady.

"What'd you see, you fuck? What'd you fucking see?" Vanni Fucci punctuated the second question with an extension of the revolver, as if he meant to thrust it through Bremen's face.

Bremen said nothing. A part of him was very calm. He thought of Gail during her last days and nights, surrounded by instruments in the intensive care ward, her body invaded by catheters, oxygen tubes, and intravenous drips. All thought of the elegant dance of sine waves had vanished with the gangster's shouts.

"Get in the fuckin' boat, motherfucker," hissed Vanni Fucci.

Bremen blinked again, honestly not understanding. Fucci's thoughts were white-hot, a torrent of heated obscenities and surges of fears, and for a long moment Bremen did not know that Vanni Fucci had spoken aloud.

"I said, get in the fucking boat, you motherfucker!" cried Vanni Fucci, and fired his pistol into the air.

Bremen sighed, lowered his hands, and stepped carefully into the skiff. Vanni Fucci waved him into the front of the flat-bottomed craft, gestured him to a sitting position, and then clumsily began poling with one hand while the other held the pistol.

Silently except for the cry of birds disturbed into flight by the single shot, they moved toward the opposite shore.

EYES

I am interested in death. It is a new concept to me. The idea that one could simply *cease* is perhaps the most startling and fascinating idea that Jeremy has brought to me.

I am fairly certain that Jeremy's own first realization of mortality is a particularly brutal one: the death of his mother when he was four. His telepathic ability is rare and undisciplined then— little more than the intrusion of certain thoughts and nightmares he would later realize are not his own—but the talent takes on a rare and unkind focus the night his mother died.

Her name is Elizabeth Susskind Bremen and she is twenty-nine years old on the night she dies. She is returning home from a "girls' night out" that they have renamed poker night in deference to the prissy sound of the earlier name. This group of six to ten women have been meeting once a month for years, most since before they were married, and this night they have gone into Philadelphia to catch a Wednesday-evening opening at the art museum and to go out to listen to jazz afterward. They are careful to appoint a designated driver, even though that name has not yet come into popular use, and Elizabeth's lifelong friend Carrie has not had any alcohol before the drive home. Four of the friends live within a half hour's drive of one another near where the Bremen home is in Bucks County, and they are carpooling in Carrie's Chevy station wagon the night the drunk jumps the median on the Schuylkill Expressway.

The traffic is heavy, the station wagon is in the left-most lane, and there is no more than two seconds of warning as the drunk comes over the median in a stretch where the guardrail is being repaired. The collision is head-on. Jeremy's mother, her friend Carrie, and another woman named Margie Sheerson are killed instantly. The fourth woman, a new friend of Carrie's who has attended poker night for the first time that night, is thrown from the car and survives, although she remains paralyzed from that day on. The drunk—a man whose name Jeremy is never to recall no matter how many times he sees it written in years to come—survives with minor injuries.

Jeremy slams awake and begins screaming, bringing his father running upstairs. The boy is still screaming when the highway patrol calls twenty-five minutes later.

Jeremy remembers every detail of the following few hours: being brought to the hospital with his father, where no one seems to know where Elizabeth Bremen's body had been sent; being made to stand next to his father as John Bremen is told to look at female corpse after female corpse in the hospital morgue in order to "identify" the missing Jane Doe; then being told that the body has never been brought in with the other victims', but has been transferred directly to a morgue in an adjoining county. Jeremy remembers the long drive through the rain in the middle of the night, his father's face, reflected in the mirror, lighted from the dashboard instruments, and the song on the radio—Pat Boone singing "April Love"—and then the confusion of trying to find the morgue in what seems an abandoned industrial section of Philadelphia.

Finally, Jeremy remembers staring at his mother's face and body. There is no discreet sheet to raise, as in the movies Jeremy watches in years to come, only a clear plastic bag, rather like a clear shower curtain, through which Elizabeth Susskind Bremen's battered face and broken body gleam almost milkily. The sleepy morgue attendant unzips the bag with a rude motion and accidentally pulls the plastic down until Jeremy's dead mother's breasts are exposed. They are still caked with not-quite-dry blood. John Bremen pulls the plastic higher in a motion familiar to Jeremy from hundreds of tucking-ins, and his father says nothing, only nods identification. His mother's eyes are open slightly, as if she is peeking at them, playing some game of hide-and-seek.

Of course, his father does not take him along that night. Jeremy has been left with a neighbor, tucked into a sofa bed in the neighbor's guest room smelling of carpet cleanser, and has shared each second of his father's nightmare ordeal while lying between clean sheets and staring, wide-eyed, at the slowly moving bands of light on the neighbor's guest-room ceiling as passing cars hiss by on wet pavement. It is more than twenty years later, after he has married Gail, that Jeremy realizes this. In truth, it is Gail who realizes it—who interrupts Jeremy's bitter telling of that evening's events—it is Gail who has access to parts of Jeremy's memory that not even he can reach.

Jeremy did not weep when he was four, but he does this night twenty-one years later: he weeps on Gail's shoulder for almost an hour. Weeps for his mother and for his father, now gone, who has died of cancer unforgiven by his son. Jeremy weeps for himself.

I am not so sure about Gail's first telepathic encounter with death. There are memories of burying her cat Leo when she is five, but the remembered mindtouch during that animal's final hours after being struck by a car might be more a mourning for the absence of purring and furry warmth than any real contact with the cat's consciousness.

Gail's parents are fundamentalist Christians, increasingly fundamentalist as Gail grows older, and she rarely hears death spoken of in any terms other than "passing over" to Christ's kingdom. When she is eight and her grandmother dies—she has been a stiff, formal, and odd-smelling old lady whom Gail rarely visits—Gail is lifted up to view the body in the funeral home while her father whispers in her ear, "That's not really Grams . . . Grams is in heaven."

Gail has decided early, even before Grams's passing over, that heaven is almost certainly a crock of shit. Those are her Great-Uncle Buddy's words—"All this holy-roller stuff, Beanie, it's all a crock of shit. This heaven and choirs-of-angels stuff . . . all a crock of shit. We die and fertilize the ground, just like Leo Puss is doing out in the backyard right now. The only thing we know that happens after we're dead is that we help the grass and flowers grow, everything else is a crock of shit." Gail has never been sure why Great-Uncle Buddy called her Beanie, but she thinks it has to do with a sister of his who died when they were children.

Death, she decides early, is simple. One dies and makes the grass and flowers grow. Everything else is a crock of shit.

Gail's mother hears her sharing this philosophy with a playmate —they are burying a hamster who has died—and Gail's mother sends the playmate home and harangues Gail for over an hour about what the Bible says, how the Bible is God's Word on earth, and how stupid it is to think that a person simply ceases to be. Gail, stubborn, stares and listens, but refuses to recant. Her mother says that Great-Uncle Buddy is an alcoholic.

So are you, the nine-year-old Gail thinks, but does not say aloud. She does not know this through her mindtouch ability—that will come under her control four years later when she enters puberty— but has deduced it through finding the can opener under the towels in the bathroom, from hearing her mother's usually precise diction slurred and loud late at night, and from listening to the voices rising up the stairs from the parties her parents throw for their born-again friends.

Ironically, the first person close to Gail to die after she comes into the true birthright of her telepathic ability is her Great-Uncle Buddy. She has taken the bus all the way across Chicago to visit Uncle Buddy in the hospital where he lies dying. He has been unable to talk, his throat catheterized for the breathing tubes that keep air flowing past the cancer-ridden throat into the cancer-riddled lungs, but fifteen-year-old Gail remains there for six hours, long past visiting hours, holding his hand and trying to project her own thoughts to his through the shifting veils of pain and painkillers. There is no sense that he hears her mindtouch messages, although she is all but overwhelmed by the complex tapestry of his daydreamed memories. Through them all there has been a sense of sadness and loss, much of it centered around the sister, Beanie, who was Uncle Buddy's one friend in a hostile world.

Uncle Buddy, Gail sent over and over, *if it's not all a crock of shit . . . heaven and all . . . send me a sign. Send me a thought.* The experiment thrills and terrifies her. She lies awake for three nights wishing she had not sent the thought to her dying friend, half expecting his ghost to awaken her each night, but on the fourth night after Buddy died, there is nothing in the night—no whisper of his husky voice or warm thoughts, no sense of his presence "elsewhere"—only silence and a void.

Silence and a void. It remains Gail's conviction of death's dominion through the rest of her life, including these final weeks when she cannot hide the bleakness of her thoughts from Jeremy. He does not try to dissuade her from that view, although he shares sunlight and hope with her even while he sees little of the former and feels nothing of the latter.

Silence and a void. It is Gail's sense of death.

Now it is Jeremy's.

Where the Deadmen Left Their Bones

Vanni Fucci led Bremen from the skiff to the shore, from the shore through the screen of trees, and from the trees to the roadside where a white Cadillac was parked. The man kept the revolver down at his side, but visible, as he opened the car door on the passenger side and waved Bremen in. Bremen did not protest or speak. Through the shield of cypress he could see the small store where Norm Sr. was drinking his second cup of coffee and where Verge was sitting and smoking his pipe.

Fucci slid into the driver's seat, started the Caddy with a roar, and peeled onto the tarmac, leaving a cloud of dust and a pattering of gravel on foliage behind them. There was no other traffic. The low morning light touched treetops and telephone poles. Sunlight glinted on water to their right. The gangster set the pistol near his left leg on the plush leather seat. "You say one fucking word," he said in an urgent whisper, "and I'll blow your fucking head off right here."

Bremen had no urge to say anything. As they continued to drive west, the Cadillac idling along at an easy fifty-five, he settled back into the cushions and watched the scenery go by to his right. They left the swamp and forest behind and entered an open area of saw grass and scrub pine. Weathered farmhouses sat back in the fields and, closer to the highway, perched the occasional roadside stands, empty of produce and people. Vanni Fucci muttered something and turned on the radio, punching buttons until he found a station with the right blend of rock and roll.

Bremen's problem was that he hated melodrama. He did not believe in it. Gail had been the one to enjoy books and television and movies; Bremen always found the situations unlikely to the point of absurdity, the action and characters' reactions unbelievable, and the melodrama banal in the extreme. Occasionally Bremen would argue that human beings' lives revolved around carrying out the garbage, or setting the table, or watching TV— not around car chases and threatening others with guns. Gail would nod, smile, and say for the hundredth time, "Jerry, you've got the imagination of a doorknob."

Bremen had imagination, but he disliked melodrama and did not believe in the fictional worlds that depended upon it. He did not believe all that much in Vanni Fucci, although the gangster's thoughts were clear enough. Unstructured and frenzied, but clear.

It was a shame, Bremen thought, that people's minds were not like a computer, that one could not call up information at will. "Reading people's minds" was more analogous to trying to read hasty scrawls on scraps of paper scattered on a bobbing sea than calling up clean lines of information on a VDT. People did not go around thinking about themselves in neat flashbacks for the benefit of any telepath who might encounter their thoughts; at least the people whom Bremen had met did not.

Nor did Vanni Fucci, although Bremen had learned the man's name easily enough. Fucci *did* think of himself in the third person, in a totally self-absorbed but strangely removed way, as if the petty gangster's life were a movie that only he was watching. *Well, Vanni Fucci got rid of that miserable fuck* had been the gist of the first thought Bremen had encountered on the island. The clothes and hair of Chico Tartugian had still been sending bubbles of trapped air to the surface.

Bremen closed his eyes and concentrated as they drove west, then north, then west again. It seemed an important thing to do, concentrate, although Bremen's heart was not in it. He disliked melodrama.

Vanni Fucci's thoughts jumped around like an insect on a hot griddle. He was in some turmoil, although his emotions were not touched by the dumping of Chico's body or the probability that this stranger would have to be killed as well. It was just that he, Vanni Fucci, did not want to have to do the killing.

Fucci was a thief. Bremen caught enough images and shreds of images to glean the difference. In what seemed to be a long career as a thief—Bremen caught an image of Fucci in a mirror with long sideburns and the polyester leisure suit of the seventies— Vanni Fucci had never fired his gun at a person except for that time when Donni Capaletto, his so-called partner, had tried to rip him off after the Glendale Jeweler job and Fucci had taken away the punk's .45 automatic and shot him in the kneecap with it. His own gun. But Fucci had been angry. That wasn't a professional thing to do. And Vanni Fucci prided himself on being a professional.

Bremen blinked, fought back nausea at trying to read these flittering shards on the sea of Fucci's turbulent thoughts, and closed his eyes again.

Bremen learned more than he wanted to know about being a gangster in this last decade of the century. He glimpsed Vanni Fucci's deep and burning desire to be made, gleaned what "to be made" meant to a petty Italian gangster, and then Bremen shook his head at the mean lowness of it all. The teenage years running messages for Hesso and selling cigarettes out of the back of Big Ernie's hijacked trucks; the first job—that liquor mart on the south side of Newark—and the slow acceptance into the circle of tough, shrewd, but poorly educated men. Bremen caught glimpses of Fucci's deep satisfaction at that acceptance by these men, these stupid, mean, violent, selfish, and arrogant men, and Bremen caught deeper glimpses of Vanni Fucci's ultimate loyalty to himself. In the end, Bremen saw, Fucci was loyal *only* to himself. All the others—Hesso, Carpezzi, Tutti, Schwarz, Don Leoni, Sal, even Fucci's live-in girlfriend Cheryl—they all were expendable. As expendable in Fucci's mind as Chico Tartugian, a Miami nightclub owner and petty thug whom Fucci had met only once at Don Leoni's supper club in Brooklyn. It had been a favor to Don Leoni that had brought Fucci south; he hated Miami and hated to fly.

It had not been Fucci who pulled the trigger, but Don Leoni's son-in-law, Bert Cappi, a twenty-six-year-old punk who thought of himself as the next incarnation of Frank Sinatra. Cappi had been hired as a singer by Tartugian as a favor to Don Leoni, and even though the patrons booed and even the bartenders objected, Tartugian kept the kid on, knowing that Cappi was a spy even while Tartugian continued to rake off the top of the south-side numbers collections, trusting Cappi to place his musical career above his loyalty to his uncle.

Cappi hadn't done that. Bremen caught a glimpse of Vanni Fucci waiting in the alley while Cappi went in to talk to Chico Tartugian after the last show. The three .22 shots had been short and flat, leaving no echo. Fucci had lighted a cigarette and waited another minute before going in with the shower curtain and the chains. The kid had made Tartugian kneel in the shower stall in his private bathroom, just as Don Leoni had instructed. There was no mess that thirty seconds of running the water wouldn't clean up.

"What the *fuck* were you doing there, huh? What the *fuck* were you doing out in that fucking swamp at fucking sunrise, huh?" Fucci asked.

Bremen looked at him. "Fishing," he said . . . or thought he said.

Vanni Fucci just shook his head in disgust and turned the music up. "Fucking civilian."

They were passing through a town now, something larger than the few villages in the Everglades that they had passed through before, and Bremen had to shut his eyes at the onslaught of neurobabble. It was especially bad passing the trailer parks, the mobile-home villages, the retirement condominiums. There, the rasp of the thoughts of the elderly struck Bremen's scoured consciousness with the unpleasant force of listening to an old person next door hawk up his morning's chestful of phlegm.

No letter, no phone call. Shawnee just isn't gonna call till I'm dead. . . .

Just a little lump, Marge said. Just last month she said that. Just a little lump. Now she's dead, gone. Just a little lump, she said. And now who am I gonna play mah-jongg with?

Thursday. It's Thursday. Thursday is pinochle night at the community center.

Not always in words, frequently not in words, the anxieties and sadnesses and surlinesses of old age and frailty and abandonment struck Bremen as the Cadillac moved slowly down the now widened highway. Thursday, he discovered, was pinochle night in most of the trailer parks and condominiums, in this town and the next they traveled through. But hours of daylight and pain and heavy Florida heat lay ahead for so many of these people before the humid coolness of the evening and the safety of the community center. Televisions flickered in a thousand thousand mobile homes and condos, air conditioners hummed, as the retired and discarded rested their bones and waited out the day's heat in the hopes of another evening with a dwindling circle of friends.

Bremen saw in a sudden, out-of-context flash of Vanni Fucci's choppy musings that the thief was angry at God. Terribly angry at God.

Same fucking day that Nicco . . .

His younger brother, Bremen saw, with the same dark hair and dark eyes, but more handsome in a quiet way.

Same fucking day that Nicco takes his vows, I broke into fucking St.

Mary's and stole the fucking chalice. Same fucking chalice I useta hand Father Damiano when I was a fucking altar boy. Same fucking chalice. Nobody wanted the fucking thing. No fence would touch the fucking thing. Fucking crazy, man . . . Nicco taking his fucking vows and me wandering the fucking streets of Atlantic City with that fucking chalice in my gym bag. Nobody wanted the fucking thing. Images of a weeping Vanni Fucci burying the silver cup in a tidal marsh north of the casino strip. Images of Fucci's arms rising toward the sky, fists clenching, of his thumb between first and middle fingers on both hands. *The fig . . . fica . . .* Bremen understood. Vanni Fucci giving God the fig, the most obscene gesture the young thief knew at the time.

Fuck you, God. Fuck you up the ass, old man.

Bremen blinked and shook his head to escape the neurobabble of the trailer park they were passing. He did not think Vanni Fucci was going to kill him. Not yet. Fucci did not want the aggravation, was already wishing that he'd left this dazed fuck behind on the island. Or had brought Roachclip along. Roachclip woulda whacked this crazy fuck right from the skiff and never looked back.

Bremen thought of clever strategies. Using what he'd gleaned already, he could start talking to Vanni Fucci, say that he— Bremen—had also been sent south by Don Leoni, that he knew Bert Cappi had whacked Chico Tartugian and—hey!—it was all right with him. Don Leoni just wanted a confirmation, that was all. Bremen imagined himself answering questions. Roachclip? Yeah, sure, he knew the crazy little Puerto Rican fuck. He remembered the night Roachclip had taken out the two Armansi brothers —the big one with the plastic leg left over from World War II and the skinny younger one with his sharkskin suit. Roachclip hadn't used a gun or a knife, just that fucking lead pipe he carried around in the trunk, coming up behind the Armansi brothers after driving them to the meeting place in the Bronx and then bashing their skulls in right there on the street, right in front of that Polish babushka with her fat white face and black scarf, her little plastic shopping bag from the fucking old country spilling oranges onto the slushy pavement. . . .

Bremen shook his head. He would not do that.

They had passed through lake country and into ranchland where egrets followed cattle, watching for insects stirred up by bovine hooves, when suddenly Vanni Fucci pulled over by a roadside phone, lifted the pistol until the muzzle was inches from Bremen's eyes, and said softly, "You fucking move outta the fucking car, and I swear to Christ I'll kill you here. You unnerstand?"

Bremen nodded.

The phone conversation, while not audible, was easy to overhear. People tended to concentrate heavily on language while on the phone.

Look, I'm not gonna whack the miserable fuck here. It ain't my goddamn business to . . .

Yeah, I know he saw me, but it's not my fucking business. It's Cappi's and Leoni's fucking problem and I'm not going to let some fuck out fishing set me up for a . . .

Yeah . . . no . . . no, he's no fucking problem. Goddamn geek. I think he's fucking retarded or something. Wearing these fucking pants that are too short and a fucking safari-shirt thing and fucking Florsheims, like a retardo dressed by another retardo.

Bremen blinked and looked down at his clothes. He was wearing the work pants and khaki shirt he'd bought three days ago in Norm Sr.'s store. The pants *were* short and his dress shoes were caked with dust and mud. Suddenly Bremen patted his pockets, but the roll of cash—most of the $3,865 he'd taken out of the savings account—was still in his suitcoat pocket draped over the chair in the tiny bedroom in the fishing shack. Bremen remembered transferring a few twenties and maybe a fifty or two to his billfold when buying provisions, but he did not check now to see how much was there. He felt the lump of his wallet against his buttock, and that was enough for now.

Yeah, I'll make the fucking meeting on time, but I'll be dragging retardo along. Just as long as . . . hey, don't interrupt me, goddamn it . . . just as long as Sal knows that this fuck is their fucking responsibility. Got it? . . . No, wait, I said fucking got it? Okay. Okay. I'll see you in an hour to two then. Yeah.

Vanni Fucci slammed the receiver down and walked to the edge of the highway, kicking gravel into the grass and clenching his fists. His white coat was getting dusty now. Fucci spun around and glared at Bremen through the windshield, the sunlight gleaming on the black silk of his shirt and the oil in his black hair.

Do him now. Now. No fucking traffic. No fucking houses. Just whack him here and get on with it.

Bremen glanced at the ignition, knowing without looking that Fucci had taken the keys. He could roll out the door and take off across the fields, weaving, hoping that he could outdistance Fucci and the range of the short-barreled .38 . . . hoping that another car would come along, that Fucci would give up the chase. Fucci was a smoker and Bremen wasn't. Bremen set his hand on the car door and took a breath.

Fuck it, fuck it, fuck it. Vanni Fucci had decided. He came around the driver's side, got in, set his hand on the grip of his pistol in his waistband, and glared at Bremen. "You do anything cute, say anything to anybody where we're goin', and I swear I'll whack you in front of a crowd. Got it?"

Bremen only stared. His hand left the door handle.

Vanni Fucci started the Cadillac and screeched out onto the road. A truck passed with a blare of air horns. Fucci gave the driver the fig with his left hand.

They drove north another ten miles on Highway 27 and then accelerated up a ramp onto Interstate 4, heading northeast now.

Bremen caught a glimpse of their destination in the churn of Vanni Fucci's thoughts, and he smiled despite himself.

EYES

Jeremy and Gail celebrate their honeymoon on a canoe-and-backpacking trip.

Neither has canoed or backpacked before, but they do not have enough money for their first choice, Maui. Or for their second choice, Paris. Or even for their eighth choice, a motel in Boston. So, on a bright day in August, hours after their wedding in the garden of a favorite country inn, Jeremy and Gail wave good-bye to their friends and drive west and north to the Adirondacks.

There are closer camping spots: they have to drive through the Blue Mountains on the way to the Adirondacks, passing half a dozen state parks and state forests on their way, but Jeremy has read an article about the Adirondacks and wants to go there.

The VW has engine problems . . . it *always* has engine problems . . . and by the time the car is fixed in Binghamton, New York, they are eighty-five dollars behind their budget and four hours behind schedule. They spend that night at Gilbert Lake State Park, halfway between Binghamton and Utica.

It rains. The campground is small and crowded, the only spot left is next to the outhouse. Jeremy sets the twenty-four-dollar nylon tent up in the rain, and then goes over to the grill to see how Gail is doing with dinner. She is using her poncho as a tarp to keep the rain from dousing the few sticks they've scrounged for firewood, but the "fire" is little better than burning newspaper and the smoldering of wet wood.

"We should've eaten in Oneonta," says Jeremy, squinting into the drizzle. It is not yet eight P.M. but the daylight has bled away through the gray clouds. The rain does not seem to discourage the mosquitoes, who whine under the tarp at them. Jeremy fans the fire while Gail fans the mosquitoes away.

They feast on half-heated hot dogs on soggy buns, kneeling inside the entrance to the tent rather than admit defeat by retreating to the comparative luxury of the car.

"I wasn't hungry anyway," lies Gail. Bremen sees through mindtouch that she is lying, and Gail sees that he sees.

He also sees that she wants to make love.

They are in their zipped-together sleeping bags by nine P.M., although the rain chooses to let up then and the campers on either side of them roll out of their Winnebagos and Silverstreams, cranking radios up high while they cook late dinners. The smell of charcoal-grilling steak comes to Jeremy and Gail through the inward-turning spiral of foreplay, and they both giggle as they sense the other's distraction.

Jeremy lays his cheek on Gail's stomach and whispers, "Think they'd give us some if we tell them we're newlyweds?"

Hungry newlyweds. Gail runs her fingers through his hair.

Jeremy kisses the gentle curve of her lower belly. *Ah, well . . . a little starvation never hurt anybody.*

Gail giggles, then stops giggling and takes a deep breath. The rain starts again, gentle but insistent on the nylon above, driving away the insects, the noise, and the smells of cooking. For a while there is nothing in the universe but Gail's body, Jeremy's body . . . and then a single body owned totally by neither.

They have made love before . . . made love that first night after Chuck Gilpen's party . . . but it is never less wonderful or strange, and this night, in the tent in the rain, Jeremy truly loses himself, and Gail loses herself, and their flow of thoughts becomes as joined and intermingled as the flow of their bodies. Eventually, after aeons of being lost in one another, Jeremy feels Gail's enfolding orgasm and celebrates it as his own, even while Gail rises on the growing wave of his impending climax, so different from the seismic inward intensity of her own, yet hers now, too. They come together, Gail feeling, for a moment, the sensation of her body cradling itself in his body as he relaxes in her mind while her arms and legs hold him in place.

When they roll apart on the flattened sleeping bags, the air in the nylon tent is almost foggy with the moisture of their exhalations and exertions. It is full dark out now as Gail undoes the tent flaps and they slide their upper bodies out into the soft drizzle, feeling the gentle spray on their faces and chests, breathing the cooling air, and opening their mouths to drink from the sky.

They are not reading each other's minds now, not visiting the other's mind. Each *is* the other, aware of each thought and sensation as soon as he or she feels it. No, that is not accurate: there is no he or she for a moment, and that gender consciousness returns only gradually, like a morning tide receding slowly to leave artifacts on a fresh-washed beach.

Cooled and refreshed by the rain, they slip back inside, dry themselves with thick towels, and curl between the layers of goosedown. Jeremy's hand finds a resting place on the small inward curve of Gail's back as she rests her head on his shoulder. It is as if his hand has always known this place.

They fit perfectly.

The next day they have lunch in Utica and head north again, into the mountains. In Old Forge they rent a canoe and paddle up through the Chain of Lakes that Jeremy has read about. The lakes are more built up than he had imagined, the hiss and crackle of neurobabble is just audible from houses along the shores, but they find isolated islands and sandbars to camp on for the three days they are canoeing and portaging, until a two-day rainstorm and a two-and-a-half-mile portage drives them in from Long Lake on their fifth day.

Gail and Jeremy find a pay phone and ride back to Old Forge with a bearded young man from the canoe-rental place. Back in the sputtering VW, they head deeper into the mountains, making the seventy-some-mile loop up through Saranac Lake and down into the village of Keene Valley. There Jeremy buys a trail guide, they hitch up their backpacks for the first time, and head off into the boonies toward something called Big Slide.

The guidebook insists that the trip is only 3.85 miles via a moderate trail called the Brothers, but the word "moderate" is an obvious misnomer as the trail leads straight up rocks, past water-falls, across ridges, and over minor peaks, while Jeremy is soon cursing that the "3.85 miles" was obviously measured by an air-craft, not a biped. Also he acknowledges that he may have overpacked. Gail suggests taking out the bag of charcoal or the second six-pack of beer, but Jeremy discards several bags of gorp and insists on keeping the essentials for a civilized trip.

At 2.20 miles they pass through a beautiful stand of white birch and scramble onto the summit of the Third Brother, a low peak that just manages to get its rocky snout above the undulating ocean of leaves. From there they get a glimpse of their destination —Big Slide Mountain—and between gasps for air, Jeremy and Gail grin at each other.

Big Slide Mountain is a smaller and much more secret version of Yosemite's El Capitan. While one side rises in a gentle, wooded arc, the other drops off in a sheer rock wall to culminate in a tumble of house-sized boulders.

"That's our destination?" pants Gail.

Jeremy nods, too winded to speak.

"Can't we just take a picture of it and say we were there?"

Jeremy shakes his head and lifts his pack on with a groan. For half a mile they drop down into a col, the trail occasionally cutting back and forth in a gentle switchback, more frequently dropping straight down rock formations or steep slopes. Just below the Big

Slide summit cliffs they hit the last section of trail, and the last three-tenths of a mile seems to be straight up.

Jeremy realizes that they have made the summit only when his downcast eyes see no rock in front of him, only air. He falls backward and sprawls on the pack with arms and legs askew. Gail politely removes her own pack before collapsing on his stomach.

They stay sprawled for almost fifteen minutes, commenting on cloud formations and the occasional hawk as they get enough breath back to whisper. Then a rising breeze makes Gail sit up, and as Jeremy watches the wind ruffle her short hair, he thinks, *I'm always going to remember this,* and Gail turns to smile at him, seeing her reflection in his thoughts.

They set up their tent back away from the south ledge, in among the weather-stunted trees along a rock overhang, but they lay their foam pads and sleeping bags along the edge of the drop-off itself. They prepare the charcoal in a natural hollow in the rocks along the tree line; the grill fits perfectly. Gail takes the steaks out of the small ice chest and Jeremy pulls one of the three cold beers out and pops the tab. Gail has already set the foil-wrapped corn on the cob in the embers, and now Jeremy oversees the cooking while Gail sets fresh radishes, salad, and potato chips on the two plates. She produces a pack-within-a-pack wrapped in towels and filled with paper, and carefully removes the two wine-glasses and bottle of BV cabernet sauvignon from within. She sets the bottle to chill with the remaining beer.

They eat as the summer evening settles toward sunset, both perching along the sheer ledge, boots hanging out over space. There are just enough clouds to ignite the sky to the west in a blaze of pinks and deep purples. The ledge lies along the south face of the mountain, and they watch in that direction as true twilight deepens into night. There is much steak, and they eat it slowly, refilling the wineglasses often. Gail has brought two large slices of chocolate cake for dessert.

A night wind comes up as they are cleaning the cooking area and stowing the paper plates in their garbage bags. Jeremy does not want a campfire and he scatters the dead coals in among the crevices in the rock, leaving as little sign as possible that they had cooked there. They pull on fleece jackets while they are brushing their teeth and attending to private business back among the trees along the north ledges, but they are in their sleeping bags along the south ledge again by the time the stars come out.

This is right comes the image, and for a moment neither one of them knows who thought it first. To the south there is only forest and mountains and darkening sky as far as they can see. No highways or houselights mar the purple length of the valley, although now a very few campfires are visible. In ten minutes the sky is lighter than the valley as stars fill the dome above them. The stars' brightness is undiminished by city lights.

The two bags have been zipped together, but there is little extra space as Jeremy and Gail shrug out of their clothes. They stack things in neat piles under the foot of their bags so underthings will not blow away if the breeze grows stronger in the night, and then they duck their heads in and huddle together, all smooth flesh and warm breath, defying the cold gale beyond their sleeping bags. Their lovemaking tonight is slow in the starting, gentle in the extreme, and promising more violent ecstasy than they have known before.

Always. Jeremy can tell it was Gail who sent the thought this time.

Always, he whispers back, or does not whisper.

They settle lower, intertwined, warm and out of the wind, while, overhead, the stars seem to blaze with the intensity of the universe's affirmation.

In the Twilight Kingdom

They parked in a row labeled GRUMPY and took the long towed shuttle to the park's gate. Vanni Fucci had taken off his white jacket and was carrying the .38-caliber revolver under it. "You do anything stupid," he said softly to Bremen as they waited for the shuttle, "and I'll whack you right here. I swear to fucking Christ I will."

Bremen looked at the thief, sensed the resolve warring with irritation there.

Vanni Fucci mistook the look for disbelief. "You don't fucking believe me, I'll whack you right here in the fucking parking lot and be in fucking Georgia before anybody realizes you've been fucking shot!"

"I believe you," said Bremen, feeling the surges of the man's excitement. There was something about a public killing, especially *here,* that did appeal to Vanni Fucci, although the little thief would prefer that crazy Bert Cappi or his equally crazy buddy Ernie Sanza would do the deed. Either way, him or Bert and Ernie, it'd make a fucking hell of a story . . . whacking this citizen *here.*

The shuttle arrived. Bremen and Vanni Fucci piled on, the

barrel of the .38 pressing through the coat into Bremen's side. During the short ride to the gate, Bremen was able to pick out more of Fucci's plan.

The meeting here had been prearranged for other reasons; more precisely, had been arranged between Don Leoni's main man down here, Sal Empori, with Bert and Ernie as backup, and some of those crazy fucking Colombians . . . that was how Vanni Fucci thought of them each time, those crazy-fucking-Colombians . . . to exchange a briefcase of Don Leoni's money for a suitcase of the crazy fucking Colombians' best smack for the nigger trade up north in Vanni Fucci's territory. They had been making the swap in Walt Disney World for some years now.

Sal'll take care of this fucking geek. No sweat, no fucking muss, no mucking fuss.

"Pay your own fucking way in," Vanni Fucci whispered as he bought his ticket and prodded Bremen in the ribs.

Bremen pawed through his pockets. He *had* stuck some of the fifties in there three days earlier. Six fifties, to be exact. He slid one across the counter, had to specify that he wanted only a single day's entry coupon, and waited for his change, which was less than he would have guessed.

The thief moved him through the crowds, one hand on Bremen's arm, the other hand out of sight under the jacket. It looked suspicious as hell to Bremen, but no one else seemed to be noticing.

Bremen hardly looked up as Vanni Fucci led him onto a monorail that took them around some lagoons and toward a distant congregation of spires, structures, and at least one artificial mountain. The monorail stopped, the thief pulled Bremen to his feet and out the door, and the two men moved into thickening crowds. The neurobabble around Bremen had risen from whisper to scream, from scream to incessant roar. And the roar had a particular and peculiar quality to it, as different from the rasp of normal neurobabble as the rush of Niagara Falls must be from the sound of a lesser waterfall. And the peculiar quality here was one of a frenetic and widely shared sadness, as pervasive and powerful as the smell of decaying flesh.

Bremen staggered, raised his hands to his temples, and covered his ears in a futile attempt to block out the waves of nonsound, nonspeech. Vanni Fucci shoved him onward.

Not like I thought it'd be . . . been waiting thirty-five years for this . . . not like I hoped it'd be . . .

More places to see! More rides to go on! Not enough time! Not ever enough time! Hurry . . . hurry them up, Sarah! Hurry!

Well, it's for the kids. For the kids. But the goddamn kids seem hysterical half the time, dazed like goddamn zombies the other half. . . . Hurry up! Tom, hurry, we're gonna be at the back of the line. . . .

Bremen shut his eyes and let Vanni Fucci direct him through the crowd while wave after wave of desperation washed over him like a heavy surf. It was as if all the urgency in the park . . . to have fun, to *by God have fun!* . . . was hitting him like heavy breakers pounding on a narrow beach.

"Open your eyes, you fuck," whispered Vanni Fucci in his ear. The muzzle of the pistol dug deep into Bremen's side.

He opened his eyes, but remained almost blind because of the pain of the neurobabble . . . the urgent, frenzied, centerless, harried, hurry-up-goddamn-it-we're-gonna-be-at-the-back-of-the-line will to have fun come hell or high water. Bremen gasped for air through his open mouth and tried not to get sick.

Vanni Fucci hurried him along. Sal and Bert and Ernie should have made the connection with the crazy fucking Colombians now, and Vanni Fucci was supposed to hand over the geek at the Space Mountain thing. Except Vanni Fucci wasn't a hundred percent sure where the fucking Space Mountain thing was; the swap was usually done at the fucking Jungle Ride, so he'd always gone straight to Adventureland during his other trips here, picked up the suitcase from Sal, and gone straight out on the monorail. He didn't know why Sal had to change the fucking meeting point to fucking Space Mountain, but he knew the mountain was in fucking Tomorrowland.

Vanni Fucci tried to orient himself. *Okay, we're on fucking Main Street out of dear dead Walt's childhood. Right . . . this is a wet dream of a childhood fantasy, man. A fucking wet dream. No Main Street never looked like this fucking place. Main Street where I grew up was fucking factories and fucking franchises and fucking '57 Mercs up on fucking blocks because their fucking tires had been boosted by the fucking niggers.*

Okay, we're on fucking Main Street. That fucking castle's north. The fucking sign says that fucking Fantasyland's over beyond the fucking castle. Which way from Fantasyland to fucking Tomorrowland, huh? You'd think they'd put up a fucking road map or something.

Vanni Fucci made a circle of the big fiberglass castle, caught a glimpse of a spaceship and some futuristic crap way off to his right, and shoved Bremen along in that direction. Another five minutes and he'd hand this geek over to Sal and the boys.

Bremen stopped. They were in Tomorrowland, almost in the shadow of the vaguely old-fashioned structure that housed the Space Mountain roller coaster, and Bremen stopped cold.

"Move, you son of a bitch," hissed Vanni Fucci under his breath. He pressed the .38 deeper into Bremen's ribs.

Bremen blinked but did not move. He did not mean to defy Vanni Fucci; he simply could no longer concentrate on the man. The migraine onslaught of neurobabble lifted him out of himself in an avalanche of otherness, on a cresting wave of alienation.

"Move!" Vanni Fucci's spittle struck Bremen's ear. Bremen faintly heard the hammer of the revolver being thumbed back. His last clear thought was, *I am not destined to die here. The path continues downward.*

Bremen watched himself through a middle-aged woman's eyes as he stepped away from Vanni Fucci.

The thief cursed and covered the pistol again with his jacket.

Bremen continued to back away.

"I fucking *mean* it!" shouted Vanni Fucci, appearing to lift both hands under the jacket.

A family from Hubbard, Ohio, stopped to blink at the strange procession—Bremen backing slowly away, the little man following him with both arms raised, the lump under the jacket pointing at Bremen's chest—and Bremen watched incuriously through their curious eyes. The younger daughter gnawed away a bit of cotton candy and continued to stare at the two men. A wisp of white-spun sugar clung to her cheek.

Bremen continued to back away.

Vanni Fucci began to leap forward, was blocked for a moment by three laughing nuns passing by, and started to run as he saw Bremen backing across a patch of grass toward the wall of a building. The thief let the muzzle of the pistol slide free. He'd be damned if he'd ruin a perfectly good jacket on this fucking geek.

Bremen saw himself reflected as if from a score of twisted fun-house mirrors. Thomas Geer, nineteen, saw the exposed pistol and stopped in surprise, his hand pulling free from Terri's hip pocket.

Mrs. Frieda Hackstein and her grandson Benjamin stumbled into Thomas Geer and Bennie's Mickey Mouse balloon floated skyward. The child began to cry.

Through their eyes, Bremen watched himself back into a wall. He watched Vanni Fucci raise the pistol. Bremen thought nothing, felt nothing.

Through little Bennie's eyes Bremen saw that there was a sign on a door behind him. It read AUTHORIZED PERSONNEL ONLY and, beneath that, EMPLOYEES USE SECURITY ACCESS CARD. There was a slot in a metal box on the wall, presumably for security access cards, but the door had been left propped open an inch by a small stick.

Mrs. Hackstein stepped forward and began shouting at Thomas Geer for making them lose Benjamin's balloon. For a second she blocked Vanni Fucci's view.

Bremen stepped through the door, kicked the stick away, and clicked the door shut behind him. Dim lights showed a concrete stairway descending. Bremen followed it down twenty-five steps, followed a turn to the right, and descended another dozen steps. The stairway opened onto a long corridor. Mechanical sounds echoed from far away.

Morlocks, thought Gail.

Bremen gasped as if struck in the stomach, sat on the third step for a moment, and rubbed his eyes. *Not Gail. No.* He had read about the phantom pain amputees suffered in their amputated limbs. This was worse. Much worse. He rose and moved down the corridor, trying to look as if he belonged there. The ebbing of neurobabble left him even emptier than he had been a moment before.

The corridor crossed other corridors, passed other stairways. Cryptic signs on the walls pointed arrows toward AUDIOANIMLABS 6–10 or TRANSWASTEDISP 44–66 or CHARACTLOUNGES 2–5. Bremen thought that the last sounded least threatening and turned down that corridor. Suddenly a giant insect whine rose from an intersecting corridor and Bremen had to hustle back a dozen paces and step up onto an empty stairway while a golf cart hummed by. Neither the man nor the partially disassembled robot in the cart looked Bremen's way.

He descended to the corridor and moved slowly, ears straining for the sound of another golf cart. Suddenly laughter echoed around the next turn and Bremen took five steps and turned into what he had hoped would be another stairway, but which was only a much narrower corridor.

He walked down the hallway, hands in his pockets, resisting the urge to whistle. The laughter and conversation grew louder behind him as someone turned into the corridor he had just vacated. He realized their destination and his mistake at the same moment.

The hallway ended at two broad doors, above which the sign read: BE SURE TO REMOVE YOUR HEAD BEFORE ENTERING. The doors were stenciled CHARACTER LOUNGE 3 with a no-smoking sign under the stenciling. Bremen could hear more conversation from the other side of the doors. He had about three seconds before the voices behind him reached the hallway.

To his left was a windowless gray door with a single word: MEN. Bremen stepped through just as three men and a woman turned into the long hallway behind him.

The rest room was empty, although a tall figure on the far wall made him jump. Bremen blinked. It was a Goofy suit, at least six and a half feet tall, hanging on a hook near the sinks.

Voices rose outside the door and Bremen slipped into a toilet stall and closed the door, latching it with a sigh of relief. No one would demand an ID badge in here. Doors opened and the voices receded into the Character Lounge.

Bremen lowered his head into his hands and tried to concentrate.

What the hell am I doing? His mind's voice was barely audible above the constant roar of neurobabble from the tens of thousands of fun-seeking souls above him.

Running, he answered himself. *Hiding.*

Why?

The neurobabble hissed and surged.

Why? Why not just tell the authorities what happened? Lead the police back to the lake? Tell them about Vanni Fucci.

Hurry up, hurry up, hurry up, let's have fun, goddamn it, these three days are costing me a fortune. . . .

Bremen squeezed his temples.

Uh-huh. Tell the authorities. Let the cops call to confirm your identity and find out that you're the guy who just burned down his house and disappeared . . . then you just happen *to be on hand when a gangster dumps a dead body. And how, pray tell, sir, did you happen to get both the gangster's and corpse's names?*

Why did I burn down the house?

No, later. Later. Think about that later.

No cops. No explanations. If you think this place is hell, try a night or two in a holding cell. Wonder what's in your bunkmates' little craniums . . . do you want a night or two of that, Jeremy old boy?

Bremen unlocked the stall, walked to the urinal against the wall, tried to urinate, couldn't, zipped up, and went over to the sink. The cold water helped. He was startled as the pale, sick face rose up in the mirror in front of him.

To hell with the cops. To hell with Vanni Fucci and his pals. Just go away from here. Go away.

There were more voices in the hall. Bremen whirled, but although the door to the ladies' rest room across the hall banged open, no one came in here. Not yet.

Bremen stood there a second, flicking water from his cheeks. The trick, he realized, was not just getting out of this labyrinth unchallenged, but getting out of the park itself. Vanni Fucci would have met up with the other gangsters by now—Sal, Bert, and Ernie, Bremen remembered—and they would be watching the exits.

Bremen found a paper towel and dried his face. Suddenly he froze and lowered the towel. There were two faces in the mirror, and one of them was grinning at him.

The golf cart came up behind Bremen in one of the main corridors. The heavyset man behind the wheel said, "Wanta ride?"

Bremen nodded and got in. The cart hummed ahead, following a blue stripe in the concrete. Other carts passed going the other way, following a yellow stripe. The second one that passed carried three security guards.

The driver shifted an unlit cigar to the other side of his mouth and said, "You don't have to wear your head down here, you know."

Bremen nodded and shrugged.

"It's your sweat," said the man. "Headin' out or in?"

Bremen pointed upward.

"Which exit?"

"The castle," said Bremen, hoping his voice was suitably muffled.

The driver frowned. "The castle? You mean Forecourt B-four? Or the A side?"

"B-four," said Bremen, and stifled the urge to scratch his head through the heavy material.

"Yeah, I'm goin' by there," said the driver, and turned right down a different corridor. A minute later he stopped the cart by a stairway. The sign read FORECOURT B-4.

Bremen slid out and gave the man a friendly salute.

The driver nodded, shifted his cigar, and said, "Don't let the little fuckers stick any pins in you like they did Johnson," and then he was gone, the cart whining into the dim distance. Bremen went up the stairway as quickly as his limited visibility and oversized shoes would allow.

He was almost out, down the phony length of Main Street and out, when the children began to gather around.

At first he kept walking, all but ignoring them, but their shouts and his fear of being noticed by adults made him pause and sit on a bench for a moment, letting them circle him.

"Hey, Goofy, hi!" they cried, pressing in. Bremen did what he thought characters were supposed to do . . . overacted, stayed silent, and raised his fat-gloved, three-fingered hand to his bulging pooch nose as if embarrassed. The kids loved it. They crowded closer, trying to sit on his lap, hugging him.

Bremen hugged them back and acted like Goofy. Parents took pictures and shot video. Bremen blew them kisses, hugged a few more kids, got to his oversized, cartoon feet, and began shuffling away toward the exits, waving and blowing kisses as he went.

The pack of kids and their parents moved away, laughing and waving. Bremen turned and confronted a quite different group of children.

There were at least a dozen. The youngest might have been about six, the oldest no more than fifteen. Few of them had any hair, although most wore caps or bandannas, and one girl—Melody—wore an expensive wig. Their faces were as pale as Bremen's had been in the rest-room mirror. Their eyes were large. Some were smiling. Some were trying to smile.

"Hey, Goofy," said Terry, the nine-year-old boy in the last stages of bone cancer. He was in a wheelchair.

"Hi, Goofy!" called Sestina, the six-year-old black girl from Bethesda. She was very beautiful, her large eyes and sharp cheekbones emphasizing her fragility. Her hair was her own and set in precise cornrows; she wore blue, green, and pink ribbons. She had AIDS.

"Say something, Goofy!" whispered Lawrence, the thirteen-year-old with the brain tumor. Four operations so far. Two more than Gail had had. Lawrence, lying in the dark of postop and hearing Dr. Graynemeir telling Mom in the hallway that the prognosis was poor, three months at the most. That had been seven weeks ago.

Seven-year-old Melody said nothing, but stepped forward and hugged Bremen until her wig was askew. Bremen—Goofy—hugged her back.

The children surged forward in a single movement, an orchestrated motion, as if choreographed far in advance. It was not humanly possible, even for Goofy, to hug them all at once, to find room in the circle of his arms for them all, but he did. Goofy embraced them all and sent a message of well-being and hope and love to each of them, firing it in laserlike telepathic surges of the sort he had sent to Gail when the pain and medication made mindtouch the hardest. He was sure they could not hear him, could not sense the messages, but he sent them anyway, even while encompassing them with his arms and whispering soft things in each of their ears—not Goofy-like nonsense, although in Goofy's voice as best as he could imitate it—but secret and personal things.

"Melody, it's all right, your mother knows about the mistake with the piano music. It's all right. She doesn't care. She loves you."

"Lawrence, quit worrying about the money. The money's not important. The insurance isn't important. *You're* important."

"Sestina, they *do* want to be with you, little kitten. Toby's just afraid to give you a hug because he thinks you *don't like him.* He's shy."

The parents and nurses and trip sponsors . . . a woman from Green Bay had been working on this Dream for two years . . . all stood back while this strange hugging and huddling and whispering continued.

Ten minutes later Goofy touched the children's cheeks a final time, waved jauntily, and walked down the rest of Main Street, rode the monorail around its circuit, stepped off at the Transportation and Ticket Center, walked out past the ticket booths, saluted Sal Empori and Bert Cappi and a red-faced Vanni Fucci where they stood watching the crowd, sauntered out to the parking lot, and boarded a chartered bus just leaving for the Hyatt Regency Grand Cypress. The elderly tourists on board the bus cheered and patted Goofy on the back.

Bert Cappi turned to Vanni Fucci. "You believe this goddamn place?"

Vanni Fucci's gaze never left the crowd streaming out toward the shuttles. "Shut the fuck up and keep fucking looking," he said.

Behind them the bus for the Hyatt pulled away with a hiss and a roar.

At the Violet Hour

A little over half of Bremen's remaining money would buy him a bus ticket to Denver. He bought it and slept in the park across from the Hyatt where he had dumped the Goofy suit. The bus departed Orlando at 11:15 that night. He waited until the last minute to board, coming in through a maintenance entrance and walking straight to the bus, his head down and collar up. He saw no one who looked like a gangster; more important, the surge and rasp of neurobabble had not been punctuated by the shock of recognition from any of the bystanders.

By one A.M. they were halfway to Gainesville and Bremen began to relax, watching out the window at the closed stores and mercury vapor lamps lining the streets of Ocala and a dozen smaller towns. The neurobabble was less this late at night. For years Bremen and Gail had been convinced that much of the effect of the so-called circadian rhythm on human beings was nothing more than nascent telepathy in most people sensing the national dream sleep around them. It was very hard to stay awake this night, although Bremen's nerves were jumping and twitching with the ricocheting thoughts of those two dozen or so people still awake aboard the bus. The dreams of the others added to the mental din, although dreams were deeper, more private theaters of the mind, and not nearly so accessible.

Bremen thanked God for that.

They were on Interstate 75 and headed north out of Gainesville when Bremen began to ponder his situation.

Why hadn't he gone back to the fishing shack? Somehow his home of the past three days seemed like the only haven in the world for him now. Why hadn't he returned . . . for his money if nothing else?

Bremen knew that part of it was that it seemed almost certain that Vanni Fucci or Sal Empori or some of their cronies would be watching the place. And Bremen had no desire to get Norm Sr. or the old man Verge in trouble with gangsters on his account.

He thought of the rental car parked there. But Verge or Norm Sr. would have found him missing by now. And found the money in the cabin. That would certainly settle the bill with the rental people. Would Norm Sr. call the police about his disappearance? Unlikely. And what if he did? Bremen had never given his name, never shown his driver's license. The two men had respected Bremen's privacy to the extent that there was little they could tell the police about him other than his description.

A more practical reason for Bremen not returning there was simply that he did not know the way. He knew only that the fishing shack was somewhere closer to Miami than to Orlando, on the edge of a lake and a swamp. Bremen thought about phoning Norm Sr. from Denver, asking that the bulk of the money be wired to a P.O. box in Denver, but he remembered seeing no name on the little store and Norm Sr. had never thought of his own last name when Bremen was eavesdropping. The refuge of the fishing shack was lost forever.

It was only two hundred and fifty–some miles from Orlando to Tallahassee, but it was after five A.M. by the time the bus pulled through the rain-silent streets of the capital and hissed to a stop. "Rest break!" called the driver, and quickly disembarked. Bremen lay back in his seat and dozed until the others reboarded. He already knew his fellow passengers very well and their return echoed in his skull like shouts in a metal pipe. The bus pulled out at 5:42 A.M. and leisurely found its way back to Interstate 10 West while Bremen squeezed his temples and tried to concentrate on his own dreams.

Two rows behind him sat a young marine, Burk Stemens, and a young WAF sergeant named Alice Jean Dernitz. They had not met until boarding the bus in Orlando, but they were quickly becoming more than friends. Neither had slept much during the past seven hours; each had told the other more about his or her life than either had ever revealed to their mates, past or present. Burk had just gotten out of fourteen months in the brig for assaulting a noncommissioned officer with a knife. He had traded a dishonorable discharge from the Marines for the final four months of his sentence and was now on his way home to Fort Worth to see his wife, Debra Anne, and his two infants. He did not tell Alice Jean about Debra Anne.

Sergeant Dernitz was two months away from a quite honorable discharge from the Air Force and was spending the bulk of that time on leave. She had been married twice, the last time to the brother of her first husband. She had divorced the first brother, Warren Bill, and lost the second, William Earl, four months ago; he had been killed when his Mustang went off a Tennessee mountain road at eighty-five miles per hour. Alice Jean hadn't cared too much by then. She and brother number two had been separated for almost a year before the accident. She did not tell Burk about either Warren Bill or the late William Earl.

Burk and Alice Jean had been inching toward intimacy since Gainesville, and by Lake City, just before I-75 encountered I-10, they had ceased swapping barracks stories and gotten down to the business at hand. As they passed Lake City Alice Jean was pretending to nap and had let her head fall on Burk's shoulder, while Burk had put his arm around her and let his hand "accidentally" fall to her left breast.

By the suburbs of Tallahassee both were breathing shallowly, Burk's hand was inside her blouse, and Alice Jean's hand was on Burk's lap under the jacket he had spread like a robe across both of them. She had just unzipped his pants when the driver announced the rest break.

Bremen had been prepared to spend the rest break in the tiny bus station rather than suffer the next stage of their slow and painful foreplay, but luckily Burk had whispered in Alice Jean's ear and both had left the bus, Burk holding his jacket rather clumsily in front of himself. They had thoughts of trying their luck in a storeroom or . . . if all else failed . . . in the ladies' rest room.

Bremen tried to doze with the other sleeping passengers aboard the bus, but Burk and Alice Jean's contortions—it had been the ladies' rest room—assaulted him even from a distance. Their lovemaking was as banal and short-lived as their loyalty to their current and former mates.

By the time the bus was approaching Pensacola it was almost ten A.M. and everyone aboard was awake and the highway sounds had taken on a new timbre. Storm clouds lay heavy in the west, the direction they were headed, but a thick, low light from the east painted the fields on either side in rich hues and threw the shadow of their bus ahead of them. The neurobabble was much louder than the hiss of tires on asphalt.

Across the aisle and three rows ahead of Bremen were a couple from Missouri. As far as Bremen could sort out, their names were Donnie and Donna. He was very drunk; she was very pregnant. Both were in their early twenties, although from the glimpses Bremen got through the seats ahead—and occasionally from Donnie's perception—Donna looked at least fifty. The two were not married, although Donna considered their four-year relationship a common-law marriage. Donnie didn't think of it that way.

The couple had been on a seventeen-day odyssey across the nation trying to find the best place to have the baby while having welfare pay for it. They had ricocheted east from St. Louis to

Columbus, Ohio, on the advice of a Missouri friend, had found Columbus no more generous in its welfare policies than St. Louis, and then had started on an endless series of bus trips—charging it all to Donna's sister's husband's borrowed credit card—going from Columbus to Pittsburgh, Pittsburgh to Washington, D.C. . . . where they were shocked at how poorly the nation's capital treated its deserving citizens . . . and then from Washington to Huntsville because of something they had read in the *National Enquirer* about Huntsville being one of the ten friendliest cities in America.

Huntsville had been terrible. The hospitals would not even *admit* Donna unless it was an emergency or proof of their ability to pay was shown in advance. Donnie had started drinking in earnest in Huntsville and had dragged Donna out of the hospital while shaking his fist and hurling curses at doctors, administrators, nurses, and even at a cluster of patients staring from their wheelchairs.

The trip to Orlando had been bad, with the credit card approaching its max and Donna saying that she was definitely feeling contractions now, but Donnie had never seen Walt Disney World and he figured that they were close, so what the hell?

Brother-in-law Dickie's card lasted long enough to get them into the Magic Kingdom, and Bremen noticed through Donnie's drunken memories that the two had been there while he had been fleeing Vanni Fucci. Small world. Bremen pressed his cheek and temple to the glass hard enough to drive thoughts away, to form a barrier between these new wavelengths of foreign thoughts and his own bruised mind.

It did not work.

Donnie hadn't enjoyed the Magic Kingdom much, even though he'd waited his whole life to go there, because goddamn spoilsport Donna refused to go on any of the real rides with him. She'd ruined his fun by standing, ponderous as a cow heavy with two heifers, and waving as he'd boarded Space Mountain and Splash Mountain and all the fun rides. She'd said it was because her water broke an hour after coming into the park, but Donnie knew it was mostly to spite him.

She'd insisted on going into Orlando that evening, saying the pains were starting in earnest now, but Donnie had left her wedged in one of the TV chairs in the bus station while he checked out the hospitals by phone. They were worse than Huntsville or Atlanta or St. Louis about their payment policies.

Donnie had used the last of Dickie's credit card to get them tickets from Orlando to Oklahoma City. A toothless old fart sitting near the phone banks in the bus station had overheard Donnie's angry queries on the phone and—after Donnie had slammed the phone down for the last time—had suggested Oklahoma City. "Best goddamn place in the goddamn country to get born for free," the old fart had said, showing an expanse of gums. "Had me two sisters and one of my wives who calved there. Them Oklahoma City hospitals just put it on Medicare and don't bother you none."

So they were off to Houston with connecting tickets for Fort Worth and Oklahoma City. Donna was whimpering more than a little now, saying that the contractions were just a few minutes apart, but as Donnie drank more sour mash he grew increasingly certain that she was lying just to ruin his trip.

Donna was not lying.

Bremen felt her pain as if it were his own. He had timed the contractions with his watch, and they had moved from almost seven minutes apart in Tallahassee to less than two minutes separating them by the time they crossed the state line into Alabama. Donna would whimper at Donnie, tugging at his sleeve in the dark and hissing invective, but he would shove her away. He was busy talking with the man across the aisle, Meredith Soloman, the toothless old fart who had suggested Oklahoma City. Donnie had shared his sour mash until Gainesville, and Meredith Soloman had shared his own flask of something even stronger from there onward.

Just before the tunnel to Mobile, Donna had said, loud enough for the entire bus to hear, "Goddamn you to hell, Donnie Ackley, if you're gonna make me drop this goddamn kid here on this bus, at least give me a swig of what you're drinkin' with that toothless old fart."

Donnie had shushed her, knowing they'd be thrown off the bus if the driver heard too much about the drinking, had apologized to Meredith Soloman, and had let her drink heavily from the flask. Incredibly, her contractions slowed and returned to pre-Tallahassee intervals. Donna fell asleep, her dimmed consciousness rising and falling on the waves of cramping that flowed through her for the next few hours.

Donnie continued to apologize to Meredith Soloman, but the old man had shown his gums again, reached into his soiled ditty bag, and brought out another unlabeled bottle of white lightning.

Donnie and Meredith took turns drinking the fierce booze and sharing views on the worst way to die.

Meredith Soloman was sure that a cave-in or gas explosion was the worst way to go. As long as it didn't kill you right away. It was the layin' there and waitin', in the cold and dank and dark a mile beneath the surface with the helmet lights fadin' and the air getting foul . . . that had to be the worst way to go. He should know, Meredith Soloman explained, since he'd worked in the deep mines of West Virginia as man and boy long before Donnie'd been born. Meredith's pap had died down in the mines, as had his brother Tucker and his brother-in-law Phillip P. Argent. Meredith allowed as how it was a terrible shame about his pap and brother Tucker, but no cave-in had served humanity better than the one that took that low-life, foulmouthed, mean-spirited Phillip P. in 1972. As for sixty-eight-year-old Meredith Soloman, he'd been caved in on three times and blown up twice, but they'd always dug him out. Each time, though, he'd sworn he was never goin' down again . . . no one could make him go down again. Not his wives . . . he'd had four, one after the other, y'understand, even the young things don't last too long back in the hollers of West Virginia, what with pneumonia and childbirth and all . . . not his wives, or his kin . . . real kin, not bastards-in-law like Phillip

P. . . . nor even his own children, them grown up nor them still in bare feet, could talk him into goin' back down.

But he did, finally, talk himself into goin' back down. And he'd continued goin' down until the company its own self made him retire early at age fifty-nine just because his lungs were filling up with coal dust. Well, *hell,* he explained to Donnie Ackley as they passed the bottle back and forth, everybody who worked down there had lungs clogged black like one of them old Hoover vacuum bags that hadn't been changed in years, everyone knew that.

Donnie disagreed. Donnie thought that dying underground in a cave-in or gas explosion wasn't nearly the worst way to go. Donnie started listing terrible ways he'd seen and been around. The time when that biker, Jack Coe, the one him and the others called the Hog, had been working for the highway department and had rolled backward off his mower on an incline and gone under the blades. Jack Coe'd lived on in the hospital for another three months until pneumonia'd got *him,* but Donnie didn't hardly call it living what with the paralysis and the drooling and all the tubes carrying stuff into him and carrying stuff out.

Then there'd been Donnie's first girlfriend, Farah, who'd gone down into niggertown to a bar and gotten gang-raped by a bunch of black bucks who ended up using things other than their dicks on her—their fists and broom handles and Coke bottles and even the sharp end of a tire iron, according to Farah's sister—and . . .

"Don't tell me she died'a gettin' raped," said Meredith Soloman, leaning across the aisle and taking the bottle back. His voice was soft and slurry, but Bremen could hear him as if in an echo chamber . . . first the slow, drunken structuring of the words in Meredith's mind, then the slow, drunken words themselves. "Hell no, she didn't die of getting raped," said Donnie, and laughed at the idea. "Farah killed herself with Jack Coe's sawed-off shotgun a couple of months later . . . she was living with the Hog then . . . and that's what made Jack go and get a job with the highway people. Neither one of them never had no luck."

"Well, a shotgun ain't a bad way to go," whispered Meredith

Soloman, wiping the mouth of the bottle, drinking, and then wiping his own mouth as some of the moonshine dribbled out onto his sharp chin. "The tire iron an' stuff don't count 'cause none of that ain't what killed her. And none of the shit you're talkin' about's near as bad as layin' there in the dark a mile underground with your air runnin' out. It's like bein' buried alive an' lastin' for days."

Donnie started to protest but Donna whimpered and tugged at his arm. "Donnie, hon, these pains're coming real close now."

Donnie handed her the bottle, pulled it back after she had taken a long drink, and leaned across the aisle to get back to his conversation. Bremen noticed that the pains were only a minute or so apart now.

Meredith Soloman, it turned out, was on a quest not terribly dissimilar from Donnie and Donna's. The old man was trying to find a decent place in the country to die: someplace where the authorities would give his old bones a decent burial at county expense. He'd tried going home, back to West Virginia, but most of his kin were dead or moved away or didn't want to see him. His children—all eleven if you counted the two illegitimate ones by little Bonnie Maybone—fell into the last category. So Meredith Soloman had been on a quest to find some hospitable state and county where an old boy with his lungs clogged as thick as two Glad bags full of black dust could spend a few weeks or months duty free in a hospital somewhere and . . . when the time came . . . have his bones treated with the respect due to bones belonging to a white Christian man.

Donnie began an argument about what happens to the soul once you die . . . he had specific views on reincarnation that he'd got from Donna's brother-in-law with the credit card . . . and the two men's urgent whispers turned into urgent shouts as Meredith explained that heaven was heaven, no niggers or animals or insects allowed.

Four rows in front of the arguing drunks, a quiet man named Kushwat Singh sat reading a paperback by the light of the small reading light above him. Singh was not concentrating on the

words in the book; he was thinking about the slaughter at the
Golden Temple a few years before—the rampage of Indian government troops that had killed Singh's wife, twenty-three-year-old
son, and his three best friends. The officials had said that the
radical Sikhs had been planning to overthrow the government.
The officials had been right. Now Kushwat Singh's mind, tired
from twenty hours of traveling and sleepless nights before that, ran
over the list of things he was going to buy at that certain warehouse near the Houston airport: Semtex plastic explosive, frag-
mentation grenades, Japanese electronic timing devices, and . . .
with a little luck . . . several Stinger-type, shoulder-launched
ground-to-air missiles. Enough matériel to level a police station, to
cut down a gaggle of politicians like a sharp blade scything
wheat . . . enough killing technology to bring down a fully
loaded 747 . . .

Bremen stuffed his fists tight against his ears, but the babble
continued and grew louder as the mercury vapor lamps switched
on along the darkening interstate exchanges. Donna went into
labor in earnest just as they crossed the Texas line and Bremen's
last glimpse of the couple was in the Beaumont bus station just
after midnight, Donna curled up on a bench in great pain as the
contractions racked her, Donnie standing with boots planted wide
apart, weaving, the empty bottle of Meredith's moonshine still in
his right fist. Bremen actually looked into Donnie's mind then,
extending his telepathic probe through the surrounding neurobabble, but pulled it back quickly. Except for the drunken fragments
of the earlier argument with Meredith still rattling around in
there, there was nothing in Donnie Ackley's mind. No plan. No
suggestion of what to do with his wife and the infant trying to be
born. Nothing.

Bremen actually sensed the panic and pain of the baby itself as
it . . . she . . . approached her final struggle to be born. The
infant's consciousness burned through the gray shiftings of the bus
station neurobabble like a searchlight through a thin fog.

Bremen stayed aboard the bus again, too exhausted to flee the cauldron of images and emotions boiling around him. At least Burk and Alice Jean, the horny Marine just out of the brig and the equally horny WAF, had disembarked to find a room somewhere near the bus station. Bremen wished them well.

Meredith Soloman was snoring, his gums gleaming in the reflection from sodium vapor lamps as they pulled out of Beaumont at midnight. The old man was dreaming of the mines, of men shouting in the cold damp air, and of a clean, white, painless death. Donna's birthing pains receded in Bremen's mind as they left the downtown and climbed onto the interstate access ramp. Kushwat Singh touched his money belt where the hundred and thirty thousand dollars in Sikh cash waited to be converted into vengeance.

The seat next to Bremen's was empty. He pulled the armrest back and curled up in a fetal position, drawing his legs up onto the seats and hugging his fists against his temples. At that second he wished that he had his brother-in-law's .38 back; he wished that Vanni Fucci had succeeded in delivering him to Sal and Bert and Ernie.

Bremen wished—with no melodrama, with no shred of self-consciousness or regret—that he was dead. The silence. The peacefulness. The perfect stillness.

But, for now, trapped in his living body and tortured mind, the roar and onslaught of mindrape continued, even as the bus moved southwest on causeways above swampland and pine forest, tires hissing on wet pavement now as the late-night rains came down in earnest. Bremen felt himself slowly being released to sleep now that the others slept, the small universe of sleeping humanity within the bus falling with him in the night, their muted dreams flickering like snippets of old film projected on an unwatched wall, the entire sealed cabin of them tumbling like the shattered *Challenger* shuttle in midnight free-fall together toward Houston and Denver and the deeper regions of darkness that Bremen knew that he was, for some reason he could not fathom, condemned to live to see.

EYES

Of all the new concepts that Jeremy has brought to me, the two most intriguing are love and mathematics.

These two sets would seem to have few common elements, but, in truth, the comparisons and similarities are powerful to someone who has experienced neither. Both pure mathematics and pure love are completely observer dependent—one might say observer generated—and although I see in Jeremy's memory the assertion by a few mathematicians like Kurt Gödel that mathematical entities exist independently of the human mind, rather like stars that would persist in shining even if there are no astronomers to study them—I choose to reject Gödel's *Platonism* in favor of Jeremy's stance of *formalism:* i.e., numbers and their mathematical relationships are merely a set of human-generated abstracts and the rules with which to manipulate these symbols. Love seems to me to be a similar set of abstracts and relation-of-abstracts, despite their frequent relationship with things in the real world. (2 apples + 2 apples did indeed = 4 apples, but the apples are not needed for the equation to be true. Similarly, the complex set of equations governing the flow of love does not seem dependent upon either the giver or recipient of that love. In a real sense I have rejected the *Platonic* idea of love, in its original sense, in favor of a *formalist* approach to the topic.)

Numbers are an astonishing revelation to me. In my former existence, prior to Jeremy, I understand the concept of *thing* but never dream that a thing—or several things—have the ghost echo of numerical values sewn to them like Peter Pan's shadow. If I am allowed three glasses of apple juice at lunch, for instance, for me there is only juice . . . juice . . . juice, and no hint of quantification. My mind no more counts the juices than my stomach would. Similarly, the shadow of *love,* so attached to a physical object yet simultaneously so separate, never occurs to me. I find that property connected to only one thing in my universe—my teddy bear—and my reaction to that one thing has been in the form of pleasure / pain response with the bias toward the pleasurable, so that I "miss" teddy when he is lost. The concept of "love" simply never enters the equation.

Jeremy's worlds of mathematics and love, so often overlapped before he comes to me, strike me like powerful lightning bolts, illuminating new reaches to my world.

From simple one-to-one correspondence and counting, to basic equations such as $2 + 2 = 4$, to the equally basic (for Jeremy) Schrödinger wave equation that had been the starting point for his evaluation of Goldmann's neurological studies:

$$i\hbar\partial\psi/\partial t = \hbar^2/2\mu\nabla^2\psi + V(r,t)\psi \text{ or } i\hbar\partial\psi/\partial t = H\psi$$

All is revealed to me simultaneously. Mathematics descends upon me like a thunderclap, like the Voice of God in the biblical story of Saul of Tarsus being knocked off his horse. More importantly, perhaps, is that I can use what Jeremy knows to learn things that Jeremy does not consciously know. Thus, Jeremy's basic knowledge of the logical calculus of neural nets, almost too elementary for him to remember, allows me to understand the way that neurons can "learn":

$$N_3(+) = .S[N_1(t)VN_b(t)] \equiv .S\{N_1(t)VS[SN_2(t).{\sim}N_2(t)]\}$$

Not my neurons, perhaps, given Jeremy's rather frightening understanding of holographic learning functions in the human mind, but the neurons of . . . let's say . . . a laboratory rat: some simple form of life that responds almost exclusively to pleasure and pain, reward and punishment.

Me. Or at least me, pre-Jeremy.

Gail does not care about mathematics. No, that is not quite accurate, I realize now, because Gail cares immeasurably about Jeremy, and much of Jeremy's life and personality and deepest musings are about mathematics. Gail loves that aspect of *Jeremy's* love of mathematics, but the realm of numbers itself holds no innate appeal for her. Gail's perception of the universe is best expressed through language and music, through dance and photography, and through her thoughtful and often forgiving appraisal of other human beings.

Jeremy's appraisal of other people—when he takes time to appraise them at all—is frequently less forgiving and often downright dismissive. Other people's thoughts, on the whole, bore him . . . not out of innate arrogance or self-interest, but due to the simple fact that most people think about boring things. Back when his mindshield—his and Gail's combined mindshields—could separate him from the random neurobabble around them, he did so. It was no more a value judgment on his part than if another person in deep and fruitful concentration had risen to close a window to shut out distracting street sounds.

Gail once shared her analysis of Jeremy's distance from the common herd of thoughts. He is working up in his study on a summer evening; Gail is reading a biography of Bobby Kennedy down on the couch by the front window. The thick evening light comes through the white cotton curtains and paints rich stripes on the couch and hardwood floor.

Jerry, here's something I want you to see.

? ? ? Mild irritation at being removed from the flow of the equation he is scrawling on the chalkboard. He pauses.

Bobby Kennedy's friend Robert McNamara said that Kennedy thought the world was divided into three groups of people—

The world's divided into two groups of people, Jeremy interrupts. *Those who think the world's divided into groups, and those who are smart enough to know better.*

Shut up a minute. Images of the pages fluttering and Gail's left hand as she searches for her place again. The breeze through the screen smells of newly mown grass. The thick light deepens the flesh tones of her fingers and gleams on her simple gold band. *Here it is . . . no, don't read it!* She closes the book.

Jeremy reads the sentences in her memory as she begins to structure her thoughts into words.

Jerry, stop it! She concentrates fiercely on the memory of root-canal work she'd suffered the summer before.

Jeremy retreats a bit, allows the slight fuzziness of perception that passes for a mindshield between them, and waits for her to finish framing her message.

McNamara used to go to those evening "seminars" at Hickory Hill . . . you know, Bobby's home? Bobby ran them. They were sort of like informal discussion sessions . . . bull sessions . . . only Kennedy would have some of the best people in whatever field there when they talked about things.

Jeremy glances back at his equation, holding the next transform in his mind.

This won't take long, Jerry. Anyway, Robert McNamara said that Bobby used to sort of separate people into three groups. . . .

Jeremy winces. *There are two groups, kiddo. Those who—*

Shut up, wise guy. Where was I? Oh, yes, McNamara said that the three groups were people who talked mostly about things, people who talked mostly about people, and people who talked mostly about ideas.

Jeremy nods and sends the image of a hippo yawning broadly. *That's deep, kiddo, deep. What about those people who talk about people talking about things? Is that a special subset, or can we create a whole new—*

Shut up. *The point is that McNamara said that Bobby Kennedy didn't have any time for people in the first two groups. He was only interested in people who talked about . . . and thought about . . . ideas. Important ideas.*

Pause. *So?*

So that's you, *silly.*

Jeremy chalks the transform in before he forgets the equation that follows it. *That's not true.*

Yes, it is. You—

Spend most of my waking hours teaching students who haven't had an idea in their heads since infancy. QED.

No . . . Gail opens the book again and taps long fingers against the page. *You teach them. You move them into the world of ideas.*

I can barely move them into the hall at the end of the class period.

Jerry, you know what I mean. Your removal from things . . . from people . . . it's more than shyness. It's more than your work. It's just that people who spend most of their thinking time on anything lower than Cantor's Incompleteness Theorem are boring to you . . . irrelevant . . . you want things to be cosmological and epistemological and tautological, not the clay of the everyday.

Jeremy sends, *Gödel.*

What?

Gödel's Incompleteness Theorem. It's Cantor's Continuum Problem. He chalks some transfinite cardinals onto his blackboard, frowns at what they have done to his wave equation, erases them, and scrawls the cardinals onto a mental blackboard instead. He begins framing a description of Gödel's defense of Cantor's Continuum Problem.

No, no, interrupts Gail, *the point is only that you're sort of like*

Bobby Kennedy that way . . . impatient . . . expecting everyone to be interested in the abstract things that you are . . .

Jeremy is growing impatient. The transform he holds in his mind is slipping slightly. Words do that to clear thinking. *The Japanese at Hiroshima didn't think that $E = mc^2$ was particularly abstract.*

Gail sighs. *I give up. You're not like Bobby Kennedy. You're just an insufferable, arrogant, eternally distracted snob.*

Jeremy nods and fills in the transform. He goes on to the next equation, seeing precisely now how the probability wave will collapse into something looking very much like a classical eigenvalue. *Yeah,* he sends, already fading, *but I'm a nice insufferable, arrogant, eternally distracted snob.*

Gail does not comment, but gazes out the window at the sun setting behind the line of woods beyond the barn. The warmth of the view is echoed by the warmth of her wordless thoughts as she shares the evening with him.

In Rats' Alley

Bremen was beaten and robbed fifteen minutes after he had gotten off the bus in downtown Denver.

They had arrived late, after midnight of the third day, and Bremen had wandered away from the lights of the bus station, hunkering into snow flurries from the west, wondering at how cold it was here in mid-April, his hands in his pockets and his head down against the cold wind from the west, when suddenly the gang was around him.

It was not a real gang, only five black and Hispanic boys—none of them yet twenty—but in the seconds before their fists and boots flew, Bremen saw their intention, felt their panic and hunger for his money, but—more than that—sensed their eagerness to give pain. It was an almost sexual thrill, and if he had been attentive to the tone of the nighttime neurobabble surging around him, he would have felt the knife-edge intensity of their anticipation. Instead, he was taken by numbed surprise as they surrounded him and moved in, herding him into an alley mouth. Through the cascade of their half-articulated thoughts and adrenaline-rushed eagerness, Bremen could see their plan—get him into the alley to beat and rob him, kill him if he made too much of an outcry—but there was nothing he could do but back into the darkness there.

Bremen went down quickly when the fists lashed at him, tossing his remaining bills at them and curling into a tight ball. "It's all I have!" he cried, but even as he spoke he read their lack of caring. The money was incidental now. It was the giving of pain that preoccupied them.

They did that well. Bremen tried to roll away from the boy with the blade . . . even though the knife was still in the youth's hip pocket . . . but each way he rolled, a boot met him solidly. Bremen tried to cover his face and they kicked him in the kidneys. The pain was beyond anything Bremen had experienced. He tried covering his back and they kicked him in the face. Blood gushed from his broken nose and Bremen raised one hand to cover his face again. They kicked him in the scrotum. Then their fists returned, knuckles and the heels of their hands pummeling him in the skull, neck, shoulders, and ribs.

Bremen heard something crack, then something else crack, and then they were pulling off his shirt, ripping at his pants' pockets. Bremen felt the blade slash at his lower belly, but the boy who wielded the knife had done so while backing away and the cut was a shallow one. Bremen did not know that at the moment. He knew very little at that moment . . . then he knew nothing at all.

It was an hour until someone found him, two hours more until someone took the trouble to call the police. The police arrived when Bremen was struggling up to a half-conscious state; they seemed surprised to find him alive. Bremen heard the car radio squawk as one of the officers called for an ambulance, he closed his eyes for a brief second, and when he opened them, there were paramedics around him and they were lifting him onto a wheeled stretcher. The paramedics wore clear plastic gloves and Bremen noticed how they worked to keep from getting his blood on themselves. He did not remember the ride to the hospital.

The emergency room was crowded. A team consisting of a

Pakistani doctor and two exhausted interns dealt with his knife slash, gave him a hurried injection, and began stitching before the local anesthetic took effect. Then they left him to deal with some other patient. Bremen drifted in and out of consciousness for an hour and a half while he waited for them to return. When they did, the Pakistani doctor was gone, replaced by a young black doctor with rings of exhaustion under her heavy-lidded eyes, but the interns were the same.

They pronounced his nose broken, set a metal bar in place there with tape, found two broken ribs and taped them, prodded his bruised kidneys until he almost fainted with the pain, and then had him urinate into a plastic bedpan. Bremen opened his eyes long enough to see that his urine was pink. One of the interns told him that his left arm was dislocated and made him hold it up while they rigged a sling. The doctor returned and peered in Bremen's mouth. His lips were so swollen that the touch of the tongue depressor made him stifle a cry of pain. The doctor announced that he had been lucky—only one tooth had actually been knocked out. Did he have a dentist?

Bremen grunted an answer made more vague by his swollen lips. They gave him another shot. Bremen could feel the medics' fatigue as palpable as a thick tent canvas covering them all. None of the three had slept more than five hours during the past thirty. Their exhaustion made Bremen sleepier than the shot had.

He opened his eyes to find a police officer there. She was stolid, her gunbelt, belt radio, flashlight, and other items swinging from heavy hips. She had smudged eyes and blotchy skin. She asked Bremen again for his name and address.

Bremen blinked, thought of the authorities and Vanni Fucci, although he had to strain to remember through the painkiller haze who Vanni Fucci was. He gave the officer the name and address of Frank Lowell, the head of his department at Haverford. His buddy who was busy saving Bremen's job for him.

"You're a long way from home, Mr. Lowell," said the officer.

Bremen's left eye was swollen shut and his right one was too blurry to read the name tag over her badge. He mumbled something.

"Can you describe the assailants?" she asked, rooting in her blouse pocket for a pencil. Bremen's vision focused long enough for him to make out the childish scrawls in her notebook. She dotted her *i*'s with small circles, like the less mature students he had taught at Haverford. He described his assailants.

"I heard one of them call the other . . . the tallest . . . Red," he said, knowing that they called each other nothing during the attack. But one of them had *been* Red, he had garnered that.

Suddenly Bremen realized that the neurobabble around him was a distant thing. Even the surges of pain and panic from the other patients in the emergency room, the mental cries and catcalls from the dark rooms stacked above him like crates of misery . . . all were muted. Bremen smiled at the officer and blessed the painkiller, whatever it had been.

"Your wallet is missing," said the cop. "Your ID is gone, your insurance card, everything. . . ." The officer eyed him, and even through the fog of medication Bremen could feel her suspicion: he looked like a derelict, but they had checked his arms, thighs, and feet . . . no track marks . . . and while his urine had held ample blood, there had been no immediate trace of drugs or alcohol. Bremen felt her decide to give him the benefit of the doubt.

"You'll spend the night here in observation, Mr. Lowell," she said. "You told Dr. Chalbatt that you had no one to call here in the Denver area, so Dr. Elkhart isn't too keen on turning you loose tonight without supervision. They'll book you in as soon as there's a room available, monitor the bruised kidney overnight, and take another look at you tomorrow. We'll send someone over in the morning to go over the assault and battery with you."

Bremen closed his eyes and nodded slowly, but when he opened his eyes again, he was alone on a gurney in an echoing hallway. The clock read 4:23. A woman in a pink sweater came by, adjusted his blanket, and said, "There should be a room available anytime now." Then she was gone and Bremen fought going back to sleep.

He had been an idiot to give the police officer Frank Lowell's name and address. Someone would call Frank's home in the morning, a description would be given, and Bremen would be sitting in custody, answering questions about his burned farm-house . . . and possibly about a body found in a Florida swamp.

Bremen moaned and sat up, swinging his legs off the edge of the gurney. He almost fell off. He stared at his bare toes and realized that he was in a paper-thin gown; there was a plastic hospital bracelet on his left wrist.

Gail. Oh, God, Gail.

He slid off the cart, went to his knees, and used his good hand to feel around on the shelf under the cart. His clothes were stacked there, bloodstained and ripped though they were. Bremen checked the hall . . . it was still empty, although rubber soles squeaked just out of sight around the corner . . . and then he was hobbling to a supply closet down the hall, dressing painfully . . . finally giving up and draping the shirt over his slinged arm like a cape . . . and then out. Before he left the supply closet, he rum-maged in a hamper of soiled clothing, came up with a white cotton intern's jacket, and tugged it on, knowing how little warmth it would give out in the streets.

He checked the hall, waited until there was no noise, and moved as quickly as he could to a side door.

It was snowing outside. Bremen scurried away down an alley, not knowing where he was or where he was headed. Overhead, between the dark cliffs of buildings, the sky showed no hint of dawn.

EYES

I do not mean to suggest that Jeremy and Gail are the perfect couple, never disagreeing, never arguing, never disappointing one another. It is true that sometimes their mindtouch is more of an invitation to discord than a binding force.

Their closeness acts like a magnifying mirror for their smallest faults. Gail's temper is fast to ignite and even faster to burn; Jeremy grows quickly tired of that. She cannot stand his slow, Scandinavian evenness in the face of even the most absurd provocation. Sometimes they fight about his refusal to fight.

Each decides early in the marriage that couples should be given biorhythm exams before the wedding rather than blood tests. Gail is an early-to-bed, early-to-rise type who enjoys the morning above all else. Jeremy loves the late night and does his best work at the chalkboard after one A.M. Mornings are anathema to him, and on those days when he does not have classes, he rarely stirs before 9:30. Gail does not enjoy mindtouch with him before his second cup of coffee, and even then says that it is like achieving telepathy with a surly bear half-risen from hibernation.

Their tastes, complementary in so many important areas, are

flatly divergent on some equally important things. Gail loves reading and lives for the written word; Jeremy rarely reads anything
outside his field and considers novels a waste of time. Jeremy will
come down from the study at three A.M. and happily plop down in
front of a documentary; Gail has little time for documentaries.
Gail loves sports and would spend every fall weekend at a football
game if she could; Jeremy is bored by sports and agrees with
George Will's definition of football as the "desecration of autumn."

With music, Gail plays the piano, French horn, clarinet, and
guitar; Jeremy cannot hold a tune. When listening to music, Jeremy admires the mathematical baroqueness of Bach; Gail enjoys
the unprogrammable humanity of Mozart. Each enjoys art, but
their visits to galleries and art museums become telepathic battle-
fields: Jeremy admiring the abstract exactitude of Josef Albers's
Homage to the Square series; Gail indulging in the Impressionists
and early Picasso. Once, for her birthday, Jeremy spends all of his
savings and most of hers to buy a small painting by Fritz Glarner
—*Relational Painting, No. 57*—and Gail's response, upon seeing it
in Jeremy's mind as he drives the Triumph up the drive with the
painting in the boot, is *My God, Jerry, you spent all our money on
those . . . those . . . squares?*

On political issues Gail is hopeful, Jeremy is cynical. On social
issues Gail is liberal in the finest tradition of the word, Jeremy is
indifferent.

Don't you want to end homelessness, Jerry? Gail asks one day.

Not especially.

Why on earth not?

*Look, I didn't make these people homeless, I can't make them not-
homeless. Besides, most of them are refugees from asylums anyway . . . tossed out by a liberal do-goodism that condemns them to a
life on the streets.*

Some of them aren't crazy, Jerry. Some are just down on their luck.

Come on, kiddo. You're talking to an expert on probability here. I may know more about why luck doesn't exist than anyone in the commonwealth.

Perhaps, Jer . . . but you don't know much about people.

Agreed, kiddo. And I don't especially want to. Do you want to go deeper into that morass of confusion that most people call thoughts?

They're people, Jerry. Like us.

Uh-uh, kiddo. Not like us. And even if they were, I wouldn't want to spend time brooding about them.

And what would you spend time brooding about?

$$\sum_\beta [\sum_\mu (\gamma\mu)\ \alpha\beta\partial/\partial_x\mu + {}^{mc}\!/\hbar\delta\alpha\beta]\psi\beta = 0,$$

$$\chi^\mu = \vec{\chi}, ict$$

Gail gleans what the equation is all about by patiently waiting for some language-equivalent translation to cross Jeremy's mind. *Big deal,* she sends, honestly angry, *you and some guy named Dirac can do a relativistic wave equation. How does that help anyone?*

It helps us understand the universe, kiddo. Which is more than you can say for eavesdropping on the confused mullings of all those "common folk" you're so hot to understand.

Gail's anger is unfiltered now. It washes over Jeremy like a black wind. *God, you can be arrogant sometimes, Jeremy Bremen. Why do you think electrons are more worthy of study than human beings?*

Jeremy pauses. *That's a good question.* He closes his eyes a second and ponders the thought, excluding Gail as much as possible from his deliberations. *People are predictable,* he sends at last. *Electrons aren't.* Before Gail can respond, he continues. *I don't mean that people's actions are all that predictable, kiddo . . . we know how perverse people's actions can be . . . but the* motivations *for their actions make up a very finite set, as does the range of the actions resulting from those motivations. In that sense, the uncertainty principle applies much less to people than to electrons. In a real sense, people are boring.*

Gail forms an angry response, but then stifles it. *You're serious, aren't you, Jerry?*

He forms an image of himself nodding.

Gail raises her mindshield to think about this. She does not shut herself off from Jeremy, but the contact is less intimate, less immediate. Jeremy considers following up on the exchange, trying to explain further, if not justify, but he can feel her absorption with her own thoughts and he decides to save the conversation until later.

"Mr. Bremen?"

He opens his eyes and looks out at his class of math students. The young man, Arnie, has stepped back from the chalkboard. It is a simple differential equation, but Arnie has missed it completely.

Jeremy sighs, swivels in his chair, and proceeds to explain the function.

Rat's Coat, Crowskin, Crossed Staves

Bremen lived in a cardboard box under the Twenty-Third Street overpass and learned the litany of survival: rise before sunrise, wait, breakfast at the Nineteenth Street Salvation Army outlet, after waiting at least an hour for the minister to arrive and cajole them with motivation, then another half an hour for the prewarmed food to arrive . . . then, out by 10:30, shuffle twenty blocks to the Lighthouse for lunch, but not before more waiting. There is a job call at the Lighthouse and Bremen must line up for work in order to line up for lunch. Usually only five or six out of the sixty or so men and women are tagged for work, but Bremen is chosen more than once in April. Perhaps it is because he is relatively young. Usually it is unskilled, mindless work—cleaning up around the Convention Center, perhaps, or sweeping out the Lighthouse itself—and Bremen does it uncomplainingly, pleased to have something fill his hours other than the endless waiting and walking from meal to meal.

Dinner is at the JeSus Saves! near the train station or back at the Salvation Army storefront on Nineteenth. JeSus Saves! is actually the Christian Community Service Center, but everyone knows it by the name on the cross-shaped sign out front where the middle *S* on the horizontal *JeSus* is the beginning *s* on the vertical *Saves!* Bremen often stares at the empty area above the *S* on the vertical stem of the cross and wants to write something in there.

The food is much better at JeSus Saves!, but the preaching is longer, sometimes running so late that most of the waiting audience is asleep, their snores mixing with the rumbles of their bellies, before Reverend Billy Scott and the Marvell Sisters allow them to queue up for dinner.

Bremen usually joins some of the others for a walk along the Sixteenth Street Mall before returning to his box by eleven P.M. He never panhandles, but by staying near Soul Dad or Mister Paulie or Carrie T. and her kids, he sometimes receives the benefit of their begging. Once a black man in an expensive Merino wool overcoat gave Bremen a ten-dollar bill.

That night, and most nights, he stops by AlNite Liquor and picks up a bottle of Thunderbird, carrying it with him back to his box.

April had been a bitch in the Mile High City. Bremen realized later that he had almost died during those last weeks of Denver's winter, especially during his first night out from the hospital. It had been snowing. Bremen wandered through a cityscape of black alleys and slush-filled streets, the buildings dark. Finally he had found himself in a block of burned-out row houses and had crawled in among the blackened timbers to sleep. He hurt everywhere, but his battered mouth, fractured ribs, and dislocated shoulder were like volcanic peaks of pain rising above an ocean of generalized ache. The shot he'd received hours earlier no longer diminished the pain, but still served to make him sleepy.

Bremen found a niche between a brick chimney and a fire-blackened beam and had crawled in to sleep when he awoke to a vigorous shaking.

"Man, you ain't got no fucking coat. You stay here, you gonna fucking die and that the flat truth of it."

Bremen had swum up to semiconsciousness. He blinked at the

face scarcely illuminated by a distant streetlight. A black face, wrinkled and lined above an unkempt, twin-spiked beard, dark eyes just visible below the soiled stocking cap. The man wore at least four layers of outer clothing and they all stank. He was pulling Bremen to his feet.

"Lemmelone," Bremen managed. His few moments of sleep, while not dreamless, had been more free of neurobabble than any time since Gail had died. "Lemmefuckalone." He pulled his arm free and tried to curl into the niche again. Snow was falling softly through a hole in the shattered ceiling.

"Uh-uh, no way Soul Dad lettin' you die jes' 'cause you a stupid little honkie fuck." The black man's voice was strangely gentle, somehow appropriate to the softening night and the silent sweep of snowflakes against black beams.

Bremen let himself be lifted, moved toward the loose boards of the doorway.

"You got a place?" the man was asking over and over. Or perhaps he asked it only once and his thoughts echoed in both their skulls . . . Bremen was not sure. He shook his head.

"All right, this once you stay with Soul Dad. But just till the sun's out and you got your brains back in your head. Okay?"

Bremen staggered alongside the black man for countless blocks, past brick buildings illuminated by the hellish orange light of the city reflected back from low storm clouds. Finally they came to a tall highway bridge and slid down a frozen slope of weeds to the darkness beneath. There were packing crates there, and sheets of plastic spread like tarps, and the ashen remains of campfires be-tween abandoned autos. Soul Dad led Bremen into one of the larger structures—a veritable shack of plastic and packing crate, with the concrete buttress of the overpass serving as one wall and a sheet of tin as the door.

He led Bremen to a pile of smelly rags and blankets. Bremen was shaking so fiercely now that he could not warm himself, no matter how deep in the pile he burrowed. Sighing, Soul Dad removed his outer two layers of topcoat, draped them over

Bremen, and curled close himself. He smelled of wine and urine, but his human warmth came through the rags.

Still shaking, but less fiercely now, Bremen fled again to dreams.

April had been cruel, but May was little better. Winter seemed reluctant to leave Denver, and even on the milder days the night air was cold at 5,280 feet of altitude. To the west, occasionally glimpsed between buildings, the real mountains rose steeply, their ridges and foothills less white from day to day, but their summits snowy into June.

And then, suddenly, summer was there and Bremen made his food rounds with Soul Dad and Carrie T. and the others through a haze of heat waves from the sidewalks. Some days they all stayed in the shade of the overpasses near their plastic tent village far across the tracks near the Platte River—the cops had rousted their more comfortable village under the Twenty-Third Street overpass in mid-May, "spring cleaning" Mister Paulie had called it—and ventured out only after dark to one of the open-late missions up beyond the state capitol building.

The alcohol did not cure the curse of Bremen's enhanced mindtouch, but it dulled it a bit. At least he believed that he dulled it. The wine gave him terrible headaches, and perhaps the headaches themselves dulled the neurobabble. He had been drunk all the time by late April—it had been a type of self-destruction that neither Soul Dad nor the usually solicitous Carrie T. seemed to care about, since they also practiced it—but, using the illogic that if a little bit of addiction is good, more would be better, he had almost killed himself, physically and psychically, by buying crack from one of the teenage dealers down near the Auraria campus.

Bremen had gotten the cash from two days on the Lighthouse work program, and he returned to his box with great anticipation.

"What you smiling through your poor honkie excuse for a beard for, anyway?" Soul Dad had asked, but Bremen ignored the old man and scuttled into his box. Bremen had not smoked since his teenage years, but now he lighted the pipe he'd bought from the kid near Auraria, flipped the glass bubble over the end of the pipe as instructed, and inhaled deeply.

For a few seconds there had been peace. Then there was only hell.

Jerry, please . . . can you hear me? Jerry!

Gail?

Help me, Jerry! Help me get out of here. Images of the last thing she had seen: the hospital room, IV stand, the blue blanket at the end of her bed. Several nurses were gathered around. The pain was worse than Bremen had remembered . . . worse than the hours and days after his beating as bones healed poorly and bruises bled into his flesh . . . Gail's pain was beyond description.

Help me, Jerry! Please.

"Gail!" Bremen screamed aloud in his box. He writhed to and fro, battering the cardboard walls with his fists until they ruptured and he was battering concrete. "Gail!"

Bremen screamed and pounded for almost two hours on that waning April day. No one came to check on him. The next morning, shuffling to Nineteenth Street, none of the rest of them would meet his eyes.

Bremen did not try crack again.

Soul Dad's thoughts were a haven of slow harmony in a sea of mental chaos. Bremen stayed around the old man as much as possible, trying not to eavesdrop on the other's thoughts, but always calmed when Soul Dad's slow, rhythmic, almost wordless musings came through Bremen's ineffective mindshield and curtains of alcohol-induced stupor.

Soul Dad, Bremen discovered, was named after a prison the old man had spent more than a third of the century in. In his youth Soul Dad had been filled with a fierce violence—a street-gang member decades ahead of his time: knife carrying, grudge holding, confrontation seeking. One of those confrontations in the late 1940s in Los Angeles had left three younger men dead and Soul Dad serving a life sentence.

It had been a life sentence in the truest sense of the word: conferring life. Soul Dad had shaken off his street mannerisms, the false bravado, the zoot-suit shallowness, the sense of worthlessness and self-pity. While quickly acquiring the deep toughness needed to survive in the toughest wing of the toughest penitentiary in America—a willingness to fight to the death rather than be trespassed upon in the slightest way—Soul Dad had gained a sense of peace, almost serenity, there in the midst of that penitentiary madness.

For five years Soul Dad spoke to no one. After that he spoke only when necessary, preferring to keep his thoughts to himself. And his thoughts were active. Even in the bits of accidental mindtouch, Bremen saw the remnants of those days and months and years of Soul Dad's working in the prison library, reading in his prison cell: the philosophy he had studied—beginning with a brief conversion to Christianity, and then, in the sixties with its influx of a new breed of black criminal, a second conversion to the Black Muslim creed, and then moving beyond dogma into real theology, real philosophy. Soul Dad had read and studied Berkeley and Hume and Kant and Heidegger. Soul Dad had reconciled Aquinas with the ethical imperatives of the mean streets and had discarded Nietzsche as just another pimp-rolling, self-justifying zoot suiter with a chip on his shoulder.

Soul Dad's own philosophy was one beyond words and images. It was something closer to Zen or to the elegant nonsense of non-linear mathematics than to anything else Bremen had ever encountered. Soul Dad had rejected a world rampant with racism and sexism and hatred of every sort, but he had not rejected it with anger. He moved through it with a kind of stately grace—an elegant Egyptian barge floating amid the carnage of some wild naval battle between Greeks and Persians—and as long as his peaceful and wordless reverie was not invaded, he allowed the world to tend to the world while he tended to his garden.

Soul Dad had read *Candide*.

Bremen sometimes sought out the haven of the old man's slow thoughts in much the same way that a small ship would seek shelter in the lee of a solid island when ocean seas grew too wild.

And usually the seas were too wild. Too wild even for Soul Dad's solipsistic musings to offer shelter for long.

Bremen knew better than anyone alive that the mind was not a radio—neither receiver nor transmitter—but as the summer passed in the underbelly of Denver, Colorado, Bremen felt as if someone had tuned his mind to darker and darker wavelengths. Wavelengths of fear and flight. Wavelengths of power and self-induced potency.

Wavelengths of violence.

He drank more as the neurobabble turned to neuroshouts. The fuzziness helped a bit; the headaches distracted him. Soul Dad's stolid presence was an even better shield than the drinking.

But the violent shouting continued around him and above him.

Crips and Bloods, showing their colors, cruising by in vans looking for trouble out here beyond their turfs, or pimp-strutting across the overpass in groups of three and five. Armed. Carrying little .32 revolvers and heavy .45 automatics and sawed-off shot-guns and even some plastic-feeling Uzis and Mac-10s. Out looking for trouble, seeking an excuse to be enraged.

Bremen rolled into his box and drank and held his aching head between his hands, but the violence surged in him and through him like a shot of evil adrenaline.

The lust to inflict pain. The yearning for violent action. The pornographic intensity of street violence, experienced in a rush of images and shouts, replayed in slow motion like a favorite video.

Bremen shared the powerlessness turned to power by the simple act of squeezing a trigger, of slipping a blade into his palm. He felt the vicarious thrill of a victim's fear, the taste of a victim's pain. Pain was something one offered to others.

Most of the violent people Bremen touched with his mind were stupid . . . many amazingly stupid, many compounding their stupidity with drugs . . . but the haze of their thought and memory centers was nothing compared with the blood-scent clarity of the *now,* the heart-pounding, penis-raising *immediacy* of those seconds of violence they had sought and savored. The memory of these acts was not so much in their minds as in their hands and muscles and loins. Violence *validated.* It balanced all the banal hours of waiting and suffering insults and inaction, of watching television and knowing that one could not have any of the bright baubles paraded there . . . not the cars, not the houses, not the clothes, not the beautiful women, not even the white skin . . . and, more important, these seconds of violence were the *envy* of those TV faces and movie-star faces . . . faces that could only pretend to violence, faces that could only go through the white-bread motions of sanitized television violence and the fakery of motion-picture blood bags.

In his fitful dreams Bremen pimp-strutted down dark alleys, the pistol in his waistband, searching for someone with the wrong color, the wrong expression on his or her face. He became the Giver of Pain.

Others in the plastic-tarp village ignored Bremen's cries and moans in the night.

It was not merely gang members and the inner-city poor who fueled Bremen's nightmares. As he sat in the cool shade of an alley mouth on an evening in late June, Bremen suffered the thoughts of the shoppers strolling by on the Sixteenth Street Mall.

White. Middle class. Neurotic, psychotic, paranoid, fueled by an anger and frustration as real as the impotent rage of the crack-charged Blood or Crip. Everyone was angry at someone and that anger smoldered on, fogging minds like smoke from a slow flame.

Bremen drank his wine from a brown bag, nursed his ever-present headache, and occasionally glanced out of the alley at passing forms. Sometimes it was hard to match up the blazing beacons of their angry thoughts with the gray shades of their bodies.

That middle-aged white woman in shorts and a too-tight blouse, Maxine: she had twice tried to poison her sister for the title to their father's unused land in the mountains. Twice the sister had survived and twice Maxine had rushed to her side in the hospital, bemoaning the bad luck of botulism. The next time, thought Maxine, she would take her sister up to the old house on Daddy's property, feed her an ounce of arsenic in her chili, and stay there with her until she was cold.

The short man in the elevator shoes and Armani suit: Charles Ludlow Pierce. He was a lawyer, a defender of the civil rights of minorities, a contributor to half a dozen Denver charities, a frequent face, alongside that of his beaming wife Deirdre, in the photos of the *Denver Post* society page. And Charles Ludlow Pierce was a wife-beater, extinguishing his pyre of periodic anger with his fists. Deirdre's face did not show the bruises because Charles Ludlow Pierce was careful not to administer one of his "lessons" when a charity ball or other public event was imminent . . . or if he did have to teach Deirdre a lesson then, it was, by silent assent, done with the sand in the sock and restricted to her body.

But it was the all-out, fists-in-the-face, orgasm-inducing, full-tilt "lessons" that Charles Ludlow Pierce credited with saving their marriage and his sanity. On those occasions Deirdre would be on "retreat" for a week or more at their home above Aspen.

Bremen lowered his eyes and drank his wine.

Suddenly he snapped his head up and stared out at the passing crowd until he picked out a man walking briskly by. Bremen left his bottle and brown bag behind and followed him.

The man continued east on Sixteenth Street, pausing in front of the glass-and-steel shopping concourse that was Tabor Center. The man deliberated going in to look at the suits in Brooks Brothers, decided against it, and continued east across Lawrence Street and onward down the open mall. An evening breeze from the foothills stirred the saplings along the bricked bus lane and cooled the city heat a bit. The man strolled on, taking no note of the bearded panhandler shuffling along half a block behind.

Bremen did not get his name. He did not care to know it. The rest was clear enough.

Bonnie will be eleven this September, but she looks thirteen. Shit, she looks sixteen! Her tits are filling out nicely. Her pussy hair's been in since a year last May. Carla says that Bonnie had her period last month . . . that now our little girl's a woman . . . little does Carla know!

The man was dressed in a wrinkled gray suit. He had come from one of the office buildings on Fifteenth and was waiting for his bus to Cherry Creek. It would be another eighteen minutes before he could get the bus two blocks south at the mall terminus. The man was tall, six-three or six-four, and he carried his extra weight well. His hair was tied back in a queue, one of those middle-aged male ponytails that Gail had called a dork knob.

He went into the Brass Rail, a wood-and-brass yuppie bar across from the north end of Tabor Center. Bremen found a shady place between two buildings where he could watch the wall-to-ceiling windows of the bar. Rich light streamed down Sixteenth Street and turned the glass opaque.

It did not matter. Bremen knew precisely where the man sat, what he drank.

Two years now with Bonnie and that dumb bitch Carla doesn't suspect a thing. She thinks the kid's stomachaches and tears are just adolescence. Adolescence! God bless adolescence! He raised another glass of Dewar's. He always specified Dewar's so he didn't get the crummy bar scotch these places tried to pawn off on you.

Tonight's another special night. A bonnie night. A bonnie lassie night. He laughed and waved his hand for a refill. *Of course, it's not like the first time, but what is? That first time . . .* Images of velvet skin, a coppery stubbling of hair on his daughter's small mound, the breasts . . . little more than buds then . . . and her weeping softly into the pillow. He had whispered, "If you don't tell, it'll be all right. If you tell, they'll take you away and put you in an orphanage."

It's not like the first time, but she's learning tricks . . . my Bonnie . . . my darling Bonnie. Tonight I'll make her use her mouth again. . . .

He finished his second scotch, glanced at his watch, and hurried out of the Brass Rail, walking at a rapid but unhurried clip west down Sixteenth. He was almost at the bus terminus when a wino came out of the shadows across from Gart Brothers and angled across the pavement toward him. He moved farther to the right, frowning his warning at the drunk. There was no one else in sight and the two of them were partially hidden by the berm of raised grass and concrete on the stairway below the bus stop.

"Beat it, pal," he snapped, flicking his hand dismissively as the wino came within panhandling distance. The man had a wild, blond beard, wilder eyes behind tape-patched glasses, and was wearing a full raincoat despite the heat of the day. The wino did not move away.

He shook his head and moved to go around the wino.

"In a hurry?" asked the bum, his throat thick with phlegm. It was as if the man had not spoken for days.

"Fuck off," he said, and turned toward the bus station.

Suddenly he was jerked backward, into the shadows of the stairs. He whirled around, pulling his suit free of the wino's filthy fist. "What the fuck . . ." he began.

"Hurrying home to abuse Bonnie?" said the wino in a soft rasp. "Going to do it to her again tonight?"

He stared, jaw slack. A cold claw slid down his back. He felt sweat drip from his armpit and trickle downward under his blue oxford-cloth buttondown. "What?"

"You heard me, asshole. We know all about it. Everyone does. The police probably know, too. They're probably waiting with Carla in your kitchen right now, asshole."

He continued to stare, feeling the shock turn to pure anger and begin to burn like white kerosene. Whoever this mangy fuck was, however he . . . however he knew . . . he was six inches shorter and eighty pounds lighter. He could kill this wino fuck with one hand tied behind his back. . . .

"Why don't you try to kill me then, child molester?" whispered the wino. Amazingly, the stairway and bit of sidewalk below it were still empty. The shadows were long.

"Goddamn fucking right I'll . . ." he began, and stopped as the flame of anger grew stronger, then blossomed into an explosion of pure hate as the wino began grinning through his tangled beard at him. He balled his large hands into fists and took three steps toward the bum, telling himself to stop just short of killing the little fuck. He had almost killed the kid back in college. He'd try to stop before the wino fuck quit breathing, but it would feel *so* good to sink his fists into that scabby, filthy face. . . .

Jeremy Bremen took a step back as the man rushed him, fists rising. Bremen reached under his raincoat, swept out the two-by-four, and brought it around in a left-handed swing that had helped him bat .287 during his last year of college ball.

In the last possible second the man's arms had come up to shield his face. Bremen smashed the long board into the man's upper arms, again into his shoulders as he went down on the stairs.

The big man snarled something and struggled to his feet. Bremen hit him once in the solar plexus with the board and then smashed it over the back of the man's head as he doubled over. He began rolling down the steps in awkward little jerks.

Someone near the bus terminus began shouting. Bremen did not look over his shoulder. Taking his time, he stepped closer, hefted the three-foot length of board still in his hand, and swung it like a golf club, the swing ending in the big man's open mouth. Teeth caught the last of the sunlight as they arced out over the street.

The big man spat, sat up, raised his forearms to his face.

"This is for Bonnie," said Bremen, or tried to say through his clenched jaws, and then he swung down, very hard, smashing the end of the board into the man's crotch.

The big man screamed. Someone down the walking mall screamed.

Bremen stepped forward and smashed the board into the man's head again, splintering the wood a final time. The big man began to topple forward; Bremen stepped back and kicked him, once, very hard, imagining his groin as a football held at a perfect angle for a field goal.

Somewhere close by on Larimer Street a siren wailed and fell back into silence. Bremen stepped back, let the last shard of splintered wood fall from his grubby hands, looked once at the whimpering man on the sidewalk, and turned and ran.

There were shouts and the sound of at least two people running after him.

Raincoat flying, beard flapping, eyes so wide that they appeared to be blank, white eggs set in a dirt-browned face, Bremen ran for the shadows of the railroad overpass.

EYES

Gail and Jeremy want a child.

At first, during the year or so that is their extended honeymoon, it is assumed that a child will come along soon enough, so Gail takes precautions against an unwanted pregnancy—first the Pill, then a diaphragm when health worries arise. Eighteen months after their wedding they agree to discontinue the diaphragm and to let nature take its course.

For another eight months or so there are no worries. Their lovemaking is frequent and still passionate and the making of a baby is secondary in their thoughts. Then Gail begins to worry. They did marry somewhat late . . . Jeremy was twenty-seven and Gail twenty-five . . . but her doctor assures her that she has ten years of prime reproductive time ahead of her. But three years after the wedding, a week after Jeremy's thirtieth birthday—celebrated by having friends from the college come over for a day of softball—Gail suggests that they both see specialists.

At first Jeremy is surprised. She has shielded her concern from him as well as she could conceal anything; which is to say, he had known it was there but had underestimated the strength of it. Now, lying in bed together on a summer night, the moonlight streaming between the lace curtains, both of them listening to the insects and night-bird sounds out behind the barn during the pauses in their conversation, they decide that it is time to check things out.

First Jeremy goes through the slightly embarrassing ritual of providing semen for a sperm count. The doctor's office is in Philadelphia and is part of a modern complex with a discreet sign on the service elevator: GENETIC COUNSELING SERVICES. At least ten doctors work out of the complex, trying to help infertile couples realize their dream of parenthood. The reality of it all is sobering to both Gail and Jeremy, but they laugh together when Jeremy has to go to the rest room to provide his "specimen."

Jeremy sends the visual: copies of *Penthouse, The Girls of Playboy,* and half a dozen other glossy, soft-core magazines sit in a plastic magazine-holder on the counter near the toilet. A small typed message on a folded card next to the stack reads: *Due to the expense of replacing missing magazines, we must ask that you not remove these periodicals from this room.*

In the small room where she is waiting for her doctor, Gail begins giggling. *Can I watch?*

Go away.

Are you kidding? And miss this fascinating vicarious experience? I may pick up some pointers.

I'll give you a pointer . . . a sharp stick in the eye if you don't leave me alone here. This is serious.

Yes . . . serious. Gail is actively working to stifle her giggles now. Jeremy can see the image she has of her doctor entering the examination room to find his patient doubled over with mirth, tears streaming down her face. *Serious,* sends Gail, and then, looking through Jeremy's eyes at the photos in the first magazine he picked up: *My heavens, how can those young women pose like that?* She begins giggling again.

Irritated, Jeremy does not answer. He finds the conversation distracting. He turns the pages.

Having a little trouble, Jerry?

Go away. He closes the magazine and sighs.

Let me help. She pulls a screen between herself and the door and begins undressing, watching herself in a full-length wall mirror as she does so.

Hey! What the heck are you . . .

Gail undoes the last button on her blouse and folds it carefully over the back of the chair. She gestures toward a hospital gown laid out on the examining table. *The doctor's nurse said that there would be an examination.*

Listen . . .

Hush, Jerry. Read your magazine.

Jeremy sets the magazine back on the stack and closes his eyes.

Gail Bremen is a small woman, only five feet two inches tall in her stocking feet, but her body is classically proportioned, strong, and sensual in the extreme. She smiles into the mirror at Jeremy and he thinks, not for the first time, that her smile is a large part of that sensuality. The only woman's smile that he has seen that is similar in such an engaging, provocative, but overall wholesome way is that of the gymnast Mary Lou Retton. Gail's smile has the same irrepressible involvement of jaws and lips and perfect teeth; it is an invitation to some small mischief that communicates directly to the observer.

Gail senses his thoughts and quits smiling, feigning a frown and squinting at him. *Don't mind me. Get on with whatever you were doing.*

Idiot.

She flashes the grin again and slips out of her black skirt and slip, setting both on the chair. In her simple bra and underpants Gail seems both vulnerable and infinitely alluring. She reaches to unfasten her bra with that unselfconscious feminine grace that never fails to stir Jeremy. The slight hunching of her shoulders brings her breasts closer together as the fabric over them goes slack and slides away. Gail sets the bra on the chair and peels off the white pants.

Still watching?

Jeremy is still watching. He is touched in an almost religious way at how attractive his wife is. Her hair is dark and short, parted so that it falls across her high forehead in a soft curve. Her eyebrows are thick and dark—Annette Funicello eyebrows, she once had ruefully called them—but they add a dramatic highlight to her hazel eyes. An artist who had drawn her portrait with pastels some years before on a summer outing to Monhegan Island had said to Jeremy, who was watching: "I've read about eyes being luminous, but I always thought that was a bullshit word. Until now. Sir, your lady has luminous eyes."

Gail's facial features somehow manage to be both fine and strong: finely chiseled cheekbones, strong nose, fine laugh lines around those luminous eyes, a strong chin, and a fine complexion that shows the slightest hint of sun or embarrassment. She shows no embarrassment now, although there is a hint of red high on her cheekbones as she tosses her underpants onto the chair and stands a second before the mirror.

Jeremy Bremen has never been overly attracted by female breasts. Perhaps it was the ease with which he had eavesdropped on girls' thoughts during his adolescence, perhaps it is his penchant to look at the entire equation—or in this case, organism—rather than at its constituent parts, but since he passed that inevitable sexual crisis of his adolescence, breasts have seemed a normal enough part of the human anatomy to him. Attractive, yes . . . a constant source of sexual stimulation, no.

Gail's breasts are an exception. They are large for someone her height, but it is not their size that so stirs him. The girls in the magazines laid out nearby to help the sperm donors tend to have huge breasts, but the proportions as often as not seem wrong or downright silly to Jeremy. Gail's breasts are . . .

Jeremy shakes his head, finding that he cannot put some things in words, even to himself.

Try.

Gail's breasts are sensual in the extreme. While proportionate to her athlete's body and strong back, they are . . . perfect is the only word that Bremen can think of: high but heavy with the promise of touch, much paler than the rest of her tanned skin—small veins are visible under the white near where the tan line ends—and tipped with areolae that have remained as pink as a young girl's. Her nipples rise only slightly in the cool air, and now her breasts are compressed and raised again as Gail unconsciously hugs herself against the chill, the dark hairs on her forearm visible against the white, weighty undercurve of breast.

Gail's gaze does not shift, but Jeremy allows himself to change his own perspective on her image in the mirror, thinking to himself as he does so: *I'm seeing my mind's reflection of her mind's view of her reflection. A ghost admiring ghost shadows.*

Gail's hips are wide but not too wide, her thighs strong, the V of dark hair between them rising to the cusp of her belly with all the bushy fullness promised by her dark eyebrows and the shadowed stipple under her arms. Her knees and lower legs are elegant not only in an athlete's honest way, but in the classical proportions of the finest sculptures of Donatello. Jeremy lowers his gaze and wonders why men ever abandoned their fascination with such a sexually stimulating series of arcs and curves as those that constitute such a slim ankle as this.

Gail sets the screen aside, slips her left arm in the gown—no standard hospital gown this, but an expensive artifact of combed cotton for the upscale clientele—and pauses, half-turned from him, her left breast and hip catching the soft light filtering through the venetian blinds above. *Still having problems, Jerry?* A smile. *No, I see you're not.*

Shut up, please.

He hears the doctor's footsteps beyond her door, then their

mindshields raise together, not shutting off their sharing but muting it a bit.

Jeremy does not open his eyes.

I have to intervene here to say that my first glimpse of this open sexual feeling between Jeremy and Gail was a revelation for me. Literally a revelation; an awakening of almost religious dimensions. It opened new worlds for me, new systems of thought and understanding.

I had known sexual pleasures, of course . . . or at least the pleasures of friction. The sadness following orgasm. But these physical responses were nothing out of the context of the shared love and sexual intimacy that Jeremy and Gail had known.

My awe at discovering this aspect of the universe could not have been greater had I been a scientist who stumbled upon the Grand Unified Theory of the cosmos. In a real sense the love and sex between Gail and Jeremy *was* the Grand Unified Theory of the cosmos.

Jeremy's sperm count is fine. His part of the testing is over.

Not so Gail. Over the next nine months she undergoes entire batteries of tests—some painful, most embarrassing, all fruitless. She suffers a laparoscopy and repeated ultrasound exams that seek for tubal blockage, uterine abnormalities, fibroid tumors, ovarian cysts, uterine lesions, and endometriosis. None is found. She is tested for hormone deficiencies and sperm-rejecting antibodies. None is confirmed. She is put on Clomid and sent out to buy ovulation predictor kits—at significant expense each month—so that the peak days and hours of fertility can be determined. Gail and Jeremy's sex life begins to resemble a military campaign; for three or four twenty-four-hour periods each month, the day begins with urine tests on chemically treated paper and ends with multiple bouts of intercourse followed by a time where Gail rests on her back with her hips slightly elevated and legs bent at the knee so that the slowly swimming sperm have the best chance possible of finishing their trek.

Nothing. Nine months of nothing; then another six months of the same.

Gail and Jeremy see three other specialists. In each case Jeremy is cleared on the basis of his single sperm-count test and Gail undergoes another series of tests. She becomes an expert at knowing precisely *when* she must drink the half gallon of water so that she can last through the ultrasound without wetting her hospital gown.

The tests continue to show nothing, satisfy nothing. Gail and Jeremy continue to try, eventually abandoning the daily charts and test kits for fear of destroying all spontaneity. The possibility of artificial insemination is raised and they agree to think about it, but they silently dismiss that option before leaving the clinic. If sperm and egg are all right, if Gail's reproductive system is all right, they would rather leave things to chance and the natural system of things.

The natural system of things fails them. For the next few years Gail and Jeremy continue to dream of having children, but quit talking about it. Even Gail's musings on the subject while they are in mindtouch can send them both into a depression. Occasionally, when Gail would be holding a friend's newborn, Jeremy is shocked to feel her reaction to the infant's touch and scent; her heart aches with longing . . . he understands that . . . but her entire body also responds: breasts hurting and womb seeming to throb with a physical reaction to the newborn. It is a response beyond Jeremy's experience and he marvels that two forms of human beings—male and female—can inhabit the same planet, speak the same language, and assume they can have anything in common while such basic and profound differences silently separate them.

Gail is aware of Jeremy's desire for children, but also of his reservations about having one of their own. She has always seen these snippets of concern in his mind: fear of birth defects, hesitation at introducing another heart and mind into the perfect two-point constellation that is their relationship, a basic jealousy that anyone or anything else could fill Gail's attention and affection the way he does now.

She has seen these concerns, but dismissed them as typical male hesitations about having children. But what she has missed is important.

Jeremy is terrified of having an imperfect child. In the beginning of their ordeal, when pregnancy seemed only a few weeks or months away, he would lie awake at night and catalog his fears.

Just from his brief work on genetics and probability in college he knew some of the possible outcomes of this roll of the genetic dice: Down's syndrome, Huntington's chorea, Tay-Sachs disease, hemophilia . . . the list goes on. And Jeremy had known the odds even before the doctor spoke to them that first time: a one-percent chance that a couple will have a child with a serious or life-threatening birth defect. At age twenty Gail ran a 1:2,000 chance of having a child with Down's syndrome and a 1:526 risk of some sort of major chromosomal disorder. If they wait until Gail is thirty-five, the odds shift to 1:300 for Down's syndrome and 1:179 for a significant chromosomal abnormality. By age forty the probability curve has become a steep and slippery slope: 1:100 for Down's and a 1:63 chance of having other serious defects.

The possibility of having a retarded or malformed child freezes Jeremy with horror. The inevitability of any child changing his relationship with Gail produces horror on a less urgent but equally disturbing plane. Gail has seen the former and dismissed it; she catches only the faintest reflection of Jeremy's terror at the second possibility. He shields it from her—and from himself—as best he can, using misdirection and the static jamming of his mindshield during their telepathic sharing when the subject arises. It is one of only two secrets that he holds from Gail through their entire time together.

And the other secret also has to do with their childlessness. Only his other secret is a time bomb, ticking away between them and beneath them, ready to destroy everything they have had or ever hope to have together.

But Gail dies before the second secret is discovered . . . before he can share and defuse it.

Jeremy dreams of it still.

In This Hollow Valley

Soul Dad got Bremen out.

The police had a description of the Sixteenth Street Mall assailant and were combing the shack cities under the Platte River overpasses. Word was out that the assailant's victim had not been hurt seriously, but the Sixteenth Street merchants had been complaining for months about the proliferation of panhandlers and the homeless on the mall during business hours. This attack had been the final straw and metro cops were tearing apart . . . literally tearing apart . . . all the temporary shacks and lean-tos from Market Street downtown all the way west to the barrio around Stonecutters Row on the hill above I-25, hunting for the young wino with blond hair, scraggly beard, and glasses.

Soul Dad got him out. Bremen had run back to his shack near the Platte and crawled into his tarp tent, pawing through the rags in the corner for his bottle of screw-top Night Train. He found it and drank deeply, trying to settle back into the fuzzy-edged murk of indifference and neurobabble that had been his life. But the adrenaline continued to pump through his system, acting like a strong wind blowing away months of fog.

I attacked that man! was his first coherent thought. And then, *What the hell am I doing here?* Suddenly Bremen wanted to quit playacting whatever farce he had found himself in, call Gail to come pick him up, and go home for dinner. He could see the long lane opening off the county road with the white frame farmhouse at the end, the peach trees he had planted along each side, some still held up by stakes and wires, the long line of shadows from the trees along the stream creeping toward the house as summer evening fell, the smell of new-mown grass through the open windows of the Volvo . . .

Bremen moaned, drank more of the filthy wine, cursed, and flung the bottle out through the opening of his crude tent. It smashed on concrete and someone farther out under the overpass shouted something unintelligible.

Gail! Oh, Christ, Gail! Bremen's longing at that moment was a physical ache that hit him like some tsunami that had come curling over the edge of the world without warning. He felt himself battered, lifted, dropped, and tossed around by tidal forces far beyond his control. *Ah, Gail . . . God, I need you, kiddo.*

For the first time since his wife had died Jeremy Bremen lowered his forehead to his clenched fists and wept. He sobbed, surrendering to the terrible constrictions of grief that now rose in him like great and painful shards of glass that had been swallowed long ago. Oblivious to the terrible heat under the makeshift tent of plastic and canvas, oblivious to the sounds of traffic on the highway above and to the wail of sirens in the streets up the hill, oblivious to everything but his loss and grief, Bremen wept.

"You got to move your ass or lose it, boy," came Soul Dad's slow, mellifluous voice through the thickened air.

Bremen waved him away and curled into his rags, face to the shade-cooled concrete. He continued to weep.

"No time for that now," Soul Dad said. "Be plenty of time later." He grasped Bremen under the arm and lifted. Bremen struggled to free himself, to stay in his tent, but the old man was surprisingly strong, his grip irresistible, and Bremen found himself out in the sunlight, blinking away tears and shouting something loud and obscene, while Soul Dad moved him along into the deeper shadows under the viaduct as easily as a parent moves a surly child.

There was a car idling there, a '78 or '79 Pontiac with a scabrous vinyl roof. "I don't know how to hotwire the newer ones," said Soul Dad, setting Bremen behind the wheel and closing the door. The old man leaned low, his forearm on the lowered driver's-side window and his Old Testament prophet's beard brushing against Bremen's shoulder. He reached in and pressed a wad of paper into Bremen's shirt pocket. "Anyway, this one will do you for the immediate future . . . such as it is. You drive it out of town now, hear? Find some place to stay where crazy white boys who cry in their sleep are welcomed. At least find some place to stay until they get tired of looking for you here. Understand?"

Bremen nodded, rubbing harshly at his eyes. The interior of the car smelled like heat-baked beer and cigarette ashes. The torn upholstery smelled of urine. But the engine idled well, as if all the owner's efforts and attention had gone under the hood. *This is a stolen car!* Bremen thought. And then. *So what?*

He turned to thank Soul Dad, to say good-bye, but the old man had already moved back into the shadows and Bremen caught only a glimpse of a raincoat moving back toward the shacks. Sirens growled somewhere close above the weedy ditch where the Platte trickled past, shallow and brown.

Bremen set his grime-caked fingers on the steering wheel. It was hot from the sun and he jerked his hands away, flexing fingers as if burned. *What if I don't remember how to drive?* An instant later the answer. *It doesn't matter.*

Bremen slammed the thing into gear and almost floored the accelerator, throwing gravel far out over the Platte River and having to spin the wheel lock to lock twice before gaining control and bouncing across a dirt access road and a grassy median to find the access ramp to I-25.

At the top of the on-ramp he swept into traffic and glanced

right at the tops of factory buildings, warehouses, the distant gray of the train station, and even the modest skyline of steel and glass that was Denver. There were police cars down among the tent city, police cars along the tracks and river walks, and police cars along the east-west streets running back toward the bus terminus, but no cop cars up here on the Interstate. Bremen looked at the waggling red speedometer needle, realized that he was doing almost eighty in the light midday traffic, and eased up on the accelerator pedal, dropping to a legal fifty and settling in behind an Allied moving van. He realized with a start that he was approaching an intersection with I-70. The signs gave him his choice: I-70 EAST—LIMON, I-70 WEST—GRAND JUNCTION.

He had come from the east. Bremen followed the cloverleaf up and around, settling back into traffic on the busy I-70 West. Brown foothills loomed ahead, and beyond them—the glimpse of snow-covered mountains.

Bremen did not know where he was going. He glanced at the gas gauge and noticed that there was three-quarters of a tank left. He reached into his shirt pocket and pulled out the paper Soul Dad had stuffed there: a twenty-dollar bill. He had no other money—not a cent. The three-quarters of a tank and the twenty dollars would have to get him wherever in the world he was going to go by car.

Bremen shrugged. The hot air roiling in through the open window and dusty vents cooled him as much as anything had in the past month or so. He did not know where he was headed or what he would do. But he was moving. At long last he was moving.

In This Valley of Dying Stars

Bremen was walking along the edge of the desert when the police car pulled up alongside him on the county road. There was no other traffic, so the brown-and-white vehicle moved at his walking pace for a moment. Bremen glanced once at the lone officer in the car—a square, sun-leathered face, oversized mirrored sunglasses—and then he looked back at his feet, careful not to step on any of the yucca plants or small cacti on the desert floor.

The police car pulled ahead fifty feet, turned onto the shoulder of the asphalt road with a small cloud of dust, and braked to a stop. The officer stepped out, unbuckled a strap over his revolver, and stood by the driver's side of the car, his mirrored glasses reflecting Bremen's slow approach. Bremen decided that the man was not a state highway patrolman, but some sort of county mountie.

"Come here," ordered the officer.

Bremen stopped, still six feet out into the desert. "Why?"

"Get your ass over here," said the cop, his voice still flat and low. His hand was on the grip of the revolver now.

Bremen held his own hands out, palms visible in a gesture of both acquiescence and conciliation. Also, he wanted the cop to see that his hands were empty. Bremen's oversized Salvation Army sneakers made small sounds on the soft asphalt as he came around the rear of the patrol car. A mile ahead on the empty road, heat waves rippled and broiled above a mirage of water on tarmac.

"Assume the position," said the officer, standing back now and gesturing toward the car's trunk.

Bremen stood and blinked a moment, not willing to show the cop that he understood the term too readily. The cop took another step back, gestured impatiently toward the lid of the trunk, and removed his revolver from the holster.

Bremen leaned forward, moved his legs a bit farther apart, and rested his palms on the trunk. The metal was hot and he had to lift his fingers like a pianist poised to begin.

The cop stepped forward and, using only his left hand, quickly patted down Bremen's left side. "Don't move," said the officer. He shifted position slightly and used the same hand to pat Bremen's right side. Bremen could feel the presence of the loaded revolver behind him and the tension in the cop's body, ready to spring back if Bremen whirled. Instead Bremen continued leaning on the car while the officer stepped back four paces.

"Turn around."

The policeman still held the pistol, but it was no longer aimed directly at Bremen. "That your car back at the Interstate rest stop?"

Bremen shook his head.

"Seventy-nine Plymouth?" continued the officer. "Colorado tags MHW 751?"

Bremen shook his head again.

The officer's thin lips twitched ever so slightly. "You don't seem to have a billfold," he said. "Any ID? Driver's license?"

Thinking that another shake of the head might be considered a provocation, Bremen said, "No."

"Why not?"

Bremen shrugged. He could see his own image in the mirrored

glasses—his reed-thin form in the filthy and baggy clothes, khaki shirt torn and unbuttoned now in the heat, his chest pale and shrunken, his face as pale as his chest except for the sunburned nose, cheeks, and forehead. He had paused at that first Colorado gas station minimart to buy a razor and shaving cream, but he'd left both in the trunk of the car. His bare face looked strange to him now, like an old photograph suddenly come upon in an unlikely place.

"Where are you headed?" asked the cop.

"West," said Bremen, taking care not to shrug again. His voice was very raw.

"Where you coming from?"

Bremen squinted against the glare. A pickup passed them in a roar and cloud of grit, giving him a second. "Salt Lake was the last place I stayed awhile."

"What's your name?"

"Jeremy Goldmann," Bremen said without a pause.

"How'd you get way out here on this county road without a car?"

Bremen made a motion with his hands. "I hitched a ride on an eighteen-wheeler last night. I was sleeping this morning when the guy woke me up and said I had to get out. That was back up the road a ways."

The officer holstered his pistol, but did not come closer. "Uh-huh. And I bet you don't even know what county you're in, do you, Jeremy Goldstein?"

"Goldmann," said Bremen. He shook his head.

"And you don't know anything about a stolen car with Colorado plates back at the Interstate rest stop, do you?"

Bremen did not bother shaking his head again.

"Well, this state has laws against vagrancy, Mr. Goldstein."

Bremen nodded. "I'm not a vagrant, officer. I'm looking for work."

The officer nodded slightly. "Get in the back seat."

Through his headache and two-day hangover Bremen had been

catching glimmers of the man's thoughts. Flat certainty that this wimpy-looking beanpole was the car thief who had dumped the Colorado Plymouth back at the rest stop. Probably caught a lift to Exit 239 and hiked down this road in the dark, not knowing that the nearest town along it was another thirty-four miles. "In the back," he said again.

Bremen sighed and got in the back. There were no door handles back there. The windows had wire mesh rather than glass in them and there was a double-mesh partition between the front seat and back. The gaps in the mesh were so small that Bremen didn't think that he could get a finger through. It was very hot and the vinyl flooring smelled as if someone had vomited there recently.

The police officer had gotten in the front and was talking on a radio when a Toyota 4×4 that had been headed east pulled to a stop next to them. A woman leaned out her window. "Howdy, Deputy Collins. Got a live one back there?"

"How do, Miz Morgan. He's not too lively right now."

The woman peered at Bremen. She had a long thin face with sharp bones angling against skin more sun-beaten than the deputy's. Her eyes were a color of gray so light as to be almost transparent. Her hair was tied back and seemed to be a dark, not-very-natural red. Bremen guessed her to be in her late forties or early fifties.

But it was not just her appearance that struck him. Bremen had allowed himself to focus on mindtouch, but there was none. The deputy's thoughts were there . . . stolid, half-angry, impatient . . . and Bremen could even sense the neurobabble from far down the highway and even from the interstate eight miles back, but from the woman, nothing. Or, rather, where there should have been the tumbled mélange of impressions, words, and memories, there was only a loud rasping . . . a sort of neural white noise, as loud as an old electric fan in a small room. Bremen sensed *something* within or behind that curtain of mindnoise, but the thoughts were as indistinct as shifting figures on a television screen filled with electronic snow.

"Couldn't be you're arrestin' the fellow come to answer my hired-man ad, now are you, Howard?" The woman's voice was surprisingly deep and very self-assured. There was only a hint of banter in her tone.

The deputy looked up. Bremen saw the sunlight glinting on his glasses as he stared at the woman. The Toyota was higher than the patrol car and the deputy had to lift his head to look at her. "I doubt it, Miz Morgan. This'n is probably the fellow who left a stolen car out to the Interstate late last night. We'll take him down to the station and send his prints out on the wire."

Miz Morgan never looked at the deputy. She continued to squint at Bremen. "What'd you say his name was?"

"Goldmann," said Bremen. "Jeremy Goldmann."

"Shut up, goddamn you," snapped the deputy, turning in his seat.

"By God," said the woman, "that *was* the name of the man who wrote answering my ad." Then, to Bremen: "Where'd you say you saw it? In the Denver paper?"

"Salt Lake," said Bremen. He had not eaten in almost twenty-four hours and his head felt very light after the long walk through the darkness and desert sunrise.

"That's right. Salt Lake." She finally looked at the cop. "By God, Howard, you *do* have my hired man back there. He wrote me last week sayin' the wages was agreeable to him and sayin' he was coming out for an interview. Salt Lake. Jeremy Goldmann."

The deputy swiveled in the front seat, his gunbelt creaking. The radio rasped and crackled while he thought. "You sure the man's name was Goldmann, Miz Morgan?"

"Sure was. How could I forget a Jew name like that? It sorta tickled me, thinking of a Jewish fella working livestock."

The deputy tapped the wire mesh. "Well, he's still probably the one who abandoned the stolen car with Colorado plates."

The woman edged the Toyota forward a foot so she could stare down at Bremen. "You drive a stolen car here?"

"No, ma'am," said Bremen, wondering when he'd last called

someone "ma'am." "I hitched a ride and the fellow let me out at the last exit."

"You tell him you were headed for the Two-M Ranch?" she asked.

Bremen hesitated only a second. "Yes'm."

She backed the Toyota up a few feet. "Deputy, you got my hired hand back there. He was supposed to be here three days ago. Ask Sheriff Williams if I didn't say I was waiting for a city fellow to come down to help me with the gelding."

Howard hesitated. "I don't doubt you told Garry, Miz Morgan. I just don't remember nobody mentioning anybody named Gold-mann coming."

"I don't recollect tellin' Garry his name," said the woman. She glanced ahead down the highway as if expecting traffic at any second. There was none. "I don't recollect it being anybody's business, to tell you the truth, Howard. Now why don't you let Mr. Goldmann get in with me so I can interview him properly. Or is there a law against walkin' along county roads these days?"

Bremen felt Howard's resolve shifting on uncertain sands. Miz Fayette Morgan was one of the biggest landowners and taxpayers in the county, and Garry—Sheriff Williams—had been out to court her a few times. "I just don't have a good feeling about this guy," said Howard, removing his mirrored glasses as if in a tardy gesture of respect toward the lady staring down at him. "I'd feel better if we cleared his name and prints."

Miz Fayette Morgan's lips compressed with impatience. "You do that, Howard. In the meantime you're detaining a citizen who . . . as far as I can tell . . . has done nothing more illegal than admit to hitching a ride. If you keep this attitude up, Mr. Goldmann will think that we act like the fat-slob frontier hillbilly hick cops that we see in the movies. Isn't that right, Mr. Gold-mann?"

Bremen said nothing. From somewhere down the county road behind them a truck ground up through gears.

"Make up your mind, Howard," said Miz Morgan. "I need to

get back to the ranch and Mr. Goldmann probably wants to get in touch with his attorney."

Howard jumped out, released the door from the outside, and was back behind the wheel before the truck came into view a quarter of a mile behind them. The deputy drove off without an apology.

"Get in," said Miz Fayette Morgan.

Bremen hesitated only a second before going around and climbing up into the Toyota. It was air-conditioned. Miz Morgan cranked up her window and looked at him. This close, Bremen realized how tall she was—at least six-two or six-three unless she was sitting on a stack of phone directories. The truck passed them with a blast of its air horn. Miz Morgan waved at the driver without moving her gaze from Bremen. "You want to know why I told that cargo of cobblers to Howard?" she asked.

Bremen hesitated. He was not sure if he did want to know. At that second he felt a strong urge to get out of the cab and to start walking again.

"I don't like little assholes who act like big assholes just 'cause they got some authority," she said. The last word—authority—came out like an obscenity. " 'Specially when they use that *authority* to pick on someone who's got enough troubles, which it looks like you do."

Bremen set his hand on the door latch, but hesitated. It was at least eight miles back to the interstate and another twenty-some to the nearest town, according to the fuzzy map he'd picked up from the deputy's thoughts. There would be nothing for Bremen in the town except a possible run-in with Howard. He had kept eighty-five cents after the last gas fill-up in Utah. Not enough to eat with.

"Just tell me one thing," said the woman. "Did you steal that car Howard was talkin' about?"

"No." Bremen's tone didn't even convince him. *Technically, that's true,* he thought tiredly. *Soul Dad was the one who hotwired it.* Soul Dad, the tarp village, Denver, the man going home to his daughter . . . it all seemed light-years and real years away to

Bremen. He was very tired, having slept only an hour or two in Utah the day before. The woman's white-noise mindshield . . . neuroblock . . . whatever it was, filled Bremen's head with static. It blended with the ache from alcohol withdrawal to give him the best escape from the neurobabble he had found in four months.

Even the desert had been no refuge. Even with no people in sight and ranches visible only every four or five miles, hiking across the desert had been like wandering in a vast echo chamber filled with whispers and half-heard shouts. The dark wavelength of thought that Bremen somehow seemed attuned to now evidently had no limitations of distance; the crackling and surge of violence and greed and lust and envy had filled the interstate with mindnoise, had echoed down the empty county road, and had bounced back from the lightening sky to drown Bremen in reflected ugliness.

There had been no escape. At least in the city the closer surges of mindtouch had given him some clarity; being out here was like listening to a thousand radio stations at once, all of them poorly tuned. And now, with the white noise from Miz Fayette Morgan's mind blanketing him like a sudden desert wind, there was a certain peace.

". . . if you want it," the woman was saying.

Bremen shook himself into wakefulness. He was so tired and strung out that the late-morning sunlight coming through the tinted windshield of the Toyota seemed to flow like syrup across him, the woman, the black upholstery. . . . "I'm sorry," he said. "What did you say?"

Miz Morgan showed her impatient smile. "I said, you can come back to the ranch and try out for that position if you want to. I do need a hired hand. The fella who wrote to me from Denver never showed."

"Yes," said Bremen, nodding. Each time his chin came down it wanted to stay down. He struggled to keep his eyes open. "Yes, I'd like to try. But I don't know anything about—"

"Name like Goldmann, I wouldn't think so," said Miz Morgan with a flicker of a grin. She gunned the Toyota around in a tight turn that bounced up onto the desert sand and then back on tarmac, accelerating toward the west and the Two-M Ranch somewhere out beyond the heat ripples and mirages that floated like phantom curtains ahead of them.

EYES

Jacob Goldmann's research so excites Jeremy—and through Jeremy, Gail—that they take the train to Boston to visit the man.

It is a little less than five years before Gail will discover the tumor that will kill her. Chuck Gilpen, their old friend who was now a researcher at Lawrence Livermore Labs in Berkeley, had sent an unpublished paper on the Goldmann research to Jeremy because of its relevance to Jeremy's Ph.D. thesis on human memory analyzed as a propagating wavefront. Jeremy sees the importance of Goldmann's research at once, calls the researcher two days after receiving the paper, and is on the train north with Gail three days after that.

Jacob Goldmann had been suspicious on the phone, demanding to know how Jeremy had received a copy of a paper not yet submitted for publication. Jeremy assured him that he had no intention of trespassing on the researcher's domain, but that the mathematical aspects of Goldmann's work were so profound that the two must speak. Reluctantly, Goldmann had agreed.

Gail and Jeremy take a taxi from the train station to Goldmann's lab in a run-down industrial section miles from Cambridge.

"I thought he'd have some fancy laboratory at Harvard," says Gail.

"He's a fellow at the School of Medicine," says Jeremy. "But his research is mostly his own, I understand."

"That's what they said about Dr. Frankenstein."

Goldmann's lab is sandwiched in between offices for a wholesale religious-textbook distributor and the headquarters for Kayline Picnic Supplies. Jacob Goldmann is the only one there—it is late on a Friday evening—and he looks the part of a scientist, if not exactly a mad scientist. In his early seventies, he is a small man with a very large head. His eyes are what both Jeremy and Gail will remember later: large, brown, sad, and sunken under brows that make his intelligent gaze seem almost simian. Goldmann's face, forehead, and wattled neck are creased with the kind of wrinkles that only a lifetime of indomitable personality and internalized tragedy can impress on the human physiognomy. He is dressed in a brown three-piece suit that had involved a significant amount of money and tailoring a decade or two earlier.

"I would offer you coffee, but the Mr. Coffee does not seem to be working," says Dr. Goldmann, rubbing his nose and looking distractedly around the cluttered little cubicle that is obviously his sanctum sanctorum. The outer office and file room that Gail and Jeremy have just passed through are meticulously neat. This room and the man in it, however, remind Jeremy of the famous photo of Albert Einstein looking lost in the littered mess of his office.

He is like Einstein, shares Gail. *Have you touched his mind?*

Jeremy shakes his head as unobtrusively as possible. He has his mindshield raised, trying to concentrate on what Goldmann is saying.

". . . my daughter usually manages the coffee." The researcher tugs at his eyebrow. "She usually manages dinner as well, but she is in London for the week. Visiting relatives . . ." Goldmann peers at them from under his shaggy brows. "You aren't hungry, are you? I tend to forget about things like dinner sometimes."

"Oh, no . . . we're fine," says Gail.

"We had dinner on the train," says Jeremy.

If you count a Payday candy bar as dinner, sends Gail. *Jerry, I'm famished.*

Hush.

"You said something about the mathematics being very important, young man," says Goldmann. "You realize that the paper you saw was *sent* to Cal Tech so that the mathematicians there could look it over. I was interested to see if the fluctuations we are charting here compare to—"

"Holograms," finishes Jeremy. "Yes. A friend in California knew that I was doing some pure-math research on wavefront phenomena and its eventual application to human consciousness. He sent me the paper."

"Well . . ." Goldmann clears his throat. "It was a breach of etiquette at the very least. . . ."

Even through his tight mindshield, Jeremy can feel the older man's anger mixing with a powerful desire not to be rude. "Here," says Jeremy, and looks for a clear spot on desk or countertop to set the folder he has brought along. There is no clear spot. "Here," he says again, and opens his folder on top of a massive text of some sort lying atop a mesa of papers. "Look." He moves Jacob Goldmann closer.

Goldmann clears his throat again, but peers at the papers through his bifocals. He flips through the dissertation, occasionally pausing to look carefully at a page or more of equation. "Are these standard transforms?" he asks at one point.

Jeremy feels his heart accelerate. "That's an application of Dirac's relativistic wave equation modifying Schrödinger."

Goldmann frowns. "In the Hamiltonian?"

"No . . ." Jeremy turns back a page. "Two components here, see? I started with the Pauli spin matrices until I realized that those could be bypassed. . . ."

Jacob Goldmann steps back and removes his glasses. "No, no," he says, his accent suddenly heavier. "You cannot apply these relativistic Coulomb field transforms to a holographic wave function. . . ."

Jeremy takes a breath. "Yes," he says flatly. "You can. When the holographic wave function is part of a larger standing wave."

Goldmann rubs his brow. "A larger standing wave?"

"Human consciousness," says Jeremy, and glances at Gail. She is watching the old man.

Goldmann stands there for a full half moment, not moving, not blinking. Then he takes two steps backward and sits down heavily on a chair littered with magazines and abstracts. "My Gott," he says.

"Yes," says Jeremy. It is almost a whisper.

Goldmann reaches out one liver-spotted hand and touches Jeremy's dissertation. "And you have applied this to the MRI and S-CAT data I sent to Cal Tech?"

"Yes," says Jeremy, and leans closer. "It integrates. It *all* integrates." He begins pacing back and forth, finally stopping to tap the folder holding his now obsolete dissertation. "My work was originally just about *memory* . . . as if the rest of the mind were just hardware running a RAM-DOS retrieval system." He laughs and shakes his head. "Your work made me *see*. . . ."

"Yes," whispers Jacob Goldmann. "Yes, yes." He turns to stare blindly at a cluttered bookcase. "My God."

Later they discover that none of them has actually eaten dinner and plan to go out for a meal as soon as Jeremy and Gail are given a quick tour of the laboratory. They leave five hours later, well after midnight. In the time between introductions and their late meal, realities are shattered.

The offices are the tip of a rather significant research lab. Behind the suite of offices, in what had been a small warehouse area, lies the room within a room, grounded, shielded, and wrapped in the nonconducting equivalent of a Faraday Cage. In the room itself are the oddly streamlined sarcophagi of two magnetic-resonance-imaging units and a much less tidy cluster of four mutated-looking CAT scanners. Unlike the usual tidiness of an MR-imaging room, this lab floor is cluttered with additional shielded equipment and ungainly cables snaking into the floor, ceiling, and walls.

The room beyond is even more cluttered, with more than a dozen monitors displaying data to a master console where four wheeled chairs sit empty. The conglomeration of cables, stacked computer components, empty coffee cups, jerry-rigged patch circuits, dusty chalkboards, multiple EEG rigs, and massed oscilloscopes suggests that this is a research project that has never been touched by the tidy minds of NASA.

Over the next few hours Jacob Goldmann explains the origins of the research based upon the crude experiments done during neurosurgery in the 1950s in which patients' brains were touched by an electrical probe. The patients were able to recall events in their lives complete with full sensory input. It was as if they were "reliving the experience."

Goldmann does not do neurosurgery here, but by measuring, in real time, the electrical and electromagnetic fields in their research subjects' brains, and by using the wide variety of modern and experimental medical imaging equipment in this laboratory, he— he and his daughter and two assistants—has been charting avenues of the mind undreamed of by neurosurgeons.

"The difficulty," says Jacob Goldmann as they stand in the quiescent control room that night, "is in measuring areas of the brain while the subject is involved in some activity. Most MRI scans are done, as you know, with the patient immobilized on the sliding gurney in the machine itself."

"Isn't that immobility necessary for the scanning process?" asks Gail. "Isn't it like taking a photograph with one of those old cameras where any motion produces a blur?"

"Precisely," says Goldmann, beaming at her, "but our challenge was to bring an entire array of such imaging techniques to bear while the subject is doing a task . . . reading, perhaps, or riding a bicycle." He gestures toward the television picture of the imaging room. In one corner there is an exercise bicycle with an array of consoles and cables above it, all converging on a black dome into which a person's head might fit. Black neck clamps give the apparatus the look of some medieval instrument of torture.

"Our research subjects call it the Darth Vader Helmet," says Dr. Goldmann with a slight chuckle. Then, almost absentmindedly, "I have never seen that motion picture. I must rent a videotape of it someday."

Jeremy leans closer to the TV monitor to study the Darth Vader Helmet. "And this gives you all the data of the larger magnetic-resonance imagers?"

"Much more," says Dr. Goldmann softly. "Much, much more."

Gail is biting her lip. "And who are your subjects, doctor?"

"Call me Jacob, please," says the old man. "Our subjects are the usual volunteers . . . students from the School of Medicine who wish to earn a modest stipend. Several of them, I confess, are my graduate students . . . bright young men and women whose wish is to score a few points with their elderly teacher."

Gail is looking at the array of threatening instruments in the MR room. "Is there any danger?"

Dr. Goldmann's bushy brows move back and forth as he shakes his head. "None. Or rather, no more than any of us would be exposed to if we were to have a CAT scan or MRI done. We make sure that none of the subjects are exposed to magnetic fields greater or more extensive than those allowed at any hospital." He chuckles. "And it is painless. Other than the boredom suffered while equipment is constantly being repaired or tampered with, the subjects have none of the usual research discomforts of blood being drawn or the danger of being exposed to embarrassing situations. No, we have quite a long list of eager volunteers."

"And in exchange," whispers Jeremy, touching Gail's hand, "you are mapping uncharted regions of the mind . . . capturing a snapshot of human consciousness."

Jacob Goldmann seems lost in reverie again, the sad, brown eyes observing something not in the room. "It reminds me," he says softly, "of the spirit photography in vogue during the last century."

"Spirit photography," says Gail, who is a talented photographer herself. "You mean when the Victorians tried to photograph ghosts and pixies and things? The kind of hoax that bamboozled poor old Arthur Conan Doyle?"

"Ja," says Goldmann, his eyes regaining focus and his subtle smile returning. "Only our ghost photography is all too real. We have stumbled upon a means to capture an image of the human soul itself."

Gail frowns at this mention of a soul, but Jeremy is nodding. "Jacob," Jeremy says, his voice all but vibrating with emotion, "you see the ramifications of my wave-function analyses?"

"Of course," says the old man. "We expected some rough equivalent of a hologram. A crude, fuzzy analog to the patterns we were recording. What you have given us is a thousand thousand holograms—all crystal clear and three-dimensional!"

Jeremy leans close to the other man, their faces only inches apart. "But not just of their *minds,* Jacob . . ."

The eyes are infinitely sad under their simian brows. "No, Jeremy, my friend, not just their minds . . . but of their minds as mirrors of the universe."

Jeremy is nodding, watching Dr. Goldmann's face to make sure that the scientist understands. "Yes, mirrors, but more than mirrors—"

Jacob Goldmann interrupts, but he is speaking to himself now, oblivious to the presence of the young couple. "Einstein went to his grave believing that God does not play dice with the universe. He became so insistent on making that point that Jonny von Neumann . . . a mutual friend . . . once told him to shut up and quit speaking for God." Goldmann moves his large head until it is cocked at a defiant angle. "If your equations are true—"

"They are true," says Jeremy.

"If they are true, then Einstein and all of the others who rejected quantum physics were incredibly, terribly, magnificently wrong . . . and triumphantly correct!"

Jeremy collapses into one of the chairs at the console. His arms and legs are rubbery, as if someone has cut his strings. "Jacob, do you know the theoretical work of Hugh Everett? I think it was published in fifty-six or fifty-seven . . . then forgotten for years until Bryce DeWitt from the University of North Carolina picked it up in the late sixties."

Goldmann nods and lowers himself into a chair. Gail is the only one in the room left standing. She tries to follow the conversation through mindtouch, but both men are thinking primarily in mathematics now. Jacob Goldmann is also thinking in phrases, but the phrases are in *German*. She finds an empty chair for herself. The conversation is giving her a headache.

"I knew John Wheeler at Princeton," says Dr. Goldmann. "He was Hugh Everett's adviser. He urged Everett to give a mathematical basis to his theories."

Jeremy takes a deep breath. "It solves everything, Jacob. The Copenhagen interpretation. Schrödinger's cat. The new work that's being done by people like Raymond Chiao at Berkeley and Herbert Walther in Frankfurt—"

"Munich," Dr. Goldmann says softly. "Walther is at the Max Planck Institute in Munich."

"Whatever," says Jeremy. "Sixty-five years after the Copenhagen interpretation and they're still messing around with it. And still finding that the universe seems to work by magic when they try to observe it directly. Lasers, superconductors, Claudia Tesche's goddamn squid . . . and they're still finding magic."

"Squid?" says Gail, grasping a word more reliable than "magic." "What squid?"

"A superconducting quantum interference device," recites Jacob Goldmann in his raspy old-man's voice. "A squid. A way to let the quantum genie out of the microbottle, into the macroworld we think we know. But they still find magic. The curtain cannot be drawn. Look behind it . . . and the universe changes. Instantly.

Totally. One side or the other. We cannot see the workings of things. Either particle or wave . . . never both, Gail, my young friend. One or the other, never both."

Jeremy rubs his face and remains bent forward, palms over his eyes. The room seems to move around him as if he has been drinking. He rarely drinks. "You know, Jacob, that this way may lie madness . . . pure solipsism . . . the ultimate catatonia."

Dr. Goldmann nods. "Yes. And also . . . perhaps . . . the ultimate truth."

Gail sits up. Since her childhood when her parents became born-again Christians and born-again hypocrites, she has hated the sound of a phrase like "the ultimate truth."

"When do we eat?" she says.

The two men make a sound somewhere between a laugh and an embarrassed cough.

"Now," cries Jacob Goldmann, glancing at his watch and rising to his feet. He bows toward her. "By all means, discussions of reality can never match the indisputable reality of a good meal."

"Amen," says Jeremy.

Gail crosses her arms. "Are you two making fun of me?"

"Oh, no," says Jacob Goldmann. There are tears in his eyes.

No, kiddo, affirms Jeremy. *No.*

The three of them leave together, Jacob locking the door behind him as they go.

This Is Cactus Land

The Two-M Ranch was not in the desert proper but set several miles up a shallow canyon that rose toward wooded foothills. Beyond the foothills snowcapped peaks were visible through the haze of heat and distance.

"Ranch" was hardly an adequate word for Miz Fayette Morgan's spread. The main house was a modern Spanish hacienda perched between two boulders the size of low apartment buildings. The sprawling hacienda was set on a shelf of land that looked out over the grassy fields and cottonwoods of the stream-fed canyon toward the desert beyond. Half a dozen large dogs came baying at the Toyota; they ceased their growls and howls only when Miz Morgan stepped out and shouted at them. She patted each in turn as it groveled its way to her legs. "Come on into the main house for a beer," she said. "It's the only time you'll be invited up here."

The house was furnished with expensive southwestern antiques, decor, and art in a finished, interior-designed way that would have looked at home in a spread from *Architectural Digest*. It was air-conditioned and Bremen stifled an urge to lie down on the thick Stark carpet and go to sleep. Miz Morgan led the way through a gourmet cook's kitchen into a breakfast nook that looked out through bay windows at the south-facing boulder and the barns and fields beyond. She twisted the caps off two cold Coors, handed one to Bremen, and nodded toward the bench across the table as she sprawled out in a sturdy captain's chair. Her denim-covered legs were very long and ended in snakeskin cowboy boots. "To answer your unasked questions," she said, "the answer is yes, I do live alone except for the dogs." She took a swig of beer. "And no, I don't use my hired men as stud service." Her eyes were such a light gray that they gave her a strangely blind appearance. Blind, but in no way vulnerable.

Bremen nodded and tasted the beer. His stomach growled.

As if in response to the growl Miz Morgan said, "You do your own cooking. There's adequate supplies in the bunkhouse and a full kitchen there. If we run out of something you want . . . basic stuff, not booze . . . you can put it on the list when you go in to shop each Thursday."

Bremen took another swallow, feeling the beer hit him hard on his empty stomach. That and the fatigue made everything seem to have a faint, hazy halo of light around it. Miz Morgan's dyed-red hair seemed to burn and flicker in the midday sun through the yellow curtains. "How long do you need a hired hand?" he asked, taking care to enunciate each word.

"How long you intend to stay in these parts?"

Bremen shrugged. The white-noise mindroar surrounded the woman like a constant crackle of some wild electrical apparatus— a Van de Graaff generator perhaps. Bremen found the effect soothing, like a constant wind that drowns out lesser sounds. The release from the whisper and burble of neurobabble made him want to weep with gratitude.

"Well," said Miz Morgan, finishing her beer, "until Deputy Dawg gets some wanted poster on you, we'll see if you can do any useful work around here."

"Deputy Dawg?"

"Howard Collins," she said, rising. "Deputy Dawg's what most folks around here call him when he ain't within range. Thinks he's a tough character, but he hasn't got the brains of Lettie . . . that's the dumbest of my dogs out there."

"About the dogs . . ." began Bremen. He got to his feet, his beer only half-finished.

"Oh, they'll tear your arm or leg off, all right." Miz Morgan smiled. "But only on a command from me or if you're someplace where you shouldn't be. I'll introduce you to them on the way down to the bunkhouse so they can start gettin' to know you."

"Where is someplace I shouldn't be?" asked Bremen, holding his beer bottle tightly as if it could steady him. The glow around things had turned into a pulsing now and he felt the liquid in his stomach slosh and shift somewhat alarmingly.

"Stay away from the main house," she said, not smiling. "Especially at night. The dogs'll go for anything that comes up here at night. But I'd stay away during the day, too."

Bremen nodded.

"There are a few other places that're out of bounds. I'll point them out when I show you around the spread."

Bremen nodded again, not wanting to set the beer bottle on the table but uncomfortable holding it. He was not sure if he could get through an afternoon of ranch work the way he felt now. He was not completely sure that he could stay on his feet the way he felt now.

Miz Morgan paused in the doorway as he followed her back outside. "You look like shit, Jeremy Goldmann."

Bremen nodded.

"I'll show you the bunkhouse and you can make yourself something to eat and settle in. We'll start work at seven tomorrow mornin'. Wouldn't do to break in the hired man by killin' him."

Bremen shook his head. He followed her out into the heat and light, into a world made luminous and almost transparent by exhaustion and relief.

EYES

Gail and Jeremy take the train home from Boston on Sunday, not talking about the experience of the weekend with Jacob Goldmann, but communicating about it almost all the way home.

Did you mindtouch the part about his family dying in the Holocaust?

Holocaust? Jeremy had felt the power of Jacob Goldmann's intellect, and had occasionally lowered his mindshield to glimpse a concept or experimental protocol for clarification during their long talks, but mostly he had respected the older man's privacy. *No.*

Ahhh, Jerry . . . Gail's sadness is like a maroon shadow stealing over a sunny landscape. She looks out the window at the urban wasteland flickering by. *I didn't mean to pry, but every time I tried to understand what you two were saying by peeking, I'd get more images, more memories.*

What images, kiddo?

The gray sky, gray buildings, gray earth, gray watchtowers . . . the black barbed wire against the gray sky. The striped uniforms, shaved heads, skeletal figures lost in rough and baggy wool. The morning lineup in the milky light of dawn, the breaths of the prisoners rising like a fog above them all. German SS guards in their thick, wool overcoats, leather belts, and leather boots looking rich and oily in the wan light. Shouts. Cries. The marching bare feet of the forest work detail.

His wife and son died there, Jerry.

Is it Auschwitz?

No, a place called Ravensbruck. A small camp. They survived five winters there. Separated, but in touch by notes sent through an underground mail network. His wife and son were shot two weeks before the camp was liberated.

Bremen blinks. The clacking of metal wheels on metal rails is vaguely hypnotic. He closes his eyes. *I didn't know. But what about his daughter . . . Rebecca? . . . The one who was in London this weekend?*

Jacob remarried in 1954. His second wife was British . . . she had been in the medical unit that liberated the camps.

Where is she now?

She died of cancer in 1963.

Jesus.

Jerry, he is so sad! Didn't you feel it? There is a sadness there deeper than anything I've ever felt.

Bremen opens his eyes and rubs his cheeks. He had not shaved that morning and the stubble is beginning to itch. *Yeah . . . I mean I got a sort of sense of general sadness. But his excitement is real, too, Gail. He's really excited about the research.*

As are you.

Well, yeah . . . He sent an image of Jacob and himself in Stockholm, accepting their shared Nobel Prizes. The humor did not quite click.

Jerry, I didn't understand all of the stuff about quantum physics. I mean, I understood how some of the relativity stuff related to your dissertation . . . a lot of that was probability and uncertainty theory, too . . . but what does it have to do with Jacob's work with charting the brain?

Bremen turns to look at her. *I could take you through the simpler math again.*

I'd prefer you to take me through the words.

Bremen sighs and closes his eyes. *Okay . . . you understand about how Jacob's work translates through my math? How the neurological wave actions he's recording end up as sort of superholograms? Complex, interacting fields?*

Yeah.

Well, there's another step. And I'm not quite sure where it's going to take us. To even work with the data properly I'm going to have to learn a lot about the new nonlinear math they call chaos mathematics. That and fractal geometry. I don't know why fractals are important in this, but the data suggests they are. . . .

Stick to the point, Jerry.

Okay. The point is that Jacob's snapshots of the human mind . . . the human personality . . . in action bring up the classic "two-slit experiment" in quantum mechanics. Do you remember that from college? It led to the so-called Copenhagen interpretation.

Tell me again.

Well, quantum mechanics says that energy and matter—in their smallest chunks—sometimes behave like waves, sometimes like particles. It depends on how you observe them. But the scary part of quantum mechanics . . . the voodoo part that Einstein never really accepted . . . is that the very act of observation is what makes the observed object one thing or the other.

Where do the two slits come in?

For the last half a century experimenters have been replicating an experiment where particles . . . electrons, maybe . . . are shot at a barrier with two parallel slits in it. On a screen beyond the barrier you can see where the electrons or photons or whatever get through. . . .

Gail sits up and frowns at Jerry. He sees his face, eyes closed, frowning slightly, through her gaze. *Jerry, are you sure this is going to have something to do with Jacob Goldmann's MRIs or whatever of people's heads?*

Bremen opens his eyes. *Yep. Bear with me.* He opens two bottles of orange juice that they had packed that morning and hands one to Gail. *The two-slit experiment is sort of the ultimate test of the secrecy if not downright perversity of the universe.*

Go ahead. The orange juice is warm. Gail makes a face and sets it back in the bag.

Okay. You've got two slits . . . one is closed, electrons or particles are zapping through the other one. What would you get on the screen behind the barrier?

With only one slit open?

Right.

Well . . . Gail hates puzzles. She always has. She considers puzzles as an invention of people who like to embarrass other people. If she senses the slightest hint of condescension in Jeremy's mental tone, she's going to punch him in the solar plexus. *Well, I guess you get one line of electrons. A stripe of light or whatever.*

Correct. Jeremy's thought stream has taken on the slightly pedantic tone that he uses with his math students, but there is no condescension there. Only an eagerness to share an exciting concept. Gail does not hit him in the solar plexus.

Okay, continues Jeremy, *now, what would you get with both slits open?*

Two stripes of light . . . or electrons.

Jeremy sends the image of the Cheshire cat grinning. *Uh-uh. Wrong. That's what ordinary macro-universe common sense would dictate, but that proves not to be the case when you do the experiment. When you actually do it, with both slits open, you always get alternating bright and dark stripes on the screen.*

Gail chews a thumbnail. *Alternating bright and dark stripes . . . oh, I get it.* She does, with only the briefest glimpse at the sentences and images Jeremy is framing for her. *With both slits open, the electrons act like waves, not particles. The dark stripes are where the waves overlap and cancel each other out.*

Got it, kiddo. A classic interference pattern.

But what's the problem? You say that quantum mechanics predicts that little bits of matter and energy will act like both waves and particles. So they're doing what's predicted. Science is safe . . . right?

Bremen sends an image of a jack-in-the-box bobbing and nodding. *Yeah . . . science is safe, but sanity is in real danger. The trick is . . . after all these years . . . that the very act of observing makes those particle/wave thingees collapse into one state or the other. We've tried incredibly complex experiments to "peek" at the electron during its transit . . . shutting one of the slits while the electron's passing through the other one . . . we've tried everything. The electron . . . or photon, or whatever we use in the experiment . . . always seems to "know" whether the second slit is open or not. In a real sense the electrons behave precisely as if they not only know how many slits are open, but as if we're watching them! Other experiments . . . Bell's Inequality experiment, for instance . . . get the same reaction from separated particles flying apart from one another at the speed of light. One particle "knows" the state of its twin.*

Gail sends the image of a row of question marks. *Communication faster than the speed of light?* she sends. *That's impossible. The particles couldn't exchange any information if they're flying apart at the speed of light. Nothing can travel faster than light . . . right?*

Kee-rect, kiddo. Jeremy transmits the throbbing of his very real headache. *And it's been a headache for physicists for decades. Not only do these buggery little particles do the impossible . . . like know what their twin's doing in the two-slit experiment and Bell's experiment and others . . . but we still can't get a peek at the real substance of the universe. The particle behind the curtain with its clothes off.*

Gail tries to picture that. Cannot. *The particle with its clothes off?*

There's no way we've devised, with all our hypertechnology and Nobel Prize winners, to sneak a peek at the real stuff of the universe when it's wearing both aspects.

Both aspects? Gail's mental tone is almost querulous. *You mean both wave and particle?*

Yeah.

But why is all this quantum junk important to understanding how the human mind . . . the personality . . . is like a superhologram?

Bremen nods. Part of him is thinking about Jacob Goldmann's family in the death camps. *Gail, the stuff Jacob is getting . . . the wave patterns that I've been translating through Fourier transforms and all the rest . . . they're like reflections of the universe.*

Gail takes a breath. *Mirrors. You were talking about mirrors on Friday night. Mirrors of the . . . universe?*

Yeah. The minds that Jacob's been charting . . . those incredibly complex holographic structures, just graduate students' minds . . . what they really shake down to is a sort of peek at the fractal structure of the universe. I mean, it's like a two-slit experiment . . . no matter how cleverly we peek behind the curtain, there's the same magic.

Gail nods. *Waves or particles. Never both.*

Right, kiddo. But we're way beyond waves and particles here. The human mind seems to be collapsing probability structures in the macro as well as the micro. . . .

Which means what?

Bremen tries to find a way to limit the power of the concept to words. He can't. *It means . . . it means that people . . . us . . . you and I, everybody . . . we're not only* reflecting *the universe, translating it from probability sets to reality sets, so to speak . . . we're . . . my God, Gail, we're creating it on a moment-to-moment, second-to-second basis.*

Gail stares at him.

Bremen grabs her by the forearms, trying to get the terrible size and importance of the concept across to her through sheer pressure and force of will. *We're the observers, Gail. All of us. And without us . . . according to the math on my chalkboard at home . . . without us, the universe would be pure duality, infinite probability sets, infinite modalities. . . .*

Chaos, sends Gail.

Yes. Right. Chaos. He collapses back in his seat. His shirt is plastered to his back and sides with sweat.

Gail sits in silence for a moment, digesting what Jeremy has said. The train clacks southward. For a moment there is darkness as they enter some short tunnel, then they are in the gray light again. *Solipsism,* she sends.

Hmmm? Jeremy has been lost in equations.

You and Jacob talked about solipsism. Why? Because this research suggests that man is, after all, the measure of all things? Gail never hesitates to use "man" to stand for "people" or "humankind." She always says that she values clarity more than the feminist imperative.

Partially . . . Jeremy is thinking of Fourier transforms again, but more in an effort to hide something from Gail than to solve any problem in mathematics.

Why are you . . . who is this Everett person you're thinking about? What does he have to do with that tree you're trying to hide?

Jeremy sighs. *You remember that Jacob and I were talking about some theoretical work that a guy named Hugh Everett did some thirty-five years ago?*

Gail nods, sees Jeremy's closed eyes, and sends an image of herself nodding.

Anyway, says Jeremy, *Everett's work . . . and the stuff done by Bryce DeWitt and others in more recent years . . . it's weird stuff. It solves most of the apparent paradoxes of quantum mechanics, but it does it by getting into real deep water as far as theories go. And . . .*

Impatient, Gail goes behind the words and the shifting math images to look at the heart of what Jeremy is trying to explain. "Parallel worlds!" She realizes that she has said this aloud, almost shouting it. A man in the seat across the aisle glances over, then returns to his newspaper. *Parallel worlds,* she sends again in a telepathic whisper.

Jeremy winces a bit. *That's the sci-fi term. . . .*

Science fiction, corrects Gail. *But this Hugh Everett, he postulated a splitting of reality into equal and separate parallel worlds . . . or parallel universes . . . right?*

Jeremy still frowns at the language but glimpses her understanding of the concept. *Sort of. Uh . . . take the two-slit experiment for instance. When we try to observe the spread-out electron wave, the particle knows we're watching and collapses into a definite particle. When we* don't *watch, the electron keeps its options open . . . particle* and *wave. And the interesting part is, when it acts like a wave . . . remember the interference pattern?*

Yeah.

Well, it's a wave-form interference pattern, all right, but according to Born's terms, it's not *electrons passing through the slits that produces wave-pattern interference, but the* probability *of waves passing through. What's interfering are* probability waves!

Gail blinks. You lost me, Kemo Sabe.

Jeremy tries to draw an example, but ends up sending primitive equations:

$$I = (H + J)^2$$
$$I = H^2 + J^2 + 2HJ$$
$$not$$
$$I = I_1 + I_2$$

He sees her frown, sends *Shit!*, and mentally erases the mental blackboard.

Kiddo, it means that the particles are particles, but that the act of us observing them makes them choose *a course of action . . . this hole? that hole? so many choices! . . . and since the probability of going through one hole is the same as going through the other, we're recording* probability waves *creating the diffraction pattern on the screen behind the slits.*

Gail nods, beginning to understand.

You got it, kiddo, urges Jeremy. *We're watching probability structures collapse. Alternatives fizzle. We're watching the bloody universe sort itself out from a finite range of* probabilities *into an even more finite set of* realities.

Gail remembers the tree that Jeremy had been thinking about. *And this Hugh Everett's theory . . .*

Right! Jeremy is ecstatic. He has been wanting to share some of this with Gail for years, but has been afraid of appearing pedantic. *Everett's theory says that when we force that electron to choose, it doesn't really choose which slit or which probability, it just splits another entire reality in which we . . . the observer . . . watch it go through one slit while its equal and separate probability partner goes through the other hole.*

Gail is physically dizzy from the successful effort to understand the concept. *While the "second universe" observers watch it go through the other hole!*

"Right!" shouts Jeremy. He looks around, aware that he has shouted. No one seems to have paid any attention. He closes his eyes again to better visualize the images. *Right! Everett neatly solves the quantum paradoxes by arguing that every time a bit of quantum energy or matter is forced to make such a choice—that is, whenever we try to observe it choosing—then a new branch grows on the reality tree. Two equal and separate realities come into existence!*

Gail concentrates on remembering the blue-and-white covers of her old Ace Double Novels. *Parallel worlds! Just like I said.*

Not really parallel, sends Jeremy. *Words and images just don't do it, but imagine a constantly growing and branching tree:*

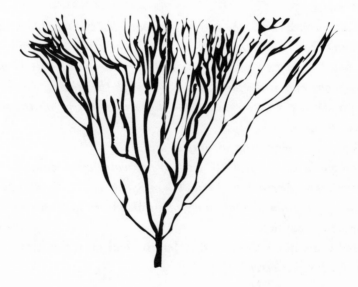

Gail is exhausted. *Okay . . . and what you and Jacob were excited and upset about was that your analysis of these holograms . . . these standing-wave thingees that you think represent human consciousness . . . they're like Everett's theory somehow?*

Jeremy thinks of his hundreds of equations at home, filling the chalkboard and enough sheets of paper to create a second dissertation. *Jacob's mapping of the holographic mind shows it breaking down reality probability functions . . . "choosing" . . . the same way the electrons do.*

Gail is irritated by the simplemindedness of his explanation. *Don't patronize me, Jerry. People don't have to choose which slit they're going to pop through. People don't end up smearing their probability waves as interference patterns on a wall!*

Jeremy sends a wordless apology, but his message is insistent and unapologetic. *They do! We do! Not just in the millions of choices we make every day . . . shall we stand? shall we sit? do we take this train or the next one? what color tie should I wear? . . . but in the more important choices of actually interpreting the data that the universe sends us through our senses every second. That's where the choices are made, Gail . . . that's where the math tells Jacob and me that the probability structures are collapsing and recombining every few seconds . . . interpreting reality!* Jeremy makes a mental note to himself to send for the most recent papers on chaos math and fractal analysis as soon as he gets home.

Gail sees the flaw in this theory. *But, Jerry, your reality and my reality aren't separate things.* We know *that thanks to our mindtouch ability. We see the same things . . . smell the same things . . . touch the same things.*

Jeremy takes her hand. *That's what Jacob and I have to investigate, kiddo. The probability structures are collapsing constantly . . . from almost infinite sets to very finite sets . . . in all of the observed standing wavefronts . . . the MR-imaged minds . . . but there seems to be some governing factor in deciding, for everyone, what that observed reality must be from second to second.*

Gail bites her lip. ???????????????????

Jeremy tries again. *It's as if some traffic manager is telling all the electrons which slit to jump through, kiddo. Some . . . force . . . some less-than-random probability delineator telling the entire human race . . . or at least the few hundred representatives of it that Jacob's tested so far . . . just how to perceive a reality that should be wildly permeable. Chaotic.*

Neither sends anything for a long moment. Then Gail offers— *God?*

Jeremy starts to smile, then does not. He senses how deadly serious she is. *Maybe not God,* he sends, *but at least His dice.*

Gail turns her face to the window. The gray brick buildings they are passing remind her of the long rows of barracks at Ravensbruck.

Neither of them attempts mindtouch again until they are home. In bed.

Consciousness is both wave + particle like light but as a group phenomenon not as individual conscious To say it another way a flock of starling appear to have a leader to direct them in their graceful aerobatics, but upon closer observation leadership constantly shifts from one to another and another. But looking even more carefully each bird must make a moment to moment decision as the chaotic swirl or turbulance puts a bird in front of his/her path requiring a mid course manuver. Second to second adjustments to its path. The slits represent the obstacles or confronting phenomena which require nanosecond decisions - a wave front of interference While the consciousness of each starling is making independant decisions moment to moment it creates a group response. The response is in regard to the things that are causing interference. At each moment a pattern or network of decision create a ne

Wind in Dry Grass

Bremen's duties were legion.

He had never visited a ranch before, never imagined the scope and variations of physical labor possible on a working ranch of some six thousand acres, surrounded, as this one was, by half a million acres of "national forest," although there was hardly a tree in sight above the relatively wet canyonlands of the ranch proper. The physical labor, he found in the coming weeks, was not just daunting, it was a backbreaking, ball-breaking, blister-making, lung-racking, sweat-inducing, blood-and-taste-of-bile-in-the-mouth level of labor. When starting, as Bremen was, from the point of a malnourished, inactive, pale and pasty shadow of a skid-row alcoholic, the level of work expected took on new dimensions of challenge.

He had imagined ranch life—when he had ever thought of it at all—as a romantic horseback riding of range land, with short intervals of herding cattle or horses, perhaps fixing the occasional stretch of wire. He did not count on the maintenance tasks around the ranch itself, the postdawn feedings of animals ranging from geese around the lake to the exotic llamas Miz Morgan collected, the long excursions by Jeep to bring in strays, the endless tinkering with the machinery—vehicles, pumps, electric motors, the air-conditioning unit on the bunkhouse itself—not to mention the gory glories of castrating animals, hauling bloated lamb carcasses out of the stream after an overnight flood, shoveling manure out of the main barn. There was a lot of shovel work: digging postholes, digging trenches for the new sewer line, digging sixty feet of new feeder ditch for the irrigation canal, digging out Miz Morgan's three-quarter-acre garden. Bremen spent hours each day on foot, in the new work boots Miz Morgan had him buy the first week, and more hours bouncing around in the dusty, open Jeep, but he never rode on horseback.

Bremen survived. The days were longer than any he had experienced since his undergraduate days at Harvard when he was trying to get a four-year degree in three years, but the dust and grit and barbed wire and muscle strain ended eventually with the sun setting behind the mountains to the west and then—while indigo shadows crept across the canyon and flowed down into the desert like slow wine—he would return to his bunkhouse, take a thirty-minute shower, fix a hot meal for himself, and collapse into bed before the coyotes started howling in the hills above the ranch. Bremen survived. The days turned into weeks.

There was a quiet here that was nothing like the true internal quiet of the Florida fishing shack; this silence was the deceptive calm at the eye of the storm. Indeed, the roar of Miz Morgan's strange mindshield of raw, white noise made Bremen think of stepping out under white-tossed skies in the false calm of a hurricane's center, where the only noise was the background rumble of the great winds pinwheeling around in their vortex of destruction.

The noise was welcome to Bremen. It shut out the dome of neurobabble that seemed to rise from the entire continent now: whispers, entreaties, shouts and declarations, midnight confessions to the soul of self, and violent justifications. The universe had been filled with these umber shiftings and selfish self-loathings, each wavelength darker than the last, but now there was only the white noise of Miz Fayette Morgan's powerful personality.

Bremen needed it. He became addicted to it. Even the Thursday trip the twenty miles into town became a punishment for him, an exile he could not bear, as Miz Morgan's protective wash of mindnoise faded and the neurobabble rushed in from either side, individual thoughts and hungers and desires and filthy little secrets slicing at him like so many razor blades to the eye and palate.

The bunkhouse was more than adequate for a home: it was air-conditioned for the August extremes of heat; its bed was comfortable, its kitchen impressive, its shower was fed by water from the holding pond half a mile uphill so the water never ran out, and it was situated in a private cul-de-sac between boulders so that the lights of the main hacienda were not visible. The bunkhouse even had a telephone, although Bremen could not call out; the phone line ran only to the hacienda and chimed when Miz Morgan wanted him to carry out some task that she had forgotten to list on the previous evening's "work list"—a single sheet of lined, yellow paper that she would leave clipped to the bulletin board on the bunkhouse's narrow porch.

Bremen quickly learned the areas out of bounds. He was not to approach the hacienda. The six dogs were well trained, they came to Miz Morgan in an instant when she shouted a command, but they were vicious. His third day at the ranch, Bremen watched them pull down a coyote that had made the mistake of coming too close in the wide pasture that ran down to the stream. The dogs had worked as a team, like wolves, surrounding and hamstringing the poor confused coyote before pulling him down and finishing him.

He was not to go anywhere near the "cold house," a low cinder-block building set back behind the boulders near the hacienda. The cold house held a cylindrical water tank on its roof and Miz Morgan had explained that first day that the fifteen-hundred-gallon tank was for fire only; she had pointed out the heavy-duty hoses and couplings at the side of the cold house. These also were out-of-bounds for hired help, unless personally directed there by Miz Morgan.

Bremen knew from the first day's tour that the cold house had its own generator, and he could sometimes hear it chugging in the night. Miz Morgan explained that she liked to dress out her own beef and the game that she brought back from her weekly hunting forays into the hills, and that the cold house held thousands of dollars' worth of prime meat. She had had problems—first with power outages that ruined a fortune's worth of beef, then with hired hands who felt that they could help themselves to a side or two of beef before departing in the night. Miz Morgan allowed no one to approach the cold house now, she said, and the dogs were trained to attack any intruder who even went up the stone walk toward the heavily padlocked doors.

Days blended into weeks for Bremen, and he soon fell into a mindless cycle of toil and sleep, punctuated only by his silent meals and his ritual of watching the sunset from the front porch of the bunkhouse. The few forays into town grew increasingly unpleasant because he was out of range of Miz Morgan's white noise and the razor blades of random thought slashed at his mind. As if sensing this, Miz Morgan began doing the Thursday shopping herself, and after his third week there Bremen never left the ranch.

One day, seeking one of the belted Galloways that had not come down to the main pasture, Bremen came upon the abandoned chapel. It sat up behind the hogback ridge, its flesh-colored walls half-hidden among flesh-colored rocks. The roof was gone—not merely tumbled in, but gone—and the wooden shutters, wooden doors, and wooden pews had rotted to dry dust and largely blown away.

The wind blew through the paneless window sockets. A tumbleweed moved across the pile of bones where the altar once had been.

Bones.

Bremen moved closer, crouching in the shifting dust to study the pile of bright, white artifacts. Bones, brittle and pitted and near petrified. Bremen was fairly sure that most of them were the bones of cattle—he saw a heifer-sized rib cage here, a cow-length xylophone of vertebrae there, even a Georgia O'Keeffe clichéd skull sunken in the tumble—but there were so *many* of them. It was as if someone had piled the corpses here, on the altar, until the altar collapsed under the weight of so much dead and decaying meat.

Bremen shook his head and walked back to the Jeep. The wind rattled dry twigs over the unmarked graves out behind the chapel.

Returning from the south range in the Jeep that same late-summer evening, Bremen saw someone up by the cold house. He slowed while driving by the barn, not approaching the cold house itself, but curious. There were no dogs out.

Fifteen yards away, along the side of the cold house where the array of hoses ran down from the water tank, Miz Fayette Morgan was bathing under a shower arranged from the fire hose on low with a sprinkler head attached. For a second Bremen did not recognize her with her hair wet and plastered back and her face turned to the spray. Her arms and throat were tanned; the rest of her was very, very white. Droplets of water on her pale skin and dark pubic hair caught the evening light. As he watched, Miz Morgan turned off the water and reached for a towel. She saw Bremen in his Jeep and she froze, one hand on the towel, half-turned toward him. She said nothing. She did not cover herself with the towel.

Embarrassed, Bremen nodded and drove on. In the side mirror of the Jeep he caught a glimpse of Miz Morgan still standing there, her skin very white against the flaked green of the cold house. She had not yet covered herself and she was watching him.

Bremen drove on.

○ ○ ○

That night Bremen drifted to sleep, the air-conditioning off, the screenless windows open to let the dead desert air creep in, and awoke to the first of the visions.

He awoke to the sound of violin strings being stretched and scratched at by carious teeth. Bremen sat up in bed and blinked at the violet light flooding the room through the swinging shutters.

The shadows near the ceiling were whispering. At first Bremen thought it was neurobabble slicing through the protective blanket of Miz Morgan's white noise, but this was not mindtouch sound, merely . . . *sound*. The shadows near the ceiling were whispering.

Bremen pulled the damp sheet up over himself, knuckles white against white cotton. The shadows were moving, separating themselves from the whispers and sliding lower along walls gone suddenly and totally black in the violent surges of stormlight through the windows.

Bats came down the walls. Bats with baby faces and obsidian eyes. They whistled and beat their wings as they came.

Outside, in the violet rage, bells tolled and a multitude of voices sang dirges from empty cisterns. Somewhere close by, perhaps from under Bremen's bed, a rooster crowed, and then the sound died off to the rattle of bones in a dry cup.

The bats with baby faces crawled head downward until they tumbled onto Bremen's bed like so many wriggling rats with leathery wings and sharp infant smiles.

Bremen screamed as the lightning stirred and the thunder dragged ahead of the rain like a heavy curtain scraping across old boards.

The next day Bremen did not eat, as if fasting would cure a feverish mind. There was no phone call from Miz Morgan, no morning note tacked to the bulletin board outside.

Bremen went south to the edge of the ranch, as far from the hacienda as he could get, and dug postholes for the new stretch of fence that would run between the woods and the pond. White noise roared around him.

On the eleventh hole, almost three feet down, his postholer bit into a face.

Bremen dropped to his knees. The dirt in the jaws of the postholer was soft, red clay. There was a bit of brown flesh and white bone there, too. Bremen took his spade and spread the hole wider, opening it out into a cone-shaped pit.

The face and skull were arched backward, almost separated from the white-wedged bones of neck and collar, as if the buried man had been trying to swim up through the soil toward air. Bremen dug out the grave as carefully as any archaeologist who had ever widened an excavation. There were tatters of brown cloth across the crushed rib cage. Bremen found bits and pieces of the left hand where the swimmer had raised it; the right hand was missing.

Bremen set the skull in the back of the Jeep and drove back toward the ranch, changing his mind just before coming into sight of the hacienda and heading up and around the hogback ridge to sit awhile and listen to the wind through the chapel windows.

When he got back to his bunkhouse at sunset, the phone was ringing.

Bremen crawled into bed, turned his face to the rough wall, and let it ring. After several minutes the noise stopped.

Bremen covered his ears with the palms of his hands, but the mindnoise continued like a great, white wind from nowhere. After it grew dark and the insect sounds from down by the stream and up by the cold house began in earnest, Bremen rolled over, half expecting the phone to ring again.

It was silent. Next to it, oddly luminescent in a sliver of moonlight through the shutters, the skull watched him from its place on the plank table. Bremen did not remember carrying it in.

It was somewhere closer to midnight than dawn when the phone did ring. Bremen studied it a moment, only half-awake, thinking for a confused second that it was the skull that was calling him.

He padded across rough boards in bare feet. "Hello?"

"Come up to the house," whispered Miz Morgan. In the background Bremen could hear a muffled stereo sounding like voices singing in dry cisterns. "Come up to the house now," she said.

Bremen put down the phone and went out the door and up through the moonlight toward the sound of baying hounds.

EYES

Jeremy and Gail love each other with a passion that sometimes frightens them both.

Jeremy once suggests to her that their relationship is like one of the plutonium pellets imploded out at Lawrence Livermore Labs by a hundred lasers on a spherical shell firing inward simultaneously, driving the plutonium molecules closer and closer together until there is no more room between discrete atoms and the pellet first implodes and then explodes in hydrogen fusion. In theory, he says. Sustained fusion hasn't actually been achieved, he says.

Gail suggests that he might find a more romantic metaphor.

But later, when thinking about it, she sees the accuracy of the comparison. Their love might have been a volatile, unstable thing without their ability, dying after a short half-life, but the ultimate sharing of mindtouch and the "driving inward" of a thousand experiences shared daily has imploded their passion into a fiery intensity rarely found outside the cores of stars.

There are countless challenges to that closeness: the human urge for privacy that each of them must compromise to such a great extent, the balance of Gail's emotional, artistic, intuitive personality with Jeremy's stable, sometimes plodding outlook on things, and the friction of knowing too much about the person one loves.

Jeremy sees a beautiful young woman on the campus one spring day—she is bending over to lift some books when a breeze tugs and lifts her skirt—and that single, sharp erotic instant is as tangible to Gail four hours later as the lingering smell of perfume or a smudge of lipstick on a collar would have been to another wife.

They joke about it. But they do not joke when Gail forms a brief but obsessive attraction to a poet named Timothy the following winter. She tries to exorcise the feelings, or at least block them behind the small remnants of mindshield still left between her and Jeremy, but her emotional indiscretion might as well be a neon sign in a dark room. Jeremy senses it immediately and cannot hide his own feelings—hurt mostly, a certain morbid fascination secondly. For over a month the brief and rapidly fading attraction Gail has for the poet lies between her husband and her like a cold sword blade in the night.

Gail's freedom with her emotions may well have saved Jeremy's sanity—he says as much sometimes—but at other times the surges of feeling distract him from his teaching, his thinking, his work. Gail apologizes, but Jeremy still feels like he is a small boat on the turbulent sea of Gail's strong emotions.

Not able to retrieve poetry from his own memory, Jeremy searches Gail's thoughts for images to describe her. He finds them frequently.

When she dies, it is one of those borrowed images that he shares silently as he spreads her ashes in the orchard by the stream. It is from a poem by Theodore Roethke:

I remember the neckcurls, limp and damp as tendrils;
And her quick look, a sidelong pickerel smile;
And how, once startled into talk, the light syllables leaped for
  her,
And she balanced in the delight of her thought,
A wren, happy, tail into the wind,

Her song trembling the twigs and small branches.
The shade sang with her;
The leaves, their whispers turned to kissing,
And the mould sang in the bleached valleys under the rose.

Oh, when she was sad, she cast herself down into such a pure
    depth,
Even a father could not find her:
Scraping her cheek against straw,
Stirring the clearest water.

My sparrow, you are not here,
Waiting like a fern, making a spiney shadow.
The sides of wet stones cannot console me,
Nor the moss, wound with the last light.

If only I could nudge you from this sleep,
My maimed darling, my skittery pigeon.
Over this damp grave I speak the words of my love. . . .

Jacob Goldmann's neural research sends Jeremy into realms of
mathematics that he would otherwise have explored cursorily, if at
all, and which now, during these last months before Gail's illness
begins, fill and change his life.

Chaos math and fractals.

As with most modern mathematicians, Jeremy has dabbled in
nonlinear mathematics; as with most modern mathematicians, he
prefers the classical, linear mode. The murky field of chaos mathematics, less than two decades old as a serious discipline, had
seemed tentative and strangely sterile to Jeremy before the interpretation of Goldmann's holographic data sent him plunging into
the realms and study of chaos. Fractals had been those clever
things applied mathematicians had used for their computer graph-
ics—the brief scene in one of those *Star Trek* films Gail had
dragged him to, occasional illustrations in *Scientific American* or in
Mathematical Intelligencer.

Now he dreams chaos math and fractals.

Schrödinger wave equations and Fourier analyses of human holographic thought models had led him into this forest of chaos and now Jeremy finds that he is comfortable in these woods. For the first time in his life and career, Jeremy craves computer time: he finally brings a powerful CD-ROM-boosted 486 PC into the sanctum sanctorum of his study at home and begins petitioning for time on the university's mainframe. It is not enough.

Jacob Goldmann says that he can get Jeremy's chaos program run on one of the MIT Cray X-MPs, and Jeremy lies awake nights in anticipation. When the run is complete—forty-two minutes of computing time, a veritable eternity of a Cray's precious time—the solutions are partial, incomplete, exhilarating, and terrifying in their potential. Jeremy realizes that they will need several Crays and more than one gifted programmer. "Give me three months," says Jacob Goldmann.

The scientist convinces someone in the Bush administration that his work on neural pathways and holographic memory function has relevance to the air force's long-standing "virtual reality" improved-cockpit research, and within ten weeks he and Jeremy have their access to linked Crays and the programmers to prepare the data.

The returns are coded in pure mathematics—even the diagrams are unreadable by anyone below the status of research mathematician—and Jeremy spends summer evenings in his study, comparing his own equations with the elegant Cray diagrams of Vague Attractors of Kolmogorov looking like dissected tube worms from the Mindanao Trench, but showing the same quasi-periodic interferometer patterns, chaos seas, and resonance islands that his own feeble math had predicted.

Jeremy does Poincaré sections of probability waves crashing and collapsing, and the Cray machines—moving through fractaled regions that Jeremy never hopes to understand—return hard data by the bale and computer images that look like photographs of some distant water world where indigo seas are mottled with sea-horse–shaped islands of many colors and infinite topological complexity.

Jeremy begins to understand. But just as it is coalescing for him . . . just as Jacob's data and the Cray fractal images and the beautiful and terrible chaos equations on his chalkboard begin to converge . . . things in the "real" world begin to fall apart. First Jacob. Then Gail.

It is three months after their first visit to the fertility clinic when Jeremy visits his own doctor for a periodic physical. Jeremy happens to mention the tests that Gail has been going through and their sadness at not having a child.

"And they did just the one semen analysis?" asks Dr. Leman.

"Mmmm?" says Jeremy, rebuttoning his shirt. "Oh, yeah . . . well, they suggested I come back for a couple more, but I've been really busy. Plus, the first one was pretty conclusive. No problem."

Dr. Leman nods, but he is frowning slightly. "Do you remember the sperm count?"

Jeremy glances down, inexplicably embarrassed. "Uh . . . thirty-eight, I think. Yes."

"Thirty-eight million per milliliter?"

"Yes."

Dr. Leman nods again and makes a gesture. "Why don't you keep your shirt off, Jerry? I'll run another blood pressure test here."

"Was there a problem?"

"No," says Dr. Leman, adjusting the cuff. "Did they tell you at the fertility clinic that they like a count of forty million per milliliter with at least sixty percent of the sperm showing good movement with forward progression?"

Jeremy hesitates. "I think so," he says. "But they said it probably was a little below average because Gail and I . . . well, we hadn't abstained quite the full five days before the tests and—"

"And they told you to come in for some averaging tests, but told you that there almost certainly wasn't anything for you to worry about, that the problem probably lay with Gail?"

"Right."

"Lower your shorts, Jerry," says Dr. Leman.

Jeremy does so, feeling the slight embarrassment that men suffer as the doctor handles his scrotum.

"Take your hand and pinch your nose and mouth shut," orders Dr. Leman. "Yes, that's right . . . no air getting through at all . . . now bear down as if you're trying to have a bowel movement."

Jeremy starts to remove his hand to make a joke, but decides not to. He bears down.

"Again," says Dr. Leman.

Jeremy winces at the pressure the doctor is exerting.

"All right, relax. You can pull up your shorts." The doctor goes to the counter, removes the plastic glove, drops it in the trash, and washes his hands.

"What was all that about, John?"

Leman turns slowly. "That was known as the Valsalva maneuver. Did you feel that pressure where I had my finger on the vein on either side of your testicles?"

Jeremy smiles and nods. He had felt it, all right.

"Well, by pressing down there, I could feel the flow of blood going through your veins . . . going the wrong way, Jerry."

"The wrong way?"

Dr. Leman nods. "I'm fairly certain that you have varicose spermatic veins in both the left and right testicles. I'm surprised that they didn't check for that at the fertility clinic."

Jeremy feels a wave of tension and clamminess wash over him. He thinks of all the embarrassing tests Gail has gone through in the past few weeks . . . all of the tests still awaiting her. He clears his throat. "Could these . . . these varicose veins . . . could they be hurting our chances for having a child?"

Dr. Leman leans against the counter and folds his arms across his chest. "They could be the whole problem, Jerry. If it is a bilateral variocele, then that could very well be dropping the motility of the sperm, as well as the actual count."

"You mean the thirty-eight million at the clinic was an anomaly?"

"Probably," says the doctor. "And my bet is that the motility study was done poorly. I'd wager that less than ten percent of the sperm were moving properly."

Jeremy feels something like anger growing in him. "Why?"

"A variocele—one of these varicose veins in your testicles—is a malfunction of one of the valves in the spermatic vein that causes the blood to flow backward from the kidneys and adrenals into the testicles themselves. That raises the temperature in the scrotum—"

"Which lowers sperm production," finishes Jeremy.

Dr. Leman nods. "The blood also carries a high concentration of toxic metabolic substances such as steroids, which further inhibit sperm production."

Jeremy stares at the wall where there is only a cheap Norman Rockwell print of a country doctor listening to a child's heartbeat. Both the child and doctor are rosy-cheeked caricatures. "Can you fix a variocele?" he asks.

"There's an operation," says Dr. Leman. "With men having sperm counts over ten million per milliliter . . . a category which you seem to qualify for . . . there's usually a quite dramatic improvement. I think the figure's around eighty-five or ninety percent. I'd have to look it up."

Jeremy moves his gaze from the Rockwell print and stares at his doctor. "Do you suggest someone who could do it?"

Dr. Leman unfolds his arms and holds his palms six or eight inches apart in a molding gesture. "I think the best thing to do, Jerry, is to go back to the clinic, tell them our suspicion of bilateral varioceles, have them do the other sperm tests, and let them recommend a good man to do the surgery." He glances down at the checklist on his clipboard. "We've drawn blood today, so I'll alert the lab to do a hormone count—testosterone, of course, but also the follicle stimulating hormone and luteinizing hormone from the pituitary gland. My guess is that these will be low and that you'd be categorized as marginally fertile or subfertile." He pats Jeremy on the back. "Harsh words, but good news, actually, because the prognosis after surgery for having children is very good. Much better than with most female fertility problems."

Dr. Leman hesitates and Jeremy reads the man's hesitation to criticize colleagues, but eventually he says, "The problem is, Jerry, that so many of these fertility-clinic doctors know that in ninety percent of the cases the female's system is at fault. They get out of the habit of looking at the man carefully once a sperm count is in. It's sort of a professional myopia. But now that they know about the variocele . . ." He stops at the door, watching Jeremy button his shirt again. "Do you want me to call them about this?"

Jeremy hesitates only a second. "No. I'll tell them. They'll probably call over for your records."

"Fine," says Dr. Leman, ready to go on to his next patient. "Jan will get back to you with the results of the blood tests sometime tomorrow afternoon. We'll have all that data ready to send over to the clinic when they ask for it."

Jeremy nods, pulls on his sport coat, and goes out through the waiting room and into the open air. Already, as he drives home, he is preparing his mindshield to bury the fact of the variocele. *Only for a while,* he tells himself as he makes the mindshield airtight and then covers it over with random thoughts and images like a trapper hiding the pit with leaves and branches. *Only for a little while, until I think this out.*

He knows even while he works to forget what he has learned that he is lying.

There Are No Eyes Here

Bremen went up the hill in the dark, past the Jeep parked some yards from where he had left it, past the baying rottweilers in their pen—they were never left in their pen at night—and through the open door of the hacienda.

The interior was dim but not dark; light came from a single brass candlestick lamp and spilled down the hallway from the direction of Miz Morgan's bedroom. Bremen felt her presence, the warm rush of white noise rising like the volume turned higher on an untuned radio. It made him dizzy and a trifle nauseated. It also excited him. As if sleepwalking, Bremen moved across the silent room and down the hall. Outside, the dogs had ceased their wild barking.

The lights in Miz Morgan's bedroom were off except for a single twenty-five-watt bulb on a table lamp, and that was covered with some fabric that bled only a bit of pink light. Bremen stood in the doorway a moment, feeling his balance shift precariously as if he were on the edge of some deep, circular pit. Then he stepped forward and let himself fall into the rush of white noise.

Her bed was a four-poster, canopied with a diaphanous gauze that caught the pink light with a silken web gleam. He could see her on the far side, the light bleeding past her, her body soft and visible under its own thin folds of open lace. "Come in," she whispered.

Bremen went in, setting his feet uncertainly as if his vision and balance were both impaired. He had started around the bed when Miz Morgan's voice came again from the shadows. "No, stop there a second."

Bremen hesitated, confused, on the verge of awakening. Then he saw her motion—a parting of lacy bed curtains, a leaning forward toward a glass or low receptacle on the nightstand, a brief movement of hand and mouth and a quick retreat. The shadows of her face seemed rearranged.

She wears dentures, he thought, feeling a pang of an emotion quite alien in his thoughts toward Miz Morgan. *She'd forgotten to put them in.*

She beckoned him forward again with a movement more of wrist than fingers. Bremen moved around to the far side of the bed, his body throwing yet another shadow across the occupant there, and paused again, unable to move forward or back. The woman may have spoken again, but Bremen's senses were filled with the white-hot roar of her mindnoise. It struck him like a torrent of blood-warm water flying from some hidden hydrant, disorienting him even more than he had been a second before.

He reached for the bed curtains, but her long, strong fingers batted his hands away. She leaned forward on her elbows in a motion at once feline and feminine and moved her face close to his legs. As her shoulders parted the curtains Bremen realized that he could see her breasts clearly through the gaps in her gown but not her face, concealed as it was by shadows and the tumble of her hair.

Just as well, he thought, and closed his eyes. He tried to think of Gail, remember Gail, but the rush of white noise drove out any thoughts except those of lassitude and surrender. Room shadows seemed to shift around him in the last instant before his eyelids lowered.

Miz Morgan set a flat hand against his belly, another on his thigh. Bremen trembled like a nervous Thoroughbred being inspected by a rough vet.

She unbuckled his belt, lowered his zipper.

Bremen started to move then, to lean toward her, but her left hand returned to his belly, restraining him and freezing him in place. The mindnoise was a hurricane of white static now, buffeting him in all dimensions. He swayed on his feet.

With a single, almost angry movement Miz Morgan tugged his trousers down his hips. He felt the cooler air and then her warm breath on him, but still he did not open his eyes. The white noise battered him like invisible fists to the brain.

She fondled him, cupping his testicles as if raising them to a kiss, then ran a warm hand with cold nails up and down his still-flaccid penis. He grew only slightly excited, although his scrotum contracted as if trying to rise into his body. Her motions became more fluid and urgent, more from her need than his. Bremen felt her head lower, felt the touch of her cheek against his thigh and the silkiness of her hair and the warmth of her brow against the cusp of his lower belly, and then the buffeting of mindnoise lessened, then ceased, and he was in the eye of the hurricane.

Bremen saw.

Exposed flesh and raw-rimmed ribs hanging from hooks. The rictus grin and frozen eyes under white frost. The migrant-family infants on their own row of hooks, turning slightly in frigid breezes. . . .

"Jesus!" He pulled back instinctively and opened his eyes the instant her mouth snapped shut with a metallic click. Bremen saw the gleam of razor steel between red lips and staggered backward again only to crash into the bedside table, knocking the covered lamp over and sending high shadows flying.

Miz Morgan opened blade-rimmed jaws and lunged again, her shoulders arching and thrusting like some ancient turtle struggling free of its shell.

Bremen threw himself to his right and struck the wall, writhing aside so that her wide-mouthed bite missed his genitals but took a round chunk out of his left thigh, just above the femoral artery. He stared as blood sprayed the curtains in the pink light and fell in droplets on Miz Morgan's upturned face.

She arched her neck in something like orgasm and ecstasy, her eyes wide and blind, her mouth opened in an almost perfect circle, and Bremen saw the healthy gum-pink of the dental prosthesis as well as the razor blades set in plastic there. His blood spattered on her red lips and on blue steel. As she opened her mouth wider for another lunge he noticed that the blades were set in concentric rows, like sharks' teeth.

Bremen leaped to his left, blind himself from the mental images now swirling in the eye of the mindnoise hurricane, crashed into the table and lamp again, and suddenly pulled back as Miz Morgan's steel teeth cut through his dangling shirttail, leather belt, and the thinner flesh of his side, scraping bone before pulling back, her head shaking like a dog with a mouthful of rat.

Bremen felt the icy shock but no pain, and then he pulled up his jeans and leaped again—not sideways, where she would certainly trap him, but straight over her—his right foot planting itself on the small of her back like a hiker finding a stepping-stone in treacherous rapids, pulling the bed curtains down behind him, then flailing through more curtains on the other side and falling, landing hard on his elbows and crawling toward the doorway even as she flopped and writhed and groped for his legs behind him.

The pain in his thigh and side struck him then, sharp as an electrical shock to the nerves of his spine.

He ignored it and crawled toward the door, looking back.

Miz Morgan had chewed her way through the gauze curtains and was on the floor, crawling after him with a great scrabbling of lacquered fingernails on the bare wood floors. The prosthesis thrust her jaws forward in almost lycanthropic eagerness.

Bremen had left a trail of blood on the floorboards and the

woman seemed to be sniffing at it as she came at him across the slick wood.

He rose to his feet and ran, bouncing off the walls of the hall- way and the furniture of the living room, leaving a red smear on the couch as he tumbled and rolled over it, got to his feet, and leaped for the door. Then he was out in the night, breathing cold air and holding his jeans closed with one hand, the other hand flat against his bleeding thigh as he ran straight-legged down the hill.

The rottweilers were going insane behind the high wire, leaping and snarling. Bremen heard laughter and turned, still running; Miz Morgan was in the dimly lighted doorway, her gown totally transparent and her body looking tall and strong.

She was laughing between the razor blades in her mouth.

Bremen saw the long object in her hands just as she made a familiar motion and he heard the unmistakable sound of the six- teen-gauge shotgun being pumped. He tried to weave back and forth, but the wound on his leg slowed him and turned the weav- ing into a series of awkward lurches, as if the Tin Man, half- rusted, were attempting an end run. Bremen felt like weeping and laughing, but did neither.

He glanced back to see Miz Morgan lean inside, the generator kicked on up behind the cold house, and suddenly the driveway below the hacienda, the bunkhouse area, the barn, and the first three hundred feet of field below the house were bathed in glare as huge arc lamps turned night into day.

She's done this before. Bremen had been running blindly toward the bunkhouse and the Jeep, but then he remembered that the vehicle had been moved and was certain that Miz Morgan had pulled the distributor cap or something equally as necessary. He tried to read her thoughts—as repulsive as that idea was—but the white noise had returned, louder than ever. He was back in the hurricane.

She's done this before. So many times before. Bremen knew that if he ran toward the river or the highway, she would easily run him down in the Jeep or Toyota. The bunkhouse was an obvious trap.

Bremen slid to a stop on the brightly illuminated gravel and snapped his jeans shut. He bent over to inspect the wounds on his leg and hip and almost fainted; his heart was pounding so hard that he could hear it like footsteps raging behind him. Bremen took deep, slow breaths and fought away the black spots that swam in his vision.

His jeans were soaked with blood and both wounds were still bleeding, but neither one was spurting the way an artery would. *If it was an artery, I'd be dead.* Bremen fought away the light-headedness, stood, and looked back toward the hacienda sixty yards behind him.

Miz Morgan had pulled on jeans and her tall work boots and come out on the porch. Her upper body was clad only in the blood-spattered nightgown. Her mouth and jaw looked different, but Bremen was too far away to tell for sure if she had removed the prosthesis.

She opened a circuit-breaker box on the south end of the porch and more arc lamps leaped on down by the stream, along the driveway.

Bremen felt that he was standing in an empty coliseum, lit for a night game.

Miz Morgan raised the pump shotgun and casually fired in his direction. Bremen leaped to the side, although he knew he was beyond critical range of the shotgun. Pellets pounded on the gravel nearby.

He looked around again, fighting the panic that joined with the roaring white noise to cloud his thinking, and then he turned left, toward the boulders behind the hacienda.

More arc lights snapped on up behind the rocks, but Bremen kept climbing, feeling the leg wound begin to bleed again. He felt as if someone had scooped out the flesh on his hip with a razored ice-cream dip.

Behind him, there was a second shotgun blast and then snarls and howls as Miz Morgan let loose the dogs.

EYES

A few weeks before Gail's headaches are diagnosed as a brain tumor, Jeremy receives this letter from Jacob Goldmann:

My dearest Jeremy:

I am still trying to get over your and Gail's most recent visit and the results of your offer to "be guinea pigs" for the deep-cortical mapping. The results continue to be—as we discussed in person and on the phone last Thursday—astounding. There is no other word.

I respect your privacy, and your wishes, and will make no more attempts to convince you to join me in a study of this so-called mindtouch that the two of you say you have experienced since puberty. If your simple exhibitions of this telepathy had not been convincing enough, the DCM data that continues to flow in would be enough to turn anyone into a believer. I certainly am. In a way, I am relieved that we will not be going down this particular detour in our research, although you must see what a bombshell this revelation has been for one elderly physicist-turned-neural-researcher.

Meanwhile, your most recent mailing of mathematical analysis, while largely beyond me, has turned out to be an even more explosive bombshell. This one may well make the Manhattan Project seem like very small potatoes indeed.

If I understand your fractal and chaos analysis correctly (and, as you say, the data hardly leaves room for an alternative hypothesis) then the human mind goes far beyond our wildest dreams of complexity.

If your two-dimensional plot of human holographic consciousness via the Packard-Takens method is reliable—and again, I have confidence that it is—then the mind is not merely the self-consciousness organ of the universe, but (excuse the oversimplification) its ultimate arbiter. I understand your use of the chaos term "strange attractor" as a description of the mind's role in creating fractal "resonance islands" within the chaotic sea of collapsing probability waves, but it is still difficult to conceive of a universe largely without form except that imposed upon it by human observation.

It is the alternate-probability scenario which you broach at the end of your letter which gives me pause. (So much so, in fact, that I have interrupted the deep cortical mapping experiments until I have thought through the tautological implications of this very possible plausibility.)

Jeremy, I wonder at the ability you and Gail share: how frequent it is, how many gradations of it there are, how basic to the human experience it must be.

You remember when we were drinking my twenty-year-old scotch after the first results of your and Gail's DC-mapping came in and you had explained the basis for the anomalies: I suggested—not after the first drink, if I remember correctly—that perhaps some of the great minds in human history had shared such a "universal interferometer" type of mind. Thus Gandhi and Einstein, Jesus and Newton, Galileo and my old friend Jonny von Neumann possessed a similar (but obviously slightly different!) form of "mindtouch" where they could resonate to different aspects of existence—the physical underpinnings of the universe, the psychological and moral underpinnings of our small human part of the universe—whatever.

I remember you were embarrassed. That was not my goal in suggesting this possibility and it is not my goal now that I repeat the hypothesis.

We are—all of us—the universe's eyes. Those of you with this incredible ability, whether blessed to see into the heart of the human soul or the heart of the universe itself, are the mechanism by which we focus those eyes and direct our gaze.

Think, Jeremy: Einstein performed his "Gendanken Experimenten" and the universe created a new probability branch to suit our improved vision. Probability waves crashing on the dry beach of eternity.

Moses and Jesus perceived new motions of those stars which govern our moral life, and the universe grows alternative realities to validate the observation. Probability waves collapsing. Neither particle nor wave until the observer enters the equation.

Incredible. And even more incredible is your interpretation of Everett's, Wheeler's, and DeWitt's work. Each moment of such "deep gazing" creating separate and equal probability universes. Ones which we can never visit, but can bring into actual existence at moments of great decision in our own lives on this continuum.

Somewhere, Jeremy, the Holocaust did not exist. Somewhere my first wife and family possibly still live.

I must think about this. I will be in touch with you and Gail very soon. I must think about this.

Most sincerely yours,
Jacob

Five days after the letter arrives, Jeremy and Gail receive a late-night call from Rebecca, Jacob's daughter. Jacob Goldmann had eaten dinner with her earlier that evening and then retired to his office "to finish some work on the data." Rebecca had run some errands and returned to the office around midnight.

Jacob Goldmann had committed suicide with a Luger that he had kept in the bottom drawer of his desk.

The Eyes Are Not Here

Limping, still bleeding, Bremen staggered uphill toward the cold house and the boulders beyond. Arc lights had come on all over the compound now, and the only shadowed places were in the crevices and crawl spaces between the rocks. Behind him, the rottweilers were free and Bremen could hear the Dopplering of their howls as they came toward him.

Not the rocks . . . it's where she wants you to go.

Bremen halted in the shadow of the cold house, wheezing and fighting away the spots in his vision again. *The memories . . . the family of illegal Mexican immigrants she had taken in when their truck broke down . . . the dogs had trapped them between the boulders . . . Miz Morgan had finished the work with the hunting rifle from the ridge above.*

Bremen shook his head. The dogs were off the road now, climbing into the loose shale and scrub brush toward him. Bremen forced himself to remember the onslaught of insane images during his seconds in the eye of the hurricane . . . anything that might help.

Frost-rimmed eyes . . . red ribs through frozen flesh . . . the dozen places of burial over the years . . . the way the runaway girl had wept and begged in that summer of '81 before the blade descended toward her arched throat . . . the ritual of preparing the cold house.

The dogs came bounding up the slope, their howls shifting down in timbre toward something more urgent and immediate. Bremen could see their eyes clearly now. Below, in the light, Miz Morgan raised her shotgun and followed the dogs up.

27-9-11. For an eternal few seconds Bremen saw only the numbers floating there, part of the ritual, important . . . but could not place their significance. The dogs were fifteen yards from him now and growling like a single, six-headed beast.

Bremen concentrated and then whirled, running for the cold house twenty feet away. The heavy metal door was securely sealed by a thick metal hasp, a heavy chain, and a massive combination lock. Bremen spun the lock as the dogs accelerated up the hill behind him. *27-9-11.*

The first of the dogs leaped just as Bremen ripped the chain free from the hasp and open lock. He dodged aside, swinging four feet of chain as he did so. The rottweiler went flying while the others came lunging, already cutting off his escape in a perfect half circle that pinned him by the door. Bremen was amazed to find that he also was growling and showing his teeth as he held the animals at bay with the blur of chain. They backed off, seeming to take turns lunging for his legs and arms. The air was filled with their saliva and the cacophony of human and canine growls.

They're trained not to kill, thought Bremen through the waves of adrenaline. *Not yet.*

He looked past the largest rottweiler's head and saw Miz Morgan striding up through the sage, the shotgun already shouldered. She was screaming at the dogs. "Down, goddamn you, down!" She fired the shotgun anyway and the dogs leaped aside as buckshot ripped into concrete block and ricocheted off the top third of the steel door.

On all fours, untouched by the blast, Bremen tugged the heavy door open and crawled into the cold darkness. Behind him, another blast slammed into the door.

In the chill blackness of the cold house he stood, swayed on his slashed leg, and tried to find a way to seal the door . . . a lock bar, handle, anything to secure the chain to. There was nothing. Bremen realized that the door was meant to be opened by a simple push whenever it was unchained on the outside. He felt for a light switch but there was nothing on the ice-rimmed walls on either side, nothing above the door.

Just audible through the thick door and walls, the howling ceased as Miz Morgan came up to the door, shouted the rottweilers into submission, and leashed them. The door was tugged open.

Bremen staggered through the darkness, bouncing off sides of beef, his work boots sliding on the frost-rimmed floor. The cold house was large—at least forty by fifty feet—and dozens of carcasses hung from hooks that slid along iron bars beneath the ceiling. Twenty feet in, Bremen paused, half hanging from a side of beef, his breath fogging the ice-pale flesh, and looked back toward the doorway.

Miz Morgan had pulled the doorway all but shut, only a sliver of light illuminating her legs and high boots. Two of the rottweilers strained silently at leather leashes in front of her, and the combined breath of the three rose like a thick cloud in the subfreezing air. With the shotgun cradled under the arm that held the leashes, Miz Morgan raised what looked to be a television remote-control unit.

Bright fluorescent lights came on all over the cold house.

Bremen blinked, saw Miz Morgan raise the shotgun in his direction, and then he threw himself behind the side of beef as the shotgun blasted. Pellets slammed into frozen flesh and ripped down the narrow corridor between the dangling carcasses, some swinging from his blundering flight a second before.

Bremen felt something tug at his right upper arm and looked at the bloody streaks there. He was panting, close to hyperventilating, and he leaned against the gutted beef carcass to catch his breath.

It was not a beef carcass. On either side of the parted, exposed ribs, white breasts were visible. The iron hook entered just behind the woman's hump of spine and came out through her collarbone, just above the point where the body had been split and pried apart. Her eyes, beneath the layer of frost, were brown.

Bremen staggered away, weaving, leaping across the open rows, trying to keep the carcasses between him and Miz Morgan. The rottweilers were baying and growling now, the sounds distorted by the cold air and long cinderblock room.

Bremen knew that there were no windows and only the one door to the cold house. He was near the rear of the room now, moving to the left of the door since there were more carcasses there, but he could hear the scrabble of the dogs' claws on the icy floor as they strained to get away and Miz Morgan moved left with him, staying near the front wall.

Bremen still held the chain, but could devise no scenario where he could use it against her unless she came into the forest of hanging carcasses. Near the back wall, the frozen, softly swaying bodies were mostly small—an entire row of children and infants, Bremen realized—and there was little cover for him there.

For a second there was silence, and then, through the rush and roar of the white noise of her insanity, Bremen caught the image of her bending over and shared her view of his own legs thirty feet away under a row of white-and-red carcasses.

He leaped just as the shotgun roared. Something kicked at his left heel as he hung, dangling by his right hand, from an iron hook that ran through what looked like the corpse of a middle-aged black man. The man's eyes were closed. The slash in his throat was so wide and so rough-edged that the frozen edges of it looked like a broad shark's smile. Bremen struggled not to drop the chain in his left hand.

Miz Morgan yelled something unintelligible and released one of the dogs.

Bremen climbed higher onto the swaying corpse as the dogs bounded down the slippery aisle and Miz Morgan raised her shotgun.

EYES

At this same moment, more than a thousand miles to the east, the thirteen-year-old blind, deaf, retarded boy named Robby Busta-mante is being beaten by an "uncle" who has lived with his mother for the last four months. The "uncle" sleeps with his mother and provides her crack and heroin for various services rendered.

Robby's crime is that he is still not toilet trained at age thirteen and has soiled his pants at a time when "Uncle" is home alone with the boy. Uncle, coming down from some bad Colombian, flies into a rage at the sight and smell of Robby, jerks him up from the pillowed corner of the small room where the boy has been rocking with his teddy bear and nodding silently to himself in the night, and begins striking him in the face with a fist that Robby cannot see coming.

Robby begins crooning a weird falsetto cry and throws palsied hands to his face to ward off the invisible blows.

This enrages Uncle further and the big man begins pounding Robby in earnest, slapping away the ineffectual, splayed-wrist hands, and punching the boy in the mouth, pulverizing the blubbery lips, smashing in the carious front teeth, breaking the boy's broad nose, smashing cheekbones and closing eyes.

Robby goes down with a spray of blood on mildewed wallpaper, but continues the falsetto crooning and begins slapping the torn linoleum with his palms. Uncle does not know it, but the child is trying to find his teddy bear.

The nonhuman noises push Uncle the last millimeter across the killing line and he begins kicking the boy with his steel-capped Redwing boots, first in the ribs, then the neck, and then, when Robby is huddled in the corner, no longer crooning, in the face.

Uncle comes out of the red place he has gone and looks down at the blind and deaf boy, still huddled in the corner but at impossible angles now—wrists and knees splayed the wrong directions, one finger rising vertically backward, the bruised and mottled neck twisted wrong on the fat pulpy body in its urine-soaked Mutant Ninja Turtle pajamas—and Uncle pauses. He has killed men before.

Uncle grabs Robby by his tuft of coarse black hair and drags him across the linoleum, down the hall, and through the small living room where MTV still blares from the black thirty-two-inch television.

There is no falsetto crooning now. Robby's pulped lips leave a trail of saliva and blood on the tile. One of his blind eyes is wide open, the other swollen shut under his scarred brow. His loose fingers flop across the floor moldings at the doorways and make pale lines in the red smears his face leaves.

Uncle opens the back door, steps out, glances around, steps back in, and uses his foot to shove Robby down the porch steps. It is like listening to a gunnysack filled with two hundred pounds of Jell-O and loose rocks fold itself down the six wooden steps.

Uncle grabs Robby by the front of his too-small pajamas and drags him across the moist grass of the yard. Buttons pop and flannel tears, Uncle curses, gets a grip on Robby's uncut hair, and commences dragging him again.

Behind the rotting garage, beyond the fallen-down fence and the abandoned lot behind it, back under the rain-dripping elms in the dark, out beyond the edge of light where a shack once had sat in the high grass not far from the river, leans the outhouse. No one uses it. A faded sheet of cardboard nailed on the door reads: KE P O T. A length of rotting rope has been tied around the door handles to keep kids out.

Uncle tears off the rope, steps into the foul-smelling darkness, rips the boards off the one-hole seat, drags Robby in, levers the boy's body into a sitting position, and then grunts and heaves to tilt the seemingly boneless mass up and over the sill where the seat had been. Robby's Teenage Mutant Ninja Turtle–patterned pajama top tears off on a nail and remains behind as his body slides into the dark pit. His bare feet seem to wave as they disappear into the hole. The noise from ten feet below is liquid and yielding.

Uncle steps out into the darkness, obviously relieved to be breathing fresh air, looks around, sees nothing, hears only a distant dog barking, finds a large rock underfoot, and then steps back into the outhouse to wipe his hands and shirt with the pajama top. Finished, he drops the rag into the reeking, rectangular hole and uses the rock to bang the seat boards back into place as best he can in the darkness.

There is no sound from the outhouse for the hour Uncle waits in the house until Robby's mother returns with the car.

Robby, of course, does not hear the voices raised in shouts, nor the brief bout of weeping, nor the quick sounds of packing and car doors banging.

He does not see the house and porch lights being switched off.

He does not hear the roar of the car's engine or the sound of tires crunching over the gravel of the drive as his mother leaves him for the last time.

Robby cannot hear the barking of the neighbor dog finally die down, like a scratched record finally being shut off, or sense the descent of silence in the neighborhood as the rains come softly,

pattering on the leaves and dripping down from tears in the corru-
gated roof of the outhouse under the trees.

All these things I have told you are true. All the things I have yet
to tell you are true.

And Saw the Skull
Beneath the Skin

The rottweiler leaped three seconds before Miz Morgan fired the shotgun.

Bremen straddled the dead black man's shoulders and wrapped the chain around the big dog's neck as the creature clambered and scrabbled up frozen flesh to get at him. The rottweiler howled. Bremen jerked the chain tight and lifted. Miz Morgan saw the dog seem to levitate between Bremen and her and she raised the barrel of the shotgun even as she pulled the trigger.

Bremen winced and almost lost his balance on the corpse and his grip on the dog as pellets slammed into the fluorescent light fixture above him and the ceiling above that. Sparks and glass flew from the light fixture. Some stray shot must have caught the rottweiler for the beast began howling with an increased frenzy and started whipping its head back and forth to bring its teeth to bear on Bremen's hands. Bremen tightened the chain until the dog's growls choked off and the howling became a high whine.

Miz Morgan pumped the shotgun, pulled the leash tight on the second rottweiler, and came down the cold aisle between softly swinging sides of meat.

Bremen was panting so hard that he was afraid he might pass out. The steel links of the chain were so cold that flesh was peeling away from his fingers and palms whenever he pulled the chain tighter or shifted position. The rottweiler was making a sound more like that of an old man gargling than that of a dog howling. Bremen knew that it would be seconds before Miz Morgan reached him; she could simply stick the barrel of the shotgun up against him and pull the trigger.

The first shotgun blast had knocked out the double row of fluorescent strip lights above him, but now there was dappled light falling on the hound's dark head. Bremen looked up, saw the depression in the ceiling above the light stanchion, and blinked at the dozen flecks of light there. Holes in wood, not cinder block. Holes letting in light from the tall arc lamp behind the cold house.

Miz Morgan moved between the corpses eight feet away. Her eyes glistened and seemed very large; her breath clouded the air between them. The rottweiler hanging from Bremen's chain was no longer struggling and its long, bony legs twitched. The sight seemed to make the other dog go insane and Miz Morgan had to cradle the shotgun for a second to hold the animal on the leash as it leaped for the black man's corpse and Bremen's dangling legs.

Bremen threw the dead rottweiler at Miz Morgan and climbed. He set his foot squarely on the corpse's shoulder, and then its head as he climbed. The light stanchion took his weight but swayed alarmingly, pieces of broken glass still dropping into the icy vapor below them. Bremen thrust his shoulders and head up into the narrow well, balanced on the icy rod of the light stanchion, and set his shoulders against the light-flecked wood.

Miz Morgan dropped the leash and raised the shotgun. She could not miss from eight feet away. The surviving rottweiler used the corpse of its mate to get a running start and all but climbed the swinging corpse of the black man to get at Bremen.

Whatever collarbone or clavicle the hook had been set under in the black man's corpse gave way then and the body came down, scrambling rottweiler and all, tumbling like a side of frozen beef onto Miz Morgan and the dead dog in the aisle.

The shotgun blast missed the narrow well but slammed into the ice-tufted cinder block inches from Bremen's left arm. He felt something rip at his left sleeve and a cold trickle, like a sudden electric current, flow through the soft flesh under his arm. Then he bent and heaved, almost slipped off the rod from the strain, then heaved again.

The trapdoor, if it was a trapdoor, was locked from the outside. Bremen could feel the resistance of the steel hasp, hear its rasping.

Miz Morgan shouted and kicked at the growling rottweiler eight feet below. The dog whirled and snapped at her in its confusion. Without hesitating a second, she lifted the shotgun and bashed the hound's skull in with the heavy stock. The rottweiler collapsed almost comically onto the corpse of its mate.

Bremen had used the six-second reprieve to catch his balance and to heave again, feeling something snap and tear in his back but also feeling the time-rotted and shotgun-weakened boards giving a bit. Cords stood out on Bremen's neck and his face grew a bright red; he heaved with enough effort of will and energy to move mountains, to freeze birds in their flight.

Bremen thought Miz Morgan had fired the shotgun again from directly under him—the blast and release of pressure was deafening—but it was only three of the broad boards splitting and flying upward above him.

Bremen lost his balance and fell then, shoes sliding off the stanchion bar, but his cold-numbed left hand came up and grabbed the edge of broken boards even as his right threw the chain out the opening and clambered for a handhold of its own. He heard Miz Morgan shout something, but then he was pulling himself up, ripping his shirt on splinters as he pulled himself through, his feet pushing off from the light stanchion.

He was blinded by the sudden glare of arc light from the water tower at the rear of the cold house's flat roof, but he rolled away from the splintered opening just as Miz Morgan fired again. Two more boards exploded skyward, showering Bremen with splinters.

Ignoring his bleeding thigh and hip and left arm, ignoring the frostbite pain from his curled hands, Bremen got to his feet, retrieved the chain from the graveled rooftop, and ran to the front of the building, leaping over a thick fire hose that ran to the south side. Four of the rottweilers were still there by the door, leashes tied to an iron pipe. They went crazy as Bremen leaped from the twelve-foot rooftop. He hit hard, felt his left leg give way, and rolled heavily on gravel and small stones.

The dogs leaped for him, their leashes pulling them back ten inches out of range.

Bremen got to his knees and staggered toward the door. It was open only a few inches; cold, rancid air flowed out like the breath of some dying demon. Bremen could hear the sound of Miz Morgan's boots on the ice-grooved floor as she ran toward the doorway.

He lunged forward, slammed it almost shut just as the weight of her struck the other side. The pressure lessened and Bremen imagined her stepping back, pumping the shotgun. The four rottweilers were leaping at him so hard that they were jerking themselves off their feet, landing on their backs. Foam and spittle struck him from three feet away.

Bremen ran the chain through the hasp, lifted the heavy padlock from the dust, and slammed it on just as Miz Morgan fired the shotgun.

It was a six-inch-thick steel door set deeply within its steel frame. It did not budge. Even the sound of the shotgun was a distant, hollow thing.

Bremen stepped back and grinned, then glanced toward the rooftop. It would take her less than a minute to slide another corpse into position and climb out the way he had come. He would not have enough time to find a ladder or material to cover the hole. He doubted if he could beat her back to the hacienda given his injuries. Bremen began limping and hobbling toward the south side of the cold house.

One of the rottweilers, a bitch, broke free then, and came lunging after him, apparently so surprised by her sudden freedom that she forgot to howl. Bremen whirled at the corner of the building, dropped to one knee to avoid the snapping jaws, and punched the animal in the gut, right under its ribs, as hard as he could.

The wind went out of the rottweiler like air from a punctured balloon. It went down, but its legs were already scrambling, claws scratching to get back on its feet.

Weeping, Bremen knelt on the big animal's back, grabbed its jaws with his swollen, throbbing hands, and snapped its neck. The surviving three went wild behind him.

Bremen hobbled around the corner. The jerry-rigged shower stall that Miz Morgan had used was still there, the five-gallon holding tank seven feet up, the heavy fire hose running to the fifteen-hundred-gallon tank above. Ignoring the pain, Bremen ran to the shower, leaped for the shower head, leveraged himself up high enough to get a grip on the holding tank, and swung up until he could get his bleeding hand around the four-inch fire hose.

The tank ripped loose from Bremen's weight and fell away to the stone pad below, but he was already eight feet up and shinnying up the now-dangling fire hose.

He swung over the edge of the roof and lay panting for a second on the gravel of the rooftop, the arc lamp on the fifteen-hundred-gallon water tank still blinding him. There were sounds from the broken vent or old skylight that he had climbed through. Bremen went over, peered down, and saw the barrel rising toward the opening just in time.

The shotgun blast went past his shoulder. The effort of raising the weapon had made Miz Morgan lose her grip and she went sliding back onto the shoulders of a young woman's corpse.

Bremen could hear the curses as Miz Morgan began climbing again, one-handed. The light stanchion squealed as the big woman swung up on it.

Bremen had to sit down or faint. Even then, his head between his knees, the arc-lighted world dwindled to a narrow tunnel between walls of black. Distantly, so distantly, he heard the noises of Miz Morgan climbing, finding her balance, resting the shotgun against the inside wall of the vent, getting to her feet. Bremen closed his eyes.

Come on, Jer. Get up! Get up now. For me.

Tiredly, sighing, Bremen opened his eyes and crawled across the tar paper and gravel to the fire hose. He left bloody handprints and a smear from his left leg as he went.

With the last of his strength—no, with strength that was not his but that he borrowed from some hidden place—he lifted the fire hose, stumbled back across the rooftop, and teetered on the edge of the hole.

Miz Morgan's head and shoulders were already out. With her eyes so white and wide, the rimming of frost on her wild hair, and her lips pulled so far back in the killing grin, she looked like something not nearly human being born. The white noise of her psychotic bloodlust was all but overridden by the sudden surge of triumph that emanated from her like warm urine. Still grinning, she struggled to raise the shotgun through the gap.

Not smiling at all, Bremen slapped the release valve open and held the fire hose steady as six hundred pounds of water pressure slapped the woman down out of sight and pounded the boards loose around the hole. He walked closer, and a stray geyser from the swiveling nozzle shot gravel fifty feet out into the night.

She had taken the shotgun with her as she fell. Bremen shut off the water and peered carefully over the rim of the hole where icicles were already beginning to form.

Miz Morgan was climbing back up, a figure wreathed in hoarfrost and sheeted with ice. She was still grinning wildly. The shotgun was in her milk-white right hand.

Sighing, Bremen stepped back, set the hose over the opening, and opened the valve all the way. He staggered toward the front of the building and collapsed on gravel just short of the low wall around the edge of the roof. He closed his eyes for a second.

Just for a second or two.

EYES

The problem is that Gail has suffered terrible migraines since puberty, so when the headaches become more frequent and more severe, neither she nor Jeremy takes adequate notice for some months. Emotional stress often triggers the migraines, and both of them suspect that Jacob Goldmann's suicide is what has triggered this most recent series of headaches. Finally, though, when Jeremy has to leave a symposium at the college, weaving with the reflected pain of her headaches, to find her vomiting endlessly in the downstairs bathroom, blinded by the pain, they see the doctor. He sends them to a specialist, Dr. Singh, who immediately schedules Gail for CAT scans and MRI studies.

Gail is nonplussed. *It's like Jacob's tests. . . .*

No, sends Jeremy, holding her hand there in Dr. Singh's office, *these are studying structures . . . like X rays . . . Jacob's scans were for the wavefront actions.*

The tests are on a Friday and Singh will not get back to them until Monday. They each see the darkest possibilities hidden behind the doctor's smooth reassurances. On Saturday, as if the tests themselves were the remedy, Gail's headaches are gone. Jeremy suggests that they take the weekend off, drop all the work around the farm, and go to the beach. It is the week before Thanksgiving, but the sky is blue and the weather warm, a second Indian summer deep into what is usually their drabbest season in eastern Pennsylvania.

Barnegat Light is all but deserted. Terns and sea gulls wheel and scream above the long stretch of sand below the lighthouse while Gail and Jeremy set their blankets amid the dunes and cavort like newlyweds, chasing each along the sliding edge of the Atlantic, playing tag and tickling—using any excuse to touch the other in their spray-wet suits—and finally coming back to drop goose-bumped and exhausted on the blankets to watch the sun set behind the dunes and weathered houses to the west.

A cold wind comes up with the dying of the light and Jeremy pulls the less-tattered of the two blankets over them, wrapping them both in a warm nest as the dune grasses and narrow fences reflect the rich russets and golds of the autumn light. The white lighthouse glows in indescribable shades of pink and fading lavender during the two minutes of perfect sunset, its glass and lamps prisming the orb of the sun across the beach like a spotlight of pure gold.

Darkness comes with the breathtaking suddenness of a curtain slamming down. There is no one else on the beach and only a few of the beach houses are lighted. The sea wind rattles dry grasses above them and stirs the dunes with a sound like an infant sighing.

Jeremy pulls the blanket higher around them and slips Gail's wet one-piece suit down from her shoulders, then lower, her breasts rising free from the clinging material and Jeremy feeling the goose bumps there, as hard as her nipples, and then he tugs the suit down over the curve of her hips, off her legs, past her small feet, and then frees himself from his trunks.

Gail opens her arms and shifts her legs, pulling him above her, and suddenly the cold wind and rising darkness are distant things, forgotten in the sudden warmth of their joining and mindtouch.

Bremen moves slowly, infinitely slowly, feeling her sharing his thoughts and sensations—and then only his sensations—as they seem to ride the growing breeze and rising surf noise toward some quickly receding core of things.

They come together and then stay together, finding each other in the returning slide of external senses and small touchings, then in mindtouch structured by language once again after their wordless swirl of feelings beyond language.

This is why I want to live, sends Gail, her mindtouch small and vulnerable.

Jeremy feels anger and the vertigo of fear rise in him almost as strongly as the passion had moments before. *You'll live. You'll live.*

You promise? sends Gail, her mental voice light. But Jeremy sees the fear-of-the-dark-under-the-bed beneath the lightness.

I promise, sends Jeremy. *I swear.* He pulls her closer, trying to stay inside, but feeling the slow withdrawal that he has no control over. He hugs her so tightly that she gasps. *I swear, Gail,* he sends. *I promise. I promise you.*

She sets cool hands on his shoulders above her, cusps her face to the salt-tinged hollow of his neck, and sighs, almost drifting off to sleep.

After a moment Jeremy shifts only slightly, lying on his right hip and side so that he can hold her without wakening her. Around them the wind blowing in from the unseen ocean has become late-autumn cold, the stars burning almost without twinkling in winter clarity, but Jeremy pulls the blanket tighter and hugs Gail more firmly to him, keeping them both warm with the heat of his body and the intensity of his will.

I promise, he sends to his sleeping love. *I promise you.*

We Are the Hollow Men

Bremen awoke late into the next day, the sun bright, his skin blistering. The gravel burned against his bare palms and forearms. His lips were chapped to the consistency of ragged parchment. Blood had caked his hip and inner thigh and run onto the hot stones beneath, congealing with the torn denim of his Levi's to a brown, sticky paste that he had to rip free from the roof. At least he was no longer bleeding.

He limped the twenty feet to the hole in the roof, having to sit down twice to let dizziness and nausea pass. The sun was very hot.

The hose still dangled into the dark hole in which cold air still stirred, but no water was dripping. The lights were out in the cold house. Bremen lifted the hose and glanced at the fifteen-hundred-gallon tank on the roof, wondering if it could possibly be empty. Then he shrugged and carried the long hose to the south edge of the roof, planning to use it as a rope to get down.

The pain upon landing was enough to make him sit on the sandstone shower slab for several minutes, his head between his legs. Then he pulled himself to his feet and began the long trip to the hacienda.

The dead rottweiler at the corner of the cold house was already bloated and pungent in the midday heat. Flies had been busy at its eyes. The three surviving dogs did not rise or growl as Bremen hobbled past, but merely watched him with troubled eyes as he moved down to the road and then up to the big house.

It took him the better part of an hour to make it to the house, to cut himself out of his jeans and clean the wounds on his hip and thigh and then stand under the shower for a blissful, gray period, to apply antiseptic—he did pass out for a moment when he dabbed at his hip—and then to dig some codeine Tylenol out of Miz Morgan's medicine cabinet, hesitate, set the bottle in his shirt pocket, find and load a rifle and a pistol from the open gun cabinet in her bedroom closet, and then to hobble down to the bunkhouse for fresh clothes.

It was early evening before he approached the cold-house door again. The dogs watched the muzzle of the rifle, whimpered, and pulled away as far as their leashes would allow. Bremen set down the large bowl of water he had brought up from the bunkhouse, and slowly the oldest bitch, Letitia, eased forward on her belly until she was gratefully lapping at it. The other two followed.

Bremen turned his back on the dogs and opened the combination lock. The chain dropped away.

The door did not swing open; it was jammed. He pried it loose with a crowbar brought up from the house and then pushed it open the last few inches with the barrel of the .30-.06 and stepped back out of the doorway. Cold air billowed out, turning to fog in the hundred-degree air. Bremen crouched, safety off, his finger on the trigger. A ridge of ice gleamed almost three feet above the level of the old floor.

Nothing emerged. There was no sound except that of the rottweilers lapping up the last of the water, some of the cattle lowing as they came in from the lower pasture, and the chugging of the auxiliary generator out behind the cold house.

Bremen let another three minutes pass and then he went in low, sliding on the raised hummock of ice and moving to the left of the doorway quickly, letting his eyes adapt to the dark and swinging the rifle in front of him. A moment later he lowered his weapon and stood up, his breath swirling around him. He walked forward slowly.

Most of the carcasses in the center rows had been knocked off their hooks, either by the water pressure from above or by the madness below. They stood now—beef sides and human bodies— in stalagmites of ragged ice. It looked as if the entire fifteen- hundred-gallon tank had been emptied in here. Bremen set his boots carefully on the rough and rising swirls of blue-green ice, both to keep his balance and to avoid stepping on any of the raw- ribbed carcasses frozen into the nightmare *mare* beneath him.

Miz Morgan was almost directly beneath the hole where sun- light shafted down through the vapor and dripping stalactites. The ice mound was at least three and a half feet tall here, and the bodies of her and the two dogs were embedded in it like some sort of pale, three-headed frozen vegetable. Her face was the closest to the surface, so close that one wide, blue eye actually was lifted above the line of frost. Her hands, with fingers still curved into claws, also rose above the general level of ice like two crude sculp- tures abandoned before the refining strokes could be applied.

Her mouth was open very wide, the frozen torrent of her last breaths like a solid waterfall connecting her to the solid sea of cold around her, and for one mad second the obscene image was so perfect that Bremen could imagine her vomiting this roomful of rancid ice.

The dogs seemed to be part of her, joined below her hips in a torrent of frozen flesh, and the shotgun rose up through the ice from one of the dogs' bellies in a caricature of an erection.

Bremen lowered the rifle and reached out one shaking hand to touch the layer of ice above her head, as if the warmth of his touch would cause her to begin squirming and struggling in her cold shroud, curved claws tearing through ice to get at him.

There was no movement, no white noise. His breath fogged the ice above her straining, open-mawed face.

Bremen turned and went out of that place, taking care not to set his boot soles above any other sunken faces with staring eyes.

Bremen left at dark, releasing the dogs and setting out enough food and water to keep them comfortable around the hacienda for a week or more. He left the Toyota where it was parked and took the Jeep. The distributor cap had been sitting atop Miz Morgan's dresser like some clumsy trophy. He took none of her money—not even the pay due him—but loaded the back of the Jeep with three shopping bags of food and several two-gallon plastic jugs of water. Bremen considered taking the .30-.06 or the pistol, but ended up wiping them clean and setting them back in the closet gun case. For a while he went around with a dust rag cleaning surfaces in the bunkhouse as if he could eradicate all of his fingerprints, but then he shook his head, climbed into the Jeep, and drove away.

Bremen drove west through the night, letting the cool desert air bring him up out of the nightmare that he had been dwelling in for so long now. He went west because going back east was unthinkable to him. Sometime after ten P.M. he reached Interstate 70 and turned west again below Green River, half expecting Deputy Howard Collins's cruiser to come roaring up behind him with all of its lights flashing. There were no lights. Bremen passed only a few cars as he drove west through the Utah night.

He had stopped in Salina to use the last of his cash to buy gas and was heading west out of town on Highway 50 when he found himself behind a slow-moving state patrol cruiser. Bremen waited until he found a road branching off—Highway 89 as it turned out —and turned south on it.

He drove a hundred and twenty-five miles south, cut west again at Long Valley Junction, passed through Cedar City and over Interstate 15 just before dawn, continued west on State Road 56, and found a place to park the Jeep out of sight behind some dry cottonwoods at a county rest stop east of Panaca, twenty miles across the state line into Nevada. Bremen made a breakfast of a bologna sandwich and water, spread his blanket out on some dust-dry leaves in the shade of the Jeep, and was asleep before his mind had time to dredge up any recent memories to keep him awake.

The next night, driving slowly south through the fringes of the Pharanagat National Wildlife Refuge on Highway 93, headed nowhere in particular, feeling the thrusts and echoes of mindbabble from passing cars, but still being able to concentrate better in the still desert air than he had in many weeks, Bremen realized that in another seventy-five miles or so he would be out of gas and out of luck. He had no money to take a bus or train anywhere, not a cent to buy food when the groceries ran out, and no identification in his pocket.

He also had no ideas. His emotions, so spiked and exaggerated during the previous weeks, seemed to have been stored away somewhere for the duration. He felt strangely calm, comfortably *empty*, much as he had as a young child after a long, hard bout of crying.

Bremen tried to think about Gail, about Goldmann's research and its implications, but all of that was from another world, from someplace left far above in the sunlight where sanity prevailed. He would not be going back there.

So Bremen drove south without thinking, the gas gauge hovering near empty, and suddenly found that Highway 93 ended at Interstate 15. Obediently, he followed the access ramp down and continued southwest across the desert.

Ten minutes later, coming across a small rise, expecting the Jeep to cough and glide to a stop any second, Bremen blinked in surprise as the desert exploded in light—rivers of light, flowing constellations of light—and in that second of electric epiphany, he knew precisely what he would do that night, and the next night, and the night after that. Solutions blossomed like the missing transform in some difficult equation suddenly coming to mind, shining as clearly as the oasis of brilliance ahead of him in the desert night.

The Jeep got him just far enough.

EYES

It is hard for me to understand, even now, the concept of mortality as Jeremy and Gail brought it to me.

Dying, ending, *ceasing to be,* is simply not an idea that had existed for me previous to their dark revelation. Even now it disturbs me with its black, irrational imperative. At the same time it intrigues me, even beckons me, and I cannot help but wonder if the true fruit of the tree denied to Adam and Eve in the fairy tales that Gail's parents taught her so assiduously when she was young had been not knowledge, as the folktale insists, but death itself. Death can be an appealing notion to a deity who has been denied even sleep while tending to His creation.

It is not an appealing notion to Gail.

In the first hours and days after the discovery of the inoperable tumor behind her eye, she is the essence of bravery, sharing her confidence with Jeremy through language and mindtouch. She is sure that the radiation treatments will help . . . or the chemo . . . or some sort of remission. Having found the enemy, identified it, she is less afraid of the darkness under her bed than she has been.

But then, as the illness and terrible ordeal of medical treatment wear her down, filling her nights with apprehensions and her afternoons with nausea, Gail begins to despair. She realizes that the darkness under the bed is not the cancer but the death it brings.

Gail dreams that she is in the backseat of her Volvo and it is hurtling toward the edge of a cliff. No one is in the driver's seat and she cannot reach forward to grab the steering wheel because of a clear Plexiglas wall separating her from the front seat. Jeremy is running along behind the Volvo, unable to catch up, shouting and waving his arms, but Gail cannot hear him.

Gail and Jeremy both awake from the nightmare just as the car hurtles over the cliff. Each has seen that there are no rocks below, no cliff face, no beach, no ocean . . . nothing but a terrible darkness that assures an eternity of sickening fall.

Jeremy helps her through the winter months, holding tightly with mindtouch and real touch as they share the terrible roller coaster of the illness—hope and suggestion of remission one day, small bits of promising medical news the next, then the spate of days with the growing pain and weakness and no glimmer of hope.

In the last weeks and days it is Gail again who provides the strength, diverting their thoughts to other things when she can, bravely confronting what needs to be confronted when she must. Jeremy draws farther and farther into himself, rocked by her pain and her growing distance from the reassuring absorption of mundane things.

Gail is hurtling toward the cliff edge, but Jeremy is there with her until the last few yards. Even when she is too ill to be physically close, embarrassed by the loss of her hair and the pain that makes her live only for the shots that help for so few minutes, there are islands of clarity where their mindtouch holds the bantering intimacy of their long time together.

Gail knows that there is something in the core of Jeremy's thoughts that he is not sharing with her—she can see it only through the *absence* his scarred-over mindshield leaves there—but there have been many things that he has been reluctant to share with her since the medical nightmare began, and she assumes that this is another sad prognosis.

On Jeremy's part, the long-hidden and shameful fact of the variocele has become so encysted that it is difficult to imagine sharing now. Also, there is no reason to share it now . . . they will have no children together.

Still, on the night that Jeremy drives alone to Barnegat Light to share the ocean and stars with Gail lying in her hospital room, he has decided to share it with her. To share all of the small slights and shames he has hidden over the years, like opening the doors and windows to a musty room that has been sealed for far too long. He does not know how she will react, but knows that those final days they are to have together cannot be what they must be unless he is totally honest with her. Jeremy has hours to prepare his revelation since Gail spends so much time sleeping, medicated, beyond mindtouch.

But then he falls asleep in the weak hours before sunrise on that Easter weekend morning, and when he wakes, there is no future of even a few more final days with her. The cliff had been reached while he slept.

While she was alone. And frightened. And unable to touch him a final time.

Yes, this idea of death interests me very much. I see it as Gail saw it . . . as the whisper from the dark under the bed . . . and I see it as the warm embrace of forgetfulness and surcease of pain.

And I see it as something close and drawing closer.

It interests me, but now, with so much opening up, the curtain opening so wide, it seems vaguely disappointing that everything might cease to be and the theater be emptied before the final act.

Malebolge

Bremen liked it here in the place where there was no night, no darkness, and where the neurobabble knew no boundaries between the penultimate, mindless surges of lust and greed and the ultimate, fiercely minded concentration on numbers, shapes, and odds. Bremen liked it here where one never had to move in the harsh glare of sunlight, but could exist solely in the warm chrome-and-wood glow of never-dimming lights, here where the laughter and movement and intensity never slackened.

He sometimes wished that Jacob Goldmann were alive so that the old man could have shared this all-too-physical realization of their research—a place where probability waves were colliding and collapsing every second of every day and where reality was as insubstantial as the human mind could make it.

Bremen spent a week in the desert town and loved every greedy, foul-minded, belly-ruling-the-mind second of it. Here he could be born again.

He had sold the Jeep to an Iranian guy out on East Sahara Avenue. The Iranian was deliriously happy to get transportation for his last two hundred and eighty-six dollars and made no demands for little things such as a pink slip or registration.

Bremen used forty-six of the dollars to check into the Travel Inn near the downtown. He slept fourteen straight hours and then showered, shaved the last of his beard off, dressed in his cleanest shirt and jeans, and then began working his way through the downtown casinos: the Lady Luck, the Sundance, the Horseshoe, the Four Queens, ending up in the old Golden Nugget. He had started the evening with a hundred forty-one dollars and sixty cents. He ended the night with a little over six thousand dollars.

Bremen hadn't played cards since his college days—and that had been mostly bridge—but he remembered the rules of poker. What he had not remembered was the Zen-deep concentration that the game demanded. The razor slashes of outside neurobabble were dulled here at the poker table because of the laser intensity of the concentration surrounding him, by the near-total absorption with the mathematical permutations that every bid and new card brought, and by the concentration demanded of Bremen himself in sorting everything out. Playing five-card stud was not like trying to pay attention to six televisions tuned to different stations; it was more like attempting to read half a dozen highly technical books simultaneously while the pages were being turned.

The other players ran the gamut: professional poker players whose livelihoods depended upon their skill and whose minds were as disciplined as those of any research mathematicians Bremen had ever met, gifted amateurs who blended real enjoyment of the high-stakes game with their quest for luck, and even the occasional pigeon sitting there fat, happy, and stupid . . . not even aware that he was being played like a cheap fiddle by the professionals at the table. Bremen took them all on.

During his second week in Las Vegas Bremen moved through the casinos on the Strip, checking into each with enough money to deposit in the safe to have his room comped and generally to be treated as a high roller. Then he would wander down to the card room and stand in line, occasionally watching the closed-circuit videos that explained how the game was played. To look the part, Bremen purchased Armani jackets that could be worn with open-collared silk shirts, three-hundred-dollar linen slacks that wrinkled if he looked at them hard, not one but two gold Rolexes, Gucci loafers, and a steel carrying case to hold his cash. He did not even have to leave the hotels to outfit himself.

Bremen tried his luck and found it good at Circus-Circus, Dunes, Caesar's Palace, the Las Vegas Hilton, the Aladdin, the Riviera, Bally's Grand, Sam's Town, and the Sands. Sometimes he saw the familiar faces of the professionals who moved from casino to casino, but more often the players at the hundred-dollar tables preferred to play at their favorite casino. The mood in the card room was as intense as that of a hospital operating room, with only the loud voice of the occasional boisterous amateur breaking the low-murmured concentration. Amateur or professional, Bremen won, taking care as he did so to win and lose with the slow accretion of gain that might be attributed to luck. Soon the professionals avoided his table. Bremen continued winning, knowing now that luck favored the telepathic mind. The Frontier, El Rancho, the Desert Inn, Castaways, Showboat, the Holiday Inn Casino. Bremen moved through the town like a vacuum sweeper, being careful not to sweep up too much from any one table.

Unlike the other games, even blackjack, where the player was pitted against the house and security against cheating, card counting, or some "system" was heavy, only the house-provided dealer usually monitored the poker players. Occasionally Bremen would glance at the mirrored ceiling where the "eye in the sky" was certainly videotaping proceedings, but since the house took its profit from a share of the winner's pot, he knew there would be little suspicion here.

Besides, he was not cheating. At least not by any measurable standards.

Occasionally Bremen felt guilty about taking money from the other players, but usually his mindtouch with the professionals at the table showed them to be similar to the casino dealers themselves—smugly confident that time would average out the winnings in their favor. Some of the amateurs were experiencing an almost sexual thrill at playing with the big boys, and Bremen felt he was doing some of these pigeons a favor by retiring them early.

Bremen did not really think about what he was going to *do* with the money; acquiring it had been his goal, his desert epiphany, and the details of how he was going to spend it could be deferred for a while. Another week here, he thought, and he could lease a Learjet to take him anyplace in the world he wanted to go.

He did not really want to go anywhere. Here, in this deepest of the tunnels he had traveled, he found some solace in the intensity of greed and lust and shallowness that surrounded him.

Walking the halls in one of the casino hotels reminded Bremen of watching the Mayor Marion Barry videotape of a few years earlier: a boring exercise in banality, ego, and frustrated sexuality. Even the high rollers in their shag-carpeted suites, rolling around in their Jacuzzis with one or more showgirls, ended up feeling hollow and frustrated, wanting more experience than the experience itself offered. Bremen found the entire town symbolized perfectly by the chrome troughs of its always-open buffets offering up heaps of underpriced, mediocre food, and by the mindtouch glimpses of its hundreds of solitary men and women alone in their hotel rooms, emotionally viscerated by the day or night's gambling, masturbating in solitude to the "adult" videos piped to their rooms.

But the five-card-stud poker tables were places of forgetting, temporary nirvanas reached through concentration rather than meditation, and Bremen spent his waking hours there, accumulating money in small but never-faltering increments. By the time he had worked his way through the larger casinos on the Strip, his steel carrying case held almost three hundred thousand dollars in cash. Bremen went to the Mirage Hotel, admired its working volcano outside and its tank of live sharks inside, and almost doubled his money in four nights of ten-thousand-dollar-entry-fee tournament play.

He decided that one more casino would be the icing on the cake and decided to finish up in a huge, castlelike structure near the airport. The card room was busy. Bremen waited like the other pigeons, bought his hundred-dollar chips, nodded hellos to the other six players—four men and two women, only one of them a pro—and settled into the night's haze of mathematics.

He was four hours and several thousand dollars up when the dealer called a halt and a short, powerfully built man in the blue-blazered uniform of the casino whispered in Bremen's ear, "Excuse me, sir, but could you come with me, please?"

Bremen saw only the command to bring this lucky player to the manager's office in the flunky's mind, but he also saw that the command would be obeyed under any circumstances. The flunky carried a .45 automatic in a holster on his left hip. Bremen went with him to the office.

The neurobabble distracted him, all those surges of lust and greed and disappointment and renewed lust adding to the background mindnoise, so that Bremen was not warned until he was waved into the inner office.

The five men were watching the video monitors when Bremen entered and they looked up with an almost quizzical humor, as if surprised to see the image on the television standing live and three-dimensional among them. Sal Empori was sitting on the long leather couch with the thugs named Bert and Ernie on either side of him. Vanni Fucci was seated behind the manager's desk, his hands clasped behind his head and a huge Cuban cigar clenched between his teeth.

"Come on in, civilian," said Vanni Fucci around the cigar. He nodded for the flunky to close the door and wait outside. Vanni Fucci gestured toward an empty chair. "Siddown."

Bremen remained standing. He saw it all in their minds. The steel case by Bert Cappi's leg was Bremen's; they had searched his room and found the cash. It was their hotel, their casino. Or, rather, it was the absent Don Leoni's casino. And it had been the thief Vanni Fucci, here on another deal entirely, who had seen

Bremen's image on the video monitor in the manager's office. Vanni Fucci had ordered the manager to take a two-day vacation, and then the thief had called Don Leoni and settled back to wait for Sal and the boys to arrive.

Bremen saw all this clearly. And he saw, even more clearly, precisely what the aging Don Leoni was going to have done to the upstart civilian who had been in the wrong place at the wrong time. First, Mr. Leoni was going to talk to Bremen back in New Jersey, where they would find out whether this civilian was really a civilian, or whether he worked for one of the Miami Families. It did not matter too much, because Bremen would then be loaded aboard a garbage truck and taken out to their favorite place in the Pine Barrens, where they would blow Bremen's brains out, put his body in the truck's compactor, and dump the parcel in the usual place.

Vanni Fucci smiled broadly and removed the cigar. "Okay, stay standing. You been real lucky, kid. Real lucky. At least up to now."

Bremen blinked.

Vanni Fucci nodded, Bert and Ernie moved more quickly than Bremen could react, he felt his arms pinned, and Sal Empori raised a hypodermic needle to the light and injected him in the arm through his seven-hundred-dollar Armani jacket.

EYES

Robby Bustamante is dying. The deaf, blind, retarded child slides in and out of coma like some sightless amphibian moving from water to air without finding sustenance in either element.

The child is so terribly and obviously damaged that some nurses find reasons to avoid his room, while others spend extra time there, tending to the dying child while trying to ease his pain through the sheer unsensed fact of their presence. On the rare occasions when Robby rises close to consciousness and the monitors above his bed register something other than REM-state dream sleep, the boy moans fitfully and paws at the bed covers, splayed fingers and stiff splints scratching at the sheets.

Sometimes the nurses gather round then, rubbing the child's brow or increasing the dosage of painkiller in his IV drip, but no amount of touching or medicine stops Robby's mewling and fevered scrabbling. It is as if he is searching for something.

He is searching for something. Robby is desperately trying to find his teddy bear, the one companion he has had through the years. His tactile friend. His solace in the endless night punctuated only with pain.

When Robby is semiconscious, he rolls and scrabbles, searching the bedclothes and wet sheets for his teddy bear. He cries out in his sleep, the falsetto croon moaning down dark hospital corridors like the cry of the damned.

There is no teddy bear. His mother and "Uncle" had tossed it and the rest of the child's possessions in the back of the car on the night they left, planning to get rid of them at the first Dumpster they passed.

Robby turns and moans and claws at the sheets during those rare times he rises toward consciousness, searching for his teddy, but those times become fewer and fewer and finally cease.

Geryon

They took Bremen to the Las Vegas airport in the middle of the night. A twin-engine turboprop Piper Cheyenne was idling outside a darkened hangar, and it was taxiing for takeoff thirty seconds after the five men boarded. Bremen couldn't tell a twin-engine turboprop Piper Cheyenne from the space shuttle, but the pilot could, and Bremen was disappointed to find that the pilot also knew exactly who his five passengers were and why they were flying back to New Jersey.

All four of the hoodlums had weapons, and Bert Cappi had carried his .45 automatic under a jacket over his arm, the muzzle of the silencer sticking out far enough to touch Bremen's right ribs. Bremen had watched enough television to know a silencer when he saw one.

They took off to the west and climbed steeply, banking around to leave the mountains behind them as they headed east. The small aircraft had two seats on each side behind the pilot's and empty copilot's seats and a bench against a rear bulkhead. Sal Empori and Vanni Fucci sat across the narrow aisle from each other in the first two seats, nearest the door; the thug named Ernie sat across from Bremen in the second row; Bert Cappi sat buckled into the rear bench directly behind Bremen, his pistol out and on his lap.

The aircraft droned eastward and Bremen set his face against the cool Plexiglas of the window and shut his eyes. The thoughts of the pilot were cool, crisp, and technical, but the four thugs offered a cauldron of dim-witted malevolence to Bremen's mindtouch. Bert, the twenty-six-year-old killer and son-in-law to Don Leoni, was looking forward to whacking Bremen. Bert hoped that the civilian would try something before they got there so he could do the asshole en route.

Wind gusts buffeted the small aircraft and Bremen felt the emptiness rise inside himself. The situation was ridiculous—cartoonish, TV stuff—but the inevitability of violence was as real as an imminent automobile crash. Until his moments of madness in Denver with the child abuser, Bremen had never hit anyone in anger. He had never bloodied anyone's nose. To Bremen violence had always represented the last refuge of the intellectually and emotionally incompetent. And now he sat in this sealed machine, the seats and doors less substantial feeling than those of an American automobile, remembering Miz Morgan's ice-filmed face while flying eastward to his fate, the violent thoughts of these violent men rubbing like sandpaper against his mind. Ironically, there was nothing personal in their eagerness to kill Bremen; it was their way of solving a problem, easing a minor potential threat. They would kill the man named Jeremy Bremen—a name they did not even know—with no more hesitation than Bremen would have in erasing a faulty transform to preserve an equation. But they would enjoy it more.

The Piper Cheyenne flew on, its turboprop engines providing a melodic counterpoint to the dark churnings coming from Vanni Fucci, Sal Empori, Bert, and Ernie. Vanni Fucci was absorbed with counting the cash in Bremen's steel case; the thief had passed three hundred thousand dollars and had a third of the stacks of

bills yet to count. Bremen noticed that Fucci's excitement at holding and counting the cash throbbed like an almost sexual arousal.

Bremen felt his depression deepen. The apathy that had governed him before his battle with Miz Morgan rose again, a cold,
dark tide that threatened to sweep him away into the night.

Into the darkness under the bed.

Bremen blinked, opened his eyes, and began to fight through
the sick neurobabble and lulling engine noise, concentrating on the
memory of Gail that rose like a solid rock he could climb above
the black tide. That memory was his North Star; rising anger
goaded him on.

They landed before dawn to refuel. Bremen saw in the pilot's
mind that the airfield was a private place north of Salt Lake, that
Don Leoni owned an entire hangar there, and that there would be
no chance for Bremen to escape.

They took bathroom breaks with Bert and Ernie holding their
silenced .45s at the ready while Bremen urinated. Then he was
back in the plane with Bert holding the pistol's muzzle against the
back of his head while the others took their time in the rest room
and getting coffee in the hangar office. Bremen saw that even if he
somehow miraculously escaped Bert Cappi, the others would hunt
him down with no worry about onlookers calling the police.

Refueled, they took off and followed Interstate 80 across Wyo-
ming, although Bremen knew this only from the pilot's distracted
thoughts; the ground itself was concealed beneath a solid cloak of
clouds fifteen thousand feet below them. The only noise came
from the engines and an occasional radio call or response from
the pilot. The late-summer sunlight warmed the interior of the
Piper Cheyenne, and one by one the thugs dozed off, except for
Vanni Fucci, whose mind was still on the money and how much of
it Don Leoni might parcel out as a reward for grabbing the civilian.

Act now! Bremen's thought caused a surge of adrenaline; he
could imagine himself grabbing a weapon from Bert Cappi or

Ernie Sanza. He had touched enough of their memories to know how to use the .45 automatics.

What then? Unfortunately, he had touched enough of their memories to know that the four thugs were tough enough and mean enough not to respond to an automatic pistol being waved around in a small aircraft flying at twenty thousand feet. If it had been just Bremen and the pilot, he might have convinced the man to divert from their route to land somewhere. The pilot—a man named Jesus Vigil—had flown drugs from Colombia and outrun DEA chase planes at treetop height before he came to work for Don Leoni, but he liked the sanity of working for the don and had no intention of dying young.

But the four hoodlums, especially Bert Cappi and Ernie Sanza, were sunk much deeper into the imperatives of machismo—or at least their Italian and Sicilian versions of it—and could never let a civilian disarm them or escape their custody. Each would let the other man die before allowing that. Neither had enough intelligence or imagination to imagine dying himself.

They landed again in late morning, this time near Omaha, but Bremen was not allowed to leave the aircraft and the other men were wide-awake now. Bremen could almost taste Bert and Ernie's eagerness for the civilian—him—to try something. He stared at them impassively.

After taking off again, Bremen catching a glimpse of a wide river before they climbed through clouds, he concentrated on the pilot's thoughts and memories, including the memory of the flight plan he had just updated in Omaha. The Cheyenne would make one more refueling stop—this one at a private airfield in Ohio—and then would continue straight to Don Leoni's own airfield a mile from his estate in New Jersey. The limousine would be waiting. There would be a very brief discussion with the don—mostly a monologue in which the man made sure that Bremen was not working for any of Chico Tartugian's Miami friends, an interrogation that might well include the loss of several of Bremen's fingers and one or both of his testicles—and then, when they were sure,

Bert and Ernie and the Puerto Rican psychopath Roachclip would take Bremen to the Pine Barrens to do what had to be done. Afterward, the garbage truck would take its trash-compacted bundle to a landfill near Newark.

The Piper Cheyenne droned on into midafternoon. Sal and Vanni Fucci spoke of business, confident that the civilian in the backseat would never repeat any of the conversation. Ernie had tried moving to the back bench to play cards with Bert, but Sal Empori had snapped at him, ordering him back to the seat across from Bremen. Ernie brooded, tried reading part of a sex novel, and then dozed off. Eventually Bert Cappi joined him in light sleep, dreaming that he was screwing one of the showgirls in Don Leoni's new casino.

Bremen was tempted to doze off himself. He had raided as much of the pilot's professional memory as he was able to find. Sal and Vanni Fucci's conversation was dying off, replaced only by the engine sounds and occasional radio rasp as they passed from one FAA flight control center to another. But instead of going to sleep, Bremen decided to stay alive.

He glanced down and saw only clouds, but knew from the pilot's thoughts that they were somewhere east of Springfield, Missouri. Ernie was snoring softly. Bert twitched in his sleep.

Bremen silently unbuckled his seat belt and closed his eyes for five seconds. *Yes, Jerry. Yes.*

He acted without further thought, moving more quickly and gracefully than he had ever managed before, rising, pivoting, sliding onto the back bench, and lifting Bert Cappi's automatic out of the gangster's hand in a single motion.

Then Bremen had his back pressed into the corner where the rear bulkhead met the fuselage and he was swiveling the weapon, first at the startled Bert, then at the snorting, awakening Ernie, and then at all of them as Sal Empori and Vanni Fucci both reached for their weapons.

"You do it," said Bremen, his voice flat, "and I'll kill everyone."

The small aircraft was filled with shouts and curses until the pilot shouted the others down. "We're pressurized, for fuck's sake!" screamed Jesus Vigil. "If anybody shoots, it's gonna be fucking bad news."

"Put down the fucking gun, motherfucker!" screamed Vanni Fucci, his hand still only halfway toward his belt.

"Stop, you fucks! Fucking freeze!" Sal Empori shouted at Bert and Ernie. Bert's hands had been rising as if he was going to strangle the civilian. Ernie's right hand was already inside his silk sport coat.

For a second there was silence and no motion except for the jerky but not panicked swiveling of Bremen's gun arm. He could hear their thoughts crashing around him like a storm-driven surf. His own heartbeat was so loud that he was afraid that he could not hear anything else. But he heard it when the pilot spoke again.

"Hey, take it easy, pal. Let's talk about this." *Shallow dive. The* pendejo *won't notice. Another three thousand feet and we won't need the pressurization. Keep Empori and Fucci between the front and the civilian so stray shots won't hit me or the controls. Another two thousand feet.* "Just take it easy, buddy. No one's gonna do anything to you." *Fuckin'* pendejo's *gonna tell me to land somewhere, I'll say okay, and then the boys'll take him out.*

Bremen said nothing.

"Yeah, yeah, yeah," said Vanni Fucci, glancing at Bert and glaring the idiot into immobility. "Don't get fucking excited, okay? We'll talk about this. Just put the fucking gun down so it don't go off, okay?" His fingers moved onto the butt of the .38 in his belt.

Bert Cappi was almost strangling on his own bile, he was so angry. If this fucking civilian survived the next few seconds, he was going to personally cut the motherfucker's balls off before he killed him.

"Just stay fucking *calm!*" screamed Sal Empori. "We'll land somewhere and . . . Ernie, fuck! *No!*"

Ernie got his hand on his pistol.

Vanni Fucci cursed and pulled his own weapon.

The pilot hunkered down and dived the aircraft toward thicker air.

Bert Cappi snarled something and lunged.

Jeremy Bremen began firing.

EYES

During the months of Gail's illness, Jeremy abandons almost all mathematics except for his teaching and an investigation into the theory of chaos. The teaching keeps him sane. The research into chaos math changes forever his view of the universe.

Jeremy has heard of chaos math before Jacob Goldmann's research data forces him to learn about it in depth, but as with most mathematicians Jeremy finds the concept of a mathematical system without formulae, predictability, or boundaries a contradiction in terms. It is messy. It is not math as he knows it. Jeremy is reassured that Henri Poincaré, the great nineteenth-century mathematician who helped stumble across chaos math while creating the study of topology, detested the idea of chaos in the realm of numbers just as much as Jeremy does today.

But Jacob Goldmann's data leaves no choice but to follow the search for holographic wavefront analysis of the mind into the jungles of chaos math. So, after the long days of Gail's chemotherapy and between the depressing hospital visits, Jeremy reads the few books available on the subject of chaos math and then goes on to the abstracts and papers, many of them translated from the

French and German. As the winter days grow shorter and then grudgingly longer and while Gail's illness grows relentlessly more serious, Jeremy reads the work of Abraham and Marsden, Barenblatt, Iooss, and Joseph; he studies the theories of Arun and Heinz, the biological work of Levin, the fractal work of Mandelbrot, Stewart, Peitgen, and Richter. After a long day of being with Gail, holding her hand while the medical procedures rack her body with pain and indignity, Jeremy comes home to lose himself in papers such as "Nonlinear Oscillations, Dynamical Systems, and Bifurcations of Vector Fields" by Guckenheimer and Holmes.

Slowly his understanding grows. Slowly his mastery of chaos mathematics meshes with his more standard Schrödinger wave analyses of holographic perception. Slowly Jeremy's view of the universe changes.

He discovers that one of the birthplaces of modern chaos math is in our failure to predict weather. Even with Cray X-MP supercomputers crunching numbers at a rate of eight hundred million calculations per second, weather prediction is a flop. In half an hour the Cray X-MP can accurately predict tomorrow's weather for all of the northern hemisphere. In a day of frenzied activity the supercomputer can manage ten days' worth of predictions for the northern hemisphere.

But the predictions begin to stray after about four days and any prediction a week into the future tends to be pure guesswork . . . even for the Cray X-MP crunching variables at the rate of sixty million crunches per minute. Meteorologists, artificial-intelligence experts, and mathematicians have all been irritated by this failure. It should not be there. That same computer is able to predict the motion of the stars *billions* of years into the future. Why then, they ask, is weather—even with its large but definitely *finite* set of variables—so difficult to predict?

To find out, Jeremy must do research on Edward Lorenz and chaos.

In the early 1960s a natural mathematician turned meteorologist named Edward Lorenz began using one of the primitive computers of the day, a Royal McBee LGP-300, to plot variables discovered by B. Saltzman in the equations that "control" simple convection, the rising of hot air. Lorenz discovered three variables in Saltzman's equation that actually worked, threw away the rest, and set his tube-and-wire Royal McBee LGP-300 humming and buzzing to solve the equations at the sedate rate of about one iteration per second. The result was . . .

. . . chaos.

From the same variables, with the same equations, using the same data, the apparently simple short-term predictions degenerated into contradictory madness.

Lorenz checked his math, ran linear stability analyses, chewed his nails, and began again.

Madness. Chaos.

Lorenz had discovered the "Lorenz attractor," wherein the trajectories of equations cycle around two lobes in apparently random fashion. Out of Lorenz's chaos came a very precise pattern: a sort of Poincaré section that led to Lorenz's understanding of what he called the "butterfly effect" in weather prediction. Simply put, Lorenz's butterfly effect says that the flapping of a single butterfly's wings in China will produce a tiny but inevitable change in the world's atmosphere. That small variable of change accretes with other tiny variables until the weather is . . . different. Unpredictable.

Quiet chaos.

Jeremy instantly sees the import of Lorenz's work and all the more recent chaos research in terms of Jacob's data.

According to Jeremy's analysis of that data, what the human mind perceives through the once-removed and distorted lens of its senses is little more than the incessant collapsing of probability waves. The universe, according to the Goldmann data, is best described as a standing wavefront made up of these churning ripples of probability chaos. The human mind—nothing more than another standing wavefront according to Jeremy's own research, a sort of superhologram made up of millions of complete but lesser holograms—observes these phenomena, *collapses* the probability waves into an ordered series of events ("Wave or particle," Jeremy had explained to Gail on the train back from Boston that time, "the observer seems to make the universe decide through the mere act of observation. . . ."), and goes on with its business.

Jeremy is at a loss for a paradigm for this ongoing structuring of the unstructurable until he stumbles upon an article talking about the complex mathematics that had been used to analyze the attitude of the orbit of Saturn's moon Hyperion after the *Voyager* flyby. Hyperion's *orbit* is Keplerian and Newtonian enough to be predicted accurately by linear mathematics now and for many decades to come. But its *attitude,* the directions in which its three axes point, is what might be politely described as a fucking mess.

Hyperion is tumbling and the tumbling simply cannot be predicted. Its attitude is controlled not by random influences of gravity and by Newtonian laws that could be plotted if the programmer were smart enough, the program clever enough, and the computer big enough, but by a dynamical chaos that follows a logic and illogic all its own. It is Lorenz's butterfly effect played out in the silent vacuum of Saturn space with lumpy little Hyperion as its confused and tumbling victim.

But even in such uncharted oceans of chaos, Jeremy discovers, there can be small islands of linear reason.

Jeremy follows the Hyperion trail to the work of Andrei Kolmogorov, Vladimir Arnold, and Jurgen Moser. These mathematicians and dynamics experts have formulated the KAM theorem (Kolmogorov-Arnold-Moser, that is) to explain the existence of classical quasi-periodic motions within this hurricane of chaotic trajectories. The diagram resulting from the KAM theorem results in a disturbing plot that shows an almost organic structure of these classical and plottable trajectories existing like sheaths of wire or plastic, windings within windings, wherein resonance islands of order lay embedded within folds of dynamic chaos.

American mathematicians have given this model the name VAK, short for "Vague Attractor of Kolmogorov." Jeremy remembers that Vak is also the name of the goddess of vibration in the Rig-Veda.

On the night Gail first enters the hospital not for tests but to stay . . . to stay until recovered sufficiently to return home, the doctors say, but both she and Jeremy know that there will be no real return . . . Jeremy sits alone in his second-floor study and gazes at the Vague Attractor of Kolmogorov.

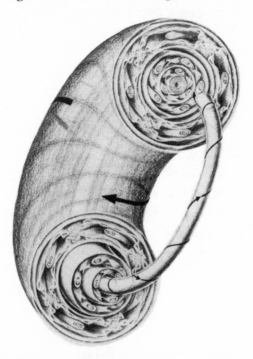

Regular quasiperiodic trajectories winding above secondary sheathings of resonances, tertiary sheathings budding in the form of more delicate multiple resonances, chaotic trajectories lashing through the organism like tangled wires.

And Jeremy sees the model for his analysis of the holographic neurological interpretation of the set of collapsing probability waves that is the universe.

He sees the beginnings of the model for the human mind . . . and for the talent that he and Gail share . . . and for the universe that has hurt her so.

And above it all the butterfly effect. The sure knowledge that the entire life of a human being is like a single day in that human's life: unplannable, unpredictable, governed by the hidden tides of chaotic factors and buffeted by butterfly wings that bring death in the form of a tumor . . . or, in Jacob's case, in the form of a bullet to the brain.

Jeremy realizes his life's ambition that evening, of discovering a profoundly new direction of mathematical reasoning and research —not for status or further academic honors, for those have been forgotten—but to advance the lighted circle of knowledge a little farther into the encroaching darkness. Islands of resonance within the chaotic sea.

But even in seeing the path of research he can take, he abandons it, tossing the abstracts and studies aside, wiping away the preliminary equations on his chalkboard. That night he stands at the window and stares out at nothing, weeping softly to himself, unable to stop, filled with neither anger nor despair, but with something infinitely more lethal as the emptiness enfolds him from within.

We Are the Stuffed Men

"Mr. Bremen? Mr. Bremen, can you hear me?"

Once, as a child of about eight, Bremen had dived into a friend's swimming pool and, instead of rising to the surface, had simply and effortlessly sunk to the bottom ten feet beneath the surface. He had lain there for a moment, feeling the rough cement against his spine and watching the ceiling of light so far above. Even as he felt his lungs tiring and watched the glory of bubbles rising around him, even as he realized that he could hold his breath no longer and would have to inhale water in a few seconds, he was loath to rise to that surface, achingly reluctant to return to that suddenly alien environment of air and light and noise. So Bremen had stayed there, stubbornly resisting recall until he could resist no longer, and then he had floated slowly to that surface, savoring the last few seconds of aquatic light and muffled noise and the silver flurry of bubbles around him.

He rose slowly now, resisting the pull back to the light.

"Mr. Bremen? Can you hear me?"

Bremen could hear him. He opened his eyes, shut them quickly at the onslaught of whiteness and light, and then, wincing, peered out from between heavy eyelids.

"Mr. Bremen? I'm Lieutenant Burchill, St. Louis Police Department."

Bremen nodded, tried to nod. His head hurt and seemed to be restrained in some way. He was in bed. White sheets. Pastel walls. The bedside trays and plastic paraphernalia of a hospital room. From his peripheral vision he could see a curtain drawn to his left, the closed doorway to his right. Another man in a gray suit stood behind the seated police lieutenant. Lieutenant Burchill was a heavyset, sallow-skinned man in his early fifties. Bremen thought that he looked a bit like Morey Amsterdam, the saggy-faced comic on the old *Dick Van Dyke Show*. The silent man behind him was younger, but his expression held the same occupational mixture of fatigue and cynicism.

"Mr. Bremen," said Burchill, "can you hear me all right?"

Bremen could hear him all right, although everything still had a once-removed, underwater quality to it. And Bremen could see *himself* through Lieutenant Burchill's eyes: wan and swaddled looking amid his blankets and bandages, left arm in a cast, his head wrapped in bandages, more bandages visible beneath the thin hospital gown, his eyes swollen and raccoon-ringed from draining blood, and fresh stitches visible beneath gauze on his chin and cheek. An IV dripped clear fluid into his left arm.

Bremen closed his eyes and tried to shut out Burchill's vision.

"Mr. Bremen, tell us what happened." The lieutenant's voice was not gentle. *Suspicion. Disbelief that this little twerp could have shot those five wise guys and landed the aircraft by himself. Curiosity about what the FBI computer said about this citizen—a college math prof, for Chrissakes—and interest in the dead wife, the arson, and this clown's connection with New Jersey's Don Leoni and his bad boys.*

Bremen cleared his throat and tried to speak. His voice was little better than a rasp. "Whermi?"

Lieutenant Burchill's expression did not change. "What was that?"

Bremen cleared his throat again. "Where am I?"

"You're in St. Louis General Hospital." Burchill paused a second and added, "Missouri."

Bremen tried to nod and regretted it. He tried to speak again without moving his jaw.

"I didn't catch that," said the lieutenant.

"Injuries?" repeated Bremen.

"Well, the doctor'll be in to see you, but from what I hear, you've got a broken arm and some bruises. Nothing life threatening."

The younger homicide detective, a sergeant named Kearny, was thinking, *Four cracked ribs, a bullet graze over one of those ribs, a concussion, and internal stuff . . . this idiot is lucky to be alive.*

"It's been about eighteen hours since the crash, Mr. Bremen. Do you remember the crash?" said Burchill.

Bremen shook his head.

"Nothing about it?"

"I remember talking to the tower about the landing gear," said Bremen. "Then the right engine started making weird noises and . . . and that's all I remember."

Burchill stared. *This asshole's probably lying, but who the hell knows? Somebody put a .45 slug right through the fuselage into the engine.*

Bremen felt the pain begin to slide in like a long, slow tide that felt no hurry to recede. Even his mindtouch and the hospital neurobabble shimmered in the wake of it. "The plane crashed, then?" he said.

Burchill continued staring. "Are you a pilot, Mr. Bremen?"

Bremen shook his head again and almost threw up from the pain.

"I'm sorry, what did you say?" asked the lieutenant.

"No."

"Any experience flying light aircraft?"

"Uh-uh."

"Then what were you doing at the yoke of that Piper Cheyenne?" Burchill's voice was as flat and unrelenting as a rapier thrust.

Bremen sighed. "Trying to land it, Lieutenant. The pilot was shot. Is he alive? Did any of the others survive?"

The thin sergeant leaned forward. "Mr. Bremen, we advised you of your rights some time ago and that Mirandizing was videotaped, but we're not sure you were completely conscious. Are you aware of those rights? Do you wish an attorney to be present at this time?"

"An attorney?" repeated Bremen. Whatever medication was in the IV drip was making his vision foggy and causing a dull roar in his ears and a fuzziness in his mindtouch. "Why'dIneed'n'torney? Didn't do anything . . ."

The sergeant let out a breath, took a laminated card from his coat pocket, and went into the Miranda litany that was so familiar from a million TV cop shows. Gail had always wondered whether police were too stupid to memorize those few lines; she said that the *audience* had them memorized.

When the sergeant finished and asked again whether Bremen wanted an attorney, Bremen moaned and said, "No. Are the others dead?"

Dead as week-old horsemeat, thought Lieutenant Burchill. The homicide detective said, "Let me ask the questions, okay, Mr. Bremen?"

Bremen closed his eyes in lieu of a nod.

"Who shot who, Mr. Bremen?"

Whom. It was Gail's voice through the fuzziness. "I shot the one named Bert with his own gun," said Bremen. "Then all hell broke loose . . . everybody except the pilot was shooting. Then the pilot was hit and I got up front and tried to land it. Obviously I didn't do too good a job."

Burchill glanced at his partner. "You flew a twin-engine turboprop with a damaged engine over a hundred miles, got it into the pattern at Lambert International, and almost landed the sucker. The tower guys say that if the right engine hadn't quit on you, you would've had it down okay. Are you *sure* you haven't flown before, Mr. Bremen?"

"I'm sure."

"Then how do you account for the—"

"Luck," said Bremen. "Desperation. I was all alone up there. Plus the controls are really sort of simple with all of the automation." *Plus reading the pilot's mind almost every second of the ten hours or so flying from Las Vegas,* added Bremen silently. *Too bad he wasn't there when I needed him.*

"Why were you in the plane, Mr. Bremen?"

"First, Lieutenant, tell me how you know my name."

Burchill stared a moment, blinked, and said, "Your fingerprints are on file."

"Really?" Bremen said stupidly. The fuzziness of the medication was less now, but the static of pain was rising. "Didn't know I'd been fingerprinted."

"Your Massachusetts driver's license," said the sergeant. His voice was as close to a monotone as a human voice could come.

"Why were you in the plane, Mr. Bremen?" said Burchill.

Bremen licked his dry lips and told them. He told them about the fishing camp in Florida, the body, Vanni Fucci . . . everything except the nightmare with Miz Morgan and his weeks in Denver. He assumed that if they had his fingerprints, they would eventually connect him to Miz Morgan's murder. That was not in the lieutenant's or sergeant's thoughts at the moment, but Bremen knew that someone would make the connections before long.

Burchill leveled his basilisk stare at him. "So they were flying you back to New Jersey so that the don himself could whack . . . could execute you. They *told* you this?"

"I picked it up from things they said. They evidently didn't mind talking in front of me . . . I guess they assumed I wasn't going to be telling anyone."

"And what about the money, Mr. Bremen?"

"Money?"

"The money in the steel attaché case." *Four hundred thousand some, schmuck. Some drug money you know something about? Maybe we're talking about a deal that went wrong at twenty thousand feet?*

Bremen just shook his head.

Sergeant Kearny leaned closer. "Do you gamble in Las Vegas very often?"

"First time," mumbled Bremen. His exhilaration at awakening still alive and relatively in one piece was being replaced by pain and a renewed emptiness. Everything was over. Everything had been over since Gail had died, but Bremen now had to acknowledge the end of his flight, his mindless, brainless, fruitless, heartless attempt to escape the inescapable.

Burchill was saying something. ". . . to get his weapon?"

Bremen filled in the rest of the lieutenant's question from the echo of mindtouch. "I grabbed Bert Cappi's pistol when he fell asleep. I guess they didn't think that I'd try anything while we were flying."

Only a madman would try something with so many guns in a light plane, thought Lieutenant Burchill. He said, "Why *did* you try it?"

Bremen made the mistake of attempting to shrug. His cast and taped ribs stopped him from completing the motion. "What was the alternative?" he rasped. "Lieutenant, I'm hurting like hell and I haven't seen a doctor or nurse yet. Can we do this later?"

Burchill looked at a small notebook in his left hand, returned his flat gaze to Bremen, and then nodded.

"Am I being charged with something?" asked Bremen. His voice was too weak to hold any real outrage. All he heard was tiredness.

Burchill's face seemed to sag into even more folds and wrinkles. The only intensity there was in the eyes; they did not miss anything. "Five men are dead, Mr. Bremen. Four of them are known criminals, and it looks as if the pilot was also connected with organized crime. Your rap sheet is clear, but there is the question of your disappearance after your wife's death . . . and the fire."

Bremen could see the shifting vectors of the lieutenant's thoughts, as ordered and precise in their way as the laser-intense concentration of the poker professionals he had been playing with less than two days before. *This guy burns his house down and disappears after his wife kicks it,* Burchill is thinking. *Then he just happens to be in Florida when Chico Tartugian is getting whacked. And then he just happens to be in Las Vegas when Chico's killer and the other Leoni boys are making a money run. Uh-huh. The pattern's not clear yet, but the elements are there—insurance money, drug money, blackmail . . . and this so-called civilian says he pulled Bert Cappi's .45 and started blazing away. Some weird shit here, but it'll sort itself out soon enough.*

"Am I being charged with something?" Bremen repeated. He felt himself sliding sideways, slipping into the haze of pained neurobabble that filled the hospital: consternation, outright fear, defiance, depression, and—from many of the visitors—guilty relief that *they* were not the ones lying in the beds with plastic bracelets on their wrists.

"Not yet," said Burchill, rising. He nodded the sergeant toward the door. "If what you say is true, Mr. Bremen, then we'll be doing some more talking soon, probably with an FBI agent present. In the meantime we'll post a guard on the room so none of Don Leoni's people can get at you." *Burchill's image of the uniformed police officer who has been posted down the hall for the past eighteen hours. This Mr. Bremen is going nowhere, either as witness or arraigned murderer or both.*

The doctor and two nurses entered as the homicide detectives left, but Bremen was fuzzy enough that he could barely concentrate on the man's terse medical chatter. He learned what Burchill's eyes had already told him—learned also that the compound fracture of the left arm was more serious than the lieutenant had known—but the rest was detail.

Bremen let himself slide away into emptiness.

EYES

At the moment Jeremy is lying in the St. Louis hospital, I am mere hours away from watching my carefully constructed universe collapse forever. I do not know this.

I do not know that Jeremy is lying in the hospital. I do not know that Gail exists or has ever existed. I do not know the paradise of shared experience or the perfect hell that this ability has brought Jeremy.

At this moment I know only the continued pain of existence and the difficulty of fleeing from it. At this moment I know only the despair of separation from the one thing that has given me solace in the past.

At this moment I am dying . . . but I am also hours away from being born.

Sightless, Unless

Bremen dreamed of ice and bodies writhing in the ice.

He dreamed of a great beast rendering flesh, and of terrible cries rising from a sulfurous night. Bremen dreamed of a thousand thousand voices calling to him in pain and terror and the loneliness of human despair, and when he awoke, the voices were still there: the neurobabble of a modern hospital filled with suffering souls.

All that day Bremen lay abed, rode the waves of pain from his injuries, and thought about what he might do next. Nothing much came to mind.

Detective Burchill returned in the early afternoon with the promised FBI special agent, but Bremen feigned sleep and the two acceded to the head nurse's insistence and left after half an hour. Bremen did sleep then, and his dreams were of ice and writhing bodies in the ice and of cries from the pain-racked darkness around him.

When he awoke again later that night, Bremen focused his mindtouch through the babble and rasp to find the uniformed officer left to guard him. Patrolman Duane B. Everett was forty-eight, seven months away from retirement, and suffered from hemorrhoids, fallen arches, insomnia, and what his doctors had called irritable bowel syndrome. This did not stop Patrolman Everett from drinking as much coffee as he wanted, although it meant long trips to the rest room on this floor. Patrolman Everett didn't mind alternating this guard duty with the other two officers working eight-hour shifts, nor did he mind taking the graveyard shift. It was quiet at night, it allowed him to read his Robert B. Parker novel, he could banter with the nurses, and there was always fresh coffee in the lounge he was allowed to use.

It was almost sunrise. Alone now in his room except for the comatose patient in the next bed, Bremen rose painfully, pulled the IV drip free, and hobbled to the window. He sat there a moment, the cold draft from the air-conditioning vent chilling him under his thin gown, and stared out the window.

If he was leaving, he should leave now. They had cut away his clothes after pulling him from the wrecked Piper Cheyenne—Bremen had seen through one of the emergency-room medics' eyes that they considered it a miracle that there had been no fire after the plane plowed into a muddy field half a mile from the airport—but Bremen knew where there were extra clothes that would fit him. He would just have to get to the interns' locker room down one flight of stairs.

He also knew from his eavesdropping that day which of the interns kept their car keys in which lockers . . . and what the combinations for those lockers were. Bremen had decided to "borrow" an almost new and fueled-up Volvo belonging to an intern named Bradley Montrose; Bradley was an emergency-room intern and probably would not notice that his Volvo was gone until he got off duty seventy-two hours from now.

Bremen leaned back against the wall and groaned slightly. His arm hurt like hell, his head ached with an improbable ferocity, his ribs felt as if splinters of broken bone were pressing against his lungs, and there were countless other pains queuing up to get his attention. Even the bites on his hip and thigh from Miz Morgan's ranch had not yet healed completely.

Can I do this? Get to the clothes? Drive the car? Stay ahead of the cops?

Probably.

Are you really going to steal the six hundred dollars in Bradley's wallet?

Probably. His mother will make up the difference before Bradley has time to tell the cops what happened.

Do you know where the fuck you're going?

No.

Bremen sighed and opened his eyes. Through the small part in the curtains here he could see the head and shoulders of the dying kid who shared his room. The boy looked terrible, although Bremen understood from the nurses' and doctors' thoughts during the day that not all of the child's dismal appearance was from his injuries. The boy—Robby something—had been blind, deaf, and retarded even before the assault that had brought him here.

Part of Bremen's nightmare that afternoon had been an echo of the anger and disgust from one of the nurses who took extra care in watching over Robby. The boy had been brought in after being discovered in an outhouse pit across the river in East St. Louis. Three boys playing in an abandoned field had heard weird cries coming from the outhouse and had told their parents. By the time paramedics had removed Robby from the flooded pit of feces, authorities estimated, the boy had been lying there for more than two days. He had been beaten viciously and the prognosis for his survival was poor. The nurse found herself weeping for Robby . . . and praying to Jesus that he would die soon.

As far as the nurses or doctors knew, the police had not found the boy's mother or stepfather. The doctor in charge of Robby did not think that the authorities were looking very hard.

Bremen set his cheek against the glass and thought about the boy. He thought about the terminally ill children he had seen in Walt Disney World and of the brief peace he had given some of them with the help of his mindtouch. During his entire purposeless, self-centered flight from himself, those few minutes were the only time that he had *helped* anyone, *done* anything except feel sorry for himself. He remembered those moments now and glanced over at Robby.

The boy lay half-uncovered on his side, his face and upper body illuminated by the medical monitors above his head. Robby's clawlike hands were curled in bizarre contortions above the sheets, his wrists so thin that they looked strangely lizardlike. The boy's head was tilted in a disturbing way, his tongue lolling from between pulped lips. His face was mottled and bruised, the nose obviously broken and flattened, but Bremen suspected that the eye sockets, which appeared the most damaged part of Robby's face, had always looked this way—sunken, blackened, with heavy lids only half covering the useless white marbles of the eyes.

Robby was unconscious. Bremen had picked up nothing from the boy—not even pain dreams—and had been shocked to learn from the nurses' thoughts that there was another patient in the room. It was the most absence of neurobabble that Bremen had ever felt from another human being. Robby was just a void, although Bremen knew from the doctors' thoughts that the monitors showed continuing brain activity. In fact, the EEG tracks showed very active REM activity—a busy dream sleep. Bremen was at a loss why he could not pick up the boy's dreams.

As if aware of being observed, Robby twitched in his sleep. His black hair rose from his skull in random tufts that Bremen might have found amusing in other circumstances. The dying boy's breath rasped out between the damaged lips in a coarse rasping that was not quite a snore, and Bremen could smell it from eight feet away.

Bremen shook his head and looked out at the night, feeling the broken-glass pain of things in the way that substituted for tears with him.

*Don't wait for Burchill and the FBI man to come back in the
morning with questions about Miz Morgan's murder. Get out now.*

And go where?

Worry about that later. Just get the fuck out.

Bremen sighed. He would leave later, before the morning shift
came in and the hospital got busy. He would take the intern's
Volvo and continue his quest to nowhere, arriving nowhere, wishing to be nowhere. He would continue to suffer life.

Bremen glanced back at the boy in the bed. Something about
the child's posture and oversized head reminded him of a broken,
bronze Buddha, tumbled from its pedestal, which Bremen and
Gail had seen once in a monastery near Osaka. This child had
been blind, deaf, and brain-damaged since *birth*. What if Robby
harbored some deep wisdom born of his long seclusion from the
world?

Robby twitched, yellowed fingernails scrabbling slightly against
the sheets, farted loudly, and resumed his snores.

Bremen sighed, slid back the curtains, and moved to a chair
next to the boy's bed.

*Patrolman Everett will be visiting the john in about three minutes.
The floor nurses are preparing medications and the station nurse can't
see me if I take the back stairs. Bradley's in ER and the locker room
probably will be empty for another hour.*

Do it.

Bremen nodded to himself, fighting the pain and the painkiller
fatigue. He would drive north toward Chicago and then into Canada, find a place to rest up and recuperate . . . someplace where
neither the police nor Don Leoni's people would ever find him. He
would use the mindtouch ability to stay ahead of them and to
make money . . . but not by gambling . . . no more gambling.

Bremen looked up at the boy again.

There's no time for this.

Yes, there was. It would not take long. He need not even estab-
lish full contact. A one-way mindtouch would do it. It was possible. A moment of contact, even a few seconds, and he could share

light and sound with the dying child. Perhaps go to the window and look at the traffic below, the lights of the city, find a star.

Bremen knew that such reciprocal mindtouch was possible—not just with Gail, although that had been effortless—but with anyone who was receptive. And most people were receptive to a determined mindtouch probe, although Bremen had never known anyone but Gail who could control their latent telepathic abilities. The only problem was making sure that the person did not *feel* the mindtouch as mindtouch, did not become aware that the alien thoughts were actually alien. Once, after days of inability to convey the meaning of a simple calculus transform to a slow student, Bremen had just *given* it to him via mindtouch and left the student to congratulate himself on his insight.

There need be no subtlety with this child. And no content. A few shared sensory impressions would be Bremen's parting gift. Anonymous. Robby would never know who had shared these images.

Robby's snore caught, stopped for an agonizingly long time, and then started up again like a balky engine. He was drooling heavily. The pillowcase and sheet near his face were moist.

Bremen decided, and lowered his mindshield. *Hurry, Patrolman Everett will be headed toward the bathroom any minute.* The remnants of his mindshield went down and the full force of the world's neurobabble rushed in like water into a sinking ship.

Bremen flinched and raised his mindshield. It had been a long time since he had allowed himself to be so vulnerable. Even though the neurobabble always got through anyway, the volume and intensity was almost unbearable without the woolly blanket of the shield. The hospital neurobabble cut directly at the soft tissue of his bruised mind.

He gritted his teeth against the pain and tried again. Bremen tried to tune out the broad spectrum of neurobabble and concentrate on the space where Robby's dreams should be.

Nothing.

For a confused second Bremen thought that he had lost the

focus of his power. Then he concentrated and was able to pick out the urgency of Patrolman Everett as he hurried toward the rest room and the preoccupied fragments of Nurse Tulley as she compared med dosages between Dr. Angstrom's list and the pink sheets on the tray. He focused on the nurse at the monitor station and saw that she was reading a novel—*Needful Things* by Stephen King. It frustrated him that her eyes scanned so slowly. His mouth filled with the syrupy taste of her cherry cough drop.

Bremen shook his head and stared at Robby. The boy's asthmatic breathing filled the air between them with a sour fog. Robby's tongue was visible and heavily coated. Bremen narrowed his mindtouch to the shape of blunt probe, strengthened it, focused it like a beam of coherent light.

Nothing.

No . . . there was—what?—an *absence* of something.

There was an actual hole in the field of mindbabble where Robby's dreams should have been. Bremen realized that he was confronting the strongest and most subtle mindshield he had ever encountered. Even Miz Morgan's hurricane of white noise had not created a barrier of such incredible tightness, and at no time had she been able to hide the *presence* of her thoughts. Robby's thoughts were simply *not there*.

For a second Bremen was shaken, but then he realized the cause of this phenomenon. Robby's mind was damaged. Entire segments were probably inactive. With so few senses to rely on and such a limited awareness of his environment, with so little access to the universe of probability waves to choose from and almost no ability to choose from them, the boy's consciousness—or what passed for consciousness for the child—had turned violently inward. What first had seemed to Bremen to be a powerful mindshield was nothing more than a tight ball of turning-inwardness going beyond autism or catatonia. Robby was truly and totally alone in there.

Bremen took a breath and resumed his probe, using more care this time, feeling along the negative boundaries of the de facto mindshield like a man groping along a rough wall in the dark. Somewhere there had to be an opening.

There was. Not an opening so much as a soft spot—the slightest resilience set amid solid stone.

Bremen half perceived a flutter of underlying thoughts now, much as a pedestrian senses the movement of subway trains under a pavement. He concentrated on building the strength of his probe until he felt his hospital gown beginning to soak through with sweat. His vision and hearing were beginning to dim in the single-minded exertion of his effort. It did not matter. Once initial contact was made, he would relax and slowly open the channels of sight and sound.

He felt the wall give a bit, still elastic but sinking slightly under his unrelenting force of will. Bremen concentrated until the veins stood out in his temples. Unknown to himself, he was grimacing, neck muscles knotting with the strain. The wall bent. Bremen's probe was a solid ram battering a tight but gelatinous doorway.

It bent further.

Bremen concentrated with enough force to move objects, to pulverize bricks, to halt birds in their flight.

The accidental mindshield continued to bend. Bremen leaned forward as if into a strong wind. There was no neurobabble now, no awareness of the hospital or himself; there was only the force of Bremen's will.

Suddenly there came ripping, a rush of warmth, and a falling forward. Bremen flailed his arms and opened his mouth to yell.

He had no mouth.

Bremen was falling, both in his body and out. He was tumbling head over heels into a darkness where the floor had been only a moment before. He had a distant, confused glimpse of his own body writhing in the grip of some terrible seizure, and then he was falling again.

He was falling into silence.

Falling into nothing.

Nothing.

EYES I

Jeremy is inside. He is diving through layers of slow thermals. Colorless pinwheels tumble past him in three dimensions.

Spheres of black collapse outward and blind him. There are waterfalls of touch, rivulets of scent, and a thin line of balance blowing in a silent wind.

Jeremy finds himself supported by a thousand unseen hands—touching, exploring. There are fingers against his lips, palms along his chest, smooth hands sliding along his belly, fingers cup his penis as impersonally as in a doctor's exam and then move on.

Suddenly he is underwater, no, buried in something thicker than water. He cannot breathe. Desperately he begins to flail his arms and legs against the viscous current until he has a sensation of moving upward. There is no light, no sense of direction except the slightest sense of gravity compelling *downward,* but Jeremy paddles against the resisting gel around him and fights against that gravity, knowing that to remain where he is means being buried alive.

Suddenly the substance shifts and Jeremy is jerked upward by a vacuum that grips his head like a vise. He is compacted, compressed, squeezed so tightly that he is sure his damaged ribs and skull are being shattered again, and then suddenly he feels himself propelled through the constricting aperture and his head breaks the surface.

Jeremy opens his mouth to scream and air rushes into his chest like water filling a drowning man. His scream goes on and on, and when it dies, there are no echoes.

Jeremy awakens on a broad plain.

It is neither day nor night. Pale, peach-colored light diffuses everything. The ground is hard and scaled into separate orange segments that seem to recede to infinity. There is no horizon. Jeremy thinks that the serrated land looks like a floodplain during a drought.

Above him there is no sky, only levels of peach-lit crystal. Jeremy imagines that it is like being in the basement of a clear plastic skyscraper. An empty one. He lies on his back and stares up through endless stories of crystallized emptiness.

Eventually, Jeremy sits up and takes stock of himself. He is naked. His skin feels as if he has been toweled with sandpaper. He rubs a hand across his stomach, touches his shoulders and arms and face, but it is a full minute before he realizes that there are no wounds or scars—not the broken arm, or the bullet graze or the broken ribs, or the bite marks on his hip and inner thigh, or—as far as he can make out—the concussion or lacerations to his face. For a mad second Jeremy thinks that he is in a body other than his own, but then he looks down and sees the scar on his knee from the motorcycle accident when he was seventeen, the mole on the inside of his upper arm.

A wave of dizziness rolls through him as he stands upright.

Sometime later Jeremy begins walking. His bare feet find the smooth plates warm. He has no direction and no destination. Once, at Miz Morgan's ranch, he had walked out onto a wide expanse of salt flats just at sunset. This is a little like that . . . but not much.

Step on a crack, break your mother's back.

Jeremy walks for some time, although time has little meaning here on this orange plain with no sun. The peach-colored levels above him neither shift nor shimmer. Eventually he stops, and when he stops, it is in a place no different than the one where he began. His head hurts. He lies on his back again, feeling the smoothness under him—more like sunbaked plastic than the grit of sand or stone—and as he lies there he imagines that he is some bottom-dwelling sea creature looking up through layers of shifting currents.

The bottom of the swimming pool. So achingly reluctant to return to the light.

Peach-colored light bathes Jeremy in warmth. His body is radiant. He shuts his eyes against the light. And sleeps.

He comes awake suddenly, totally, nostrils flaring, his ears actually twitching with the strain of trying to pinpoint a half-heard sound. The darkness is total.

Something is moving in the night.

Jeremy crouches in the blackness and tries to filter out the sound of his own ragged breathing. His glandular system has reverted to programming more than a million years old. He is ready to flee or fight, but the total and inexplicable darkness eliminates the former. He prepares to fight. His fists clench, his heart races, and his eyes strain to see.

Something is moving in the night.

He feels it nearby. He feels the power and the weight of it through the ground. The thing is huge, its footsteps send tremors through the ground and Jeremy's body, and it is coming closer. Jeremy is certain that the thing has no trouble finding its way in the darkness. And it can see *him*.

Then the thing is near him, above him, and Jeremy can feel the force of its gaze. He kneels on the suddenly cold ground and hugs himself into a ball.

Something touches him.

Jeremy fights down the impulse to scream. He is caught in a giant's hand—something rough and huge and not a hand at all—and suddenly he is lifted high into the blackness. Again Jeremy feels the power of the thing, this time through the pressure on his pinned arms and creaking ribs, and he is sure it could crush him easily if it so wishes. Evidently it does not so wish. At least not yet.

He feels the sense of being viewed, inspected, weighed on some unseen balance scale. Jeremy has the helpless but somehow reassuring feeling of total passivity one feels while lying naked on an X-ray table, knowing that invisible beams are passing through one's body, searching for malignancy, probing for decay and the seeds of death.

Something sets him down.

Jeremy hears no sound but his own ragged panting, but he can feel the great footsteps receding. Impossibly, they are receding in all directions, like ripples in a pond. A weight lifts from him and he discovers to his own horror that he is sobbing.

Later, he uncurls and gets to his feet. He calls into the blackness, but the sound of his voice is tiny and lost and later he is not even sure whether he had heard it himself.

Exhausted, still sobbing, Jeremy pounds the ground and continues to weep. The blackness is the same whether his eyelids are closed or not, and later, when he sleeps, he dreams only of darkness.

EYES I DARE

The sun is rising.

Jeremy's eyes flutter open, he stares into the distant brilliance, and he closes his eyes again before the fact fully registers.

The sun is rising.

Jeremy jerks awake and sits up, blinking at the sunrise. He is lying on grass. A prairie of soft, knee-high grass expands to the horizon in all directions. The sky is a deep violet fading to blue as the sun climbs clear of the horizon. Jeremy sits up and his shadow leaps across grasses stirring softly in the morning breeze. The air is filled with scents: grass, moist earth, sun-warmed soil, and the hint of his own skin scent touched by the breeze.

Jeremy goes to one knee, plucks a strand of the tall grass, strips it, and sucks on the sweet marrow. It reminds him of childhood afternoons spent playing in grassy fields. He begins walking toward the sunrise.

The breeze is warm against his bare skin. It stirs up the grass and sets up a soft sighing that helps ease the headache that throbs behind his eyes. The simple act of walking pleases him. He is content with the feel of grass bending under his bare feet and the play of sunlight on his body.

By the time the sun is far enough beyond the zenith to suggest early afternoon, he realizes that he is walking toward a smudge on the horizon. By late afternoon the smudge has resolved itself into a line of trees. He enters the edge of the forest just before sunset.

The trees here are the stately elms and oaks of Jeremy's Pennsylvania boyhood. He pauses just inside the woods and looks out at the gently rolling plain he has just left; the evening sunlight is burnishing the rippling grass with gold and igniting coronas around the countless tassels atop the stalks. Jeremy's shadow leaps ahead of him as he turns and moves deeper into the forest.

For the first time fatigue and thirst begin to work on him now. Jeremy's tongue is thick and swollen with dryness. He stumbles leadenly along through lengthening shadows, dreaming of tall glasses of water and checking the visible patches of sky for any sign of clouds. It is while he is looking up for a glimpse of the darkening sky that he almost stumbles into the pond.

The circle of water lies within a low ring of weeds and reeds. A cluster of cherry trees on the higher banks sends roots down to the water. Jeremy takes the last few steps toward the pond with the agonizing conviction that he is viewing a mirage in the dim light, that the water will disappear even as he throws himself forward into it.

It is waist-deep and as cold as ice.

She comes just after sunrise the next morning.

Jeremy has breakfasted on cherries and cold water and is just in the process of stepping out into a clearing to the east of the pond when he spots the movement. Not believing, he stands perfectly still, just another shadow in the shade of the tree line.

She moves hesitantly, placing her feet amid the high grass and low stones with the tentative step of the meek or the barefoot. The tasseled saw grass of the clearing brushes at her bare thighs. Jeremy observes her with a clarity amplified by the rich, horizontal sweep of morning light. Her body seems to glow, to radiate rather than absorb that light. Her breasts, the left ever so slightly fuller than the right, bob gently with each high step. Her dark hair is cut short and stirs when the breeze touches it.

She pauses in the center of the clearing and then comes forward again. Jeremy's gaze drops to her strong thighs as she walks, and he watches as they part and close with the heart-stopping intimacy of the unobserved. She is much closer now, and Jeremy can make out the delicate shadows along her fine rib cage, the pale, pink circles of areolae, and the faded old appendix scar along the lower cusp of her belly.

Jeremy steps out into the light. She stops, arms rising across her upper body in a motion of instinctive modesty, and then she moves quickly toward him. She opens her arms and he steps into their closing circle, setting his face against her neck and being almost overcome by the clean scent of her hair and skin. His hands move across muscle and the familiar terrain of vertebrae. Each of them is touching and kissing the other almost frantically. Both are sobbing.

Jeremy feels the strength go out of his legs and he goes to one knee. She bends slightly and cradles his face between her breasts. Not for a second do they relax the pressure binding them together.

"Why did you leave me?" he whispers against her skin, unable to stop the tears. "Why did you go away?"

Gail says nothing. Her cheek is against his hair as her hands tighten against his back. Wordlessly, she kneels with him in the high grass.

EYES I DARE NOT

Together they pass out of the forest just as the morning mists are burning away. In the rich light the grassy hillsides beyond the woods give the impression of being part of a tanned and velvety human torso. Gail reaches out one hand as if to stroke the distant hills.

They speak softly, occasionally intertwining fingers. They have discovered that full mindtouch brings on the blinding headaches that have plagued each of them since awakening, so they talk . . . and touch . . . and make love in the soft grass with only the golden eye of the sun watching them. Afterward, they hold each other and whisper small things, each knowing that mindtouch is possible through means other than telepathy.

Later, they walk on, and in midafternoon they cross a rise and look past a small orchard at a vertical glare of white clapboard.

"The farm!" cries Gail, wonder in her voice. "How can it be?"

Jeremy feels no surprise. His equilibrium remains as they pass the barn and other outbuildings and approach the farmhouse itself. The building is silent but intact, with no signs of fire or disturbance. The driveway still needs new gravel, but now it goes nowhere, for there is no highway at the end of it. The long row of wire fence that used to parallel the road now borders only more high grass and another gentle hillside. There is no sign of the neighbors' distant homes or of the intrusive power lines that had been set in behind the orchard.

Gail steps onto the back porch and peers in the window with the slightly guilty manner of a weekend house browser who has found a home that might or might not still be lived in. She opens the screen door and jumps a bit as the hinge squeaks.

"Sorry," says Jeremy. "I know I promised to oil that."

It is cool inside, and dark. The rooms are as they had left them —not as Jeremy had left them after his weeks of solitude while Gail was in the hospital—but as they had left them before their first visit to the specialist that autumn a year ago, an eternity ago. Upstairs, the afternoon sunlight falls from the skylight he and Gail had wrestled to install that distant August. Jeremy pokes his head into the study and sees the chaos abstracts still stacked on the oak desk and a long-forgotten transform still scrawled on the chalk-board.

Gail goes from room to room, sometimes making small noises of appreciation, more often just touching things gently. The bed-room is as orderly as ever, the blue blanket pulled tight and her grandmother's patchwork quilt folded across the foot of the bed.

After making love again, they fall asleep between the cool sheets. Occasionally a wisp of breeze billows the curtains. Gail turns and mumbles in her sleep, frequently reaching out to touch him. Bremen awakes just after dark, although the sky outside the bedroom window holds the lingering twilight of late summer.

There has been a sound downstairs.

Jeremy lies motionless for a full moment, trying not to disturb the stillness even by breathing. For the time being no breeze stirs. He hears a sound.

Jeremy slides from the bed without waking Gail. She is curled on her side with one hand lifted to her cheek; she is smiling ever so slightly. Jeremy walks barefoot to the study, crosses to his desk, and carefully opens the lower right-hand drawer. It is there, wrapped in old rags, under the empty folders he had laid atop it the day his brother-in-law had given it to him. The .38 Smith & Wesson is the same one Jeremy had thrown into the water that morning when he had come across Vanni Fucci in Florida—the nick in the stock and dullness along the lower part of the barrel is the same—but it is here now. He lifts it, breaks the cylinder, and sees the brass circles of the six cartridges firmly in place. The roughened grip is firm against his palm, the metal of the trigger guard slightly cool.

Jeremy tries to make no sound as he moves from the study to the head of the stairway, from the stairway through the dining room to the door to the kitchen. It is very dim, but his eyes have adapted. From where he stands he can make out the pale white phantom of the refrigerator and he jumps when its recycling pump chunks on. Jeremy lowers the revolver to his side again and waits.

The screen door is slightly ajar and now it swings open and then closed again. A shadow slips across the tile.

The movement startles Jeremy and he takes a step forward and lifts the .38 a second before he lowers it again. Gernisavien, the tough-minded little calico, crosses the floor to brush against his legs impatiently. Then she twitches her tail, paces back to the refrigerator, looks up at Jeremy meaningfully, and crosses back to brush against him with even less patience.

Jeremy kneels to rub her neck. The pistol looks idiotic in his hand. Taking a long breath, he sets the weapon on the kitchen counter and uses both hands to pet his cat.

The moon is rising the next evening by the time they have a late dinner. Electric lights in the house do not work, but all other electricity seems to be flowing. The steaks come from the freezer in the basement, the ice-cold beers from the refrigerator, and the charcoal from one of several bags left in the garage. They sit out back near the old pump while the steaks sizzle on the grill.

Gernisavien crouches expectantly at the foot of one of the big, old wooden lawn chairs despite the fact that she has been well fed only moments earlier.

Jeremy is wearing his favorite pair of cotton chinos and his light blue work shirt; Gail has slipped into the loose, white cotton dress she often wears on trips. The sounds tonight are the same they have heard from this backyard so many times before: crickets, night birds from the orchard, variations of frog sounds from the darkness near the stream, and an occasional flutter of sparrows from the barn. They set one of their two kerosene lanterns on the picnic table as they prepare the meal, and Gail lights candles as well. Later, as they eat, they douse the lantern so as to better see the stars.

Jeremy has served the steaks on thick paper plates and their knives make crisscross patterns on the white. Their meal consists of the steaks, wine from the still-well-stocked basement, and a simple salad from the garden with ample fresh radishes and onions.

Even with the crescent moon rising, the stars are incredibly clear. Jeremy remembers the night they had lain out in the hammock together and waited to catch a glimpse of the space shuttle floating across the sky like a windblown ember. He realizes that the stars are even clearer tonight because there are no reflected lights from Philadelphia or the tollway to dim the sky's glory.

Gail leans forward even before the meal is finished. *Where are we, Jerry?* Her mindtouch is as gentle as possible so as not to bring on the headaches.

Jeremy takes a sip of wine. "What's wrong with just being home, kiddo?"

There's nothing wrong with being home. But where are *we?*

Jeremy concentrates on turning a radish in his fingers. It had tasted salty and cool.

Gail looks toward the dark line of trees at the edge of the orchard. Fireflies blink there. *What is this place?*

Gail, what's the last thing you remember?

"I remember dying," she says softly.

The words hit Jeremy like a blow to the solar plexus. For a moment he cannot frame his thoughts.

Gail continues, although her soft voice is husky. "We've never believed in an afterlife, Jerry." *Uncle Buddy* . . . *"After we're dead we help the grass and flowers grow, Beanie. Everything else is a crock of shit."*

"No, no, kiddo," says Jeremy, and moves his dish and glass aside. He leans forward and touches her arm. "There's another explanation. . . ." Before he can begin it, the floodgates give way and they are inundated with the images he has held from her: *burning the house . . . the fishing shack in Florida . . . Vanni Fucci . . . the dead days on the streets of Denver . . . Miz Morgan and the cold house . . .*

"Oh, Jerry, my God . . . my God . . ." Gail has recoiled in her seat and now covers her face with her hands.

Jeremy comes around the table, grips her upper arms firmly, and lowers his cheek to hers. *Miz Morgan . . . the steel teeth . . . the cold house . . . the anesthesia of poker . . . the flight east with Don Leoni's thugs . . . the hospital . . . the dying child . . . a moment's contact . . . falling.*

"Oh, Jerry!" Gail sobs against his shoulder. She has suffered his months of hell in a violent moment of pain. She is suffering his own grief and the echoed insanity of that grief. Now they weep together for a moment. Then Jeremy kisses her tears away, wipes her face with the loose tail of his work shirt, and moves away to pour them each some more wine.

Where are we, Jerry?

He hands her a glass and takes a moment to sip from his. Insects chorus from out behind the barn. Their home glows pale in the moonlight, the kitchen windows warm with the light from their other kerosene lantern inside. He whispers, "What do you remember about waking up here, kiddo?"

They have already shared some of the images, but trying to put it into words sharpens their memories. "Darkness," whispers Gail.

"Then the soft light. The empty place. *Rocking. Being rocked. Being held.* And then walking. The sunrise. Finding you."

Jeremy nods. He runs his finger around the rim of the wineglass. *I think we're with Robby. The boy. I think we're in his mind.*

Gail's head snaps back as if she has been slapped. *The blind boy . . . ????????* She looks around her and then extends a shaking hand toward the table. She grips the edge tightly and the glasses vibrate. When she lets go, it is only to raise her hand to touch her own cheek. "Then nothing here is real? We're in a dream?" *I'm really dead and you're only dreaming that I'm here?*

"No," says Jeremy loudly enough that Gernisavien moves quickly under a chair. He can see her tail twitching in the soft light from candles and stars. "No," he says more softly, "that's not it. I'm *sure* that's not it. Remember Jacob's research?"

Gail is too shaken to speak aloud. *Yes.* Even her mindtouch is tiny, almost lost in the low night sounds.

Well, continues Jeremy, holding her attention with the force of his will, *you remember then that Jacob was sure that my analysis was correct . . . that the human personality was a complex standing wavefront . . . a sort of metahologram holding a few million smaller holograms. . . .*

Jerry, I don't see how this can help—

"Damn it, kiddo, it *does* help!" He leans closer again and rubs her upper arms, feeling the goose bumps there. "Listen, please. . . ."

Okay.

"If Jacob and I were right . . . that the personality is this complex wavefront which interprets a reality consisting of collapsing probability wavefronts, then the personality certainly couldn't survive brain death. The mind may work as both generator and interferometer all in one, but both of those functions would be extinguished with the death of the brain. . . ."

Then how . . . how can I . . . ?

He sits next to her again, keeping one arm firmly around her. Gernisavien comes out from under the chair and jumps on Gail's lap, eager to share their warmth. They both keep one hand busy petting the calico while Jeremy continues talking softly.

"Okay, let's just think about this a minute. You weren't just a memory or a sense impression to me, kiddo. For over nine years we were essentially one person with two bodies. That's why when you . . . that's why I went crazy afterward, tried to shut my ability down completely. Only I couldn't do it. It's as if I was tuned to darker and darker wavelengths of human thought, just spiraling down through . . ."

Gail glances up from petting Gernisavien. She looks fearfully at the darkness down by the stream. *The dark under the bed.* "But how can it be so real if it's just a dream?"

Jeremy touches her cheek. "Gail, it's *not* just a dream. Listen. You were in my mind, but not just as a memory. You were *there.* The night you . . . that night when I was at Barnegat Light . . . the night your body died . . . you *joined* me, you leaped to my mind as if it were a lifeboat."

No, how could . . .

"Think, Gail. Our ability was working well. It was the ultimate mindtouch. That complex hologram that's *you* didn't have to perish . . . you just leaped to the only other interferometer in the universe that could contain it . . . *my* mind. Only my ego sense or id or superego or whatever the hell keeps us sane and separate from all the barrage of our senses, not to mention separating us from the babble of all those minds, that part of me kept telling me that I was only sensing a *memory* of you."

They sat in silence for a moment, each remembering. *Big Two-Hearted River,* offered Gail. Jeremy could see that she did remember fragments of the time he was at the Florida fishing camp.

"You were a figment of my imagination," he said aloud, "but only in the way that our own personalities are figments of our own imaginations." *Probability waves collapsing on a beach of pure space-time. Schrödinger curves, their plots speaking in a language purer than speech. Vague Attractors of Kolmogorov winding around resonance islands of quasi-periodic sanity amid foaming layers of chaos.*

"Think in a human language," whispers Gail. She pinches his side.

Jeremy jumps away from the pinch, smiles, and holds the cat down as it prepares to leap away. "I mean," he says softly, "that we were both dead until a blind, deaf, retarded child ripped us out of one world and offered us another in its place."

Gail frowns slightly. The candles have burned out, but her white dress and pale skin continue to glow in the starlight and moonlight. "You mean we're in Robby's mind and it's as real as the real world?" She frowns again at the sound of that.

He shakes his head. "Not quite. When I broke through to Robby, I tapped into a closed system. The poor bastard had almost no data to use in constructing a model of the real world . . . touch, I guess, scent, and a hell of a lot of pain, from what the nurses knew about his past . . . so he probably didn't depend much on what little he could sense of the external world in defining his interior universe."

Gernisavien leaped away and trotted off into the darkness as if she had urgent business somewhere. Knowing cats, Gail and Jeremy both guessed that she did. Jeremy also could stay still no longer; he stood and began pacing back and forth in the dark, never getting so far from Gail that he could not reach out and touch her.

My mistake, he continued, *was in underestimating . . . no, in never really* thinking *about the power that Robby might have in that world.* This *world. When I broke through to him . . . planning just to share a few sight and sound images . . . he pulled me in, kiddo. And with me, you.*

The wind comes up a bit and moves the leaves of the orchard. Their soft rustling has the edge of a sad, end-of-summer sound to it.

"All right," Gail says after a moment. "We're both existing as a couple of your squiggly personality holograms in this child's mind." She taps the table hard. "And it feels *real.* But why is our house here? And the garage? And . . ." She gestures helplessly at the night around them and the stars overhead.

I think Robby liked what he saw in our minds, kiddo. I think he preferred our polluted old Pennsylvania countryside to the landscape he'd built for himself during his lonely years.

Gail nods slowly. "But it's not really our countryside, is it? I mean, we can't drive into Philadelphia in the morning, right? Chuck Gilpen's not going to show up with one of his new girl-friends, is he?"

I don't know, kiddo. I don't think so. My guess is that there's been some judicious editing going on. We're "real" because our holographic structure is intact, but all the rest of this is an artifact that Robby allows.

Gail rubs her arms again. *An artifact that Robby allows. You make him sound like God, Jerry.*

He clears his throat and glances skyward. The stars are still there. "Well," he whispers, "in a real sense he is God right now. At least for us."

Gail's thoughts are scurrying like the field mice that Gernisavien is probably out chasing. "All right, he's God, and I'm alive, and we're both here . . . but what do we do *now,* Jerry?"

We go to bed, sent Jeremy, and he took her hand and led her into their home.

EYES I DARE NOT MEET

Jeremy dreams of rocking back and forth in a darkness deeper than his dream can convey; he dreams of sleeping with mildewed blankets against his cheek, of rough wool against lacerated skin, and of being struck by unseen hands. He dreams of lying broken and battered in a pit full of human shit while rain drips on his upturned face. He dreams of drowning.

In Jeremy's dream he is watching with growing curiosity as two people make love on a golden hillside. He floats through a white room where people have no shape, are only voices, and where the voice-bodies shimmer to the heartbeat of an invisible machine.

He is swimming and can feel the tug of inexorable planetary forces in the pull of the riptide. Jeremy is just able to resist the deadly current by exerting all of his energy, but he can feel himself tiring, can feel the tide pulling him out to deeper water. Just as the waves close over him he vents a final shout of despair and loss.

He cries out his own name.

o   o   o

Jeremy awakes with the shout still echoing in his mind. The details of the dream fracture and flee before he can grasp them. He sits up quickly in bed. Gail is gone.

He has almost reached the door of their bedroom before he hears her voice calling to him from the side yard. He returns to the window.

She is dressed in a blue smock and is waving her arms at him. By the time he is downstairs she has thrown half a dozen items into their old wicker basket and is boiling water to make iced tea. "Come on, sleepyhead," she says, grinning at him. "I have a surprise for you."

"I'm not sure we need any more surprises," he mumbles. Gernisavien is back and moving between their legs, occasionally rubbing up against a chair leg as if offering affection to the chair.

"*This* one we do," she says, and is upstairs, humming and thrashing around in the closet.

"Let me shower and get some coffee," he says, and stops. *Where does the water come from?* The electric lights had not been working yesterday, but the taps had all functioned.

Before he can ponder the question further, Gail is back in the kitchen and handing him the picnic basket. "No shower. No coffee. Come on."

Gernisavien follows reluctantly as Gail leads them up and over the hill where the highway once had been. They cross meadows to the east and then climb a final hill that is steeper than any he can remember in this part of Pennsylvania. At the summit Jeremy lets the picnic basket drop from a suddenly nerveless hand.

"Holy shit," he whispers.

In the valley where the turnpike had been there is now an ocean.

"Holy shit," he says again softly, almost reverently.

It is the curve of beach so familiar to them from their trips to Barnegat Light along the New Jersey shore, but now there is no lighthouse, no island, and the coastline stretching north and south looks more like some remote stretch of cliffs along the Pacific than any rim of the Atlantic that Jeremy has ever seen. The hillside they have been climbing was actually the rear slope of a mountain that drops off several hundred feet on its east side to the beach and breakers below. The rocky summit they are standing on seems strangely familiar to Jeremy, and recognition slowly dawns.

Big Slide Mountain, confirms Gail. *Our honeymoon.*

Jeremy nods. His mouth is still open. He does not find it necessary to remind her that Big Slide Mountain had been in the New York Adirondacks, hundreds of miles from the sea.

They picnic on the beach just north of where the sheer face of the mountain catches the morning sun. Gernisavien has to be carried down the final stretch of steep slope, and once set down, she runs off to hunt insects in the dune grass. The air smells of salt and rotting vegetation and clean summer breezes. Far out to sea, gulls wheel and pivot while their cries make minor counterpoint to the crash of surf.

"Holy shit," Jeremy says a final time. He sets the picnic basket down and tosses the blanket onto the sand.

Gail laughs and tugs off her smock. She is wearing a dark one-piece suit underneath.

Jeremy collapses onto the blanket. "Is that why you went upstairs?" he manages between laughs. "To get a suit? Afraid the lifeguards will toss you out if they see you skinny-dipping?"

She kicks sand at him and runs to the water. Her dive is clean and perfectly timed and she cuts into the surf like an arrow. Jeremy watches her as she swims out twenty yards, treads water as another breaker rolls by under her, and then paddles in to where she can stand. He can see by the way her shoulders are hunched and by the sight of her nipples raised under the thin Lycra that she is freezing.

"Come on in!" she calls, just managing to grin without having her teeth chatter. "The water's fine!"

Jeremy laughs again, steps out of his Top-Siders, gets out of his clothes in three quick movements, and runs down the wet shingle of beach. She is waiting for him with open but goose-bumpy arms when he comes up spluttering from his dive.

After their picnic breakfast of croissants and iced tea from the Thermos, they lie back among the dunes to get out of the rising wind. Gernisavien returns to stare at them, finds nothing interesting, and goes back to the high grasses. From where they lie they can see the sun climbing higher and throwing new shadows along the uneven face of the mountain south of them.

Gail has removed her suit to sunbathe and falls asleep. Jeremy is almost asleep with his head on her thigh when he becomes suddenly and totally aware of the clean-sweat scent of her skin, and of the fine film of moisture glistening along the soft groove inches from his face where the curve of her thigh meets her groin. He turns over, rests his elbows on the blanket, and looks up beyond the compressed hillocks of her pale breasts at the undercurve of her chin, at the suggestion of dark stipple under her arms, and at the corona of light the sun is making around her hair.

Gail begins to stir, to question his movement, but he restrains her with the palm of his hand against her stomach. Her eyelids flutter and then stay closed. Jeremy shifts position, lifts himself and then lowers himself so he is lying between her legs, parts her thighs with his hands, and lowers his face to the sun-moistened warmth of her. Thinking of a line she had shared with him years before from a John Updike novel, he imagines a kitten learning to lap milk.

Moments later she pulls him higher, her hands and breathing rapid against him. Their lovemaking is more violent than any that has come before and the sharing of it goes beyond passion and mindtouch. Later, after Jeremy has lain alongside her with his head on her shoulder, their breathing slowing finally, their heartbeats receding so that they can hear the surf again, he fumbles for a towel and brushes away the sweat and traces of sand from her skin.

"Gail," he whispers finally, just as they are both ready to drop off to sleep in the shade of the dune grass, "I have to tell you something." But even as he speaks he feels the remnant of his last mindshield tighten and curl in a reflex protective action. The secret of the variocele has been hidden too deeply for too long to be surrendered so easily. He struggles for the words, or the thoughts, but neither come. "Gail, I . . . oh, Jesus, kiddo . . . I don't know how . . ."

She turns on her side and touches his cheek. *The variocele? The fact that you didn't tell me? I know, Jerry.*

The shock is like a physical blow to him. "You know?" *???? When? How long?*

She closes her eyes and he sees the moisture in the lashes. *That last night I was sick. While you were sleeping. I knew there was . . . something . . . I'd known it for a long time. But the secret of it hurt you for so long that I had to know before . . .*

Jeremy begins shaking as if from illness. After a moment he does not try to hide the shaking, but clutches at the blanket until it passes. Gail touches the back of his head. *It's all right.*

"No!" He cries out the syllable. "No . . . you don't understand . . . I *knew* about this. . . ."

Gail nods, her cheek almost touching his. Her whisper mixes with the wind in the dune grass. "Yes. But do you know *why* you never told me? Why you had to create a mindshield like a tumor in your own mind to hide it?"

Jeremy shudders. *Ashamed.*

No, not ashamed, corrects Gail. *Frightened.*

He opens his eyes to look at her. Their faces are only inches apart. *Frightened? No, I . . .*

Frightened, sends Gail. There is no judgment in her voice, only forgiveness. *Terrified.*

Of what? But even as he forms the thought he grips the blanket again as the sensation of sliding, of falling, rolls across him.

Gail closes her eyes again and shows him what had been hidden from him within the tight tumor of his secret.

Fear of deformity. The baby might not be normal. Fear of having a retarded child. Fear of having a child who would never share their mindtouch and would always be a stranger in their midst. Fear of having a child with *the ability who would be driven insane by their adult thoughts crashing into his or her newborn consciousness.*

Fear of having a normal child who would destroy the perfect balance of his relationship with Gail.

Fear of sharing her with a baby.

Fear of losing her.

Fear of losing himself.

The shaking begins again and this time clutching the blanket and the beach sand does not save him. He feels on the verge of being swept away by riptides of shame and terror. Gail puts her arm around him and holds him until it passes.

Gail, my darling, I am so sorry. So sorry.

Her mindtouch reaches beyond his mind to someplace deeper. *I know. I know.*

They fall asleep there in the shadows of the dunes, with Gernisavien stalking grasshoppers and the wind rising in the high grass. Jeremy dreams then, and his dreams mix freely with Gail's, and in neither, for the first time, is there even the hint of pain.

EYES I DARE NOT
MEET IN

Jeremy walks in the orchard in the cool of the evening and tries to talk to God.

"Robby?" He whispers, but the word seems loud in the twilight silence. *Robby? Are you there?*

The last light has left the hillside to the east and the sky is cloudless. Color leaks out of the world until everything solid assumes a shade of gray. Jeremy pauses, glances back at the farmhouse where Gail is visible making dinner in the lantern-lit kitchen. He can feel her gentle mindtouch; she is listening.

Robby? Can you hear me? Let's talk.

There is a sudden flutter of sparrows in the barn and Jeremy jumps. He smiles, shakes his head, grabs a lower limb of a cherry tree, and leans onto it, his chin on the back of his hands. It is getting dark down by the stream and he can see the fireflies blinking against black. *All this is from our memories? Our view of the world?*

Silence except for insect sounds and the slight murmur of the creek. Overhead, the first stars are coming out between the dark geometries of tree branches.

"Robby," Jeremy says aloud, "if you want to talk to us, we would welcome the company." That is only partially true, but Jeremy does not try to hide the part that denies it. Nor does he deny the deep question that lies under all of their other thoughts like an earthquake fault: *What does one do when the God of one's Creation is dying?*

Jeremy stands in the orchard until it is full dark, leaning on the branch, watching the stars emerge, and waiting for the voice that does not come. Finally Gail calls him in and he walks back up the hill to dinner.

"I think," says Gail as they are finishing their coffee, "that I know why Jacob killed himself."

Jeremy sets his own cup down carefully and gives her his full attention, waiting for the surge of her thoughts to coalesce into language.

"I think it has something to do with that conversation he and I had the night we had dinner at Durgan Park," says Gail. "The night after he did the MRI scans on us."

Jeremy remembers the dinner and much of the conversation, but he checks his memories with Gail's.

Jaunting, she sends.

"Jaunting? What's that?"

You remember that Jacob and I talked about The Stars My Destination *by Alfred Bester?*

Jeremy shakes his head even as he shares her memory of it. *A sci-fi novel?*

Science fiction, Gail corrects him automatically.

He is trying to remember. *Yeah, I sort of remember. You and he were both sci-fi fans, it turns out. But what does "jaunting" have to do with anything . . . it was a sort of a "Beam me up, Scotty" teleportation thing, wasn't it?*

Gail carries some dishes to the sink and rinses them. She leans back against the counter and crosses her arms. "No," she says, her voice carrying the slight defensive tone she always uses when discussing science fiction or religion, "it wasn't 'Beam me up, Scotty.' It was a story about a man who learned to teleport all by himself. . . ."

By "teleport" you mean zap instantaneously from place to place, right, kiddo? Well, you have to know that that's as impossible as anything in the—

"Yes, yes," says Gail, ignoring him. "Bester called the personal teleportation jaunting . . . but Jacob and I weren't talking about jaunting really, just how the writer had people learn how to do it."

Jeremy settles back and sips his coffee. *Okay. I'm listening.*

"Well, I think the idea was that they had a lab out on some asteroid or somewhere, and some scientists were trying to find out if people could jaunt. It turns out that they couldn't. . . ."

Hey, great, sends Jeremy, adding the image of a Cheshire cat's grin, *let's put the science back in science fiction, huh?*

"Shut up, Jerry. Anyway, the experiments weren't succeeding, but then there was a fire or some sort of disaster in a closed section of a lab, and this one technician or whatever just teleported right out . . . jaunted to a safe place."

Don't we wish that life were that simple. He tries to shield the memories of him clambering up a frozen corpse while Miz Morgan approached with the dogs and a shotgun.

Gail is concentrating. "No, the idea was that a lot of people had the jaunting ability, but only one person in a thousand could use it, and that was when his or her life was in absolute jeopardy. So the scientists set up these experiments. . . ."

Jeremy glimpses the experiments. *Jesus wept. They put loaded pistols to the subjects' heads and squeezed the trigger, after letting them know that jaunting is the only way they can escape? The National Academy of Sciences might have something to say about that methodology, kiddo.*

Gail shakes her head. *What Jacob and I were talking about, Jerry, was how certain things come only out of desperate situations like that. That's when he began talking about probability waves and Everett trees, and I lost him. But I remember him saying that it would be like the ultimate two-slit experiment. That's why I was interested in what you were talking about when we were going home on the train. . . . alternate realities and all. . . .*

Jeremy stands up so quickly that his chair clatters to the floor behind him. He does not notice. "My God, kiddo, Jacob didn't just kill himself out of despair. He *was* trying to jaunt."

But you said that teleportation was impossible.

"Not teleportation . . ." He begins pacing, rubbing his cheek. Then he fumbles through the junk drawer and comes up with a pen, sets the chair back up, draws it over next to Gail's, and begins sketching on a napkin. "Remember this diagram? I showed it to you right after my first analysis of Jacob's data."

Gail looks down at the doodle of a tree with its branchings and rebranchings. *No, I . . . oh, yes, that parallel-world idea that some mathematician had. I told you that it was an old idea in science fiction.*

"These aren't parallel worlds," says Jeremy, still scribbling branches from branches, "they're probability variances that Hugh Everett worked out in the 1950s to give a more rational explanation of the Copenhagen interpretation. See, when you do the two-slit experiment and look at it Everett's way without the quantum-mechanics paradoxes intact, all the separate elements of a superposition of states obey the wave equation with total indifference to the actuality of the other elements. . . ." He is scribbling equations next to the tree.

Whoa! Wait. Slow down. Think words.

Jeremy sets down the pen and rubs his cheek again. "Jacob used to write to me about his theory of reality branching. . . ."

Like your probability-wave thing? That we're all like surfers on a crest of the same wave because our brains break down the same wavefronts or something?

"Yeah. That was my interpretation. It was the only theory that explained why all these different holographic wavefronts . . . all these different minds . . . saw pretty much the same reality. In other words I was interested in why we all saw the same particle or wave go through the same slit. But while I was interested in the micro, Jacob wanted to talk about the macro. . . ."

Moses, Gandhi, Jesus, and Newton, offered Gail, sorting out his jumble of thoughts. *Einstein and Freud and Buddha.*

"Yeah." Jeremy is still scribbling equations on the napkin, but he is not paying attention to what he is writing. "Jacob thought that there were a few people in history—he called them ultimate perceptives—a few people whose new vision of physical laws, or moral laws, or whatever was so comprehensive and powerful that they essentially caused a paradigm shift for the entire human race."

But we know that paradigm shifts come with big, new ideas, Jerry.

No, no, kiddo. Jacob didn't think this was just a shift in perspective. He was convinced that a mind that could conceive of such a major shift in reality could literally change the universe . . . make physical laws change to match the new common perception.

Gail frowns. "You mean Newtonian physics didn't work before Newton? Or relativity before Einstein? Or real meditation before Buddha?"

Something like that. The seeds were all there, but the total plan wasn't in place until some great mind focused on it. . . . Jeremy abandons language as he begins seeing the math diagrams of it. Vague Attractors of Kolmogorov winding like incredibly complex fiber-optic cables, carrying their message of chaos while the small resonance-island nodes of classical quasi-periodic linear functions nestle like tiny seeds in the substance of uncollapsed probability.

Gail understands. She moves to the table on unsteady legs and collapses into a chair. "Jacob . . . his obsession with the Holocaust . . . his family . . ."

Jeremy touches her hand. "My guess was that he was trying to concentrate totally on a world in which the Holocaust never occurred. The pistol wasn't just an instrument of death for him, it was the means by which he could force the experiment. It was a probability nexus . . . the ultimate act of observation in the two-slit experiment."

Gail's hand curls around his. *Did he . . . jaunt? Did he go to one of those other branches? Someplace where his family is still alive?*

"No," whispers Jeremy. He touches his scribbled diagram with a shaking finger. "See, the branches never cross . . . there could be no way to go from one to the other. Electron A can never become Electron B, only 'create' the other. Jacob died." Even as he feels the swirl of grief from Gail, he blocks it out as a new thought strikes him. For a moment the intensity of the idea is so powerful that it is like a mindshield between them.

What? demands Gail.

Jacob knew that, he sends, the thoughts coming almost too rapidly to formulate. *He knew that he could not travel to a separate Everett-branch superpositional reality . . . a world where the Holocaust had never happened, say . . . but he could* exist *there.*

Gail shakes her head. *??????*

Jeremy grips her forearms. *See, kiddo, he could* exist *there. If his concentration were total enough . . . all-encompassing . . . then in that microsecond before the bullet took out his mind, he could have brought the Everett counter-reality into existence. And that branch . . .* Jeremy stabs at a random branch in his diagram. *That branch could have* him *in it . . . and his family who died in the Holocaust . . . and all the millions of others.*

"And his daughter, Rebecca?" Gail says softly. "Or his second wife? They were part of his . . . of *our* reality because of the Holocaust."

Jeremy is dizzy. He goes to the sink for a glass of water. "I don't know," he says at last. "I just don't know. But Jacob must have thought so."

Jerry, what kind of mind would it take to . . . what did you say? . . . encompass all of a counter-reality. Could any person really do that?

He pauses. Knowing Gail's resistance to religious metaphors, he still has to try to explain through one. *Maybe that's what the Garden of Gethsemane was about, kiddo. And maybe even the Garden of Eden.*

He does not feel the flash of anger with which Gail usually responds to a religious concept. He senses instead a great shifting in her thinking as she encounters a profound religious truth without the absurdities of religion getting in her way. For the first time in her life Gail shares some of her parents' awe at the spiritual potential of the universe.

Jerry, she shares in a mental whisper, *the Garden of Eden fable . . . the important thing wasn't the forbidden fruit, or the knowledge of sin it's supposed to represent . . . it's the* Tree! *The Tree of Life is precisely that . . . your probability tree . . . Jacob's reality branches! Mother always used to quote Jesus saying 'My Father's house has many rooms. . . .' Worlds without end.*

For a while they do not talk or share mindtouch. Each walks alone in his or her thoughts. Both are sleepy, but neither wants to go to bed quite yet. They douse the lantern light and go out front to rock on the porch swing awhile, to listen to Gernisavien purring from her place on Gail's lap, and to watch the stars burn above the hillside to the east.

EYES I DARE NOT
MEET IN DREAMS

They take a picnic lunch to the shore the next day, bypassing Big Slide Mountain to descend to the beach north of their earlier spot. The sky is a flawless blue and it is very warm. Gernisavien had wakened from her midday nap to stare at them with sleepy, disinterested eyes and had shown not the slightest interest in accompanying them. They left her behind with a command to guard the house. The calico had blinked at their foolishness.

After lunch Jeremy declares that he is going to follow his mother's admonition to wait an hour before going into the water, but Gail laughs at him and runs into the surf. "It's warm today!" she shouts from forty feet out. *"Really."*

"Uh-huh, sure," calls Jeremy, but he does not want to doze now. He gets to his feet, steps out of his shorts, and begins walking toward her.

NO!!!

The blast roars from the sky, the earth, and the sea. It knocks Jeremy into the surf and thrusts Gail's head underwater. She flails, splashes to make the shallows, and crawls gasping from the receding surf.

NO!!!

Jeremy staggers across the wet sand to Gail, lifts her, and holds her against the sudden violence. Wind roars around them and throws sand a hundred feet into the air. The sky twists, wrinkles like a tangled sheet on the line in a high wind, and changes from blue to lemon yellow to a deathly gray. Jeremy hangs on to Gail as they both fall to their knees while the sea rolls out in a giant slack tide and leaves dry, dead land where it recedes. The earth pitches and shifts around them. Lightning flashes along the horizon.

NO!!! PLEASE!

Suddenly the dunes are gone, the cliffs are gone, and the receding sea has disappeared. Where it had been a second before, a dull expanse of salt flat now stretches to infinity. The sky continues to shift down through darker and darker grays.

There is a sudden flash to the east, as if the sun is rising again. No, Jeremy and Gail realize, the light is moving. Something is crossing the wasteland toward them.

They climb to their feet again, Gail starts to break away, but Jeremy holds her tight. There is nowhere to run. The beach and mountain and cliffs behind them are gone . . . there is only desolation stretching to infinity in each direction . . . and the light moves across the dead land toward them.

The radiance grows brighter, shifts, sends out streamers that make both of them squint and shield their eyes. The air smells of ozone and the hair on their arms stands out.

Jeremy and Gail find themselves leaning toward the blaze of pure light as if toward a strong wind. Their shadows leap sixty feet behind them and light strikes their bodies like a shock wave from an atomic blast. Through their fingers they watch while the radiance approaches and resolves itself into a double figure just visible through the corona.

It is a human figure astride a great beast. If a god were truly to come to earth, this then is the perfect human form he would choose. The beast the god rides is featureless, but besides its own corona of light it gives off a sense of . . . warmth, softness, infinite solace.

Robby is before them, high on the back of his teddy bear.

TOO WEAK! CANNOT KEEP

The god is not used to limiting himself to language, but he is making the effort. Each syllable strikes Gail and Jeremy like electrical surges to the brain.

Jeremy tries to reach out with his mind, but it is no use. Once at Haverford he had gone with a promising student to the coliseum where they were setting up for a rock concert. He had been standing in front of a scaffolded bank of speakers when the amplifiers were tested at full volume. This is much worse than that.

They are standing on a flat, reticulated plain. There are no horizons. Above them levels of translucent, gray-colored nothingness cover them like the cold folds of a plastic shroud. White banks of curling fog are approaching now from all directions. The only light comes from the Apollo-like figure before them. Jeremy turns his head to watch the fog advance; what it touches, it erases.

"Jerry, what . . ." shouts Gail over the rising wind that drowns out their mindtouch.

Suddenly Robby's thoughts strike them again with physical force. He has given up an attempt at structuring language, and images cascade over them. The visual and auditory images are vaguely distorted, miscolored, and tinged with an aura of wonder and newness around a core of sorrow. Jeremy and Gail reel from their impact.

a white room
the heartbeat of a machine
sunlight on sheets
the sting of a needle
voices and shapes moving
a current pulling, pulling, pulling

With the images comes the emotional overlay, almost unbearable in its knife-sharp intensity: discovery, loneliness, an end to loneliness, wonder, fatigue, love, sadness, sadness, sadness.

Gail looks around in terror as the fog boils and reaches its tendrils for them. It is closing around the god on his mount, already obscuring his brilliance.

Gail sets her face against her husband's. *My God, why is he doing this? Why can't he leave us alone?*

Jeremy raises the volume of his thoughts above the roar all around them. *Touch him! Reach him!*

They step forward together and Gail extends a shaking hand. The fog obscures all but the fading corona. She jerks at the electric shock as her hand melds with the radiance, but she keeps her hand in place.

My God, Jerry, he's just a baby. A frightened child.

Jeremy extends his hand until the three are a circle of contact. *He's dying, Gail. He's been holding me here against terrible forces . . . he's been fighting to keep us together, but I can't stay. He's too weak to hold me . . . he can't resist the pull any longer.*

Jerry!

Jeremy pulls away, breaking the circle. *If I stay any longer, I'll destroy us all.* With that thought he steps closer and touches Gail on the cheek. Gail sees what he plans and starts to protest, but he pulls her closer and hugs her fiercely. They both feel Robby as part of the embrace, even while Jeremy's mindtouch amplifies the hug, adding to it all of the shades of feeling that neither human touch nor human language can communicate in full.

Then he pushes away from both of them and turns before he

can change his mind. The fog surrounds him almost instantly. One second Robby is visible only as a fading glow in the white mist, an Apollo child clutching the neck of his teddy bear, Gail little more than a gesturing shadow next to him, and then they are gone and Jeremy is plunging deeper into the cold whiteness.

Five paces into the fog and he can see nothing, not even his own body.

Three more paces and the ground drops out from beneath him.

Then he is falling.

Falls the Shadow

The room was white, the bed was white, and the windows were rectangles of white light. A monitor somewhere out of sight electronically echoed his heartbeat.

Bremen moaned and moved his head.

There was a plastic tube of oxygen hissing under his nose. An IV bottle caught the light and he could see the bruises on his inner arm above where the needle was hidden under gauze. Bremen's body and skull were one vast, integrated ache.

The doctors wore white. His eyes refused to focus properly, so they continued to be little more than white blurs with voices.

"You gave us quite a scare," said a white blur with a woman's voice. *Five days of an absolutely flat EEG,* came the harsher voice of her thoughts through the ragged holes in his mindshield. *If we'd been able to find any next of kin, you would have been disconnected from life support days ago. Damned weird.*

"How do you feel now?" asked a blur with the voice of one of the doctors. "Is there anyone we can contact for you?" *Better tell the police that Mr. Bremen has come out of what we told them was almost certainly an irreversible coma. He's not going anywhere for a while, but I'd better tell that detective . . . what was his name?*

Bremen groaned and tried to speak. The noise made no sense even to himself.

The doctor blur had left, but the white blur that was female came closer, did something to his covers, and adjusted the IV drip. "We're very, very lucky, Mr. Bremen. That concussion must have been much more serious than anyone had guessed. But we're all right now, a few more days here in intensive care and—"

Bremen cleared his throat and tried again. "Still alive?"

The blur leaned close enough so that he could almost make out the details of her face. She smelled of cough drops. "Why, of course we're still alive. Now that the worst is past we can look forward to—"

"Robby," rasped Bremen through a throat so raw that he could imagine the tubes that had been forced down it. "The boy . . . in my room . . . before. Is he still alive?"

The blur paused, then efficiently began tucking in his covers. Her voice was light, almost bantering. "Oh, yes, no need to worry about that little fellow. He's doing just fine. What we have to worry about is ourselves if we're going to get well. Now, is there anyone we'd like to contact . . . for personal or insurance reasons?"

And what she had thought in the second before speaking: *Robby? The blind, retarded kid in 726? He's in a much deeper coma than you were in, my friend. Dr. McMurtry says that the brain damage was too extensive . . . the internal injuries untreated for too long. Even on the respirator, they think it'll only be a few more hours. Maybe days if the poor child is unlucky.*

The blur continued to talk and ask friendly questions, but Bremen turned his face to the white wall and closed his eyes.

He made the short voyage in the early hours of the morning when the halls were dark and silent except for the occasional swish of a nurse's skirt or the low, fitful groans of patients. He moved slowly, sometimes clutching the buffer railing along the wall for support. Twice he stepped into darkened rooms as the soft tread of nurses' rubber-soled shoes squeaked his way. The stairway was difficult; several times he had to lean over the cold metal railing to shake away the black spots that swam at the edge of his vision.

Robby was in the room Bremen had once shared with him, but now the child was alone except for the life-support-system machines that surrounded him like metal carrion crows. Colored lights flickered from various monitors and LED displays flickered silently to themselves. The shriveled and faintly odorous body lay curled in a fetal position, wrists cocked at stiff angles, fingers splayed against sweat-moistened sheets. Robby's head was turned upward, and his eyes were half-open and sightless. His still-battered lips fluttered slightly as he breathed in rapid, ragged surges.

Bremen could feel that he was dying.

He sat on the edge of the bed, trembling. The thickness of the night was palpable around him. Somewhere outside, a siren echoed in empty streets and then fell away to silence. A chime sounded far down the hall and soft footsteps receded.

Bremen laid his palm gently against Robby's cheek. He could feel the soft down there.

I could try again. Join them in the wasteland of Robby's world. Be with them at the end.

Bremen touched the top of the misshapen head tenderly, almost reverently. His fingers were trembling.

I could try to rescue them. Let them join me.

He took a breath that ended as a stifled moan. His hand cupped Robby's skull as if in benediction. *Join me where? As memory wavefronts locked away in my brain? Entomb them as I entombed Gail? Carry them through my life as soulless, eyeless, speechless homunculi . . . waiting for another miracle like Robby to offer us a home?*

His cheeks were suddenly damp and he stabbed roughly with the back of his free hand, rubbing away the tears so that he could see. Robby's straight black hair stuck up between Bremen's fingers in comic tufts. Bremen looked at a pillow that had fallen to one side. He could end everything for them here, now, so that the two people he loved were no longer stranded in that dying wasteland. *Wavefronts collapsing as all possibilities are canceled. The death of sine waves in their intricate dance.* He could go to the window and join them seconds later.

Bremen suddenly recalled the fragment of some poem that Gail had read to him years ago, even before they were married. He couldn't remember the poet . . . Yeats, maybe. He remembered only a bit of the poem:

> The eyes are not here
> There are no eyes here
> In this valley of dying stars
> In this hollow valley
> This broken jaw of our lost kingdoms
>
> In this last of meeting places
> We grope together
> And avoid speech
> Gathered on this beach of the tumid river
>
> Sightless, unless
> The eyes reappear
> As the perpetual star
> Multifoliate rose
> Of death's twilight kingdom
> The hope only
> Of empty men.

Bremen touched Robby's cheek a final time, whispered something to them both, and left the room.

This Is the Way
the World Ends

It took Bremen three days and three nights to drive the intern's Volvo from St. Louis to the East Coast. He had to park frequently at rest stops along the Interstate, too exhausted to continue, too obsessed to sleep. Bradley had only three hundred dollars in his wallet when Bremen had opened his locker, but that was more than enough for gas. Bremen did not eat during the transit.

The Benjamin Franklin Bridge out of Philly was almost empty as he crossed it an hour before sunrise. The double strip of highway across New Jersey was quiet. Occasionally Bremen would lower his mindshield a bit, but always flinched and raised it again as the roar of neurobabble lashed at him.

Not yet.

He blinked away the migraine pain and concentrated on driving, occasionally glancing at the glove compartment and thinking of the rag-covered bundle there. It had been at a rest stop somewhere in Indiana . . . or perhaps Ohio . . . when the pickup had pulled in next to him and the sallow-faced little man had hurried in to the rest rooms. Bremen had flinched at the cloud of anger and distrust that had surrounded the man, but he had smiled when he was out of sight.

The .38-caliber pistol was hidden under the driver's seat of the man's pickup. It looked almost like the weapon that Bremen had thrown into the Florida swamp. There were extra bullets under the seat, but Bremen had left those. The one in the chamber would be all that he needed.

The sun was not up, but morning light was paling above the rooftops when he drove onto Long Beach Island and took the road north to Barnegat Light. He parked near the lighthouse, set the revolver in a brown bag, and carefully locked the car. He set a slip of paper with Bradley's name and address under the windshield wiper.

The sand was still cool when it lopped over the tops of his sneakers. The beach was deserted. Bremen sat in the curl of a low dune so that he could see the water.

He took off his shirt, set it carefully on the sand behind him, and removed the pistol from the bag. It was lighter than he remembered and smelled faintly of oil.

No magic wand. No miracle worker. Only an absolute end to that mathematically perfect dance within. If there is anything else, Gail, my darling, you will have to help me find it.

Bremen dropped his mindshield.

The pain of a million aimless thoughts stabbed behind his eyes like the point of an ice pick. His mindshield rose automatically, as it had since he first knew he had the ability, so as to blunt the noise, ease the pain.

Bremen pushed down the barrier, and held it down when it tried to protect him. For the first time in his life Jeremy Bremen opened himself fully to the pain, to the world that inflicted it, and to the countless voices calling in their circles of isolation.

Gail. He called to her and the child, but he could not sense them, could not hear their voices as the great chorus struck him like a giant wind. To accept them he must accept all of them.

Bremen lifted the pistol, set the muzzle to his skull, and pulled back the hammer. There was little friction. His finger curled on the trigger.

All the circles of hell and desolation he had suffered.

All the petty meannesses, sordid urges, solitary vices, vicious thoughts. All the violence and betrayal and greed and self-centeredness.

Bremen let it flow through him and around him and out of him. He sought a single voice in the cacophony now rising around him until it threatened to fill the universe. The pain was beyond enduring, beyond believing.

And suddenly, through the avalanche of pain-noise, there came a whisper of the other voices, the voices that had been denied Bremen during his long descent through his psychic hell. These were the soft voices of reason and compassion, the encouraging voices of parents urging their children in their first steps, the hopeful voices of men and women of goodwill who—while far from being perfect human beings—spent each day trying to be a better person than nature and nurture may have designed them to be.

Even these soft voices carried their burden of pain: pain at the compromises life imposed, pain at the thoughts of their own mortality and the all-too-threatening mortality of their children, pain of suffering the arrogance of all the willing pain-givers such as those Bremen had encountered in his travels, and the final, ineluctable pain at the certainty of loss even in the midst of all the sustaining pleasures life offered.

But these soft voices—including Gail's voice, Robby's voice—gave Bremen some compass point in the darkness. He concentrated on hearing them even as they faded and were drowned by the cacophony of chaos and hurt around them.

Bremen realized again that to find the softer voices he would have to surrender himself totally to the painful cries for help. He would have to take it all in, absorb it all, swallow it like some razor-edged Communion wafer.

The muzzle of the pistol was a cool circle against his temple. His finger was taut against the curve of trigger.

The pain was beyond all imagining, beyond all experience. Bremen accepted it. He willed it. He took it into and through himself and opened himself wider to it.

Jeremy Bremen did not see the sun rise in front of him. His hearing dimmed to nothing. The messages of fear and fatigue from his body failed to register; the increasing pressure on the trigger became a distant, forgotten thing. He concentrated with enough force to move objects, to pulverize bricks, to halt birds in their flight. For that briefest of milliseconds he had the choice of wavefront or particle, the choice of which existence he would embrace. The world screamed at him in five billion pain-filled voices demanding to be heard, five billion lost children waiting to be held, and he opened himself wide enough to hold all of them.

Bremen squeezed the trigger.

For Thine Is
Life Is
For Thine Is The

From down the beach comes a young girl in a dark suit two seasons too small. She has been running along the edge of wet-packed sand, but now she pauses as the sun rises and breaks free of the sea.

Her attention is on the water as it teases the land with sliding strokes and then withdraws, and she moves closer to dance with the surf. Her sunburned legs carry her to the very edge of the world's ocean and then back again in a silent but perfectly choreographed ballet.

Suddenly she is startled by the sound of a shot.

Suddenly she is startled by the . . .

Suddenly she is startled by the screaming of gulls. Distracted, she halts her dance, and the waves break over her ankles with the cold shock of triumph.

Above her the gulls dive, rise again, and wheel away to the west, their wings catching the flare of sunrise. The girl pirouettes to watch them as salt spray teases her hair and splashes her face. She squints, rubbing her eyes gently so as not to rub the salt in, and pauses to watch three figures emerge from the dunes up the beach. It looks as if the man and woman and the beautiful child between them have no suits on, but they are far enough away and her eyes are blurred enough from sea spray that the girl cannot tell for sure. She *can* see that they are holding hands.

The girl resumes her waltz with the sea, while behind her, squinting slightly in the clean, sharp light of morning, Jeremy, Gail, and Robby watch the sunrise through newly opened eyes.